A LONG ROAD
TO SALAMANCA

························

P A BREINBURG

To. Ken
Best wishes
March 2007

Perkoully.

THE AUTHOR

Like her main character, Petronella Breinburg is from a mix-cultural, bilingual and catholic background, with roots in South America. She travelled across the Venezuela/Guyana border, visited Brazil before travelling first to the UK then to other European countries. In her travels she met and interacted with people from various cultures and beliefs, including taboos.

She arrived in the UK in 1961, where she attended the University of London; where she retired as senior lecturer many years later. She obtained her PhD from Keele University in Staffordshire. In the UK she taught in the primary, secondary and tertiary sector prior to becoming a lecturer in higher education; including teachers education.

She has published a long list of books for children, short stories in anthologies, and papers in scholarly journals.

Her working languages are Dutch, English and Sranan with some knowledge of other languages such as Spanish and dialect such as Ndjuka, in use in South American.

Further information may be found on the internet.

ACKNOWLEDGEMENTS

I am greatly indebted to quite a number of people. First, my family and friends, who acted as sounding boards. I cannot thank Tessa and her two daughters enough for sustaining me with hot meals and drinks during the writing of this story.

My thanks to my young friends of Elena and Chris's age, particularly Antonia, in the UK and Eunice in the Netherlands who read and commented on selected pages for me. Nurse Maduagwu –Paris for answering my endless questions. Special thanks to Karen Scott of New Writers Consultancy for her support without attempting to change my words and how I wanted to express them. A special thank you to the two Canadian reviewers for their positive and constructive comment on INSTEAD OF ROSES AND RINGS, of which this book is the second of a trilogy in process. Perhaps my greatest gratitude goes to Jenny, an editor, who had seen the synopsis and the opening chapters of this book and had found nothing positive to say about it. Strangely, her negativity send me back to the drawing board where I worked with more determination to tell a story as I saw it and how I chose to tell it.

My greatest thanks to Mike Wilson for his time, moral support and computer skills, in preparing my work for publication.

Last, but not least, thanks to Ursula Troche for the use of her photograph from which the front cover was designed.

PA Breinburg
31st January 2007

PUBLICATION INFORMATION

Published in 2007 by Petrojass Publications
PO Box 27966 London SE7 8WY
Email: petrojass@btinternet.com
ISBN 0-9549992-1-5
British Library Cataloguing in-Publication Data.
A Catalogue record for this book is available from British library.

Copyright © 2007 PA Breinburg
Cover design © Courtesy M F Wilson
Cover photograph © Courtesy Ursula Troche
Digital and Editorial layout Courtesy M F Wilson

Printed and digitally produced in a Standard Specification in order to
ensure its continuing availability by Catford Print Centre

Catford Print Centre
PO Box 563
Catford
London
SE6 4PY
Telephone: 020 8695 0101

DEDICATION

*FOR
ALL THOSE
ON A
LONG ROAD
TO SOMEWHERE*

THE PROLOGUE

Standing here on my birthday, I couldn't help looking back to it all, especially to that other birthday. Then there were no candles. There were only that pair of eyes, which had hit mine across the room on my first day here. Yet it was my...well, my coming of age, not the day I leapt out my mom's belly. But looking back, that was my other birthday.

There was that day. It kept coming back to me. Especially after I agreed to write my 'auto bio as Fiction' for the English part of my Special Study project. I remember it well as if it happened yesterday. On that day I was glad to get Mom out of the house that morning. She had already taken two days off work. Her boss didn't mind much since Mom was one of her workers, paid hourly. No work no pay! Thing was that Mom worried too much. When she was not worrying about Kevin's asthma, she worried about me.

'This is no place for a young girl to grow up in,' Mom went on and on, 'It no place for any child, but for girls it worst.'

Sometimes Mom's grammar got shaky; after all, English was not her mother tongue.

'Back-street schools,' Mom would continue, 'Factory bench or if you lucky, supermarket checkout then baby-mother to a string of useless good-for-nothing, absent daddies.'

Mom repeated those lines like a song, perhaps, trying to imprint them on my brains. She was warning me of how much worse my situation would be.

Yet in spite of our situation we still were able to joke. I remember how we roared when I said that at least the good-for-nothing visit the mother in hospital and carry a paper bag of cheap deady-deady grapes they got from the market. Mom had learnt that good-for-nothing phrase from my Guyanese dad, though she herself was from Venezuela. And I had learnt the deady-deady talk from him.

'And they take flowers that they nicked from the park, don't forget the flowers.' Kevin would say.

As a family we had little choice but to use comedy as a coping mechanism for dealing with our misfortune, at least for a time. I often tried to reassure Mom. I will not be anyone's baby-mother because I had no interest in the opposite sex.

At that Mom would grunt a 'Mm' and shrug.

My brother Kevin used to pull out grey hair strands from the side of Mom's head. She was beginning to look older than her real age. Anyway, each time Kevin pulled out one strand he wanted to be paid but was prepared to accept an IOU. He would then tell Mom that when things got better for her, and they would, she must remember that she owed him money. Our Kevin would certainly be a businessman if he had a chance, so I often thought. But what chance did he have? What chance for me, living in a run down neighbourhood and, to crown it all, in a damp basement? We were on the housing list for many years but did not have the points needed to be re-housed. Once, Mom was offered a flat in a housing estate notorious for crime with police sirens constantly blaring due to murders; high numbers of lone mothers, some still in their teens, gang warfare and more.

'No thanks,' said Mom, 'not for my two kids.' Mom then explained that we were better off where we were until something came along from back home.

Mom was still hoping that her brothers back in Venezuela would have mercy and not keep all the land of their father for themselves. The social worker meanwhile called Mom choosy and left. Nothing more was heard about us being re-housed. This was even though Kevin's asthma should have given us a few re-housing points. But because of Kevin, Mom did get us some help from a church charity. But we still had to live some number of metres under a five-storey Victorian house. There Mom slept in the kitchen/cum bedroom. Kevin and I slept on a bunk bed given to us by the charity people; bless them, in what was a living/bedroom all in one. The landlord was threatened with court action if he did not install a gas fire. And so he did. That gas fire and cans of soup from the charity people helped me to recover. Mom had insisted though that I took another couple of days off Hill Croft Community College. Reluctantly I agreed that I needed a few more days at home.

Anyway, as I was saying, on that particular day, I managed to get Mom out. I was feeling very much better after what the doctor said was a touch of pneumonia. I promised her that I'd rest. When hungry, I'd heat up a can of soup. I'd have soup and bread, my favourite.

After both Mom and Kevin left, I made myself some Swank, as me dad called that drink. The children in Guyana made it by squeezing lemon or lime in water sweetening it with brown sugar and you could add ice cubes. I didn't have ice cubs so I had my Swank warm. I half laid down on my part of the bunk bed. After a while I must have fallen into a slumber. Something woke me up. For a moment a sharp fear went through my spine and made me shudder. There had been talk of breaking and entering further up the road. There were better houses there. But here? Who would want to break into this dump? Steal what, for Christ sake? I rested my head again on the pillow.

'Mm!' I muttered. I heard something again. Ah it's only Jean bunking off classes. I shrugged and relaxed on the bed. Jean was my best mate of those days. We had much in common. Her dad had left home years ago: 'Pressure of life.' Jean often made excuses for her dad. My own daddy had also left; this time the reason given was racism from both sides. On one side the whites of those days called him racist names like Pakki-bastard, when he had no connection with Pakistan. On the other side there were the African Caribbean who saw him as a Coolie-man when he was as much Caribbean as they were. Dad often moaned about that double-edged racism.

Another thing that Jean and I had in common was that neither of us wanted to be baby-mothers to anyone. In fact we were determined not to ever be and kept away from those who did not seem to mind that trend of baby-mother. Those others called us two weird, even funny. Jean and I talked a lot about boys and that, 'all what they wanted was to get their hands up your knickers.', we joked.

But back to that day. I was so sure that it was Jean but when I heard nothing more, I assumed she was in the kitchen helping herself to bread or whatever she could find to eat. I then thought that she was going to play some trick on me. Well, Miss Jean, two can play games. I wanted to hit her with something that would not hurt her, only frighten her. I picked up my cheap pillow made up of rags not feathers. That will do, I thought.

I tiptoed to the back. Jean was not there. Ah ha! I was sure then that she must be in the kitchen cum bedsit. I tiptoed to the kitchen. I raised the pillow high above my head with one hand. The other hand pushed the kitchen door open and ready to strike. I must have screamed though I was not sure if any sound came out my mouth or if I fell over from fear when I saw what I saw. Until this day, many years later, I still can't remember if I did scream. Not that any one would've heard and come to my aid. At that time of the day the place was like a ghost town. It was a hard-working street, almost like modern-day slavery as people, black, white and other, slugged away somewhere. Some left home when it was still dark. It was again dark when they return. But maybe I did scream or I just fell over; after all I'd been very ill. Maybe I just sat down on the floor and waited for what I was sure would come. Of course afterwards I'd have to gas myself. When I opened my eyes it was to shut them again, something was telling me to scream. But who would've heard me? I made to run back into the front room, but he barred my way, his eyes staring.

'Shut yuh mouth, right?' He said in a strange accent. 'Shut it or yuh get it!' Something like that he said and he sounded as if he meant it.

'Get out!' I heard myself shout. 'My friend will be here soon.'

Secretly I was hoping that Jean would have chosen that particular day to bunk off our so-called six-form college.

'Mm, nice! Two for one, eh?' he grinned. His teeth were like someone who smoked a lot. I was sure that I would never forget that smell. Meanwhile I was thinking. There was that knife on the draining board with plates and stuff Mom washed before she left for work. I can talk, get his attention away for a split second.

I'll then make a dash for the knife. I can get to it I know I could. I thought of what you see on late night TV. She distracts him, grabs the knife and sticks it in him. He drops on the floor, dead! She runs out screaming, blood trickling from the knife still in her hands, she drops the knife, she hears the police siren in a distance. I could almost see the scene flashing in front of me.

'What the hell you want here?' I shouted at him, trying not to show that I was petrified. My hands got very cold as I thought of stories in the news of what happened to young girls. The thought of him pinning me down and stick his filthy 'what's it' up me, gave me some courage. Oh God! Give me strength, I thought, but aloud I said, 'Now, enough of this shit. If you're hungry take the whole loaf of bread and piss off. And that would be the end of story. If you don't clear off someone bound to come and I'd scream the bloody place down...ah! someone coming.'

My attempt to draw his attention away from me failed. He grinned showing a row of stained teeth.

'Brave is we, eh? Been watching too much telly,' he mocked. 'Now, where you lot stack the doss you get from the social?'

'Doss, you mean money, here?' I forced myself to laugh, 'Show how you lot stupid. Money in this poverty-stricken hole, a stinking damp basement... you come for money, here?'

The knife, the knife seemed to say to me in my ear, 'get the knife.'

'Come on,' He said staring at me, 'Don't mess me about. You lot got it stacked away. You get yur social but still sneak out doing a bit a work for cash in hand.'

'Yeah and you're an intruder,' I said aloud, hoping that the boy upstairs by some striking coincidence would've bunked off school as he often did. Please God let him be hiding at home as he often did. I silently prayed.

Aloud I said, 'Look, mister, I don't know what the hell you want with us but I think you should go. Take the bread if you're hungry but go.'

'Now, what would I be doing with it?' He snorted and I noticed that his eyes were greenish like a lizard's. I was sure that I would be able to describe him in detail, after he left.

Looking back now, I could have called the police on my phone if we had one. But that was then. I had no way of calling the Old Bill. The likes of us could not afford the luxury of a telephone in the home. Strange as that may seem, at a time when every Tom, Dick and Harry had a phone, we couldn't afford one.

'I'd give you a head start, before I call the police.' I tried to humour him.

'Oh yeah, which phone you going use to call them?' He was mocking me.

I wondered if he simply wanted somewhere to hide perhaps from some gang or the law was after him. He could've attacked me so he must be hiding from some one. He was a little relaxed now. I saw my chance. I made a dash for the knife.

I got there but so did he. He grabbed my wrist and twisted so hard that I thought that he broke it. I let go of the knife. It dropped back on the sink. He picked it up without taking his eyes off me.

'You'd be dead before you can raise it, right?' He pressed the point of the knife against my flesh. He continued to hold the knife by the side of my neck.

'Look you seem a nice bloke, why don't you go? The houses up the road, they got money.' I pleaded nicely to humour him. 'We are half-starved here.'

'You think me stupid? The last place them lot will come looking for me is a Jamaican house. Them up the road...ugh!' He pulled a nasty face in the direction of the better-off houses near the park. He spat on the floor of the kitchen.

'What made you think this was a Jamaican house?'

I knew that the chance of anyone coming at that time of day was almost nil. I was on my own therefore my safety was in my own hands. All the time that I was thinking I was imprinting his face, his tobacco breath and his voice in my mind so that I could describe him later.

'You black, you're Jamaican! 'He shrugged.

Dumb ass! I was thinking but dared not voice my thoughts.

He moved the knife from pressing on the side of my neck. 'Come on. Move! Don't want to hurt no one just want bit a' cash. But I might if you messed me about.'

He waved the knife near my neck. To me the knife seemed to get larger than usual.

'Now move!' He pushed me towards the bed which was one side of the room we also used for cooking. He pointed the knife towards the mattress.

Nervously I lifted the mattress. 'See? Told you no money here!'

I again prayed silently, 'Dear God, anyone, the postman, footsteps even a dog barking.'

He marched me, still keeping the knife close to my neck. I tried to stay calm. I had to be calm, be calm, be calm, the words went on and on in my head. You can escape. Knee him the groin and run. I wasn't a champion runner at school fo' nothing. But I must get him in front. At that moment he was sideways, not in front. He marched me into the next room. He then went straight to the dressing table where we kept our stuff. He pulled out the drawer so hard that the thing collapsed. He made me pull out stuff onto the floor. He was satisfied that there was no money. He then marched me to the side door where the steps were leading to the street.

'Open that door!' he demanded.

'Nothin in there, only old broken furniture and other stuff we don't want. In the old days it was a coal bunker.'

He grunted.

'See, see for yourself. Only junk.' I pointed to the old chairs and a side table we stockpiled in there when we moved in.

The man pushed me in front of him and to my surprise he went straight to the beam holding the staircase leading to the floor upstairs. It was as if he knew where to look. He saw Mom's toffee tin on a ledge.   He grinned with glee. 'How funny, me own mother used to hide things there from me dad. Nothing changed eh?'

'You lived here once?'

'Was a long time ago.' He grunted seeming to lick his lips.

'If there's anything, wouldn't be much,' I said as calm as I could.

I remembered that even Mom didn't known how much there was. She usually gave me whatever little she could squeeze from our daily living, my job was to put it in the tin. Now this man will take it all. And even rape me on top of it. The thought of him raping me sent spiders crawling up my hands. He looked me in the face, then for whatever reason he decided to concentrate on opening Mom's toffee tin. He needed both hands to twist the lid of the tin open. He eyed me strangely then began to open the tin. He lost concentration for a split second as he opened the tin. Suddenly something got into my hands. My hands went up then down again. Then something fell out off my hands. Then nothing!

I opened my eyes. I was in the sub-post office up the nice part of our street. I knew that it was that sub-post office because I was sitting on a large box next to those red bags with huge letters saying POST. I felt cold and was shivering. I saw faces peering into mine. I heard whispering voices and advice. Someone was patting me on the shoulder, everyone seemed to be talking all at once. The police siren or the ambulance or even both were trying to blast my eardrums to pieces. Suddenly I was being driven, to somewhere. A door slammed, then darkness! I was relieved. It was only a nasty dream. I forced myself to believe that it was a dream. No, it sure was the fever. I had a very high temperature for days. There was no man, or intruder. It was the fever and no man. But it turned out that there was a man.

Then came the day I was standing in front of important people, their eyes staring at me. With mouths opening and closing they spat out questions at me. I heard angry accusations, angry voices, men and women glaring from a long table. Mom was holding my hand. I was not afraid. After all it was only a long dream.
What else but a dream? Mom's eyes were red from crying. Kevin, was it Kevin? Of course it was Kevin my baby brother. There were arguments as they glared at me. It was only a dream I kept thinking as if voices in my head were trying to convince me that it was a dream.
One voice was saying, 'No one should take the law into their own hands.'
'She has no idea where she is.' Said a second.
That second voice was wrong. I knew that I was in some court of law. But I could not answer some of the questions being asked.
'I don't known what happened. Yes, after he went to take the money ... I don't know ... yes I could've run out ... no ... yes no ... I can't remember ... yes I understand ... it is a house of correction ... yes, I am lucky and thank you madam. Thank you sir ...!

The House of Correction had a name printed at the front. It was The House of Our Lady of Grace. I had no interest in the name. The main thing for me was that something bad had brought something good. I was now in a beautiful and warm house. I noticed a well-kept drive in front and a garden at the back. I saw a small monument by a fountain where stood the statue of a lady. What's more, there seemed to be only girls and women around. I soon learnt that many of the girls were teen-age mothers. Others had trouble at home or with the law. But none of the girls was bad enough to be sent to youth prison or where ever it was that bad girls were sent. I did hear a whisper that we were all at risk.
My first few nights at that house were strange. I had never been away from my mom and my brother Kevin. Nights were bad. I had trouble falling asleep and when I did it was only brief. During that brief sleep I had the incident replayed but always with a gap between when he was going to take the money

and when I found myself in the Post Office. When awake I kept wondering and asking the white ceiling above my head, 'Did someone die?' No one died, not really. This was only a long dream caused by that high temperature I had. No one actually died or got badly hurt. The ceiling over my head could not assure me. Some of us were on stuff as prescribed. The women in charge kept all medications locked away. My own medication for my bad headache was brought to my room when needed. I shared that tiny room with Marcelle who the others said was funny. I soon noticed that Marcelle was not much liked by the others. One reason they gave, was that she showed off and put on a bogus French accent and that she pretended to have a French Caribbean mother. They were saying that Marcelle had no mother, either Caribbean one or which ever. Marcelle was a very strange girl alright. I often forced myself to laugh at some of the things she said. She kept asking me if I had ever done it. She asked so often that once I lied and said, 'Oh yes, I have.'

I said without knowing what I was supposed to have ever done.

One night Marcelle was sobbing her eyes out in bed. The visitors had all gone. As usual everyone had someone visiting. My mom came with apples and some Caribbean snacks her Guyanese friend had made especially for the visit. Kevin came armed with back numbers of women's mags. Other residents, as we were officially known, had relatives, friends or baby-fathers visiting. Marcelle was the only one of us who hadn't had visitors. But Marcelle never had visitors anyway, at least not since my arrival at the House of our Lady of Grace. So why those tears on this particular occasion?

Poor Marcelle. I felt sorry for her. I went over to her bed. I took her in my arms as if I was her younger sister. She was grateful. She kissed me on both cheeks as people do in France. I had no objection to that. It was when she kissed me on the lips and tried to force her tongue between my lips that I not only pushed her away but also threw her a back-hander that cut her lip. Marcelle ran out the room, bawling that I hit her. The carer in charge that evening rushed in grabbed hold of me and dragged me out. She muttered that I had a violent tendency, as she marched me away by the collar of my pyjama top. I was taken to one of the emergency rooms where girls who came in late at night slept until morning. I was furious and felt that it was terribly unfair. Some fight happened between two girls but only one is moved without any questions asked. I was left in that room until the following morning. That space was more like a broom cupboard than a room. It was several steps up in the building. I had the room all to myself as punishment. Funny, if only the carers knew how delighted I was! Being on my own suited me fine. I could sleep without having someone babbling to me. I was so happy to be on my own that I hoped that I would be able to stay in that tiny room for the duration of my stay at The House of Our Lady of Grace.

But Mom reacted differently. When she visited and I told her what happened, she was ready to take up arms. She wanted to have answers to why it was that if two girls had a dispute only one was punished. Was it because of the colour of the skin of the other one? I explained to her that I didn't want to get in more trouble. I had to stay at the House until I was eighteen. If Mom was to make a fuss the officials might move me to another place. Some of those places, it was rumoured, were Houses of Hell. I tried to reassure Mom by telling her that I was strong enough to make the best of anything. After a lengthy argument I managed to calm Mom down and she promised not to say anything about the event. I convinced her that in any case I preferred being on my own. The others, though they were all very nice girls, bored me stiff with talks of boys, men and so called baby-fathers.

I carried on normally. When I was not reading I spent time in the garden. I often sat by the monument and talked to the statue of Our Lady of Grace. I would ask her to look after me and bring some luck in my life. I loved the House of our Lady, but when the time came to leave I'd like a chance to make something great of myself. Of course, Our Lady looked coldly at me, after all, statutes don't talk nor do anything else for that matter.

Time went by. The book trolley from the local library came in daily in the afternoon. I was the book trolley's best customer. One day the young lady who came with the books saw me watching her. She asked me if I would like to help.

'Oh.' I hesitated. 'I wouldn't know what to do.'

The book trolley lady had an idea. She wanted me to be a sort of librarian assistant because she was pleased that I always returned my books. Some of the girls were taking books to their rooms and not returning them. Others left books in the bathroom or on the grass outside, in fact everywhere. Worse trouble was that people had been tearing out pages from books. Others had been cutting pictures out of the magazines. The book trolley lady had to do something she did not want to. She had to have a strict card system. My job would be to help keep track of the books. All borrowers had to have their card stamped. The book lady said that she'd show me how to do things.

Soon I began to chase after borrowers. I found books left everywhere. Sometimes a borrower had left without giving her books in. Funny thing was that the trolley book lady did not appear to be angry with the girls who stole books when they were leaving. She shrugged and said that she hoped they would read the books taken. I was by then a library assistant and happy. Maybe with luck I too might become a book trolley young lady. Some of the other girls began to tease. They called me the 'Book madam' or the 'Nutty professor' because I was always seen now with a book in hand, or my head buried in one. I was blissfully happy working with books and having my own little space. Then came the bad news. I was to be moved back downstairs. I was behaving very well said the report from the carer in charge. I was to come down from the tiny space to a larger room. There I was to share once more. In my desperation I went out to plead with whomever it was living in heaven but helped people on earth. Please, not Marcelle again! Please I prefer Satan himself to Marcelle. I went outside to the statue and I silently begged. Please, anyone but Marcelle. This time I'd have to knock her teeth out then I'll get in trouble with the law again. I noticed then that I was pleading with the statue and begging, 'Please, not Marcelle, she's a nut case,' the statue simply looked straight ahead.

I went from secret prayer to silent cursing. That statue was a useless freak. There was no sign of any kind that my pleading was heard. I went back indoors. If it was Marcelle, I continued thinking. I'd make it clear from the start that if she as much as touched me she'd lose her teeth. It was not Marcelle. It was worse. It was Mad Betty. At least 'Mad Betty' was what the others called her. Betty had been going up and down one of those isolated spaces to cool off. Every one at the House of Our Lady of Grace knew that she did. It was also known that Betty, when provoked, had a violent temper. But often it was the others who teased her into reacting. To be fair, at was at times Betty who was asking for the teasing. Why did she have to go on and on about her Scottish dad in a place where all the talk was about people's African roots.

'If I were you,' I told her once, 'even if I did have a Scottish dad I'd blinking keep quiet about it. I'd even lie and say that my pale skin was due to the 'throw-back' people talk about.'

But would Betty listen? No! Betty never listened. Instead, she went on and on and the more she went on the more they teased her. They would laugh and insisted that her Scottish dad goes around Scotland in a skirt. They were all 'Homos' there. Betty's asking what those girls would say if someone made nasty remarks about their black dads, was only shrugged off. I more than once told Betty to ignore the insulting remarks or reports the people who made them. I tried to make Betty laugh and said that in some countries dads go around naked, their private part dangling.

'Where's that country?' I remember Betty asking.

I could not say where because I had made it all up. Instead I said something about Betty wanting to know where it was so she can go for a peaky. On the first night that Betty and I started sharing I made it clear to her that I didn't go in for hugging and kissing. Betty's reply was that she wouldn't want to kiss me, she'd rather kiss the backside of a filthy sow.

'You call me a pig?' I threw my pillow at her.

Betty threw the pillow back at me. I went across to her bed and hit her on the head with my pillow. She hit me with her pillow. Like two little children we ended up in a pillow fight and laughing. We were heard and the carer on duty came and told us that as older teenagers we should set a good example for the younger ones. From then on Mad Betty and I became best mates. We remained mates until a nasty bully got out of hand and Betty was to go missing. But before that bullying event there came some good news for me as if out of the blue.

One day while helping with the trolley library books I was asked if I would be interested in the new Special Further Education unit. That small special unit was to be in a prefab across the field. The unit was an experimental programme for access courses of some kind. I said I'd give it a try but didn't want to let down the trolley book library lady. Six of us were chosen for an Experimental Education programme but we were not told on what grounds. I still shared with Betty but she was not chosen for that unit. Us chosen six filled in papers and the programme began.

Every weekday morning us six went in a line like French schoolgirls and taken to the unit by a tutor brought in especially for the programme. She soon became Ms Jolly rather than her difficult to pronounce French name because she was always cheerful unlike some of the teachers at my old school. Some of the girls, especially those who did not get in the unit, whispered behind Ms Jolly's back. Some said she was a man pretending to be a woman in a suit. Personally I didn't care a damn what Ms Jolly looked like or if she came in a skirt or in fig leaves. She was kind and so encouraging. She told me to consider the language of the books brought by the trolley rather than looking only at the issue dealt with. She also thought that since I said that my mother was from Venezuela I could take Spanish as a second language.

I took both of Ms Jolly's advice and soon the book trolley brought in bilingual picture books. The stories and pictures of those books were babyish but the language, which was English, and another language, made those books interesting. The trolley then brought books, which Ms Jolly called parallel text because they had English and another language such as Spanish or Urdu on each page. I decided there and then to look at parallel text in English/Spanish on each page for my project. Then to my surprise, the trolley also brought books about babies and sexual health. Suddenly the book trolley became popular indeed. Girls queued long before the book bus arrived and handed their books in so that they could borrow another. Soon I had a lot of homework for Ms Jolly who got very agitated if homework was not completed. I hated to see Ms Jolly upset that's why I asked the trolley book lady, as we still called that visiting librarian, if Betty, my roommate, could help me. The lady in charge said yes and Betty began to help but I had to show her how.

I was right about the heavy workload. Ms Jolly was pleasant but she treated us like slaves. Sometimes I liked her a lot but at times I hated her. She made me write things over and over again. Sometimes I felt that she was picking on me. She also, I believed even then, knew someone who spoke Spanish. She took my work home and that person placed lots of red marks all over my hard work. I often felt that if I knew who that person was I'd wring his or her bloody neck. However, Ms Jolly might have been a slave driver but she also gave encouragement. She began to call us 'her girls' and put big ideas in our heads. She said I could become a PR for a director of a classy company, then a company director myself. But for that I had to be fluent in more than one language. We all laughed at that. Elena Peterson, a company director?

One of us six, a girl very small for her fifteen years, had the potential of becoming a botanist. Ms Jolly told that girl off for saying that she was too dumb to be a bota-any thing. We had great fun, hard work but lots of laughter as well. And some of us admitted that coming to The House of Our Lady of Grace was a blessing. We should not have to come to the house but once there some of us were better off.

Wilma, a girl who had run away, then got caught and brought back, was now saying that she was glad that she was caught. We were content working with Ms Jolly when a disaster struck.

The day of that disaster was a terrible one for Betty. A couple of new girls came in. They were older than Betty and I were. They soon found out that Betty's real name was McCarthy. The bullies immediately took away the 'C' from Carthy and replaced it with an 'F'. I told Betty to laugh it away and they would stop. But Betty could not laugh, after the insulting remarks about her mother get her with some white thrash, the term used for white folk by some non–whites.

I wasn't there at the start of the fight because I had gone in to complain to one of the carers in charge. The house had a strict policy against racism and bullying and what the girls were saying about Betty's Scottish dad was, in my opinion, as much racist as what Julie had said about black people. The carer in charge that day was busy but she promised that she'd record it in the usual report book and deal with those bullies. She would not tolerate any one insulting any other's culture. I was satisfied and went back in the gardens. I noticed a commotion at the far end of the garden at the back of the house. I rushed there where the girls often went to settle scores. I saw a fight going on and it was vicious. It was three against one and poor Betty was losing. I intervened and Betty got a chance to crawl away, her lips bleeding. She got to some building rubbish left by the far end of the back of the building. She grabbed hold of a piece of pipe and began to swing it as if she was a deranged animal. Betty screamed obscenities. She swung the pipe right and left and not caring about whose head it connected with. Without meaning to, my school's life-saving swimming class sprang into my mind. I went behind Betty and grabbed her from behind around the waist.

I pleaded with her, 'Don't!' I begged, my own nightmare, as I shall always call it, replaying in front of my eyes.

The commotion was heard. A crowd gathered. Two carers rushed up and dragged, not the bullies, but poor Betty, away. They shook her and dragged her screaming like a wounded lioness.

'They'll send her away, wanna bet?' So began the whispers.

'Good! She's a mental case, a psycho!' Said one of the new girls.

'Too full of herself!' said someone else.

'Yeah, thinks she's better than us,' said one of the girls who believed that Betty was a snob.

'She and her bloody imaginary Scottish daddy.'

'Thinks she's white!' was another comment about Betty.

'Why don't you lot shut up!' I screamed, 'you don't know nothing.'

With that I marched to my room and stayed there for the rest of the evening. I refused to go down for supper. I felt sick anyway. I felt cold for no apparent reason. I waited for Betty but I knew that she wouldn't come. They would take her to one of those 'Quiet rooms', as they were called, high up the building.

Alone in bed that night my nightmare played again and again. It was not fair, bullies get away with things and get the best treatment. Not fair ... Not fair! That man was a criminal on the run but I wasn't supposed to hit him. And I did attack him said his lawyer. 'Not blinking fair', I muttered and turned. Yet I could not wake myself out of the nightmares. While I was going in and out of my personal nightmare my life and that of the others was in danger. It was at midnight that dreadful disaster came.

'Out! Out!' Came the shouts. 'Leave everything behind!'

The disaster was in form of a horrendous fire.

We could've all been burnt alive or killed by toxic fumes. It was the shrill noise of sirens and footsteps with doors banging that finally woke me up shaking.

I heard the words, 'Fire! Fire! Everyone out!' It was one of our carers shouting.

'Fire! Fire!' Some of the girls were shouting, running and forgetting all the fire drills we had. The fire alarms and smoke detectors were by then going mad.

'Don't run! Don't push!' one carer advised.

'Walk calmly to the back,' said another.

'Anyone seen Betty McCarthy?' A carer asked when we got to the back.

'Should be in the permission book.' The carer in charge said.

'Who went on home leave with permission?' Asked another, with the book of our names in her hand.

Betty my room mate could not be found when the list of names was read out. The fire people risked their lives going through thick smoke in every part of the building before deciding that Betty was not inside.

'I want me teddy,' Little Louise whimpered and tried to get back in the house.

'No! Stay out.' A carer held her back.

'Louise we can get you another?' I comforted her with my arm around her.

We lined up, as we had practised, at the far end of the back garden. One of the carers on duty read out our names again. Girls were found to be missing. It seemed that people were all talking at once. It turned out that Betty McCarthy was one of the missing but not in the permission book.

The fire people had arrived with two policewomen. While the firemen rushed up ladders, the policewomen asked questions. The smoke billowed intensely. The fire, so it seemed, started in the basement where our laundry was. There would have been baskets of clothing waiting to be washed or be ironed.

Rumour soon spread that the fire was started deliberately. And because it started in the basement with our laundry and in the middle of the night, the fire quickly spread. That rumour was followed by the whisper that mad Betty, now missing, had done it to burn the lot of us to death.

'Why weren't there working smoke detectors in the basement?' Or something like that I overheard the fire woman asking.

'Somebody going to be in trouble. And it is not just Mad Betty.' Someone whispered, while girls were muttering and huddled together, shivering in scanty night clothing. We were all hurried across the field to Ms Jolly's special education unit.

In that unit we were wrapped up in blankets to stop us shivering. Some girls were selected and whisked away. Most of the girls taken away wanted to go home. Some girls were taken to emergency youth places or fostering families. They could not stay in a half burnt-out and smoke-filled house. In any case it would only be temporary until repairs were done. There were murmurs that the other places for the likes of us were horrible. Nasty things, not simply a bit of punch-up, happened there. Those whispers were frightening and made some of the girls cry like babies and say that they wanted to stay at the House of Our lady of Grace. They were willing to sleep outdoors until repairs were done.

Little Louise was sniffing and calling for her mother. But she too had to go away to foster home. She was promised that it would be a short stay until her time under state protection ended, which would be soon. Still Louise wept for her mother and rubbed her eyes. Louise was taken away somewhere surely not home to her mammy. I hoped that poor Lou, as I called her, would be taken to a temporary family instead of a horrible place.

I'll remember, always, how glad I was that I was not allowed home. I never wanted to see that place again. The smell of that mouldy basement, the cold. The rat-infested disused railway at the back. What would become of me if I did? I'd rather stay forever at The House of Our Lady of Grace. I can, maybe, become a trainee carer or even an office helper like Linda. She was in big trouble when she came to The House of Our Lady. Now she's helping in the office and goes to evening classes. Only six girls were sent to stay at the experimental unit across the lawn. Emergency camp beds came from local business. The six of us who were sent were all from Ms Jolly's group, it turned out. We could not fall asleep again though so we talked about events. I was thinking all the time about Betty.

Poor Betty, I thought. What will they do to you when they catch you and the law will get you? They always do. Oh why did you do it? Why were you so stupid? I wondered if Betty was really wicked. She had caused a lot of damage.

The fire burnt out most of the lower level of the house. We girls were lucky to escape unharmed, except for some cases of smoke inhalation. Oh, Betty! Will I ever see you again? How long will they keep you in prison, oh Betty ... my poor Betty?

After that fire came many and drastic changes. There came stricter rules for a start. Friends were separated. I began to get bouts of depression thinking about things which I had once succeeded in pushing away from my mind. Things like the letters GBH, which were stamped on my life and would follow me everywhere. And there was no excuse, GBH was GBH, no two ways about that. Look how easy it could have been for Poor Betty with that pipe. I believe they'll call it arson when she was finally caught. All that struggling with my thoughts was giving me a headache and making me more depressed and my work began to suffer. What would happen to me when at the age of eighteen I had to leave the care of Our Lady of Grace? My heart felt heavy with trepidation. All that stuff about French Baccalaureate, Ms Jolly called it, might not do me any good. I should've been more realistic and gone to the Training Centre nearby and learnt computing and catering.

Ms Jolly noticed that I was falling behind. She talked a lot to me. At first she pretended that she was only a tutor and not interested in what it was that brought the girls to Our Lady of Grace's care. But I suspected that she knew. And one hard look into her eyes one day and Ms Jolly admitted that she had seen records. We were all in one way or the other only victims of circumstances. 'But the worst you can do,' she preached, 'is to remain victims.'

'Refuse to remain victims.' She insisted.

Easier said than done, I thought.

Without making a big thing of it, Ms Jolly, bless her, was working hard behind the scenes on our behalf. And if people like good old Ms Jolly wanted to help, don't give her hassle. I promised myself and buried my head in books. We had lots of books to read and make notes for homework. We were doing all sorts of projects. One project was for a Creative Writing option. Ms Jolly called it 'Autobiography as Fiction' and suggested we wrote from experience. We could change the names of the people if we wanted. We would pick up some marks and every little bit helped. We studied hard during the time that the building was being repaired.

The main building was repaired and redecorated at what looked like top speed.

Some of the girls came back and with lots of horror stories about the other places that they were sent. We, Ms Jolly's girls, were lucky to be allowed to stay to live upstairs in the Education Unit even though we went to the main building for proper meals and laundry and things. We were happy as a small group. It was like camping out.

Ms Jolly was like an angel guarding her flock. When one of us cried we all cried and made Ms Jolly cry as well. For example, when one of us six had to leave because her time at Our Lady of Grace come to an end we cried. We had a leaving party. Ms Jolly brought her friend Helen, which she called her partner, along. Her partner was a lecturer in a college linked to a university, which recognised that inter-European Qualification that Ms Jolly was trying out. The Partner explained a great deal about universities and colleges. But me, going to a proper college? No chance! I was sure of that.

We girls discussed our plans with Ms Jolly. I said that I'd like to stay at the House of Our Lady, maybe as a trainee carer or an office assistant. Ms Jolly promised that she'd look into it but felt that I should go out into the wider world. The thought of the wide world, the poverty, my hard working mother getting to look older than her age, frightened me. I began to have panic attacks. I began to have nightmares, replaying that day in my damp basement. The court scene event, though juvenile as they called it, was scary. All kept coming back into my dreams. I began to dream of a young man, a buggy, screaming and smelly babies! People with huge heads and teeth grinning at me as I pushed a screeching and rusty buggy along. I would wake up, my body damp from nervous sweating. No thanks, I rather stay here!

One-day Mom and Kevin came for the usual visit. And on that occasion they did not come armed with apples and grapes. They came smiling. I had been at the House for over two years and would soon be eighteen years old. I felt a mixture of relief and panic. Relief if I was to be freed early for good behaviour and at the same time fear that I might not be allowed to stay as a live-in worker. Then Mom broke the news with Kevin grinning like a Cheshire cat.

'Guess what?' Mom paused, then went on, 'we moving, praise the lord.' Mom seemed to have gone all religious talk.

Kevin supplied the rest. It was a small house but with three bedrooms. It was far from those rundown council flats. These were rows of little houses with little gardens at the back and small space in front for flowers. And Mom said yes, we'd take it. It all came out of the blue that very morning. A family moved to a larger council house.

'The lord Jesus finally decided to give us a break.' Mom looked up to the ceiling, where I supposed that Jesus bloke lived.

I wonder where that Lord Jesus was all the time, but I kept my thoughts to myself. Kevin supplied more information.

'Breathing problem will get better,' Kevin babbled, 'the place we lived was declared unfit as it was for humans ... we ... and ...,' Kevin's voice faded away.

Oh no! I was dreaming again. A room of my own? Kevin's breathing better?

He'd be able to play his clarinet now. A house? No more damp and smelly basement? It could not to be anything else but a dream I kept thinking. But it was no dream.

Ms Jolly was delighted for me when she heard the news. She herself had some news. No, I could not stay at the House of our Lady. Others who need it more than I did were now coming in. But Ms Jolly, with the help of her partner had an idea but could not tell me yet in case things did not materialise. From then on things moved at top speed like I was on high-speed roller skates. First Ms Jolly announced that she had sent samples of our special projects for a competition. Second, Mom was allowed to take me to see the new place. Well, it wasn't new. It was one of a set of refurbished homes for highly recommended people. In our case the place we lived, was now condemned and boarded up. Everything seemed to be happening at once.

The day I had to leave the House of Our lady of Grace arrived and I was armed with homemade cards from my friends I had made at the House. Cards came from carers. I cried inside but forbade the tears to come through my eyes. Why I wanted to cry I'd never known. Maybe it was because Ms Jolly kept away. She did so much for me, but did not bother to come and say good-bye. She left me a fancy note, that's all. She included a photograph of herself, with gloves on her hands; she was planting or tending flowers in a garden. She simply wrote, 'Good luck as you climb up the ladder of success.' signing it, Ms Jolly.

I felt the happiness of starting on a new life spoiled. None of the cards I received seemed to fully comfort me. The one person I badly wanted to be there was not. She didn't even take the trouble to come to see me off. My heart wept. I could not take it in why she didn't come. Maybe she fell ill or something. Her car could have broken down or she felt that she had done her job, so, full stop! Why oh why didn't you come to see me off, my soul cried? If she did I would have gone up and kissed her. I suppose to her I was just a stray, which she gave a helping hand to and I had to accept that. Before leaving with Mom in her Sunday best and money for a minicab, I felt that I had to go to the back of the house. I wanted to be on my own for moment. I went to the monument and statue of Our Lady of Grace but had no idea what to say. That statue was only a lump of clay anyway and can't hear me. I could not think of what else to do but to pluck a bloom from well-kept flower growing around the monument. Picking those flowers was something strictly forbidden. I would never know why I did what I did then. I'll always remember placing the bloom to my lips, and then threw it at the feet of the lump of clay moulded into a statue of Our Lady of Grace muttering, 'Take care of me, please.'

I didn't look back. I went straight to Mom where a mini-cab was already waiting to take me to what was the first step to my new life.

I got in the cab to the shouting and waving of a group of about a dozen girls, some new to the House. They circled the cab and waved frantically. Bye-bye!

We were not even quite settled in our new home when an official looking, large and bulging, envelope came. It frightened the life out of me. Just as I was thinking that I was starting a new life, the parcel came like a bolt through my head. The thought of me being sent to prison after all after being sued, flashed in front of my eyes. I was too petrified to open that parcel. That bulging envelope was redirected from The House of Our Lady of Grace. That large brown envelope was like a mini-coffin. I placed it on the kitchen table and sat by it. It was as if at any time a creature would leap out.

Without meaning to I began to mutter to some invisible person standing by me as though listing.

'It was on the telly. Even if they break into your house you're not allowed to hit them. You have to speak nicely to them or call the police and sit down and wait for the police. If you don't have a phone or you mobile ran out, well that's your business. It is your responsibility and no one else, to have phones and mobiles. You're not allowed to go around cracking people's blinking head open even if they forced their way into your home to rob you or for the fear they'll rape you. The law is the law. And hitting people was against the law. They have rights, human rights. They can sue you later.'

The words spun in my head bringing the whole horrible event back. The huge envelope on the table began to grow and started spinning around. It began to spin faster and faster, getting larger and larger. Faster it went until it burst open, ant-like creatures started crawling over my hands. I wanted to brush them away but they had eaten up my hands and both arms. I screamed but the sound stuck in my throat and did not come out. I saw Ms Jolly at the door. She was coming in my house.

'I'm home! Anyone in?' came Mom's soothing voice.

'Oh! Mom,' I threw myself at my mother. It wasn't Ms Jolly after all.

'What's the matter? You're shaking,' said Mom.

All I could do at the time was to look in the direction of the table.

'Ah! It came!' Mom was pleased. She had a message at work to say a packet for Ms. Elena Peterson was sent to her new address.

'I fell asleep.' I glanced at the envelope in front of me.

'Not surprised when you stay up all night to read all them books.' Mom shrugged.

Nervously I opened the envelope. I let out a scream.

'I got in! That place where Ms Jolly sent our work, I got in, all fees paid! It's called a bursary, Mom!' My hands holding the papers were shaking.

Mom got on her knees. She closed her eyes, folded her hands together and softly thanked Lord Jesus in Spanish. After that, everything went crazy. Mom was going mad in the catalogue until I stopped her. She was ticking off stuff she'd order for me as if there was no tomorrow. She phoned her friends, and bragged that her daughter got into a college linked to a university. She even told the grumpy neighbour next door, and twice! The days simply flew past. Then there was the interview. And before I knew it, it was registration time and I was on a bus taking me on a long road.

1

At last I was there. I was at the International University College for The Creative Arts.

There were lots of speeches and piles of documents to pick up; most of which were beyond my comprehension. I looked around several times wishfully thinking that Ms Jolly would somehow pop out from a corner. But she did not. Instead, my eyes fell on those of a tall, strikingly good-looking female as from the Massai tribe. She was obviously a mature student about twenty-three or so. She was definitely not one of those lecturers standing like generals along the side of the hall forcing those obligatory smiles on their faces. Shall I go up and say hello? She looked to be alone. Her eyes held mine and that gave me courage to walk across. But, what shall I say when I got there? Shall I say I like your earrings? It would've been a lie. The hoops dangling from her ears were like the ones hung in birdcages for the birds to swing on. Her hair was trimmed short and tinted a pinkish colour. How ridiculous! I thought.

'I am Elena,' I said as I walked up, 'Elena Peterson.'

She just looked vaguely at me but as if she was studying me. She then asked, without taking her eyes off me, 'You dance?'

I did not reply. Instead, I meekly went on the floor where others were dancing and seemed at ease. I was not much of a dancer, I just shook me bodyline, as Mom would say from a Guyanese song, as did the others. I made sure that I smiled and pretended to be at ease, even though inside my heart was beating faster than the beat of the music. I was petrified of what might be in store for me. Those others no doubt had their traditional 'A' levels. I was a special entrant with that International Baccalaureate or whatever it was that Ms Jolly called it. The piece of music stopped. More drinks and titbits, then a fast piece which I had often heard from the 'Gipsy Kings' singing in their own language. That Gipsy music seemed to drive the dancers wild. They danced around and laughed. So this is my first day in a New World I thought, accepting a plastic cup of juice from my new and strange, fellow student in higher education.

There are no candles; there is no cake, yet, a big HAPPY BIRTHDAY TO ME.

The next morning, shouldering my bag with writing pads, rulers and pens from my local 'Pound Shop'; I walked into my first lecturing day at College of the Creative Arts.

I was earlier than most. The door had just been opened by a uniformed official. A worker in a different colour uniform was putting up a sign that said; 'late comers, through the back'. There was an arrow pointing to a back staircase I had just gone past. My eyes and mind searched for that tall young woman who the day before had asked me to dance. She did not even say her name. Perhaps I should have asked?

My seat was in the middle row of what looked like a cinema with raised seats and a huge screen. Soon the lecture theatre II, as it was labelled on my map, began to fill with nervous chattering. I kept looking in front then behind me but the person I was looking for was nowhere insight. Surely if she was a first year like me then shouldn't she be here? Maybe she was a junior lecturer after all and not a mature student just starting on her first year, as I had thought. Soon the theatre was packed and I wondered how come there were so many of us in the first year. There seemed to be hundreds and many more females than males. I'll never find that young woman from the day before in this crowd, I thought, disappointedly. I was still wondering whom and from where that mature person was, when two important looking people came in. At once, the buzz of us first years stopped. The two people, a man and women, went to the podium in front of the huge screen. The man pointed to a chair while the women went to stand in front of some desk thing. She first gave her name.

'Good morning and welcome.' The woman was still speaking. 'This is your very first step ...' the voice faded away.

After a brief moment I forced my thoughts back to the lecture. I was not sure if the introduction said professor Hoopla! That's because the speaker's voice kept coming and going as my thoughts wandered. The whole theatre began to clap but the women raised her hands suggesting that we should not clap. I felt embarrassed. Already I was doing the wrong thing or so it seemed. Maybe you don't clap in lectures. Professor Van, whatever the name was, went to stand and the woman sat down.

'Learning to learn. What do we mean?' Professor Van whatever then paused.

Was he waiting for a reply? People looked round to each other but no one spoke.

And so began my first main lecture. My shoes began to pinch. The catalogue people had lied in their advert. Those shoes were not leather anything. It was some cheap and hard imitation thing that hurt because it scraped against your flesh. I planned to make a dash home during lunch and get back into my old shoes. My thoughts went once again to the lecturer or who ever it was speaking then to the woman who looked so much like Ms Jolly's friend. I had walked past very close to her when we were leaving the lecture theatre. She was standing at the door and smiling or nodding to us as we filed out. She did not appear to recognise me. If she did she was very good at hiding it.

Come lunchtime I had to change my mind about rushing home and getting back. If I did, I might get back late for my two-o'clock seminar of my small group. I was wandering around the campus and bearing the discomfort of my shoes when I heard her. The voice came as I was checking to see if I could afford any of the items on the menu.

'You understood the lecture on learning?' she asked.

I looked around and there she was. Again, she gave, what to me was, a vague look.

'Not really, all those drawings and new words, I'd have to look them up.'

'Mmh ...' she murmured, taking a tray from the pile, handing it to me then taking one for herself.

'I don't eat much at lunchtime. It'll make me sleepy,' I lied.

'You mean you can't afford to.' She had read my thoughts.

Maybe she was some witch's daughter or medicine women from Jamaica, or maybe Brazil, it was difficult to place her.

'I'll have a jacket tuna,' she said, as if demanding that I took the same.

I took a jacket potato with tuna filling as she did. I watched her take a small portion of coleslaw which she said we could share. I began to think then that she was secretly laughing at me. Did I stand out as wearing clothes from catalogues?

While we were eating our tuna- filled jacket potato and shared coleslaw amidst the chatter of students, I was thinking. Why should it bother me what she thought of me? I broke the silence, well someone had to, between us.

'Err...I forgot your name, silly me!' I found enough courage to say.

'You can't forget what you didn't know in the first place.' She shrugged.

'Today,' I began, in order to change the subject, 'I saw someone that looked like someone what had visited my old place.'

I waited for her to ask me what old place. I could tell though that she was thinking about what I said but her simple response was, 'Mmh...is that so?'

She did not even look up from the paper cup she was bringing to her lips.

Blast! I thought; hope you're not going to say Mmh ... every time.

Even your accent is not the Jamaican talk I heard in the streets and at the House of Our Lady of Grace. Maybe you're the daughter of some rich African Chief, over here for English Education which them overseas lot like.

She managed a smile and picked up both trays.

Oh God, I forgot that she reads people's thoughts! I must be careful not to think anything about her in her presence.

We walked together; or rather I followed slightly behind her, towards the square where there were a number of students in small groups, chatting.

Then she turned and said, 'You following me or som'ink?'

Her face was expressionless.

'Sorry! I didn't mean...err...didn't realise I was, err...following you.' I stammered.

I felt rejected and she must have noticed.

'See you around.' She walked away from me and didn't even turn to look back leaving me standing and thinking that she obviously did not want to be friends.

I felt very alone .There was no one around that I knew. At least some of the students who were laughing and chatting were probably from the same school, even same 'A' Level classes. That's why they found it easy to form small groups. I was still standing there like a fool when I heard a male voice.

'Hi!' He greeted. 'You're new, aren't you?' he asked.

'Yes, I'm first year.'

'Ah, never mind. You'll soon make friends. I'm Andre, *et tu?*'

'Elena, and I don't speak French, sorry.'

I found myself walking along while he talked and offered to show me around. I said a polite thank you but secretly wished he would go away.

'I must rush to the library and grab a couple of books before my afternoon seminar.' I had made my excuse but it didn't work.

'That's where I'm heading,' he said with a broad grin, which irritated me.

'What year are you then?' I asked as we walked up to the huge building called, according to the fancy lettering, Nelson Mandela Research Centre.

'I've just jumped into my third year,' he replied.

Wow! So it's your last year then?'

'No, I am on the Continuing Ed. Program. I'm going stay on for an extra year for my Masters. I can even stay on for my doctorate if I so wish and that would be another three years,' he explained, as proud as peacock.

Christ! You'll be here for five years. I didn't think that I would want to stay at one place for five years.

But I kept my thoughts to myself. I went to sit by the computer to begin to search for books on my list. I hoped that he would take the hint and walk away but he just went to sit nearby. It suddenly came to me how that mysterious mature student must have felt about me hanging around her. Now the table was turned and an unwelcome and rich looking person was following me.

'See you.'

I rushed away from him.

Two o'clock came and I went to my seminar feeling sure that my mysterious lady would be there. She was not. We had been divided into small groups of twelve to discuss the morning's mass lecture. There was a lively discussion about what 'Learning' meant to us. On and on the discussion went, at times heated and with disagreement as to what the Professor had said or did not say. I found myself joining in and loving it even though the class had become very noisy. I wondered, however, and somewhat anxiously, to which other small seminar my mystery mature student had gone. Soon it was four in the afternoon and the end of my first seminar. I dashed out and went to sit on the stone wall outside the main entrance of the library. I watched students go in and out with piles of books in hand. All the students seemed to have someone with them. Perhaps they were second or third year and knew each other. I suddenly missed the girls of the House of Our lady of Grace. Some of them said stupid and boring things but we did have some laughs. Why was it that I was the only one that came to this university college? Where did the others of Ms Jolly's group go? My project 'Biography as Fiction' could not have been the best. Suddenly I felt that I had enough for one day and made my way home.

Mom was early home especially for my first day. She made my favourite of fried okra with lots of onions and tomatoes on a bed of rice. She had kept everything warm and waiting for when I arrived. Mom could not wait until I had finished eating to ask how it all went. Kevin was also home early because he had decided to skip his After School Clarinet session. I rebuked him.

'You must not skip lessons. You will never get anywhere in life if you go skipping lessons.'

Kevin said he wanted to be there for when I got home but he would not do that ever again. I gave him a hug and said how lucky I was to have him and Mom behind me and nothing was going to stop me.

'Any of them friends you made at the home, got in?'

Mom began to bombard me with questions as she sat and watched every mouthful of food I stuck in my mouth.

'Not really, maybe they've gone somewhere else,' I muttered while I chewed.

'Oh! My Elena,' Mom said with pride in her voice and eyes. 'My Elena, she is so clever, yes? 'Mom leaned over and gave me a hug.

'Ah!' I teased 'All parents claim that their child is clever.'

'Yeah, wonder...is there a single not-bright child in the world?' Kevin replied before leaving the family table.

He went to his room to practise his clarinet and drive the neighbours mad.

I smiled and counted myself lucky to have such a nice and loving family even without a dad who deserted us. Nothing can stop me; nothing in the world can put brakes on me now. I thought of a poem I read at the House of Our Lady of Grace. It was done in fancy lettering and framed. Ms Jolly had stuck it on the wall of our special unit.

It was written by a woman, who said, 'On those rocks, I shall clamber to success.' And she went on to list some of rocks thrown in her path, yet she climbed.

I rose and began to clear the table. After helping with the dishes I had a short rest then started scanning that lengthy reading list. It would take me years to read all those books, of that I was sure. I had to read one particular book and prepare for the next seminar. That seminar was to be for the lecture on Postcolonial Literature, whatever that was. There was also something to prepare for Spanish. No trouble, my Spanish had taken off since Ms Jolly suggested I took that as my second subject. Mom was helpful though. What she knew was the Latin American Spanish of her childhood school days in Venezuela. It was the post-colonial stuff that looked like gibberish and leapt up from the paper hitting me in the eyes. I read a while but couldn't make out the argument of the chapter I had to prepare. I also had to keep checking words in my dictionary. For example, the difference between a *Paradox* and a *Parody*. I was sure though that knowing my luck I'll learn the difference and then when it came to exam time, if they appear on the exam papers, I'm bound to get the two mixed up. Our seminar 'learning to learn' tutor had already explained that we would be covering 'Words at Work' because if you got one word, which you do not under stand or misinterpreted, you might give the wrong answer to a question. She gave an example of someone who got *Affluent* mixed up with *Effluent*...Ugh!

Soon my thoughts wandered off from *parody* and *paradox* to that mature student. If she was from African or Caribbean parents, she's bound to tell me her name when she is good and ready. The next day came, and the next.

I buried my head in books at the same time looking out for my mysterious mature student. I also had to be dodging one other student by the name of Andre. There was something about him that annoyed me. He appeared a bit too sure that any female would fall for him. Not Elena, I'm here to work hard, get qualification, then a push job!

One day, after I had been at college for three weeks, something happened. I was at my bus stop at the back of the college. Suddenly a voice said, 'Hi.'

'Oh! Hi, 'You make me jump.' I said laughing.

'You mean I startled you?' She corrected.

'You been away?' I asked nervously.

'Mmh,' she grunted, leaving me to wonder if it was Mmh for yes or Mmh for no.

Christ if she says one more Mmh…I'll have to kick her, I thought, as if I could. She'll probably throw me on the ground and stamp on me as an elephant would. The bus came and we both got on. There was only one vacant seat and she indicated that I should take it. I went like a meek little puppy and sat down. She stood up until a vacant seat was available. We did not speak until I got to my bus stop and we both got off.

'I didn't know you lived in this area.' I frowned.

'Did I say I did?' she replied coolly.

'No you didn't.'

'Was your preparation, OK?' she asked, and then crossed the road to the bus stop for going in the direction from where we just came.

I shook my head thinking what a strange young woman this was. The way she looked at me as if she was studying me. Maybe she was learning how to analyse people. She was probably training to be a counsellor. Main thing was that the bus trip was to be the first of many. It was on the second such trip that I demanded that I must know her name. I couldn't be on the road home with someone, whose name I didn't know.

'Mmh,' she grunted, muttering with a shrug, 'it's Esmay!'

'It's nice name?' I meant well but apparently offended her.

'That's what people say to patronise a little child!' she sneered.

'Sorry, I didn't mean to patronise or offend.'

One day we had a late seminar. It was nearing Christmas and darkness came early. Esmay got off the bus with me as usual. On that occasion, however, she didn't dash across the road. Instead she walked me home. I tried to stop her because she would have to go back on her own, but she insisted and waited at the road-side by my house until I turned the key and went in. I waved from inside the door-way. I knew then that I would invite her in but first I had to tell Mom. When I did, mom was cautious. She felt that the mature student sounded a bit too old for me. Might I not do better going round with students of my own age? I disagreed. I said that Esmay was a nice person. As planned, I invited Esmay home for the Xmas vacation.

It was Esmay, however, who first took the step to let me meet her family.

It all started when one of Esmay's aunts was planning a 'Hair Day' as a Show Case to publicise her 'Hair Care Centre' as she called it. Esmay and I were sitting on the grass of the college's green. We were chewing my mom's homemade sandwiches when out of the blue Esmay asked, or rather stated in a matter-of-fact way, 'You can be one of my models.'

'Model? What, me a model?' I stopped chewing.

'Mmh, well, you see my auntie got this publicity day yeah, it's for her 'Hair Care Centre' and we the helpers must bring two contrasting models.'

'Ah! You mean, do me hair and show it off?'

'Yep!' Esmay said, looking at my head, 'And your hair sure looks terrible, shame,' she continued. 'Long wavy hair but kept like dry grass.'

'Well, some of us can't afford hair dressers you know?'

'This one is a free hairstyle for all the models.'

Esmay paused then continued, 'Plus their faces in the press. Who knows what might come out of it?'

The Hair Day soon came and Esmay performed miracles with my hair and that of Joy. We were all at the Centre from midday until the early evening when the show started. Nervously, Joy and I waited with the other models. Two of the others were elderly ladies, one bluish rinsed grey hair, the other grey hair with silver strands. I had my hair pinned up high while two twisted curls trickled down the side of my face to each of my shoulders. Esmay did something to make my curls look very dark brown in places and lighter brown in others. Joy had blond extensions with strands of yellowish hair. When I saw myself in the mirror I got a sudden urge to go up and kiss Esmay. Instead, I went up to her and said thank you. All she did as response was to use two of her fingers to pull the two tiny curls she had left hanging by each side of my face into place. I wonder then if she would throw me a back hander if went up and I kissed her, as I did to poor Michelle that time. Esmay was not the hugging and kissing type, unlike other students.

We all waited nervously as names of presenters were called and they went up with their models. Esmay was the last on the list. I felt my hands getting colder and colder. When our turn finally came I whispered to Joy, who was holding on to my hand.

'Don't you dare pass out?' I whispered, as I felt her hand go cold.

The poor girl was shaking. Finally it was our turn to model a hairstyle. Joy and I walked out with me holding my head high and Joy shaking like a leaf. There was a tremendous roar. People were clapping like mad. Some began to chant.

'Contrast, Contrast!' Some rose to their feet. Cameras were clicking. Joy and I, still hand in hand, took a bow. The chant changed to, 'we want the presenters, we want the presenters, we want...' on and on they went until Esmay came out. She was followed by a line of presenters. The models came out to more roars with cameras flashing. After what seemed like hours and several bows by us, the models, we returned backstage. There, more reporters appeared this time asking for our names.

Some asked each of us what we wanted to do next. Most of the others said that they wanted to be models or singers. Joy, however, perhaps out of spite, said that she wanted to look after old people. I followed her in teasing the media lot and said that I would like to be a lady pirate like Anna Bonny who we learnt about in a special seminar about NOTORIOUS LADIES. One reporter was certainly disgusted at our reply and left.

It was at that stage that poor Joy broke down suddenly. The day had become too much for her. I had to take her in my arms merely to comfort her.

Esmay's auntie, the owner of the centre, invited all the presenters and their models to her home where she had organised a garden party. It was at that party that I plucked up courage and gave Esmay a congratulation kiss on her cheek. Again that Mmh grunt from her before she announced that from now on she was in charge of my hair. It was at that party that I was properly introduced to Esmay's close relatives. The party itself, with soft drinks for us models, lots of jerk chicken, jerk veggies and loud music blaring from inside, went on until late. It was great fun especially since Esmay did not throw me a back-hander When we were away from the others I gave her that congratulation kiss. She just grunted her usual Mmh!

Nearing midnight, Mom said we had to leave because she still had some last minute Xmas shopping to do. One of Esmay's numerous cousins offered to drive us home. Mom politely declined with a nice thank you .Instead, we went up the road to a tatty looking mini-cab place. We got in some rattling old car and managed to get home in one piece. Mom paid ten quid for the ride. Once we were alone, Kevin remarked yawning, 'That driver picked that motor up from the junkyard.'

'Yeah! And took Mom's ten quid.' I joined in.

'And bin looking our Elena up in his mirror,' Mom said, 'Pig!'

'Hi! You sayin' that only pig men look at me?' I asked Mom.

'Pig or not, them better keep them filthy roving eyes off my Elena.' Mom warned.

We laughed, as we usually did, even when we had very little money.

The next day was Xmas Eve morning. As arranged, Esmay was coming to my house for the first time. She arrived at the exact hour that we had said. She rang my doorbell. I was expecting her and she had met my family before, yet I felt very nervous. I went and opened the door and let Esmay in. She had a bunch of flowers with her. She said good morning to mom and handed her the bunch of flowers.

'*Muchos Gracia*' said Mom as she took the flowers.

I led Esmay to a chair. I still feared that Mom would ask her all sorts of personal questions. Who were her family, were they Jamaican or *Bajans*, the term used for Barbadians. Mom was sure that she could tell a Barbadian a mile away because of the accent. My fear was unfounded. After some polite conversation with Esmay and a glass of cold juice, Mom announced that she had to get some spices. She already had the meat for the *pepper-pot* but needed the right spices. Kevin wanted to go with her but Mom insisted that he stayed behind and practiced his music for the evening carol service. After Mom left for the shops and Kevin went upstairs to practice his clarinet piece for the evening service, Esmay and I were left alone.

'My mom seemed to like you.'

I was sitting opposite Esmay by the table.

'Mmh!' … Esmay said, almost to herself, 'I wonder why your mother thinks that you need a chaperone?'

Esmay also wanted to know what *pepper-pot* was. I explained that it was a meat dish boiled for hours, in pepper and *Cassareep*, which was fermented cassava juice. Mom had got the recipe from some Guyanese woman.

'I think she cooks and eats it to remember her man. He is Guyanese.' I said.

'She didn't look like she had a man when she came to the Hair Fair.'

'He's me dad. He left us. He's gone back but she secretly still thinks of him.'

Esmay changed the subject abruptly. She talked about her trip to the US and that she'd be away for weeks working on some scheme for disadvantaged kids.

'So, you really are going?' I failed to keep the sadness from my voice.

'Look, we've been through this, ok? I need the money for my fees.'

Esmay and I had discussed the summer job in the US. She had pointed out that what she got for helping in her aunts Hair Centre couldn't cover the fees and get her books, feed and cloth her and pay government Community Charge. I understood yet I felt very sad. A lump grew in my throat.

'Three weeks is a long time. Also, if you work, when will you do your studies for the essays we have to hand in at the beginning of term?' I pointed out.

We had gone, after a snack, for a stroll in the park. We had been walking in silence when Esmay suddenly stopped. I stopped walking also.

'You'll be away for a long time.' I said, without knowing why I was feeling so heavy hearted.

'Look,' she said softly, 'Three weeks will fly.'

She then playfully wrapped her fingers around one of my curls.

'Just brush it until I get back and tend it proper.'

It was then something came to me. I remembered what Ms Jolly often told us.

'Listen! Ms Jolly, I told you about her before. Well, she reckoned that you must use your experience, good or bad, to your advantage. Why not write up your trip to the US for your independent project?' I suggested as we began to make the return trip to my house.

'Actually, I was thinking of doing something English, reading a couple of books like...you know ...for that project.'

'Well, listen and make notes on how the Americans talk. They have different names for things.' I suggested.

'Do they?' Esmay asked.

'They do! Washroom is really toilets and gasoline is really petrol, so I believe.'

Still laughing at the things Americans said and wrote we arrived back home.

Mom had returned and made us tea. It was Esmay's first tea at my house. Mom and Kevin were present. We ate, then Mom and Kevin wished Esmay good luck in the US.

It was getting late. So with a heavy heart I took Esmay to the bus stop. I badly wanted to say goodbye but that might be too final. Goodbye means that the person was going forever. I wanted her to come back. She noticed my hesitation and said as she got on the bus, 'Three weeks is a short time,'

The bus drove off and I waved.

Heavy hearted I got back home. Mom began to ask questions.

'What about boy friend? Surely at her age she must have a man friend? Did she have kids? At her age, most them girls have kids.'

Mom then questions me about male students at the college.

'Any nice young man showed an interest in my pretty Elena?'

I said there was one but I suspected that he might be the kind that's looking for a baby-mother.

'I have no intention of being any man's baby-mother. No thanks. I'm at college to work hard, get a qualification, then get me a top PR job. No mother to any man's baby you be sure.' I told mom.

'*Si,* Keep you head till a good young man comes,' Mom said, then added, 'Mind you what good did me being a good girl do for me? I still end up alone fending for us three.'

Sadness came over mom, 'I pray our holy mother to protect you and give you two a better chance.'

I went up and kissed mom on the top of her head which was forming a grey patch.

'We managing Ok and things will get better and better, you'll see.'

That night I got to bed still thinking of Esmay. What if she never came back? There was talk of better opportunities in the US for educated black people than there were in London. She might decide to stay and train as a nurse or something like that.

She'll earn more than she could dream of getting in the UK. She might be tempted to stay and not return to England!

2

Christmas and all its fuss and over-eating came and went. Then, on New Year's Eve, we all went to the house of a family where a great deal of both Spanish and Portuguese were spoken. Other guests spoke all sorts of versions of Spanish on top of versions of English. Anthony, for example, was from somewhere in Africa and his Portuguese was an African version, which he mixed with English. He was introduced to us as a business management student. He was going back to manage his family's large enterprise.

'So, you want to learn English?' I asked and smiled while thinking, take me for a big jackass, eh! Want to learn English, me foot!

My mom on the other hand was very impressed by this, apparently well-mannered, young man, asking my mom's permission for me to show him around. Mom was swallowing every word he said and the polite manner in which he said them.

'English is very nice. I really like the English language and must practice.' He smiled.

Watching him, I wondered if that's the way a cat grinned before it grabbed the mouse for its supper. No chance, I thought, you grabbing this mouse here. I outwardly smiled back to him. That outward reaction of mine pleased Mom, I could tell. I could almost hear the wedding bells chiming in her ears. Her only daughter is to marry some African chief's son. Not on your Nelly as my grumpy neighbour would say in her Cockney slang she brought over to the new residence. This lone daughter is going to be a top-class professional, maybe even an entrepreneur.

'I would like to hear from your parents, that's how we do things in, err where I come from.'

Mom appeared to be over the moon.

'Yes, I am very delighted you say that. Your daughter was respectfully brought up as my sisters are and...' his voice faded away as my thoughts turned to what Esmay might be up to in the US.

On our way back home, which was by then New Years Day, Mom went on and on about Mr Alowally, being very polite and a gentleman with a positive future and no doubt from a respectable family, and the family we went to for 'Old Year's Night', as Mom called it, speak highly of him. Therefore, there was no harm in him visiting us and if he asked to take me out; Kevin would go along as well. And that was how Anthony, Mr Alowally to Mom, began to visit our house.

Every time Anthony visited, he either brought flowers for Mom or a CD or some little gift for Kevin. I usually made an excuse that I had too much reading and note taking to do, and could not possibly find the time to show him around. Mom, on the other hand, seemed to want me to go out with him. She said that I was doing too much reading without a break. In addition, Mom was always smartly dressed when her Mr Alowally came and the more he visited and Mom made a fuss of him the more depressed I became. I began to ask myself if the press and others who made such a hullabaloo about Asian arranged marriages were ever aware of other groups in London who do the same but in a more discreet manner. Thing was, I would not want to hurt my Mom. She had worked so hard to feed and clothe us, single-handed. At the same time I didn't want any boy friend to come block my way. I was soon beginning to despair and struggling with not wanting to hurt Mom but at the same time I was bored with her Mr Alowally, as polite as he was. Then, one afternoon I got a text on my mobile. I had to use all my will power not to jump up and down and shout. Esmay was on her way back! I wanted to shout but held back. I didn't want Mom to know how delighted I was. But I was not sure why I did not want her to know.

It was nearly the end of January when Esmay returned. She had missed a whole week of the new term of college and I was worried that she would have fallen behind. She had arrived in the afternoon and after dumping her bag home she came round to my house. I was so glad to see her that I flung myself at her for a hug and fought back my tears of happiness.

'Tell me all about it. How was it in New York?'

'Well, for one thing, there are two New York's, the state and the city.'

Esmay went on to give a lengthy explanation about her stay in the US.

And so began a very long evening that continued well after midnight until Esmay had missed the last bus back home. We went to my room. There, I tried on the present Esmay had brought me. We laughed, because the label said that it was an African wrap, the funny thing was it was made in the US. But once in my room, away from Mom's ears, I wanted to know personal details including if Esmay had met a handsome and rich young man. At the mention of young man, Esmay merely looked at me and gave the usual 'Mmh' which could have meant anything or nothing in particular. Esmay then changed the subject abruptly to working with rough kids. Her voice began to fade away. She was falling asleep across my bed, her legs dangling over the side. When Esmay finally stopped talking, I gently took off her trainers and placed her legs properly on the bed. On tiptoe, I went downstairs. There I found Mom, her head rested on the table, and fast asleep.

'Get to bed, Mom.' I said, waking her up, 'You'll get a stiff neck.'

When Mom learnt that Esmay was so tired from jetlag that she fell asleep on my bed, Mom being Mom, wanted to give up her own bed. She promptly said she could sleep happily in the large armchair as long as her feet were on the footstool. She had fallen asleep like that before. I could sleep in her bed and Esmay could sleep on mine. But we had to phone Esmay's mom to let her know that Esmay had fallen asleep here and would be safe until next morning.

'That's the duty of any good Venezuela *madre;* you protect other people's children as you protect yours,' Mom insisted, using her Spanish philosophy as usual. I agreed to phone but did not agree with Mom giving up her own bed. I put it, however, that there was a danger that Esmay might wake up. She'd think that she was a bother and sneak out. She would tiptoe out to try and find a mini-cab.

'What if she did and something bad was to happen to her?' I pointed out.

In the end Mom agreed but still felt that my single bed was too small for two grown-up young women. Mom made me collect all cushions off the armchair. She then gave me spare bedding to make a bed on the floor of my room. Mom even tiptoed into the room and watched me make up the bed. To my surprise, as soon as Mom left the room, Esmay whispered, 'She gone?'

I whispered back, 'Yes, but she may come back.'

I explained that my door did not have a lock. And that my mom often peeped in to see I was OK. That was our first 'sleep-over', Esmay and I, though with one of us on cushions and bedding on the floor.

The next time Esmay and I spent the night together was at the beginning of the second year at college and the start of a long term of sharing time together after lectures.

That second 'sleep-over' was at Esmay's after a nasty row I had with Mom. It was horrible. I had never quarrelled with my mother before. We've had disagreements but this one was a big bust up. Kevin got very upset and ran off to his room. The row started when I found out that Mom had, against my wishes, written to my dad about me going to a university college. She told him that I had been doing very well for myself.

Suddenly, he showed interest. I was livid. He hadn't cared a damn when we were in the slimy basement or when I was in the home and with the possibility of being sued hanging over my head. Now he'd heard I was doing well he suddenly wanted to be a caring father? I called him a bastard and Mom hit me. How dare I call my own daddy a bastard? I immediately apologised to Mom but insisted that he was conning her. He was waving Canada under her nose and she was falling for it.

'He dumped you in London with two kids,' I bawled, my hands shaking from the rage I felt at a man who had left his wife and kids to struggle like we had. And now that same wife was going all gooey-eyed over him. Well, he can stuff his Canada, so I thought, but kept to myself until Mom broke into my train of thought.

'Was me. I didn't want to take you back. Go back to what? I told him *sé* you children had a better chance here. There...nothing, not a thing...no *ha nada*! So I say I stay, for the children...give them a good chance. It be my fault if we'd starved,' Mom moaned, breaking into her natural 'tongue' as she often did when upset.

'Oh Mom...Mom...open your eyes.'

I tried to persuade her, 'He probably thinks that you saved some money so he wants you back.'

'How dare you! How dare you talk likes that bout you own father. Get out me sight!'

Mom screamed at me like an angry animal which was very much out of character.

'Mom, listen...!

'He *brang* you in this world,' said Mom, using the East-End slang, *get out me sight.*'

I knew then that Mom was secretly concerned though she forced herself not to agree with what I said.

I went to my room, packed an overnight bag, and as I got to the front door, I heard Mom shout, 'Where the hell you think you going?'

'Getting out your sight.' I shouted, slamming the front door behind me.

'Get back here.' Mom's voice thundered from behind the door.

'Elena, come back here at once, you hear me?' she bellowed.

I ignored her, running through our little gate. Like an angry mare escaping from somewhere or something. I made my way to the bus stop. Only when I was at the bus stop did I question where was I going?

There was nowhere but Esmay's. At that time she was still living at home but was on the list for a room in Block A on the campus. That block was meant for mature students needing a quiet environment to study. I was in a terrible emotional state by the time I arrived at Esmay's house and pressed the bell. For a while I was crying so much that no one was able to make any sense of why I was weeping. In fact even I myself didn't know why the mention of my own dad and my mom sapping up to him after the way he treated us brought such angry tears.

Esmay's mom was very understanding and said that I could stay the night but she must let my mother know where I was and that I was safe until next morning. I was made up the sofa bed in the living room. Esmay sat on the floor by me and held my hand under the covers. It was our second night together though we again slept separately.

I must have fallen asleep because when I opened my eyes again I could hear whispers and smelt coffee. After a spell in the bathroom I had a cup of strong coffee and a slice of toast. Esmay's mom said she'd drive me home. Esmay was told by her mother to let her deal with things. It meant that Esmay was left behind. We got to my house and Esmay's mom came in with me to talk to Mom. She told my mom that I was very sorry for whatever it was that happened. Of course I would apologise. I did. Mom said that I had never behaved like that before. She thanked Esmay's Mom for looking after me and bringing me home. After Esmay's Mom left, my mom said I must never run off again. We must discuss things. Anyway, things would be all right from now on.

But things weren't OK. Mom gradually became obsessed with Canada.

My dad had been writing to relatives there and going on about how well Guyanese people were doing over there. Mom read part of the letters to me. According to what my dad wrote, many Caribbean people, who got their qualifications in England, packed their bags and cleared off to Canada and the US. At those letter-reading times I suspected from Mom's voice that I was to take note about the supposed good life in Canada once I get 'my bits of papers' as she's been referring to my studies. On and on Mom went about Canada, especially Toronto, where, according to dad, half of the Guyana-Asian population had moved to settle. I began to feel that if Mom didn't stop going on she'd do me blinking head in. Kevin was also worried. He told me that it would be a disaster if Mom took us to Canada. Of course I was of age and she could not force me, but she could force Kevin to go.

Kevin once frightened me. He said he'd throw himself out the aeroplane if Mom forced him. I said I would have a quiet talk with Mom. But before I had a chance to have a quiet talk, she broke the news, which increased Kevin's fear.

Mom told us that our dad was going to live with cousins in Toronto. His cousins had got a job lined up for him. As soon as he settled a bit he'd send for us. I could be trained as a nurse. Me, with my bits of university papers from England, would have no trouble getting into nursing. Many Guyanese women are nurses and drive flash cars and have their own apartments. Nursing is a high-class job there, so my dad wrote to Mom.

Ugh! I thought. All those bedpans full of poo, blood all over the place, women screaming their heads off as they pushed a head the size of a water melon out of their tiny vagina. Jesus, the pain! I shuddered...couldn't bare watching their agony and hearing the screams. Me, a nurse? *Nunca,* as Mom would say. Any case, nursing not part of my dream of success, although I respect those who want to do it.

A few days later I discussed the Canada and nursing talk by Mom with Esmay. Had she ever thought about being a nurse, I asked her.

'Nah!'...she grunted, 'enough nurses and midwives among my relatives.'

'What of the pain? How can anyone listen to that day in and day out? Of course, those with money can go private and have caesareans.'

'Your 'woman part' stretches anyway,' said Esmay, 'women are made so that they can stretch down there.'

'Knowing my luck, mine would refuse to stretch.' I said, 'No thanks, no babies for me, ever!'

We both laughed as the conversation went from being a nurse to childbirth. But some of my sniggering was embarrassment at my ignorance of things. I was gone eighteen year old. Some of my age group already had two, even three kids hanging on to their skirts. I asked many more questions of Esmay. In fact, we talked a lot those days. I often came up with things to do with sex mainly from books or watching late-night telly. Esmay often had to put me right that those moans and groans of people having sex as shown on telly were only to tantalise. In reality, it was nothing like that.

'How you know? You ever...err...had a boyfriend?'

'Mmh...I'm no virgin, but for me, it was the most boring and disappointing thing I did. Anyway, why you asking all these questions?'

'Curious, that's all.'

In spite of my sometimes irritating questions, Esmay and I were getting very close. At the same time Mom was spreading the news about Canada to everyone, including Anthony. He had heard it already anyway from the family who had introduced him to our family. Anthony began visiting more often. Sometimes he came on Sunday lunchtime. He began to have tea with us some evenings. Mom was obviously encouraging the visits. Mom was trying hard, as hard as ever, to bring Anthony and me together. But the harder she tried the more I hated him because I knew what Mom was thinking; she was offering two choices, neither of which I fancied. I had to talk to someone so I talked to Esmay about Anthony's visit and him going on and on about his father's business which was getting on my nerves. Esmay then suggested that I told my

Mom how I felt. Keeping secrets was bad for everyone. If I was not happy with this Anthony's visits, say so. I had to find a good time when Mom was in a good mood and tell her. Don't keep feelings secret she insisted. But as I listened to Esmay's advice I thought, how strange. Esmay had her own secrets. I was sure that there was something about her which she wasn't telling me. I couldn't work out what it was though. Sometimes, she got very moody and didn't want to talk. Sometimes, she missed a whole day's lessons but wouldn't say where she went and why. At the same time she was finding fault with the way I dressed. She said more than once that I looked like I had sprung straight out the pages of a low-standard shopping catalogue. I felt insulted at that and made that clear to her.

One Saturday, Esmay dragged me to one of the shops where they sold remnants. She made me spend my few pennies for a couple of pieces .She then dragged me along a couple blocks to one of her many aunts. This one, known in her community as The Seamstress, made up outfits for people who brought their own fabric. When I asked how much for making me two skirts, the seamstress looked at Esmay then said that Esmay would tell me. As soon as we got back outside in the street I asked Esmay about cost because I was worried that Mom already owed the catalogue people.

'Don't worry, it's all settled.' Esmay said casually.

'But how? You're not paying for me! Mom'll do what she can.'

'Stop worrying, like some old woman, for Christ sake!'

About two weeks later I saw myself in the skirts The Seamstress had made. I was shocked. True, I had agreed to the style that everyone was into around campus; however, I was not prepared for how short it would look on me. Perhaps my long legs were to blame. But looking in the mirror, I looked like some doll out of a child's toy collection, but one with two pale brown sticks for legs.

'My mom will get a heart attack!' I told The Seamstress.

'You look beautiful, very pretty.' Esmay muttered softly, turning me round as if I was a *maniquí* in a shop window.

Once we get back in the street I said, 'You want me to look like some stupid git while you live in jeans and baggy palazzos.'

'Mmh...we'll get you a pair of peddle pushers OK? So stop putting yourself down. You look very pretty.'

I nervously got home. I found Mom in a good mood. She'd got the latest letter from Dad. His cousins had organised a pay-later plan for him to travel from Guyana to Canada. Mom looked very happy when she told Kevin and me. I thought it was good time to show off my new outfit that actually made me look less like a pauper of one of those low-cost catalogues. I went to my room, dressed, and then came back down to the living room. Kevin was plastering jam on a slice of bread. He saw me. He stared at my mini skirt and gasped, 'Jesus Christ!'

Kevin put the knife and the slice of bread down and said, 'Oh! Err...got to practise with me mate up the road.'

He gave a nervous look in the direction of the kitchen and rushed away, had a brief change of thought, and went back to the table.

Kevin picked up the knife, looked again in the direction of the kitchen where Mom was happily humming a tune and left the house with the knife in his hand.

I took a deep breath and went to the kitchen door. I forced a smile on my face, 'Mom,' I called, 'My new outfit, you like it? It's the latest fashion on campus.'

I spun around, forcing myself to be calm though I was really petrified. What if she was to throw a saucepan at me? Mom stopped what she was doing turned round, and her mouth went wide open. I had no idea that her mouth could open that wide. Her face got funny. Her eyes got bigger. I got scared for her safety. What if she fainted or had a fit or even dropped dead.

'You alright Mom?' I heard my voice asking stupidly.

Mom stared from my waist to the end of my skirt then she roared like a lioness, 'Up those stairs, up those stairs at once!'

'Mom, what's...I mean everyone...'

I never completed that sentence because Mom moved towards to me while dangerously brandishing the wooden spoon she had in her hand.

'Upstairs! Take that indecent thing off before I rip it off.'

This time her voice was not a roar but more threatening. She had gone very pale and was breathing heavily.

Mom didn't drop dead but we did have a second nasty row. I insisted that I was a young woman now. She couldn't let me go on dressing like a page from a catalogue. It was a nasty thing to say. Mom could only afford things on monthly payments. I regretted it and apologised right away. But after that Mom went silent. My mom hardly said anything for weeks. I tried my best behaviour, cooked at weekends, helped with the ironing, yet Mom seemed to avoid any conversation with me. It was horrible. Kevin seemed to keep out of my way as if afraid to upset Mom if he was too friendly with me.

Esmay became my only real companion. I did make friends with other students but most of the time I was with Esmay. She made me laugh with some of the things she came up with and her serious face that went with them. For most of the time we buried our heads in our books while at the same time Esmay had to work Saturdays and two evenings to earn some money. When she was away I had to study alone. I also had to keep Andre and the likes of him at bay. There seemed to be a race on by the second and third year males to date first year students. Some were genuinely friendly, others were not. Andre especially was openly flirting. There were still those rumours that he kept a checklist and ticked off the names of his conquest. Esmay said that it was up to me but she felt that it would be a shame if my name were to get on that list. She was sure that someone with my innocence would be terribly hurt if he got me then dumped me.

But Andre kept trying with his smart talk. He seemed to appear wherever I was especially when I was not with Esmay. Poor me, at home I had Anthony to hold off, at college it was Andre. I had to please my Mom as well. I took down the skirts' hems a little making them less provocative. It was a depressing time for me and without the support of Esmay I might not have been able to cope with all that and my studies. Esmay decided to deal with Andre on my behalf but insisted that the problem at home I had to deal with between my mother and myself. One afternoon, as Andre followed us uninvited, Esmay had a verbal confrontation with him. She barked, 'Can't you take a hint? She does not want to be on your list of conquests.'

She warned him that if he did not stop bothering me, she'd have to lodge an official complaint about sexual harassment.

Andre got very annoyed then and called Esmay names, something about a roaster, the meaning of which I did not quite know but guessed that it was something rude. It was then that Esmay shrugged and 'kissed her teeth' at him.

Andre laughed, perhaps not understanding the meaning of the teeth-kissing.

'Come on you two. Look, I have no time at present for...err...men. I'm behind with my studies as it is. I'll have to work hard to catch up.' I said as nicely as I could.

'Well...your keeper must let you loose one day I suppose.'

With that Andre went his way and I kept my toes crossed that we would just say hello as fellow students, nothing more.

3

At home I told Mom that I wanted to talk to her about something important.

At first she continued to do her ironing. I took the iron from her and said, 'Sit down Mom.'

I led her to the nearby chair. I pulled a chair up and sat beside her.

'Mom, I'm a woman now and you're a woman, and my loving mother. So I want to tell you things.'

Mom gave me a strange look. I read her thoughts, from the sudden fear in her eyes.

'No, Mom, I didn't go get myself pregnant...I'm still your virgin daughter and I want to stay that way.'

'*Bien*! My Elena wait till she gets a good man, then marry.'

A smile came to Mom's face for the first time in weeks.

'Oh yes.' I humoured her for a moment then continued with what I really wanted to say.

'Please don't encourage Anthony to our home. I don't want to be with him or any man at the moment.'

Secretly, I thought not now, not ever...I'm going to be a top-class professional and be independent, that I swear!

Mom nodded agreement to what I had said. She patted me on the hand.

'Is like this...I can't go away and leave my Elena in England. But you're right. You finish study, get you bit of paper then we travel, OK? Your father's family said that over there, it is your qualification not the colour of your skin...and...and...that matter...so...'

Mom's voice faded away as my thoughts wandered too. I was thinking, I didn't want a man, I didn't want to go to Canada neither where I would have to face the man who dumped us in the slums. If I did I'd probably spit in his face! Anyway, I'm English, born English shouldn't have to go to no Canada or be Miss Nigeria neither for that matter to get to my dreams.

When the following Sunday came, Anthony turned up for his usual lunch. I had a long talk with him. I had invited him so we could go for a walk in the park. There I told him what I had already told Mom. He was not too disappointed and said he'd wait for me. I nodded but was thinking that he'll wait forever if he was that dumb as not to get the hint that I was not interested in him. But if I thought I had got rid of Anthony as easy as that, I was wrong.

His next sentence sent a chill through my spine. We can get engaged, he suggested. His father would get me the biggest diamond ring he could afford, and it would not be a cheap one. Shit, I thought, so I will be marrying your dad as well! Aloud I said, 'Yes, that would be very nice but let's wait until, say, after I get through at least my second year exams.'

I was secretly hoping that by then his eyes would catch someone else.

Reluctantly, Anthony agreed but kept coming on Sundays. That Sunday visit infuriated me and made me begin to think of leaving home. Perhaps share with some other student. But how would I pay my share of the rent? It was then that the idea of getting in touch with the House of Our lady of Grace occurred to me. I did promise when I left to keep in touch. Maybe I could live there, work for my keep, say at weekends, though that was never the plan for the House of Our lady. It was for distressed young women in trouble at home or with the law but not bad enough to be sent to prison.

'Mmh' Grunted Esmay when I told her.

'I wouldn't want to tell a lie, nor give the real reason for wanting to live there.'

'You could smash that Andre's blinking face in and get in trouble with the police,' said Esmay sounding serious, 'You know what he asked me the other day, that scum bag?'

'What?'

'He asked me for a date? No other male on this campus would dare!'

I was sure that Andre would not be so stupid.

'He wouldn't dare!'

'No! He first said that you're very pretty and fresh. Then asked some nonsense 'bout did I think that you might be a bi?'

'A what?' I screeched, stopping Esmay in her tracks. 'What did that good-fo-nothing ask you about me?'

'Oh, don't bother with him. I mentioned it so you'd know the kind of man he was. To think you'd like both male and female, that stupid jackass.'

'Don't worry? I'm going to look for him right now.' I fumed.

'You don't have to. I told him worse than anything you ever know to tell him.'

'That filthy-minded bore. You known he tried it on with our Joy?'

'Don't worry. He will not trouble you again. True, some of what I called him was in heavy Jamaican slang, which he did not understand anyway.'

'Well, I'll sure tell him in plain English, his mother tongue as it's called.'

'Look, don't drag yourself to his level. Be the perfect lady.' said Esmay.

'Don't know bout being a lady. He can't go round saying those things.'

'Look, leave Andre to me, right? He'll stop pestering, aright!' Esmay insisted.

'No, you look! Don't go get your brothers in trouble! No Andre is worth that.'

'You're right. Let's get our head round this wretched exam coming.'

'Esmay, tell me something, and the truth. What is it with me? Do I look easy game or what? At home Anthony, here Andre, why? Do I look gullible?'

'You're a pretty young woman and obviously still untouched. Men can tell that from a mile and some walking with their tongue sticking out, dying to be the first.'

'Oh yeah?' I sneered, 'they can try!'

After that, Esmay and I worked hard. During that time we had no trouble from Andre. He often came and sat across me in the library and I could almost read his thoughts. He was so sure of himself that he'd have me sooner or later. Mentally, I sent my own message. No chance. No man going to come between me and my dreams of success. Anthony too, was less forceful. I think Mom had spoken with him. He still dropped by to chat with Mom and give presents to Kevin.

Soon, that first-year exam came and went. All that was left was the long and nervous wait. I spent many hours wide awake thinking I might have failed.

I was sure that the only paper and project I was sure to shine in was Spanish. The English lit paper was a nightmare for me. All that stuff about '*The Nonnes Preestes Tale*' by Chaucer was hell. I should not have attempted that question. But I thought it was only the prologue I had to discuss and should have been easy.

'Dear God! Why didn't I try question four instead?'

For poor Esmay it was that complicated theory about Culture and Imperialism. She was heartbroken when she said that she could not answer any of the questions in full. Poor Esmay; what will happen if she fails and I pass, or the other way around? Secretly I prayed, 'Please, holy mother of God, let's both pass or both fail.'

We both wanted holiday jobs but could not concentrate enough to try for anything because of the result thing hanging over our heads. Then, suddenly, the exam results, which we had to pass to move to the second year, were posted. We had both passed. I was delighted. Esmay was shocked because she never thought that she'd pass .Mom hugged me several times and told everyone who wanted to listen that her daughter had passed her first university exam. Anthony brought me a huge bunch of flowers to congratulate me. Kevin also had something to celebrate. He had passed his clarinet exam. He was now doing well in all subjects since we moved to our new place. For Kevin's sake, I agreed to go to the cinema to sit through what I thought was no more than a lot of noise and special effects, no particular story line. What's more, Anthony kept holding my hand. That annoyed me though I tried to be polite and smiled, easing my hand away. Anthony showed no sign of being offended whenever I took my hand away. Once he whispered, 'You're shy, that's good, and my sister also is good. She is very shy like you.'

Blast! Seems like I would be marrying his whole family, sister and everybody, no thanks!

Back at college my only sadness was that I had gained higher grades than Esmay. I tried to explain that for one thing we took different subjects. I personally couldn't cope with all that stuff she wrote about culture and people.

'Phew!' I teased, 'What a load of garbage! Oh, sorry, didn't mean garbage, but all that theory is a bit up in the sky, not very down-to-earth .You did extremely well to get through all of that.'

'Don't patronise me, OK.' Esmay was in one of her bad moods.

'Look, you had to work and study to pay your way. I didn't. I have a sponsorship from somewhere or other. I had more time to read and things like that. Come on now.'

I placed my arm around her shoulders, trying to plant a kiss on her check, but she pushed me away.

'None of that soppy stuff, please!' she said.

And so, time went by. I spent time at home and going through the vacancy lists in the newspapers. It was then that I decided to write to the House of Our Lady of Grace. I asked if there were any holiday jobs available but no reply ever came.

In the end both Esmay and I found holiday jobs. I got a job in a bookshop, while Esmay worked in the Afro-Euro International Beauty Centre. The pay was good even for trainees like Esmay. It was interesting work but the hours were long and there were troublesome women who had more money than manners, according to Esmay. Yet, she seemed pleased to see so many black young women in their designer suits and being in a position to step into that Centre. The hair care unisex was above an expensive boutique, with its own security-protected car park at the back.

'I'll be one of those women one day.' I nodded to no one in particular.

Time went by. Soon, it was the end of our summer vacation but the upside was that Esmay had some very good news. She was offered a room in the block for mature students needing a quiet place to work. Esmay didn't waste any time. She went straight to the accommodation office and managed to persuade the accommodation officer to let her share with me even though I did not qualify as a mature student. She lied and said that I could not study properly at home because of a reason she was not in a position to reveal. I could almost see the sad face she put on for the benefit of the equality officer of the college when she pleaded on my behalf. I was also very pleased because it would be a chance to get away from home and that Anthony problem.

After that letter about the sharing with her, Esmay came to my house and once more put her natural creative skills in action. She soon managed to talk her way into my mother's trust when she said that I would benefit from the intellectual academic environment. Everyone there studied hard. Also, the college library and its huge computer space stayed open until ten at night, which would be too late for me to bus it home. Once I got my qualification I could travel to anywhere in the world to work. Mom need not fear. Esmay went further and said that she would take care of me. She herself did not mess about with men so Mom needs not worry that any monkey business would take place. To my surprise Mom swallowed it all and agreed that I could share a room on campus with Esmay but come home weekends. She warned though that we girls must be careful whom we let in our room

During the first week of that September at the start of our second year at college, Esmay and I moved in together, with both our Moms' blessing. We were busy arranging our things. Esmay was given one of the rooms where two students could share.

There were two single beds, each with a bedside table and night lamp. But it also had a desk with a study lamp. Overhead, by the desk, was a board for sticking paper with a warning note not to stick anything on the walls of the room. There, by a window, were some built-in shelves where we placed our books and special photographs. We left the placing of our clothing in the built-in wardrobes until later while we inspected the communal kitchen and the laundrette in the basement.

'Very cosy and homely,' I said to Esmay.

'Yeah! And self-catering. Hope you can cook,' she said.

'Hope you can iron,' I replied.

It was like a real home and I felt that I had become a real woman, no longer mommy's little baby. Maybe I was not on my own but at least I was away from mother's nest. This was the first rung of my independent ladder. After we had put our things in place I went up to Esmay and threw my arms around her neck kissing her on the cheek and danced around the room with her. It was then that she gave me her usual grunt of 'Mmh' and I asked, 'You do want me to share with you, don't you?'

'What stupid questions some people ask!' Esmay grunted and gently took my hands from around her waist.

I was disappointed but simply said softly, 'I'm happy to be sharing with you and hope that you're happy to share with me. We can be like a couple.'

'Careful how you use that word, here.' she warned.

'Why?' I asked, puzzled.

'Couple means something special here on campus.'

'What?' I said, throwing myself backwards on the bed.

'Which of the beds you want?'

Esmay changed the subject.

'This one is soft and spongy.' I bounced happily up and down, like on a trampoline. Esmay and I had become partners sharing a home and all expenses. Later we went to one of the student bars and celebrated.

Our second year was somewhat different to the first. Me and Esmay were now studying and living together during the week. We each went home to our Moms on Sundays, often taking a pile of laundry along with us. I had my Saturday job in the bookshop where I had worked during the summer. Esmay had two nights a week student's bar work and helped her aunt on Saturday mornings. She always got home first on Saturday and prepared something for our supper. For me, Saturday was a long day. We started at 8:30am though the bookshop opened at 9:00am and we, the assistants, often stayed long after closing time which was 5:00pm to unpack boxes or fill shelves. It was different work to when I was just part-time during the summer. Then, I was given light work. Now I had to work hard. Now it was back-aching work. There were times when Esmay had to massage the back of me leg and lower back because they ached.

Sometimes Esmay argued that I should give it up because I was not accustomed to such hard work. It was not as though I was just selling books but I had to work at the back before and after opening time. She thought that I was being exploited. I should not have to open boxes and fill shelves. I was there to sell books. However, I refused to give up the job. I was sure that I was learning a lot about books and cataloguing.

Some Saturdays I came home so tired that I would fall asleep with my supper still in front of me on the table. At those times Esmay looked after me, got me to take a shower and tucked me in bed. She would sit and read to me any lesson I had.

She'd read until I dropped off to sleep. It was on one of those tired nights that I had the most bizarre dream that then turned into a horrendous nightmare.

In the dream, a group of us students were on some sort of field trip. I found myself alone walking along the top of a narrow concrete wall. The wall went on and on. Way down below the wall other people were laughing and messing about. When I got to the end of the wall I could see a forest ahead with a lane that had flowers on both side. The flowers were waving side-to-side as if they were alive.

When I looked sideways I saw what appeared to be a green field. It was then that I heard a voice telling me not to go there. It was a bad place. Alongside that field ran a sort of wide stream or river. Across the river were some grass-roofed houses. A group of women and children were just sitting, some walking along on the opposite side of the river. I was trying to draw their attention but first I had to walk across the field. I jumped down off the wall and began walking on the grass to get to the stream to call out. Suddenly, I noticed that the grass was full of snakes of all colours and sizes. I was unable to run back. Those wriggling creatures surrounded me. It was then a small machete found itself in my hand. I began to chop my way through; left, right, in front I chopped frantically .Yet they wriggled. It was as if my chopping was having no effect. The creatures never tried to bite; they just wriggled around my feet. I thought that one of the women saw me and threw what looked like a bunch of keys to me. I stretched out to grab them. Someone held me back and I lashed out.

'Heh! Heh! Wake up!' Someone with a familiar sounding voice was holding and shaking me.

'Snakes! Snakes!' I heard myself cry out.

'Shush! ...There ain't no snakes here.' That someone was holding me tightly.

I opened my eyes and there was Esmay. I threw my arms round her.

'Shush! You had a bad nightmare. It's all them books you're seeing at work.'

'It was so real.' I said shaking.

Esmay wiped the cold sweat off my forehead.

'It's because you're overtired.'

Esmay was rocking me like a baby. That was when she gently slid in beside me to reassure me.

It was the first time that we had shared the same bed. The next night, Esmay crawled in with me again but this time asking if I had any objection.

'You can say so if you do.'

I had no objection but the bed was really too small. I suggested then that we pull the two beds close together to form one bed with the table reading lamps on opposite sides. And so we did and I was happy. But the next morning there was some embarrassment. We were at the table having some toast smeared with peanut butter. Our milk was stolen so we had to have '*Cafe solo*', as we often said when there was no milk. Somehow I picked up courage to start a conversation

'Essy,' it was the first time that I had called her Essy, 'I like it when you reassure me and console me till I fall asleep but...'

I could not get the words out.

'But what?'

'What happened last night...I mean...I like you caressing and things but I 'm dead set to stay virgin, whatever else happens. Maybe one day Mom will persuade me to get married. What if I agree just to please her? She'd drop dead if she thought no decent man would want me, because I wasn't...you know?'

'Jesus Christ, Virgin? Your Mom living in early nineteenth century or what? You better keep your mouth shut about that around here. Girls eight and nine years old already at it.' Esmay sniggered.

'That's for them. I don't want to. I wouldn't want to shame me Mom. She worked very hard to keep us after me dad pack his bag and clear off.'

'But you did go on about you didn't want a man to come between you and your dream. Now you're talking about virgin marriage. I think you're confused because it's first thing in the morning.'

'Oh, I don't know...I just don't want certain things to happen, that's all.'

'Don't worry, I wouldn't do anything to hurt you or spoil your chances of being a virgin bride to the son of some wealthy chieftain, or whoever.'

'Funny. Ha! Ha! Me! Elena! Me as a Mrs Chief wife.' I mimicked.

'Whatever, got to run.'

Esmay pulled a sweater around her shoulders ready to leave, 'See you this afternoon.'

'See you later.' I said, watching her dash away, that strange friend of mine.

After that woman-to-woman talk, we worked, lived and studied happily together, Esmay and me. We were now partners, or lovers, whichever of the two terms our friends wished to use at a particular time.

We mingled a bit more. We attended extra-curriculum and political meetings. We were a happy couple.

4

One day in the summer break a letter came to Esmay advising that she was one of the two students entering the third year who had won a competition. That annual event was in memory of a head of the college who had died many years ago. One of our tutors had sent in good pieces of writing from needy students. I did not qualify because I already had a sponsorship. Other mature students, some from overseas, had there pieces of work entered.

Esmay, being one of the three winners, would have the rent for her residence on the campus paid for a year. The funds were not for those renting outside of the college's residence. Not having to pay rent meant that she only had to pay tuition fees.

We were told that the rent was actually for a room but sharing was not normally allowed. However, because I was already sharing and I was also a third year student, the accommodation officer might make an exception. Once again, Esmay put on a good show. I even told her afterwards that she should be in the theatre. She was such a good actress. She joyfully corrected me that there's no such thing as an actress. They're all actors now, male or female. Actress or not Esmay was terrific. I thought at one stage that the accommodation officer might burst into tears at my plight. I was allowed to share the room and we moved in as partners, rent free, at least for a year.

Time went by. Esmay and I were happy, most of the time anyway, and had no idea of the change that was to come like a thunderbolt into our lives. Esmay was having fewer mood swings. And when she did it amounted to nothing serious. She just sulked for hours, sometimes for a whole day, came back and refused to answer questions about where she went and why. Another problem was also developing. It was jealousy! She seemed to get worked up if anyone, male or female, got too close to me. We had a couple of rows about that, especially at that time when she was so terribly rude to one male student who had been asking me for a date. And so Esmay and I argued. I made up with her and she promised never to be rude again to anyone. She even crossed her heart and hoped to die and burn in hell if she did. But she often broke her promise. I even began to tease her and said that she was jealous even of the neighbour's ginger cat that seemed to take to us and came begging for titbits.

Soon we were at the start of our final year. We had agreed that, because of the pressure of academic work, we must cut down on going out to earn money. Esmay would be helping her aunt in the Hair Centre. I was going to help out in the student union for expenses only. In particular, I was to help with new 1st year students who came from Spanish speaking countries. It was while I was helping in the students union, when one day that thunderbolt came.

It was during the first week of my work in the student union that the call came. I was in the back room unpacking leaflets when a call came from the front desk, 'Elena, Spanish!'

I walked to the front desk to be confronted by the most frightened young man I had ever seen. He looked totally out of place. He could not be more than barely nineteen.

His two, light greenish eyes, seemed to be screaming at me, 'Help I'm totally lost!'

'*Hola, ¿qué tal?*' I stuck out a hand in friendship.

'*Bien, me jamás...err...esta...Chris.*' He said it very slowly as they do in Spanish for beginners as well as the wrong use of a verb.

I nearly burst out laughing but held back. Instead, I suggested we used English, but pointed out that to know a language well he had try to speak it. I led him to one of the union's hand-me-down settees.

'Yu speak very good English for a Spanish girl.'

'I'm not really Spanish. My Mom is from Venezuela. My dad is from Guyana and I was born in the East End of London. A right mixture of dialects, eh?' I laughed to put him at ease.

After sitting briefly in silence, he began to talk. He told me about being new and that the place looked scary to him. Everyone looked so clever. He didn't think he'd make it here. Maybe he should leave. He'd made a fool of himself and people took the Mickey.

'Why Spanish?' I quickly chanced the subject. I wanted to known more about this soft-spoken young man, quite the opposites to people like Andre and his kind who were so full of themselves.

'I was, err...they sent me here for experience and things in that language unit place, like...you know. I would look a real idiot. I can't even speak English proper. All that grammar stuff does me head in. Anyhow, must leave and thanks...'

'You'll be OK. Everyone here is friendly. And if I can help in anyway?'

'Nah, they'll call me a stupid git or something worse.'

While Chris talked I was thinking that if he was a couple of years younger he could've been my brother Kevin, especially when he had all that trouble with asthma and looked so weak. I noticed the ill-fitted, obviously charity shop stuff on him. Dressed better, he would be quite handsome.

Suddenly Esmay burst in as if from nowhere. She was fuming like an angry bull.

'There was me stood there waiting for you. Why the hell didn't you say you had a date?'

'Sorry! I lost track of time,' I apologised.

'I can see that!'

'Essy, this is Chris, a new student. He'll be taking Spanish as his second subject. Chris this is Esmay.'

'*Hola, me jamma esta Chris Newman.*' He started his *jamma* thing again and offered a hand and a smile.

Esmay ignored his hand of friendship and stormed out.

'Yu friend, she don't like white boys?'

'Doesn't,' I tried to correct him, 'like any boys, black, white or otherwise.'

'Oh!' Chris frowned, 'she looking after you then?'

'We share a room, as many students do.'

'Better go. Don't want to get you in no trouble.'

'It's alright. I know her weak spot, but I better go,' I said, rising.

'Err...thanks again. I feel bit better now,' he said, and got ready to leave.

'You're welcome. *Adios, hasta luego.* I'll be at the student union again tomorrow lunchtime. And if you want some help with Spanish just shout.'

'OK, see you *de semana*,' He smiled, 'you said to learn I must speak.'

'Be careful how you use Spanish words, some are tricky.' I laughed. 'But don't worry, you'll soon learn.'

With that we parted and I rushed back to our block to find that Esmay was not there. I was not too concerned about her absence. All that she'd do was perhaps go somewhere to some debating meeting.

I tried the supper she had prepared but couldn't eat. For one thing the chips had gone cold. Also, I was concerned about Esmay going on her own to some meeting. She'd shout her controversial views which often got her in trouble. She said what she thought without thinking. For no apparent reason I began to wonder, as I had never done before. Why didn't Esmay get herself some young man friend, then she wouldn't hold on so tightly to me? She'll smother me if she didn't get herself a man friend. Thing was, there was no way even Esmay or I could have foreseen how the arrival of a nervous and poorly dressed young man would've affected our lives and that of others.

I waited a long time for Esmay to return. While waiting, I found myself talking to the cat, like a sort of confidant.

'Hey,' I said, 'today your friend Elena saw a very, well, a potentially, handsome young man. Hair, after a good shampoo, will be mouse colour. And you know, this young man in second-hand drabs...take him out of them, put

61

him in a decent suit and by God the girls will swoon at his feet. And do you know?' I said, stroking the cat by then at my feet, 'hardship is colour-blind. When life's cruel hammer wants to strike, it doesn't look at the colour of your skin.

'Oh! Holy Mary!' I shouted, pushing the poor cat away.

Esmay! Blast, we were to go somewhere! I suddenly remembered that Esmay and I were to have an early meal and go out. It was to one of those usual campus residents' meetings. Oh, she'll kill me I thought, looking at my watch. No wonder she was so mad. Anyway it was too late now.

She should not, as she was doing at the present time, be so possessive of me. I seemed to be the only close friend that she had. Perhaps if she did not look so sure of herself she would find someone. Again, I thought if she didn't give young men on campus that stand-off look…well…it makes men afraid of her…unless, she did not want any man.

Like me she was ambitious. She had spoken about wanting to open a hair business of her own. Round and round my thoughts went and I must have fallen sleep as I did not hear Esmay come in. She often tiptoed if she came in and saw me already in bed and probably already asleep. I woke and stretched my arm out as usual to her side of the bed but she wasn't there. I turned my head and saw that she had pulled out some bedding and made a bed for herself in the armchair.

Good, I shrugged, if you want to sulk, go head see if I care.

Next day, Esmay was having one of her moods. She left without breakfast. I took no notice. I was accustomed to her resentment when anyone came too near me. I was due at the student union during lunchtime, hence, could not go for lunch with her as we usually did. But she knew that when I helped in the students union during our lunch break I got a free sandwich. On such occasions she would drop in, say 'hi, how you doing' and leave. On this occasion she did not. Instead I had another visitor. It was Chris. He came to the union as I had suggested he did. Once again he seemed ill at ease. I made him sit with me in a corner, as I was allowed to do if a student came that seem to have a problem. We should better deal with it in private.

'*Hola*! How are things?' Our supervisor at the union taught us not to greet the student with the phrase 'What's wrong?'

'He hates me, 'said Chris.

'Who hates you? And what makes you think whoever it is hates you?'

'Is that doctor bloke. I suppose to work with him and he can hardly bear to look at me. Do I smell or something?'

'Don't talk daft. You are tidier than most here that go around with big holes in their jeans.'

'He's right not to like me. I am too low down Him being very senior or something, he's so clever, knows loads of languages and they send him some dumb white kid.'

'Listen, how long since you been here?'

'A few days.'

'How can he hate you within a few days of meeting you?'

'Dun know. I don't think I want to stay. First I thought I'd like it here, yeah? Now I err...don't seem to fit in.'

'Now you listen to me. You'll stay if I have to tie you down.' I attempted a joke.

'The room, err...his office, is a tip. Magazines, papers, books everywhere.'

'Well, there's your chance. Tidy it all up. Impress him. He'll love you for it.'

'I can't. Some are in foreign writing. I don't know what goes with which.'

'Ask him to give you labels and show you how to use them.'

'I thought maybe I go to the supermarket and get some boxes. Write things on them. Would you show me? French and Spanish look the same to me. Only English look OK, is it looks?'

'I can, but you should ask your supervisor and trainer.'

I was thinking that this young man's knowledge of English tenses would have to be improved. I was no expert but could help him.

'I'm a bit scared of him.'

'But why? He's Human like you.'

'Yeah! But he's clever and talks like, well, like how French people talk English.'

Chris went on to explain about his boss and mentor.

'He's very serious, like, you know? He looks at me like he thinks here's another white trash they sent me...look, I better go, see you!'

'Don't you dare call yourself that? Where did you get that word from anyway?'

'Some of them on the estate say it.'

'Well don't you use it? Just because stupid people say dumb things, doesn't mean you must say it as well. It's only stupid American talk.'

'Thing is, nearly all them whites left, so I'm an ethnic minority now!'

He succeeded in producing a wry smile.

'Tell you this, anyone call <u>me</u> black trash to m'face gets it in the blinking mouth.'

He laughed and looked at me as if he was sure I couldn't even punch a baby.

His laugher sounded soft and beautiful and I felt there was a something here. Not only was he just good looking, he had a sort of baby-like appearance. I wondered if he had even started to shave properly yet. If he had, he was very clean-shaven. But why was I thinking about what he looked like? He needed support and I should give it. I was sure that good old Ms Jolly didn't think about whether I was good looking or not.

Chris left after we arranged to meet again the next day.

5

After Chris left I kept seeing that pale face in my mind and thinking how much he reminded me of my own past. Perhaps he's recently out of a boy's version of The House of our Lady of Grace. He probably had his own version of Ms Jolly who helped him and got him into the college. Poor devil, I thought, as I hurried along the back lane to my mature students' block. Once inside, I thought that I had better make something for dinner because I was first home. We did have a list of who did what on which day but it soon became who got home first made a meal. Esmay had diced some vegetables for one of her specialities. I chose to make her something she liked. She was mad about anything with coconut milk in it, and grated ginger and bits of lemon grass. 'Mm...' Elena will knock her Essy dead with a South American dish.' I told Ginger, who was purring and brushing my leg with his furry body.

Soon the aroma of a vegetable curry filled the air but no Esmay. After waiting until dark and still no sign of her, I began to worry. I tried her mobile but she had switched it off. I thought of phoning her mother then decided against that in case her mother got concerned. After an anxious wait, I went out to see if I could find her.

I went to the students' bar but she wasn't there. Then to the library but she was nowhere to be found. Stop mucking about, I thought. No doubt she wanted to teach me a lesson for being late home that first day with Chris. Unless of course, she was mad at me, as she often was, if she saw me having a friendly chat with anyone. Surely she wasn't jealous of that shy and harmless boy with the mousy coloured hair. He was barely an adult. He probably wouldn't even know what to do if you'd tied him to the bed and flung a girl on top of him...or would it be under him?

Now, how the devil would Elena Peterson know who goes where or who does what? As unusual as that was, all she knew was what she had learned from hearsay and what she had heard in the school playground. I sniggered all the way back to our room. Once there I kept thinking of Esmay's jealousy. She was not unduly concerned about macho Andre. Even Anthony didn't worry her, she even grinned whenever his name was mentioned. But Chris? He's like a younger brother you take into your arms, cuddle and kiss any sadness or pain, away. And if Miss High and Mighty has a problem with that, then she could go to bloody hell. If she gives me grief, I'd simply pack m'things and go back to my Mom's. My room was as I had left it. Mom would never sublet even though we could do with the money. So go to hell Ms Esmay, I can love Chris if I want to and there's nothing you can do about that. So there, bloody there!

It was well after ten at night when Esmay came in.

'What happened? I was worried.' I greeted.

Esmay did not reply or even look at me.

I followed her around the room and asked, 'What's wrong? Talk to me.'

She continued to ignore me. She picked up a towel and her wash bag, and went out the room to the communal showers. I knew then that she was in one of her foul moods, so I ignored her. I took a book, went to lie on my back on the bed we shared. But I wasn't reading. I was only turning the pages. I could not concentrate.

I kept wondering what could have happened. Why did she look so angry? Something very bad or disappointing must have happened. Surely it couldn't be about me and Chris? Someone or something else must have upset her. I was fairly sure. But who and what? It was definitely a personal thing she didn't want to tell me. We were supposed to be friends and partners as she called it, yet there seemed to be things she preferred to keep to herself. When she ignored the meal I had prepared and took the trouble to warm up for her, I chucked it in the bin thinking that two could play this game. I went back to bed. But again I turned restlessly from side-to-side thinking about what could have upset her so. She had gone off before but had never come back so upset.

I heard her return from her shower. After pretending to read at the table for a while she put down the book and went to get the spare bedding we had and began to make up a bed using the armchair. Then she got ready.

'No you don't!' I was using the opportunity to get her to speak to me. 'I'm not letting you sleep in no armchair. I'll take the chair.'

'Get off my bloody bed then.' She said angrily.

'Oh, we can speak, can we?' I sneered. I made no attempt to get off her bed and that provoked her.

She grabbed my legs to drag me off. We began pulling and tugging.

'Watch it, yeah! I'll blinking have you for assault.'

I forced a serious tone into my voice. She stopped trying to drag me off the bed, gave me a murderous look, and went to get an old blanket, which we often used as a rug, from the bottom of the cupboard. She sat herself down on the old hand-me-down armchair silently making it clear that she intended to spend the night in that chair.

'Get yourself a stiff neck by morning. See if I care a damn.' I barked.

But I did care. I could not let her spend the whole night in that chair. After trying to ignore her for some time, I gave up. I got up and kneeled by her feet.

'What's so wrong that you can't tell me, eh?'

'Nothing's wrong. OK? Leave me alone. Give me some space.'

'Ok! Ok! I'm sorry. I thought we were mates. Anyway, sorry.'

With that I returned to bed. I tried hard to go to sleep, even counting sheep as I used to when I was a little girl and after a while eventually dropped off. I even had one of my ridiculous dreams. In this one, I had peed myself while sitting on a bus going home. Of course my mom, or one of her friends, would have found a meaning in such a dream.

The next morning we had coffee and a slice of toast in silence. Both of us had an early Seminar, but in different rooms because we were reading different subjects. At lunchtime, I began my usual two hour stint at the student union before my 2:30 tutorial. I was at the union for half an hour when a call came through that I had a visitor. At first I thought it might be Esmay. But it was not.

'*Hola Chris*! *Como estas*?' I greeted my visitor.

'*Buenos dias, Elena*.' He replied with that usual shy but infectious smile.

'Actually,' I began, showing him to a seat, 'in Spanish, after 12 noon, it is, *Buenas tardes*.'

'Sorry, still learning but improved a lot since you're helping me.'

'*Tardes*' means afternoon until early evening. Mind you, there are, I suppose, regional differences not only within Spain but also between Spain and South America. Any way, *poco-poco* and you master *da idioma, si*?' I said, putting on a phoney voice.

We sat down and talked a great deal. For instance, how I could help him with his *deberes*. I waited for him to try and work out what *deberes* might mean.

'Ah! Don't you mean homework! But shouldn't it be *trabajo e casa*? Sometimes I get things mixed up.'

'Well, *trabajo* is the verb *work* but it has a different meaning to *deberes*. *Trabajar* is more like working in an office or doing housework, to work. *Deberes*, is more like working at home on your essay.'

'Christ! I'll never remember all them stuff.' He drifted into the use of *them*, a word commonly used on the London streets.

We both felt at ease. I admitted that I was no expert. I too was a student taking Spanish language and culture as an option. I had a big advantage over Chris though, my mom left Venezuela many years ago but still speaks what she and her friends call Latino. Also, I was in my final year. We agreed that because I was two years ahead of him, I could let him have some of my earlier notes to look at. But it might be better to stick to homework set by his tutor. He asked where we could meet. He did not mind if we worked in the Union. But I pointed out that it would be too noisy here and people would keep coming in distracting us. I suggested that he could, if he wanted, come to the bed-sit that I shared with my friend.

'That would be great. But I don't want to get you into trouble.'

Without even thinking about Esmay's reaction, I said that Wednesday evenings would be fine. I had time on Wednesday because it was a study half-day. It was much later that I realised that it was actually an evening when Esmay was working at the student bar.

'You friend don't mind then?' He enquired, showing some concern.

'Nah! She'll be OK with that.'

We talked some more while he drank from a can of diet-coke he got from the machine. I didn't want a drink. I only wanted to talk as there was something fascinating about him.

'Look, during the week, if I see you I will say something to you in Spanish, if you don't understand, I will explain again in English, OK?'

'That'll be great. You are so kind. Oh...'

He stopped, as if remembering something. 'How much will it cost? I don't have much.'

'Money? Who said anything 'bout money? I want to help. I know that people offering help advertise on the union notice board, but I have my own work and I didn't want to be bogged down with a long list of crazy students.'

'Don't be mad. I'm sorry I mentioned payment. I always open me gob and things jump out.'

Chris then mentioned how he often said the wrong things, and how with his supervisor, Dr Alexis, you could never tell if you had upset him. He just gave you a vague look, which could mean anything.

It could be as far back as those early days with Chris that I began to wonder if his supervisor saw him as I did. A young, even helpless innocent with a pale face, dressed in charity shop clothes.

'Sometimes he looked at me as though he was studying me, like those counselling people.'

Chris jerked me back to reality.

'You mean shrinks,' I chuckled. 'I doubt if the college have them.'

'They need them for people like me, I suppose. They called me a weirdo and a freak at school.'

'Why?' It was a stupid reply, even though he was not exactly feminine he did look soft and gentle, the kind that would attract school bullies.

'Because I was skinny and didn't want to do PE or football. But them teachers, they made me.' He said in a voice that would make anyone laugh.

As Chris spoke it was as if I could almost see him in that situation. I knew those schools; by god I knew them alright and only too well. He went on to relate how the other boys used to deliberately trip him up on the football pitch, and how they would deliberately stamp hard on his foot when the game's teacher was not looking. They said that if he told anyone, he'd get his head kicked in after school. It was a typical story of bullying, but the way he was describing his school experience made it difficult for me to keep a straight face.

I got home that afternoon and rebuked myself. How could I have laughed at his stories? They were not merely anecdotes for cheap laughter. They were awful experiences. I felt as if my heart was going out to him .He came across as such a lovely person. He should not have been put through that hell. Pity he was not black. If he had been black, half the country would have stood up for him and shouted 'racism'.

The more I thought of his miserable experiences at school, the more I felt that I'd like to go up to him, take his face between my hands and kiss his check, as I would my little brother's. I made up my mind there and then that I would be his best pal, and if Ms Esmay didn't like it that would be her problem, not mine.

Before the start of the Wednesday sessions I told Esmay about Chris. True, I should have asked her what she thought about the arrangement first. I did try to 'break the ice', so to speak, by telling her about Chris's school experience. I told her how they bullied him just because he did not like games and all that stuff. I told her how the others had tripped him up and stamped on his feet when the teachers forced him to play games or do PE. The stories brought a smile and the usual grunted 'Mm' from her.

Then she muttered, 'Very clever young man. He could run circles round that Andre with all that private education and his string of 'A' levels.'

'What you mean by that?' I asked, puzzled.

'Mmh! Nothing!' She grunted again, sneering, 'good luck teacher.'

On the Wednesday, Chris arrived during the evening when Esmay was out. He brought with him a stack of Spanish books. Most of the books were at a level too high for a foundation year student. At first Chris talked mainly about Dr Alexis, who he said had warned him not to take on too much extra work, but I managed to persuade him to go over the homework that he had for Spanish. He had to memorise a list of the most common vocabulary that he would need for every day conversation. I went over them with him and then let him try to make up short sentences. I could not help but notice his blushes when he got something wrong, and was not surprised when he declared that he was relieved that Esmay was not in. He was sure that if she had been there she would have laughed at him for being stupid. I rebuked him again for calling himself stupid.

On the second Wednesday that Chris came round, Esmay stayed in. I didn't need to ask her about her job at the Student's Bar; I knew for sure that she had changed her evening so she could keep an eye on Chris and me. As soon as Chris arrived, she planted herself on the bed and pretended to be reading a textbook. I could tell that Chris was ill at lease with Esmay there listening in.

'It's Ok, Chris. We all had to start somewhere and we all got things wrong at first.' I said, not only for Chris's benefit but also Esmay's. Esmay too was once a beginner.

'No problem, I've got my list of sentences.'

Chris handed me a list.

I had told him to let me see them before he handed in his homework. I looked at the first sentence he had made up and grinned.

'Oh dear, I see you're going to order sandwiches filled with soap?'

'Not soap, with ham!' He pointed out.

'No! In Spanish, that word is not ham, its soap.'

'But our teacher, she said it was ham.'

'His teacher's gone loco!' Esmay said in a nasty tone of voice.

'Shut up! If you're going to interfere, you'd better go out.' I warned Esmay.

'It's all right; she's only teasing. She could be one of me big sisters.'

Chris lapsed into a speech pattern which was certainly not the cockney I heard around the market street near where I grew up.

'Sorry Chris, but sandwiches with soap did sound a bit funny.'

Strangely enough, that broke the ice but Esmay decided to go out anyway.

'I'll leave teacher Elena to teach 'bout sandwiches and, err...let me see...'

I threw a cushion at her as she left.

'She's not in a bad mood today then?' Chris remarked.

'She just has mood swings, that's all, anyway, let's look up soap and ham, and I'll show you the difference.

We worked for over an hour putting together a list of words that in Spanish might look similar, or even be spelt exactly the same, except for a little accent at the top, which gave the words a different meaning.

'Look here,' I said, pointing to some examples, *Pero/perro, porque/por que,* see?'

'When I learn more, I'll make a funny poem with those words.'

'You like poetry, then?'

'Only the easy, funny ones, nothing posh like. I don't have the education to write posh ones.'

And so the conversation continued about poetry, then his boss.

I caught him smiling at something he was reading. When he noticed me watching he got serious again.

Chris obviously had great affection for his boss.

'You like him, don't you?'

'I'd do anything to please him. I'd even polish his boots. But sometimes I get frightened. What if I said something, you know, something to upset him. He'd get me kicked out, wouldn't he?'

He went on talking about his boss.

I could not put my finger on it. Was it something that he said or the way he was talking about his boss?

Suddenly I had a thought, Oh my God. No! Nah!

I quickly brushed that idea away with an explanation. He is young and had a hard life and would respond like that to any show of kindness to him!

While he continued talking, I began to wonder what it would feel like if he were to think of me as he appeared to be thinking about his boss. True, I was nothing like the things he was saying about his boss-cum-mentor. I was not good-looking and from the French Caribbean or anything like that, I did not have black hair. Above all, I didn't have white skin, if there was such a thing as white skin.

When Esmay returned, Chris packed up his books and left.

'You going to tell me?' Esmay asked.

'Oh, he talked more about pleasing his boss than about Spanish he has trouble with.'

'Is he aware that you fancy him like mad?' Esmay changed the subject abruptly.

'Don't be daft! You think everybody's like...well, perhaps not like you because you don't fancy anybody.'

'You think so?' Esmay shrugged, moving towards the biscuit tin.

'I like him as a brother, what's wrong with that, eh?'

'Mmh...call yourself that often enough and you'll come to believe it. Want a bicky?' She handed me a chocolate biscuit.

I took the biscuit and for a while I silently asked myself questions. What if Esmay was right? What would that make me, not that I knew what I was. My relationship with Esmay and all that stuff in bed some nights, what did it all mean? I certainly didn't feel like one of those ladies I had heard or read about. Christ, Mom would kill me! She'll force me to go to confession at once, and let the priest give me a thousand *Holy Mary's* to recite as punishment or at least pray to cleanse my sinful soul. But why hadn't I thought of all that before?

As time went by, Chris and I were getting closer and seeing each other more often than just on Wednesday evenings. He often dropped in at the students union when I was on duty there. In any case, he had to go past it to get to the staff refectory for a sandwich for his dark-eyed boss. Most of the time he talked about work. There was a great deal of computing work to be done. His boss was constantly writing applications with complicated lists of figures for project money and was not very good with computers and got angry. He swore under his breath once when things were not adding up and other times he was funny.

Once, Chris said he caught him shaking a fist at the computer and calling it names in French. He could tell that it was not very nice French from the look on his boss's face.

Again, I could not miss the look of affection on Chris's face when he was talking about his boss. I tried to get him to talk about his young Spanish tutor who was a young woman, but no luck. I asked him about the computer Help Desk, where he had to spend part of his work time at the college, but again no luck. All that he said was that the head of Computer Help Desk was called 'De beer' behind his back because he drank so much. There was always a pungent smell of stale alcohol when he came near you.

Strange, I thought, on the one hand I liked to hear Chris talking about his boss-cum-mentor with such feeling, and on the other I sometimes found his babbling about this man aggravating. I wished he would talk about me sometimes. Once I asked him bluntly what he thought of the idea of me modelling hairstyles for Esmay's aunt. He looked at my hair and said that he thought that it looked lovely since I had had it done. I felt greatly insulted because I hadn't had my hair done yet. My hairstyle modelling was the following Saturday. I was only going to continue with it because the little bit of cash came in handy. In fact, I had begun to feel like some olive coloured doll with flowing curls and dress for a showcase.

The closeness that was developing between Chris and me was worrying Esmay, that I could tell. But strangely, unlike in the case of Andre, she didn't threaten to go and 'stink him up', her phrase for the use of strong language to tell him to leave me alone. She had no concerns about Anthony either. She even joked and said that I'd look well in my posh African wrap with a long line of servants looking after me. She promised that when I became Mrs Anthony, she'd apply for a post as my chambermaid. Yet, when it came to Chris, Esmay got sulky at times and for no apparent reason. One evening, when we were both in, she said that we should talk.

'What is it?' I asked, seeing the seriousness on her face. I went and sat opposite her at the table.

Esmay took a deep breath before she said, 'Look, if you fancy this young man or any man I wouldn't dream of standing in your way. You're not like me. You want to marry and make grandchildren for your mother. Something I could never give to mine.'

'Wait a moment. If I wanted a man, could you stop me? So once and for all stop this nonsense about men or it will be the end of our friendship, *sabes*?'

I felt very angry at her suggestion about me wanting a man. True, a man and a woman was the natural thing but I had never taken an interest in the male species. Then along comes a pale and skinny young man dropping in at the students union. But even he was only a friend, or more like a little brother of mine. Poor devil, he looked as if he was lost and needed a friend.

While Esmay was listening to my explanation, I was thinking that if I were so inclined, Chris would have been the type of young man for me. But it so happened that I was not. But what was I? Again and again, I kept asking myself that question. Was there a name for people like me? Are there any people like me who are not really interested in the opposite sex at the same time the *chica y chica* thing was, well...a bit of a joke. They all get married in the end, I suppose.

After our woman-to-woman talk, Esmay went from being aloof to being relaxed. On one evening in particular she was more relaxed than normal because she had managed to keep Chris talking about little else than about his boss. Who had said this or who had said that. Esmay kept probing him. I was sure that she did this because she detected that I was getting annoyed with having to listen to so much about his boss. That man came over as an angel dropped out the French Caribbean sky.

That evening, after Chris had left with his Spanish homework I had helped him with, Esmay came up with one of her ideas.

'I'm dying to meet that man?' She said.

'What the blinking hell for?'

'Mm...want to see what he's like. Could it be the same Caribbean man that was barred from an African-Caribbean students meeting because of his white skin?'

'Don't you go stirring up an old can of worms, right?'

'Right! But you are his volunteer helper and...Jesus!' Esmay shouted, 'By God! I got it! Listen...'

'I'm not listening.' I said to deaf ears.

'You got to listen. This is what we do. We invite Chris to one of our poetry readings, right? We tell him to invite his Doctor, whatever his funny name is, along to see how his Chris is getting on.' Esmay winked.

'You forget that those stuffed shirts don't mingle socially with students.' I reminded her.

'Come on, don't be such a wimp. How else can we meet Mr wonder man, eh?'

'Hang around his office door and see him when he comes out, perhaps?' I suggested as a joke.

'Of course, why the hell don't I use me blinking brains?'

Esmay had yet another of her bright ideas.

'We wait until we're sure that Chris is not there. We knock at that guy's door and say we have come to invite Chris to lunch at the Tapas Bar? Chris got to practise his Spanish, see?'

Esmay, pleased with herself, poked me in the ribs.

I was not sure about knocking at the office door but went along with Esmay's plan. So, the following lunchtime, we waited until we saw Chris going to the main building, then in the direction of the staff canteen.

'Quick, hurry, before he gets back.' said Esmay.

Reluctantly, I went with her to the language unit, which was across the lawn. We hurried up a flight of stairs, looked at several office doors until we came to one saying, Dr Sylvere. Esmay prodded me again, and made me knock at the door.

'Come in.' came a soft voice from inside the office.

We walked in to be faced by what I thought was one of the most handsome men I'd ever seen, except a film star, maybe. I thought, this man may have a whitish skin but there was certainly something else about him.

'Did you ladies have an appointment?' He began to check a list pinned to the white board in front of his desk.

'No! We came to invite Chris...we're his friends, ain't we?'

Esmay turned to look at me and all I could do was to nod in agreement.

While Esmay explained why we were there, all sort of things were going round in my head. The man was exactly as Chris had described. He had a white person's skin but with a sort of olive colouring. I recalled Chris's description with some amusement. Very black wavy hair, unless it was dyed and permed. Chris came in. I noticed that he did not knock.

'Here is Mr Newman now.' said Dr Sylvere, looking at Esmay and me, as if he was studying us both.

'What you doing here?' Chris was obviously shocked to see us there.

'I didn't invite them.' He glanced nervously at his boss-cum-mentor.

'It would be up to Mr Newman. But fine with me, Miss...'

'Esmay will do fine and this is my friend Elena.'

'The young lady that helps Mr Newman with his Spanish?'

'Yes, and, as you can see, he needs to practice talking Spanish for his role-play in class Doctor...err...Silver.' Esmay explained, stammering a little, perhaps because she was looking at the man as though studying him in return.

'Why not just say Dr Alexis. You seem to have some difficulty with Sylvere.'

A rather nervous Chris was finally persuaded that it was alright for him to go to the Tapas Bar with us.

'We'll bring him back in one piece, Dr Alexis.' Esmay reassured.

Once we were outside, Esmay could not keep her mouth shut.

'Jesus! What a dish! If I were into men I'd go for him!' She said seriously.

'Do you think all young women think like you do?' Chris said tenderly, 'I'm not sure, but maybe that's why they sent me instead of a young woman to work for him?'

'Mm...'Esmay grunted. 'Terrific!'

I knew what Esmay was thinking and didn't want her to voice her suspicions. I changed the subject abruptly. 'His accent is definitely French, but more like French Africa, or Belgium maybe?'

'Well, as I said, it's not French, like in Paris.'

Chris was obviously proud that he knew the details.

'It's really Caribbean, white French Caribbean in fact. His family lived there for many centuries. They got land and stuff like that.'

'Hey, don't go on about land, all right? Black people here would hate him. They'll call him a descendant of murderous slave owners, or similar. So zip up your lips about that, OK?'

Chris promised not to talk any more about Alexis Caribbean family. He then asked us not to let Alexis know what he had told us about his Caribbean background. Some of which Alexis had told him, some of which he worked out for himself.

We got to the Tapas Bar and found a table, and who should walk up, but that pest, Andre.

'That's all we need.' Esmay muttered between her teeth.

'Hi, ladies.'

'Hi!' I replied. Esmay said nothing.

'Cor! Esmay, where have you been hiding this cutie,' Andre smiled, like a lizard about to attack some unsuspecting prey.

'This is private.' Esmay placed the book she was holding on the vacant chair.

'Since when do we book tables here?' Andre was still looking at Chris.

Andre's bad reputation did not necessarily exclude young males. There was also that rumour that he went for new arrivals on campus. Of course, it could all only be rumours. One of the students acting as *Camareros,* sporting a Mexican hat, came to take our orders.

'I'm Andre, a friend of Esmay and Elena.' He stuck his hand out, which Chris ignored with a shy grin.

When the *Camarero* went away with our order, Esmay whispered to Andre.

'Why don't you go sling your hook elsewhere?'

'You his protector then?' Andre smiled, rather macho and full of self confidence.

'We're looking after him for someone. So you keep your roaming eyes and filthy paws off, right?'

'Ok! Mother hen is we? First, you keep me from Elena and now,' he turned to Chris, 'didn't catch your name luv.'

'He didn't give it.' I finally had to say something.

'It's all right, Elena. It's Chris, Christopher Newman.'

I was thinking that if Andre dared to say, 'what a nice name', I'd get up and slap him, so help me God. He did not; instead, he asked what Chris was having and said it in very bad Spanish.

Because it was a Spanish Tapas bar, people attempted to speak Spanish and often did so very badly.

'He's got his own money to get what he wants, thank you all the same.'

I felt myself protecting Chris now. He was not saying anything. Instead, he had a look on his face which suggested that he was amused. I, on the other hand, was concerned. What if Chris fell into the hands of that experienced and evil Andre? Poor lad, he'd be totally vulnerable.

'It's OK, Ellie; I won't let Andre get your Chris.' Esmay had read my thoughts.

After Andre left to pester someone else, Esmay warned Chris, 'You keep well away from that one you hear me? He may come over as a comic but he's deadly.'

'Yeah, you stick with your Dr Alexis.' I added.

The rest of the lunchtime was very pleasant. There was a lot of Spanish being spoken and orders were being given in Spanish. The menu was also in Spanish. The music was soft and a bit romantic; a mixture of Mexican and Flamenco sounds.

Back at Dr Alexis's office we handed Chris over. Esmay pretended to return the small change left from the £20 note Dr Alexis had 'loaned' Chris because he felt that a young man must not have his lunch paid for by young ladies. As Esmay suspected, Dr Alexis told her to keep it. Chris was going to pay it all back, anyway, he said, and in any case, how did we manage to feed all three of us on that? I suddenly remembered something Chris had said about him not smiling as he spoke. You could tell that he was scrutinizing us. He also appeared to be avoiding looking directly at Chris, unless it was my imagination.

'Snacks are cheap at the Tapas bar.' Esmay explained.

On our way back, Esmay asked if I had noticed something.

'Like what?'

'The way he wasn't looking at Chris. Mm...somebody gwan,' Esmay attempted her made-up Patwa, 'get she nose knock out ah' place.'

'Why don't you stop being stupid? You know damn well it is <u>her</u> nose not she nose. You go round Brixton saying that you're talking Patwa and they'd laugh at you.'

I said this because I didn't want Esmay to know that I knew that she meant that someone, meaning me, was going to be disappointed. That was because she had it in her thick skull that I fancied Chris.

The days following that first meeting with Chris's Dr Alexis turned into weeks. We all worked hard at our studies. Chris got help with his Spanish homework from me, and apparently help with his English from his Dr Alexis. Chris once told Esmay and me that his Dr Alexis had said that Chris's Elena, meaning me, would make a good teacher and that she should think about that.

'Me, a teacher? No thanks! I might end up strangling some kid.'

'Get some pistol and threaten them, eh!' He laughed, and I thought how lovely he sounded even on a serious matter.

'You lot behave or I'll blow your brains out.' I joked.

Esmay continued to encourage Chris to talk a great deal about his work with Dr Alexis, and how hard he worked and I kept thinking, longingly, about what it would've been like if I was Dr Alexis. If I were in his place I would have sent Chris roses, not the usual red roses meaning love, but golden ones. Gold in colour that is. I might not have had the cash for real gold roses. The gold would have been a ring on his little finger. The fantasy got to the stage where I began to have a recurring dream about me chasing a teenager who was himself chasing someone. The three of us were running along a seemingly endless road. I went further and began to battle with two Elena's; one was sensible and saw Chris as a mate, the other Elena carried on daydreaming about what could never be.

While I moped about what could not and should not be, I had failed to note that Esmay was getting very moody again. When I did notice it, I put it all down to her studies. She was not doing very well. She had resumed her disappearing act, once for two days, and I became worried and rang her mom. She said that Esmay had probably gone to stay with an aunt but couldn't give me the address. When Esmay returned she made it clear that she was not in the mood to tell me why she went and where she had gone and told me off for phoning her mother. I apologised and told her that I was concerned. If she did not do her work, she would not pass the final examination, and without that she would not get on the post grad teaching 'Earn as you Learn' scheme.

'Don't give a shit!' She barked at me.

'Of course you do. Please tell me what's wrong.' I pleaded.

'Why the bloody hell don't you go to your man and leave me alone?'

'Oh! Not that again?' I responded, trying to laugh it off. 'You're not still with that Chris thing? I can't understand why you are so bothered about Chris. What if I went off and married Anthony instead?'

'No chance! Mr Anthony? You better don't hold your breath, mate.' She sneered.

A few days passed and Esmay calmed down again. I had made it clear that I would not stop helping Chris, and if there was a problem for her, I could move back home to mom's. Chris and I continued to meet and talk, partly in English and partly in Spanish, in order for him to practise for his oral. In any case, he was making amazing progress. Even his use of English was getting more formal. It was as if there was another Chris inside him trying to get out, and in such a short time. Then, one day, I received a very disturbing phone call from Chris. He had called me on the home phone instead of my mobile. That told me that it would be a long talk.

'There is trouble. I've been stupid.'

Chris was in a state of severe distress.

'Calm down Chris. What's happened?'

Esmay grabbed the phone from me.

'Who, what? We can't help if we can't understand you.'

I took the phone back from Esmay and suggested that we meet him at the Tapas bar.

'If that Andre's messed him up, I'll kill him.' Esmay said furiously.

'We don't know if it was that. Anyway, you confuse me. Shouldn't you be pleased if he went off with Andre?'

'Nobody deserves a pig like Andre.'

Esmay and I made our way to the meeting place. On the way there, Esmay asked, 'You think Chris was so naive as to go for a drink or something with Andre?'

'I doubt it. Even if Andre had gone after Chris, he'd have to drug him to get him from that Dr Alexis. No, don't think it was Andre, bad as he might be.'

We got to where Chris was waiting and he practically threw himself at me.

'It's gone wrong. Everything's gone wrong and it was my bloody fault.'

'Come and sit down. Tell us what's gone so wrong.' I said, leading Chris to a bench.

'Everything's wrong. And they were right at school to call me a useless freak. I wish I was dead.'

He dragged the back of his hand across his dripping nose.

'You will be if you don't calm down and tell us...' Esmay forced him to sit down.

We sat on either side of him.

'We can't help if we don't know what it is that has upset you so much.'

I placed an arm across his shoulder.

'Yeah, take a deep breath.' Esmay encouraged him.

'Now tell us about it.' I took his hand in mine but resisted the temptation to kiss him.

'He didn't do nothing wrong. Now he's going to lose his job. That Jimmy's going to tell lies. Well, they want to get rid of him, and now I have given them a chance.'

'Chris, what are you on about?' Esmay was never the one for tact.

'Let him take his own time, for Christ's sake!'

'OK, I'll leave. You want to talk to Elena alone?' Esmay made to get up.

'No, please stay. You must both help him, doesn't matter 'bout me.'

'Him! Him who, the Pope?' Esmay enquired.

In between wiping his nose with the back of his hand, even when his nose did not need wiping, Chris told us in disturbing detail what had happened. He had done very well in his assessment interview, but then, Dr Alexis suddenly, and without telling him why, was arranging to send him away. He was now to work with another lecturer as his supervisor and mentor.

'He didn't have the guts to tell me so himself.' Chris sniffed and again nervously wiped his nose.

Chris went on further to reveal what was, on the one hand, a serious matter, but on the other, funny. After a third party had told him about the arrangement he went ballistic. He admitted that he was on record for smashing things up in his classroom when some bullies pushed him too far. He had also been in trouble when he was twelve years old. He had chucked a brick at the image of God on the church in his road. It was after he was told that his mother had gone to heaven. He was sure that Dr Alexis had all of this on record and that was why his boss tried to calm him down.

'I began to throw things and kicked over a chair. That's when he forced me to sit down and said that it would be OK, I didn't have to go anywhere if I didn't want to.'

'What happened then?' I asked.

'He tried to silence me but I wouldn't listen. I hated it that he didn't tell me himself. I believe I kicked his leg, hard. That's when he kissed me.'

'Mm...' Esmay gave one of her grunts.

'He what?' I exclaimed.

I felt like a dagger was being pushed through my heart. This is it then, I thought. It has started. If you had any ideas about him, you can forget it for a start.

'He only kissed me on the forehead. But it was just then that the troublemaker, Jimmy, walked in. Someone next door had heard the commotion and called him.'

Esmay had gone very quiet and I knew what she was thinking.

'Oh! No!' I was shocked by what I was hearing.

'That Jimmy even tried to drag me out of Dr Alexis's office but I refused to let him. And he couldn't make me. Now he's going to say that Dr Alexis was trying something bad.'

'He's not supposed to kiss you, Chris, whether on your forehead or where ever.'

'What a stupid man! You're an adult,' Esmay muttered, 'If he wanted to snug you, why didn't he throw you in his motor, take you somewhere, and snug you then, eh?'

'Esmay! The man is his boss and mentor?'

'So? A number of people here have married their boss, or a professor.'

'Anyway, it wasn't a snug. It was like kissing his little cousin or somebody like that.'

'And you? What was it for you?' Esmay was probing, that I could tell.

'It doesn't matter 'bout me.'

Chris didn't answer Esmay's question.

'He's the one that's going to lose his job. They're people here who don't like him and I gave them their chance to kick him out.'

'They wouldn't, dare! We'll mobilise the anti-discrimination group, won't we, Elle?'

'I don't know about that, Essy. A lot would depend on what that Jimmy man reported that he saw.'

'Look, since you've been here, weren't there weddings, one between my own Head of Department and a secretary from another department?'

'That was a woman marrying a man' said Esmay.

'Please don't make a fuss. Dr Alexis shouldn't even know that I told you two about anything.' Chris pleaded.

It was the end of Chris's lunch break, and he left.

Esmay and I talked about the incident and what that might lead too. What if she was right about the first time we met Dr Alexis? Would there be a scandal if the Jimmy man chose to say more than he actually saw?

There was nothing else we could do but wait for Chris's feed back. We both agreed on that. We also agreed that Dr Alexis was bound to have a big time lawyer to look into the matter if worse came to worst.

6

The days and weeks following Chris's revelation about the 'kiss on the forehead' event, and his fear of the possible consequences, were dismal ones. The weather was saying that winter was on its way. The trees were beginning to shed their leaves as if shouting *hasta luego* to summer. Eight o'clock in the morning looked like midnight with thick, freezing fog. I got my cardigan out and put on a pair of jeans in place of one of those tiny skirts Esmay had me wearing.

In my head there was turmoil. Mom was one reason for that turmoil. I could tell that she was still secretly hoping that I'd become the fiancée, then wife, of Anthony. He was still visiting Mom for his Sunday lunch, going on and on about his successful father, and his ever-so-good sister. Not that Mom wanted to get rid of me. She was holding on to the hope that my dad would go to Canada and then send for us. Since she knew that she could never persuade me to go Canada with her to live with the man who dumped us, she was pushing the Anthony line. Why me, I had asked Mom more than once. He has many girls hanging around him at his business college. He had even told me that there was one female student there who fancied him and he liked her too. Mom was sure that Anthony could tell that I was the kind of respectable and untainted girl that his family would welcome. Most of the other girls my age had already 'been at it' with men, and long since became teenage-mothers. Mom would then quote the television show, which features these young mothers talking about when they first had sex.

On one or two occasions, Mom looked rather strangely at me when she was talking about the fact that I was a pure young woman. I said, jokingly, that if I were ever to become sexually active, she'd be the first to know. Her response was that I should always remember that no good man would want me if I had gone and messed myself up. I dared not voice my thoughts to ask her whether she had been a good girl and why my dad left us to cope alone in London.

During those weeks and months it was as if I had become an outsider, standing back and eavesdropping on two Elena's arguing about the situation between Chris and me. One was saying; if you want him, go for him. The other was saying, what if he doesn't want you? What of him and his boss...eh? Then there was a third Elena questioning the relationship with Esmay. Was that experience in bed with Esmay not considered to mean being sexually active?

Was that bed romp all that women are up to? Of course, Esmay, with all her apparent bravado, could be as green about these matters as her Elena was. What of words of love? Men do tell women how beautiful they look. Men give women flowers and chocolates and stuff like that. The only time that Elena got a bit of chocolate was after Esmay had stuffed most of the chocolate bar herself. Or did things just happen on that night after a nightmare about snakes. In that nightmare, one of the Elena's had wandered off to a sort of field full of snakes which were trying to get her. Esmay had climbed into bed with her to reassure and comfort her, and that's how it began, and that is how it still was, the second Elena pointed out.

I left the two Elena's arguing and went back to thinking about Chris. It was as if an image of him was permanently stuck in front of my face. I kept seeing his boyish smile that turned to concern for his Dr Alexis's possible trouble over that kiss. The washed but wrinkled shirt he came to college in made it clear that Chris could not be living with anyone or even have access to an iron. Not that I'd want to iron his clothes. What would I want then? I asked myself over and over again.

Before long it was Xmas break. We did our Carol signing in English, German and Spanish. Some of our overseas students shouted greetings in their own language. It was great fun, though it was an extremely cold English winter. We missed not having Chris at the actual event. He had taken a full time holiday job in a large bookshop. He apologised and explained that it was back breaking work. He went home too tired to do anything else but grab something to eat and jump into bed. Esmay found out that Chris would be alone at Christmas. His Dr Alexis had to make the obligatory visit to the Sylvere family gathering in France. There were relatives coming over from St. Marten, Dominica Republic and Canada. Dr Alexis would not dare to be absent. When Esmay's mom heard that Chris would be alone at Christmas, she promptly invited him over. She said that where she came from no one was left but Chris had politely turned down the invitation. He had explained that he had promised to spend Christmas with an elderly neighbour who was a friend of his grandma before the grandma died.

Christmas came and went. It was a lovely Christmas, though my family did not have all the goodies that other people had. I had even managed to be very polite to Anthony whom Mom had invited for Boxing Day. January came and we woke up to a white blanket of snow covering everywhere. It was as if we had all migrated to the North Pole. It was like a sort of magic land, very white and with a sweet, almost hypnotic smell, coming from the snow. The young children, out on toboggans, some on bits of planks or in boxes, could have been little Elves dropped from the sky.

The final year students were advised to get back immediately after New Year's Day because we had much to do. The library and all its facilities would be open for us.

I arrived at college very early on the second of January to find that Esmay was already there, and fretting. Our whole block was unbearably cold. Even the library was freezing. The heating system had either broken down or the maintenance people had turned it off to save fuel.

'Blast those mean bitches,' Esmay swore under her breath, 'They tell us to return early and then don't bother to turn the heating on before we arrive.'

Other students, some of them wrapped up like creatures from outer space, began to arrive. The first one that we noticed was Chris. I ran up to him and gave him a hug.

'*Hola.*' I kissed him on both cheeks; they felt like blocks of ice.

'*Como estas?*' He kissed me once on each cheek.

'Hi Esmay.'

Chris attempted to kiss her but she moved away. Esmay didn't believe in all that kissing stuff. She thought kissing was soppy.

'Hey Chris. How was your Christmas?' Esmay asked.

'*Muy Bien.*' He replied.

'Less of that funny language! That's some coat you're sporting.' Esmay ran her fingers lightly over the sleeve of Chris's winter coat.

'Well, it was, err...was a Christmas present.' Chris blushed as he said it.

'From?' Esmay enquired.

'Esmay! It's none of your business.' I rebuked her.

'I gave it to me myself. It was cheap.'

'Look! Joy. Hey! Joy!' I called out. I was trying to change the subject. I didn't want Esmay to cause Chris's face to explode like a smashed ripe tomato but I failed.

'Looks expensive. What did you pay for it?' Esmay insisted on knowing.

'It's from that shop that sells designer things cheap.'

'Oh! Yeah? Fell off the back of a lorry, more like it!' said Esmay.

'You saying I go round nicking stuff?'

'Not you, them, they do, then flog it to the likes of us at car boot sales.'

After Chris left, Esmay remarked, 'Bloody liar! He was given that coat. And we all know by who or should it be, by whom? You're the brainy one Elle boo...'

Esmay blew cold wind onto the side of my neck.

'Eh! What! What did you say?'

'Look...why don't you go for him and get him out your system?'

'Don't you think of anything else?' I responded, walking away angrily.

85

I could feel Essay's eyes on my back as she muttered, 'It's in your eyes, and as they say, eyes don't lie.'

Stupid jackass I thought, but was not sure who the jackass was, Esmay or me.

We were all working flat out on our studies and at the same time mingling with other students on extra-curricula activities. Soon the week leading to Valentine's Day arrived. It was a good excuse for reading poetry, and stuffing ourselves with food and cheap booze. Esmay was asked to organise the event. And she in turn made me compare for the evening. It was mainly Esmay who drew a crowd together. Some were going to read in other languages, not just in so-called Standard English. The reader would give a summary in English for the benefit of those who did not understand that language. Soon the event was billed as a 'Bilingual-literary' event. The names of the contributors and the languages they would read in came to me and included Jamaican Patwa, Ghomalo from Cameroon, Yorkshire dialect and Brazilian Portuguese. We also had listed Polish and Italian. We invited Chris. He accepted and said that he had found a book on Cockney Rhyming slang, and that his grandma used to say things like, 'apples and pears' for stairs. He promised to try and read some. We did suggest to Chris that he invite Dr Alexis along, but he said that he didn't dare. Esmay dared and did invite him! She said that the invitation was because Chris had mentioned that Dr Alexis spoke several languages. However, Dr Alexis apologised saying he had a previous engagement. Esmay, who was supposed to have the knack of knowing when people were telling a lie concluded, 'Blinking liar. He doesn't want to mingle with the likes of us.'

She soon was to find out that she was wrong about him, when a couple of days before the event, Dr Alexis phoned. He asked to meet us in confidence. He wanted a big favour from us. He spoke first to Esmay.

'Oh! I see.' said Esmay, handing the phone to me.

At first I feared that it was more trouble about the 'kiss on the forehead ' saga but it was not that. It was something else, but Dr Alexis preferred not to say what it was on the phone. He also didn't want Chris to know about any meeting.

'I see...yes! Yes, we will be there and in strict confidence.' I promised. The day before the literary event arrived, Esmay and I met with Dr Alexis as arranged. Chris was not with him. He had been left behind to finish some work in the office. That extra work involved waiting by the phone for any important calls. We were both apprehensive when we met Dr Alexis by the entrance of The Golden Rose, a Chinese tea shop, no doubt very expensive judging from the type of cars parked nearby. He was his usual serious self, which had frightened Chris when they first met. He said very little and I secretly wished that he would at least smile a little to put us at ease, since neither Esmay nor I had ever had tea with a head of a department before. Esmay, usually good with small talk that made people either laugh or argue, was silent.

It was after he fed us on Chinese tea and exotic cakes, that Dr Alexis explained first of all, that he did in fact have a pre-planned meeting but did have something else in mind for the event, but needed to have our trust. He told us briefly that he wanted to say a special thank you to Chris. He went on at length to describe how hard Chris worked, often staying on long after hours and did much more than the pennies offered to him by the college. Esmay was agreeing with everything Dr Alexis said but I know that once we two were away from him she'd make some snide remark.

Dr Alexis asked what time we thought that the literary event would finish. I explained that we had permission for late opening of the hall. So it would be midnight before those unpleasant security people came to throw us out.

'*Bien*,' he said, 'a car will call for Mr Newman at around 11:45, if that is all right with you, ladies?'

'Ok with us, ain't... err, isn't' it, Elle?'

'Yes.' I nodded my agreement.

'Not a word mind. It must be a surprise.'

'Mm...trust us.' Esmay promised.

On our way back, Esmay came out with it, as I knew she would.

'For Chris's hard work, me arse!' Esmay swore, 'Who that man think he was talking to? Just 'cause we came in without A' levels some people think we're thick.'

'I don't know, maybe he didn't trust us enough to tell us the whole truth.'

'No, it's not just that. They don't give credit to us street-wise kids. Put him without money or shelter in London and that man, with all his posh education, wouldn't last a week.'

'Esse?' I changed the subject abruptly.

'Mm?'

'You ever had real sex?'

'What in Christ's name yu mean _real_ sex? You ask 'bout that sex rubbish before. Now it's _real_ sex. What the hell yu on about?'

'Well, with a man, or boys, you know?' I questioned her, somewhat embarrassed to even be thinking what I was beginning to think in relation to Chris.

'So, only sex with a man is _real_, eh?'

'Well, that...err...you know, that entering thing.'

'Penetration, that what yu mean?'

'Err...yes. Have you?'

'You know, sometimes I wonder where yu head bin all this time. The things you ask, unbelievable.'

'Well...have you...you know...'

Even with Esmay I found it hard to bring out the words to explain what I was beginning to think about.

'What would it be like if...?'

'Didn't I answer that question before?' Esmay seemed to know my thoughts. 'I said that I was no virgin?'

'How old are you anyway, still a kid?'

'What has age got to do with it? And don't call me kid, I'm no baby goat,' Esmay retorted, 'if you must know I'm twenty.'

'Mm, either you're a good actress or just a dumb twenty-year-old.'

'I am not dumb. But some of them school stories sound a bit far-fetched now. Mind you, that one about hearing a scream on me sister's wedding night might not have been a lie. Me sister was probably sewed up when she was little to make sure that on her wedding night her husband got maximum pleasure from fighting his way in. Oh, those poor women!'

'It's their culture, nothing to do with us here.' Esmay went further. 'I for one still think, as I told you before, that the whole sex thing with a man is overrated. A couple of quick stabs and it's all over but for the sticky mess and the stench. Plus...'

'All right! All right. No need to get vulgar!' I said, wanting her to stop.

'I believe in plain talk. Anyway, if you're thinking about that young man you'd better make a move.' She mocked.

'Ta! You can be real *tonto* at times!' I said, using a Spanish word for being foolish.

'Yeah, cuss-me up in your funny language, but I still can see someone else's making a move. Not that you have a chance, mind you.'

Esmay was taunting me.

'Go to hell! I'm sleeping on my own tonight.' I gave Esmay a filthy look and marched off.

'No more, no more...' she chanted in a funny voice, trying to make it sound like an American gospel song.

I had to admit to myself that Dr Alexis was appeared to be making moves towards Chris. I had no doubt that somehow; the young and obviously innocent man was getting to the older man. But how would Chris respond if he came on to him? If it was rejection, then there would be a chance for me and that would wipe the grin off Esmay's face. I knew she did not want me to make a move on

Chris. But why? Was it because she wanted me to remain unattached so that I would stay with her? I had no one else in my life except for my mother and brother. But what if it was a yes to the Doctor man? Funny, I would still have feelings for Chris but if I still loved him, what would that make me? There must be a name for a young woman who hangs around a young man even if he turned out to be with another man? There was something in one of the tabloids about wives who stayed with their husband even after they found out that they were seeing a man.

I suppose that I could go to some web site and find things out. But what the devil was I thinking? There were many young men around if I wanted one. There was Mom's Anthony for one. Ugh!...Me! A Nigerian wife? The thought of me wanting to marry or anything like that? No thanks! I was going to be an independent professional with my own car and a posh apartment. Yet, there was Chris and something about him got to me. Was it because he looked so gentle and was soft spoken? His voice had that ring to it, not a high-pitched soprano type but nowhere near a tenor either. I was thinking in terms of a range of voices on the scale, perhaps because of all that talk around campus about the music week at the end of the spring term. He was to me, if put in Spanish, more *bonito* than *guapo*.

As I lay alone in my bed that night, things went round and round in my head. That whole thing with Esmay was neither one thing or the other. Esmay did not love anyone. I was just her property, maybe a sort of doll, which she never had as a child.

Esmay was also domineering, the kind of person who 'wore the trousers in the house'. If anything, I wanted to be the one who wore the trousers.

'Why the devil don't you go right up to him and say you fancy him?' asked that other Elena. 'But you wouldn't dare would you?' replied another. He may reject your advances and say that he wants Alexis, not you.'

It was morning and I could smell coffee. Esmay was already up and chewing a partly burnt piece of toast.

'Why didn't you wake me? It's gone eight!' I said, yawning, before taking a piece of toast.

'What! And spoil your beautiful dream?'

'Yeah, slept like a log as they say.'

'Better watch it though. You talk in your sleep. Did you know that?' She said in matter of fact way.

She got up, picked up her books, and left the room.

'What!' I exclaimed, 'Nah! Yu havin' me on, you always do.'

Then a sudden fear came over me. What if I did talk in my sleep? There would be all hell let loose if I slept at Mom's and she heard me muttering all the things that had been going round in my head. Anyway, I thought, Esmay could just be lying in order to wind me up.

The night of the literary event arrived. We were all there but for one person. We had already started reading, discussing, disagreeing and clapping when, as on cue, Chris made a dramatic entrance. Joy had just begun to read from John Beaumont.

'Shush...' I motioned Chris to a nearby cushion.

All eyes had turned towards him as he approached. I noticed that he was wearing a pair of rather tight jeans, which were smartly ironed. From his neck hung a joke tie, which almost fell down over his crotch. Joy's voice brought me back to the poem.

'Hope and love are twins;
Hope gone, fruition now begins...'

The reader's voice faded as my thought once again turned to Chris. I failed in my attempt not to think of the surprise awaiting him. Esmay and I knew only about the car that had been arranged to pick him up. What would happen after that, neither of us had a clue? My thoughts ran wild. All I could think about was the romantic scene that might take place. Or was it just a friendly gesture towards a young man who had worked so hard for his boss-cum-mentor?

The loud cheers jerked me back to the event.

'Where were those lines from?' Esmay's question stopped the cheering.

'Easy peasy, it is from 'The Definition of Love'.' a voice from the floor shouted.

'Good. Now who was The Definition of Love by, then?' I asked.

People looked at each other .No seemed to be able remember the name of the poet.

'Bet our latest arrival knows.' Andre the joker replied, nodding in Chris's direction.

'He's a newcomer on campus, give him a break.' I said, quickly coming to Chris's aid. I then went on to introduce Chris to everyone.

'Hi, Chris!' came a chorus of welcome.

'I love that tie.' said one girl.

'*Si me gusta La Corbata.*' said someone who was obviously from the beginners in Spanish course.

'It's from France.' said Chris with a glow of happiness on his face.

'It's by Donne, John Donne.' Someone took us back to the poem.

'Wrong!' said an overseas EAL student. 'It's by Sir John Beaumont. It's a poem from his book, I believe. He wrote, 'Love is full of Fire'.'

'That's right, John Beaumont it was.' Esmay clapped in the direction of the overseas student. Everyone, except for Andre, cheered.

'Who's next?' I asked to get things moving.

'Me! Me!' shouted a chorus of voices.

And so, our Valentine's Day literary event continued.

Reading and discussion soon turned into argument, disagreement and mucking about, as the cheap booze began to take its effect. It could have been Esmay's reading that started all the uproar. She had started with one of Shakespeare's sonnets.

'In the old days black was not counted fair.'

Others, including Chris, joined in because we all had done those sonnets in class.

'Or if it were, bore no beauty's name.'

The formal reading did not progress much further because an argument began about whether it was sonnet 127 or 146. Some people were shouting 127, others shouted 146. Then came a remark, as if from nowhere:

'Did you know that Shakespeare was gay?'

'Nonsense! He was black, not gay.'

'I heard that he came up on the list of Black Heroes, so he was black. He and Beethoven are on that list.'

'Maybe he was black and gay?'

Chris, obviously now quite relaxed and happy, joined in.

'Actually, I read somewhere that Shakespeare was Jewish. But he hated Jews that's why he wrote the Merchant of Venice.'

'Yeah! Maybe he was black and gay and Jewish?'

'And Catholic.' someone laughed.

'Don't be bloody daft! How could he have been Jewish as well as Catholic?'

'Why not? In Haiti, we can be devotees of Voodoo and Catholicism too.' One of the overseas students joined in the debate.

'Careful, you'll get bloody done by our law against inciting religious and racial hatred.'

'No strong language. Please behave yourselves.' I called above the thunder of laughter that broke out.

The evening got wilder by the minute. Some people began to sign or dance. It seemed that everyone was snogging someone. Except, that was, for Chris, Esmay and myself.

Andre grabbed Chris by his joke tie and tried to kiss him. Chris laughed but pushed him away and came to stand behind me.

Above the noise came the voice of one of the security men.

'Car for Mr Newman. Mr Christopher Newman?' The security man came in and at once people grabbed him and tried to kiss him.

'You young ones been drinking?' The man rebuked.

'Only mineral water.' said Joy, who could just about stand on her feet.

'We have to see her to her room.' I whispered to Esmay.

'We'll take her home with us.' Esmay whispered back. 'No Andre's going to get her.'

'I'm Chris Newman.'

'Ok! Come with me.' The security man led the way and we all followed. 'Gore blimey! Some motor that is!' said an unsteady voice.

A smart car had driven right up to the end of the drive.

'For me?' Chris gasped.

'Yes, I said we'd see you home didn't we Elle?' Esmay glanced at me.

I nodded my agreement

'Can I share?' Andre asked. 'Bin drinking and can't...'

'No!' Esmay shouted at him before he completed the sentence, 'Definitely not!'

'Look, I could be stopped if the old Bill saw me wobbling about on a motor bike.'

'That's your problem. Get a cab like everyone else,' Esmay said with a smirk.

'It's okay with me,' said Chris, who had no idea of the plan, 'If he's going in the same direction.'

'No Chris, Elle and I invited you; we'll see you back home, savvy?'

'It looks very expensive. I don't...' Chris whispered to me.

'It's okay. Esmay and I took care of everything.'

'But...'

'No buts. You can pay next time.' I said to lesson his obvious embarrassment.

The driver came out and held the door open for Chris and we saw him in.

We waved Chris off while I ignored the inquiring frown of Andre.

'Adios.' I said.

Others, who had since joined us, shouted a chorus of 'good nights.'

Watching Chris leave brought a pain to my chest. Was this the end of my hope? An evil thought crept into my head. I could always let the cat out of the bag, as the saying goes. In a place like this a mere whisper and the whole campus, and beyond, would know. But what good would that do me? I wondered. All that would happen is that Dr Alexis would lose his job. Because, though Chris was of the age of consent, he was still a student. There was also the question of gender. All the hidden homophobes would crawl out of their present hiding places which they occupied because of the college's anti discrimination policy. Worst scenario would be that the man's trouble would only push Chris closer to him. So Ms Elena, go and do your worst, and watch your evil doing actually back fire on you I argued with the other Elena in me.

Round and round things went, like little creepy crawlies in my head. I became moody and I decided to go home for the weekend after the literary evening.

Going home for the weekend was something I had not done for a while in order to avoid Anthony. Somehow, I preferred going home, where I'd have to be polite to Anthony, to not going and putting up with Esmay's sniping remarks about Chris and me. She seemed to twist every word I uttered. She was trying to get me to reveal how I actually felt about Chris. In fact, I could write my Monday morning presentation for Spanish class based on my weekend. We were usually asked what we did at the weekend. A lot of what we wrote about doing was lies anyway, and the professor knew it. But he was mainly interested in our mastery of the conjugation of Spanish verbs.

I could, I thought, fabricate a story under the title, 'El fin de semana pasada.'

I'd write that I spent the weekend with my boyfriend. The class liked to hear those kinds of stories. I'd write that my boyfriend and I went to see a film. After the cinema we went for a meal at an Italian restaurant. He then, like a gentleman, took me home, where my mom waited up for us. Here I would get some sniggering because it would not be the ending they expected. I could not help grinning to myself at the thought of the disappointed looks on their faces. Afterwards they would corner me outside and say that I was a bloody liar. Going home to Mom waiting up, what big pokies you tell, Elena!

My lies never materialised.

Going home for that weekend was perhaps the biggest mistake I had made. Not only was Anthony there, what he said made me want to pack my things and flee. But where could I go? Run back to Esmay who would smirk and make me feel that I had nowhere else to go?

That Sunday's fried chicken and rice was difficult to swallow. I had suspected that something was amiss when Anthony arrived with a larger than usual bunch of flowers for Mom. Blast, I thought, again and again, why me? There are hundreds of young women around, why me?

After we had eaten and were relaxing with glasses of pineapple juice, he just happened to mention that, 'My aunt is coming to London on business and would like...' His voice faded away.

'That's nice, isn't it?' Mom's voice brought me back to the present.

'Oh, what did you say, Mom?'

'Anthony's aunt...asked to meet you...err...to meet us.' Mom was openly excited at the prospect of meeting Anthony's aunt. 'Isn't that nice?' Mom repeated.

Mom apologised to Anthony for me being miles away.

That was because I worked very hard at my studies and often I walked around with my essays in my head.

'When are they expected?' I asked.

Secretly, I was planning to be miles away even If I had to break my own leg. I'll be in the hospital, then. Christ, no, they'll visit me in hospital, I mused. Now I'll have to find another reason for being away. That Sunday evening was the most miserable I've ever had. Anthony kept smiling every time he looked in my direction even though he was playing a game with Kevin. He had brought Kevin an expensive mobile phone which Mom could never have afforded. After Anthony left, Mom sang his praises. He was a good young man. His parents must be very proud of him. He was nothing like them Caribbean men who stick the baby in you and disappear.

'Don't you worry, Mom? Your Elena wouldn't go with a Caribbean man and become his baby mother. I'd rather go for a Polish young man. There are a couple of them at our college.' I teased, but at the same time wondered if deep down my mom could be a secret racist. If that were the case all hell would break loose if she found out what I was thinking about Chris, a white, English young man.

'Or, wait a minute, an Eskimo.' Kevin joined in. 'Any Eskimos at your college?'

'Get yourself to bed, Kevin!' Mom chastised poor Kevin again.

'Okay, okay, going, but I want to be the best man at the wedding...'

'I'll give you best man, get up those stairs this minute or else...' Mom shouted, shaking her head from side to side.

I threw a cushion at Kevin as he pulled faces from the stairs. I was thinking what a happy family we were even without much money. No Anthony should come and spoil that. I'll deal with Anthony. I had told him before that I was not ready for young men. Well, that didn't work. Now I'd have to shock him. I'd fabricate a boy next door who I had sex with when I was thirteen...no, when I was eleven and did it many times with him. After all, I bet that I was not the only one at school who lied so that we did not look square. I'd lie and say that I was also doing it. Anyway, once Anthony had been shocked I'd put on a serious face and say that his parents should know that I was not the virgin they thought I was. If that didn't work I'd tell him about Esmay and me. We slept together and kissed and things. That should be shock enough to keep him away. Of course, he might tell Mom, but I'd deal with that when the time came. With that plan in mind, only to be used if I had too, I managed to scribble a few notes in Spanish for the Monday morning presentation before I went to bed.

It was the Monday after the Valentine's event. I warned Esmay not to put Chris under pressure to tell us the details of what had taken place after the car had taken him away. She promised not to. But she felt that there was no harm in asking Chris if he had had a Valentine's card. And if he had gone to another party after he left us. I remained concerned though that if Esmay might, directly or indirectly, make Chris say things and they got out. That Dr Alexis might be in big trouble. Even Esmay would not want that to happen, surely? But she sometimes let words fly out of her mouth without thinking. Luckily, Chris came up with a completely different story to the one I had been thinking.

We met Chris at lunch break and got ourselves a couple of muffins from the student canteen and went outside to sit on a bench away from the crowd.

'So, did you get a Valentine's card? Elle got one, didn't you Elle?'

'Yes, I did. Though God knows why anyone would send me a card.'

'I did get a card but I don't know who sent it.' Chris went pink.

'You're not supposed to know. You have to guess.' I said, but was sure that Chris could guess who the sender of his card might be.

'Did you go to another party?' Esmay could no longer hold her tongue.

'Nah! He...the driver, took me straight home.'

'He did? And what happene...?' Esmay did not get further because I stamped hard on her foot.

'Thank you both for the cab. But I was never so ashamed in m'life.'

'Why?' Esmay and I asked in unison.

'What appened,' said Chris, dropping his 'H', 'was embarrassing?'

Oh my God, No! I thought. The Doctor hadn't made a move and embarrassed Chris?

Luckily, Chris came up with something that I did not expect.

'The driver insisted he took me straight to my place. I was ashamed for him, driving such a posh car to the dump I live in. He was calling me 'sir' and treating me like I was a gentleman.'

Chris used what he thought was posh English.

'But you are a gentleman.' I emphasised the 'are'.

I felt strange and confused at the same time. On one hand I wanted him to be happy. And if his happiness would be with Dr Alexis then so be it. On the other hand I wanted him to be happy with me. My feelings for him were getting stronger by the day. At the same time, if he could be happy with Dr Alexis as well, I wouldn't have a problem with that. I rebuked myself. That was a crazy line of thinking. Meanwhile, Chris was talking but I was not listening until Esmay said, 'She's miles away in a world of her own.'

'Must be her exam that's coming up. Anyway, I better go. I'm boring the pants off her.' said Chris, readying himself to leave.

'No, don't go.' I apologised, 'sorry, I was thinking about how I was once ashamed of where we lived!'

'You ain't seen my dump. I told the driver to drop me at the corner. Actually, I was going to sneak through the back of those nice houses to get to my run-down, Woodland Estate. The driver refused. He said that he had to do what he was told to do because it was very late. He took me up that stinking lift, how embarrassing! Someone had been pissing in the lift. It stank! I had to tell a lie, I had to.'

'What was the lie?' I asked.

'That I really lived somewhere else but my grandma had lived there for years before she got so bad and died. I told him I was looking after the place until we got her stuff sorted out.'

'That's all?' Esmay sounded disappointed.

'Dr Alexis, he rang. He asked if I was okay. I said yes because Elena and Esmay got me a home by a nice taxi. And the driver was very kind.'

'And you just went to sleep?' asked Esmay, with a frown.

'Yes, drinks don't agree with me. I fall asleep.' He laughed.

After Chris left we looked at each other.

'Your Chris is such a big liar.' Esmay chuckled.

'Why do you think he's fibbing?'

'Come on! You mean to tell me that that man got some fancy cab to take Chris home to sleep on his own? Come on! I wasn't born yesterday.'

'And why not, may I ask?'

'This is what happened. Your Chris was driven to some fancy exclusive club where the Doctor man was waiting. They had a romantic night until early in the morning. Mm...we can imagine the rest.' Esmay gave me hard look.

'So that's how your minds working. Romantics, then slap-bang and bed.'

'Of course, you'd like to think that nothing happened. That it was merely a friendly gesture toward a hard working young man.' Esmay gloated.

'So what's it got to do with you, eh?'

'I hate to see you hanging on to something that can never be.'

Suddenly I decided that I'd had enough of Esmay going on and on about me fancying Chris.

'Of course, you'd like to believe that nothing happened between those two, eh?' Esmay went on and on.

I glared at her for winding me up. I could not take any more from her. I quietly walked away.

I should have gone to my late afternoon seminar but I could not face any lengthy analysis of English classics. I went straight to the place that Esmay and I shared and quietly took down the case I had brought my things in to share with her. When the case was full, I went to the communal kitchen and found myself a shopping bag. I crammed in all my books, writing pad and stuff like that, in the bag. With those two bags in hand, I left my key to the room on the table by the door. For one moment I was tempted to leave a note, but I decided not to do so. After all, she often went away for a whole day without leaving a note. I went to the bus stop and within forty minutes or so I was turning the key in the door to my family's home where my own room was always there for me. I called out, as we always did when we entered the house. There was no response. Mom was obviously still at work, slogging her guts out doing overtime for extra pennies for us. Kevin was still out as well. He was probably at one of those after school projects. I slammed my bag against the inside of the front door and called out again, this time as if talking to the building, the bricks and mortars, itself.

'I'm home!'

7

The week following my return home for a bit of peace and quiet was anything but peaceful. First, Esmay phoned my Mom. She said that she was worried and asked if I was okay. I overheard Mom telling her that I wanted to concentrate on my work for the final exam. Esmay wouldn't take no for an answer and insisted that she spoke to me. In the end, I picked up the house phone and talked to her.

'I'd be grateful if you left me to my work. I just want a break, a bit of space.'

'Did I do something to upset you?

'No, you didn't.' I said, thinking, stupid jackass of course you did something that upset me.

Esmay must've called on Chris for help because next I had a call on my mobile from him.

'You alright?' He asked.

'We'll talk. The mobile call charges are too expensive.'

I did not have to wait long for a call from Chris on the house phone.

'Listen, did you quarrel with Esmay because of me?'

'Of course not. What gave you such a stupid idea? See you as usual for Spanish.'

'Actually,' he said, 'I was thinking, perhaps I shouldn't take up your time. You have your own exam coming up. For you it's important because it's your final.'

Hearing Chris's voice was enough to make me want to see him. Yet I had no idea what I would say when I did. I couldn't possibly reveal that it was Esmay's nagging me about him that I returned to my mom's.

'Elena, you still there?'

'Yes, yes! But you don't have to stop coming to work with me.'

Inside, I was begging him, by telepathy perhaps, not to deny me those private moments with him. But Chris was adamant. He insisted I must have time to work on my own essays.

'Did Esmay put you up to this?' I wanted to know.

'No, but she thinks that you left because you have too much work.'

The bitch! I should've known. She somehow manipulated him so he would stop coming to get help from me with his Spanish studies. Well, Madam Esmay, you've done it now. I want nothing more to do with you.

I had phoned my personal tutor to say that I wanted to spend more time working from home .It was quieter at Mom's. I said that it was better if I concentrated on what material I already had in hand. My tutor was agreeable but Esmay was not. First she called at the house when Mom was at work. I let her in for a long talk.

'You're stalking me. I like some space, can't you understand that?'

'You're angry with me. I'm sorry, whatever it was that I've done.'

'Listen Esmay, the more you harass me the more I'll insist on staying here, so it's up to you. Leave me in peace and eventually I may come back, harass me and I won't, savvy?'

The following Sunday morning I told Mom that I was going for a long walk to help clear my thoughts. Actually, I ended up getting onto two busses then walking to the notorious Break Wood Estate. I was shocked to see how huge and depressing it appeared. All the blocks were drab and greyish in colour. The estate was worse than the Peckham estate we had lived on before moving to that damp basement in the slums of Hackney. I had no idea that these places still existed. Like on the Peckham estate, people stayed indoors. There was no one around. The eerie stillness of the place sent chills down my spine. I had no idea of Chris's actual address in what seemed like a never-ending row of blocks of large size pigeonholes. I would never find him. Not that I really wanted to knock at his door uninvited and embarrass him. If only I could get a glimpse of him, perhaps while going for a Sunday Newspaper or for a bottle of milk. I walked from where the bus had left me to what seemed to be the middle of that vast, run-down estate. I saw a play area with swings and slides but no children playing. I strolled along until my legs got tired. I saw a concrete wall and went and sat down. I gazed at the block opposite to me. I was silently willing Chris to come out onto one of the long prison-like corridors. But he did not. I noticed something odd about those grey and depressing looking blocks. There was not a single flowerpot or plant. Surely someone could plant a few daffodils to liven up the place? Instead, they left it to look like a science fiction scene in which humans and animals seemed to have disappeared. Chris deserved better than this horrible place.

I begin to realise how badly Chris needed a helping hand out of this mud pit. And there was help at hand. Of course, that man was not a sugar daddy as such. If he were, he wouldn't be stuck at the college, and dealing with all the students who needed extra help. He'd be at one of those private high-fee colleges. I was sure that with the man's olive coloured skin and French accent, he was being given the worst cases to deal with. Never-the-less, sugar daddy or not, he was in a position to help Chris out of this dump. Which meant that you, Ms Elena Peterson, should keep your paws off Chris? So, do yourself a favour and get up and go home!

I rose and walked further down the estate. I was getting more and more depressed at the sights where such a lovely and gentle young man, who was trapping my heart, was himself trapped in such a god forsaken place. My poor, poor, Chris. It's going to be hell for me but I couldn't come and stand in your way. This mean that I could never let you know how I feel. I must let you have your chance. True, you don't appear to be the type to sell your body for a better life. But even a friendship with this particular older man, even though I'm sure he's not a sugar daddy, would help. I'm sure that he loves you. To him you're more than just another of the second chance students put in his charge. True, so true, I can't claim to be experienced in those things but if that man doesn't fancy you as his young lover, I'd eat my hat, as they say.

So busy was I thinking of poor Chris that I didn't even realise that I had gone to sit by a wall at the entrance to the Wood; that was until someone coughed near me.

'Oh! Sorry! I was miles away.'

'I could see that.' The young man, perhaps about seventeen years of age, said. At least that was what I believed he said. He spoke in a broad dialect of some sort. It certainly wasn't the made up Jamaica-talk that Esmay often messed about with.

'Anyway, good morning. Have good day. I'd better be going.'

I stepped off the wall.

'Come on, saw you walking and looking.'

'You did?'

'Look, sister, you stay here.' He nodded to his right. I noticed then that a car was driving slowly past us.

I was thinking: I'm not frightened. I'm not, I'm not! He couldn't attack me, and rape me, surely? Not in broad daylight? He probably only wanted to sell me some stuff. Oh my God! Yet another side to this horrible estate. I walked away towards some stone steps leading into the woods.

'Not there? Not on your own, sister!' I was amazed how the young man switched from using broad dialect to the English of any Southeast Londoner.

'Oh! Isn't it safe then?'

'Didn't yu mama warn you not to go through woods on yuh own?'

'She didn't need too.' I was thinking that I wish he'd piss off. He smelt strongly of tobacco or something.

He began to follow me and was saying something I couldn't understand.

'What?'

'What can I do for me sister today?'

'Nothing, thank you.' Since when was I your sister? I kept my thoughts to myself.

'You name it and Brother Ben delivers.'

He was walking slowly beside me to my left. The stone steps led first to a lane I had to cross to enter the wood on my right. I felt trapped by the danger of entering the woods and the man following me or turning back and him still following me. Suddenly, the event, which had lead to my brush with the law culminating in nearly three years as a guest at what we later called, The House of our Lady Grace, sprang into my mind.

The young man appeared to read my thoughts and said, shaking his head from side to side, 'Look, me is...' He resumed that posh dialect. 'A businessman does not go round raping young women.'

'Aha, there's a bus stop!' I shouted, 'Adios!' rushing to the stop in the distance leaving him behind.

Wow! That was a close shave I thought, joining the others waiting in the queue.

A bus came and I jumped on, not caring where it was going as long as it was away from that dreadful place. Anyway, I had had enough adventure, if you could call it that, for one day. Once on the bus, I asked if it was going anywhere near a train station. It turned out I was going in the opposite direction to the train station but the correct one for the bus station. There I could ask which bus to take to my destination.

It was quite a long ride to the bus station and my mind was in turmoil. It was if I had just had an interesting but somewhat despairing adventure. I went to a land far removed from Britain, a developed country. I felt sorry for people of that backward run down country. But worst of all was that my Chris had to live there. How would he get out? Love can get him out though not yours, dear Elena. Of course he does not have to leave his Doctor Man to come to you.

My thoughts turned to Anthony and his visiting aunt. Anthony and me? No chance! Anthony or Chris? No contest! If there were, Chris would win hands down and blind folded. On and on the argument rumbled in my head. At times it was as if thousands of creatures where whispering and talking about me as if I wasn't there, the same way that adults talk about children in the presence of their child.

'She's going to stay away from him. Nah!...She wouldn't. Yeah! She'll go for him. But what if he does not want her, what if, eh, eh? She'd make him want her. Come on, she's got no experience with men. She's not stupid. She was clever; her mother told all who wanted to hear that her Elena was clever. She's only clever with book. You're right there. She can ask Esmay, ex-bed partner, for tips. Come on! Esmay, who wants her for herself going to give her tips to get a man? You're right there. And that Doctor Man, if he was to be her rival he'd win hands down! Yeah, you're right there. And what of Anthony, her mother's choice for her? The woman only wanted the best for her only daughter. Anthony, the mother was sure, would marry her daughter, the rest of the good-fo-nothings more likely to shove a baby up her and disappear. Remember all those teeny-age lone mothers? And what about Chris then, could she take him home to Mom? Nah!

'Last stop!' a voice called out. At last we had reached the bus station.

By the time I changed between three buses, one of them going past the back of our campus, I arrived home to find our visitors already there. I turned my key in the door and entered to be greeted with a wail of questions and faces of concern.

'What happened?' asked Mom, with a worried look on her face.

'We were extremely worried.'

Anthony again used his formal words to impress, yet he did have a note of sincere concern in his voice, I thought.

Kevin joined in with one of his jokes. 'Thought you got kidnapped.'

'I'm so sorry,' I said and meant it, 'I wandered off and ended up in one of the most dreadful places for any human to live. Oh Mom, you should've seen it!'

'My Elena, she makes essays 'bout people in bad conditions, don't' you Elena?' Mom said with a glow of pride on her face.

'This is my Auntie, Mrs Anjihamo, and Clara, she is my cousin. My sister could not come this time.'

'I do apologise for dropping in like this. But we were with Tony and he was coming here. He said that it was not a trouble...' said the aunt in clear English, except for her accent.

'We still sur' Americana, our door always open. Any one much welcome when they want to visit us.' Mom, in her Sunday best, reassured the aunt.

I shook hands with the two visitors.

'Our visitors had a little *tapas Y bebidas frías*.' It was one of those occasions when Mom mixed English with Spanish, often with Venezuela idioms.

'Your Elena should have her lunch. We talk later.' suggested the aunt.

'I'm okay. I had a snack in one of them greasy spoon cafés.' I lied, and found myself a seat.

I was weighing the aunt up. She was obviously a businesswoman. Probably privately educated in one of those elitist Catholic run schools we read about. What would my life be as young women from England married to her nephew? Hell. Sheer hell!

'Tony wrote and said a great deal about your daughter, Mrs Peterson.' She said to Mom as if I wasn't present. 'I understand that her father is away...'

I listened as Mom sang me praises. I wondered, at times, who that Elena was that Mom was talking about. Then it was the aunt's turn. She sang Anthony's praises. Meanwhile Saint Clara sat silently. I was sure that Clara was not an African culture name. But then they are, according to Anthony, Catholics. That poor wimp of a sixteen-year-old girl, sitting like me with her hands in her lap and saying nothing, was probably named after some Catholic female saint.

I listened to Mom and the aunt talk business. That is, Anthony's aunt was telling Mom about the business in mind.

Mom kept saying *Si, bien*. She'd nod her head and agree, '*Si, Buena* idea!'

I could not bear listening to the chat between Mom and Auntie any longer so I asked permission to leave the room. It was what any submissive daughter would be expected to do.

'May I go to the kitchen and get a cold drink.'

'*Si, Si*.' Mom nodded with pride.

The aunt also nodded and smiled at me. She was obviously impressed.

'Me too, Mom?' Kevin too was bored.

'Yes.' said Mom.

Kevin and I got to the kitchen. Once there he closed the kitchen door behind us and whispered, 'Why's Mom talking so much Venezuelan? We don't use all that Spanish at home'

'Don't know...gone bonkers over Anthony, I suspect.'

'They'll make you marry him?'

'No way! Me marrying no one? *Nunca*!'

'You could marry him then push him over a cliff. It was on telly, this girl; she married a rich man then pushed him over...'

'Elena!' Mom's voice rang out.

'Coming, Mom!' With glasses of drinks in our hands we left the kitchen.

Mom gave me one of those looks which made me ask, 'Would Clara like a drink, Auntie?'

'Yes, she would.' Anthony's Aunt spoke up for Clara.

'Auntie, may Clara come to the kitchen and choose what she wants?' I asked, humbly.

'Yes she may.'

Secretly I was thinking what a load of shit! The whole thing was like a scene from a black comedy. Looking at her I felt that the Clara girl would any moment sprout wings and fly off. Saint Clara meekly followed me into the kitchen. Once there I nearly asked if she'd had a stroke or some childhood illness that left her brain damaged, but I stopped myself. It would've been rude to ask that. Instead, I asked about her school or college.

I wanted to ask about boyfriends as we do in London. Even five-year-old girls on kid's telly programmes are asked if they have a boyfriend and boys if they have a girlfriend ugh! Why don't they ever ask if the boy had a boyfriend and girl had a girl friend? But I wouldn't dare ask Saint Clara about boy friends because I was sure that Auntie would later question her about what we had talked about. So I kept my questions to schoolwork. She was at college for 16 years and above. She was good at every subject. She couldn't make up her mind what to choose from so many choices. Auntie thought that she'd be a good businesswoman. But Pappy, Anthony's dad, wanted her to be a doctor and look after women and their problems.

'You poor thing. In a way I'm lucky,' I told her, 'I'm not very good at any thing; therefore I have no problem with choice.'

'You are very pretty. You get married soon.'

Saint Clara sipped the mineral water she had chosen for herself.

'You are very pretty as well. As for anytime soon...I doubt it.'

We were called back to the living room because Anthony's aunt was ready to leave. She said that she had to visit some people about her business link with London. Mercifully, the visit came to a close. We waved goodbye. As soon as we were on our own as a family, Kevin asked, 'Mom, you going to marry off our Elena to Anthony and his Auntie?'

'Anthony family very nice and polite.' Mom ignored Kevin's question.

'I bet they are. God help the woman who marries one of them.' I muttered, while clearing up the glasses.

'Auntie asked me if I would want to be involved with her business in London.' Mom ignored my sniping remark.

'Oh yes! And how you going to be involved?' I frowned.

'Well, house parties, dat sort o' ting. You know, some of the girls at work been having them for pots and tings but this one would be for African clothes and cards.'

'Mom! What do you know about African clothes? And why would any one come to a Venezuelan woman to buy African stuff?'

'Some of the girls from work, and neighbours and friends would.'

'Old Mrs grumpy next door would look nice in African wraps.' giggled Kevin.

Mom gave him a dirty look and went to take off her Sunday best she puts on for Anthony's visits.

'She gone funny, you think?' I whispered to Kevin when Mom left.

'Yeah! She'll soon be learning African drumming at the Community Centre.' Kevin said.

In bed that night I wondered, why me, and not a young African women? Lots of pretty ones at our college. Maybe I should introduce him to one or two of them. Perhaps even Esmay. I laughed at the thought of Esmay with a man, African or otherwise. Seriously, I wondered over and over why Mom was so keen on Anthony for me. Why keen on any man for me. Is it that she wanted to get rid of me? I wondered if her friends had been talking about me because they had never seen me with a boyfriend. They, the Spanish speaking ones, might even have been making sniping remarks about her old-maid daughter. Well over twenty and still not married, not even boyfriends? Mom was probably hinting about a Mr Anthony. Well, all of you wait and see. Elena is going to give you all a great big shock one day, you just wait! My thoughts were not about Anthony being part of that big shock. They were certainly not in the direction of Anthony but a very different person...Well, I can dream can't I?

The following Monday I went to college. I needed something I had left behind at Esmay's but dreaded going to the flat in case she was in. I remembered also that I had left her the spare key and would have to knock. I decided to leave the book and pad that I had forgotten to take from the shelf. Instead, I made for the IT building .As I was going up the stairs, Chris was coming down them.

'*Hola* Elena. *Buenas Tardes.*' He greeted me in Spanish because I had been encouraging him to practice speaking.

'*Hola* Chris, you OK?'

'Well...' he shrugged, and I knew then that there was something wrong.

'Look, let's go for a coffee.' I suggested.

The Tapas bar was now closed. We had to go along to the students' refectory and use the coffee machines. We got a cup of coffee for me and drinking chocolate, which was his favourite, for him. I was concerned and anxious to know why Chris looked so miserable.

'Let's sit outside where it's quieter.'

'Okay. Yuck!...' he grimaced, 'the drinking chocolate here is getting worse.'

We sat down but before Chris could explain, whom do we see, Esmay, walking along, pretending not to have spotted us, that was until Chris called out!

'Hi Esse, come and join us!' Chris invited.

'Thanks, but I don't want to interrupt.'

'Don't be a plonker.' Chris copied a phrase from one of the TV soaps. Esmay gave me an inquiring look.

'Sit down if you want!' I shrugged

'You two been fighting, I can tell.' Chris grinned, 'lovers tiff, eh?'

'Nah! Just a misunderstanding.' said Esmay.

'Misunderstanding? Seems rather familiar.'

Chris sounded very unhappy about something.

'Was you fighting with someone, then?' Asked Esmay, deliberately using was instead of were.

I had no choice but to sit with Chris and Esmay. I'd prefer being alone with Chris as he spoke of his troubles. But having agreed for Esmay to stay I could do nothing to stop Chris speaking out and Esmay hearing what he had to say.

Things had gone wrong. He was no longer eating in the office with his boss. He was even thinking that it would be better if he left the college at the end of his contract even though it was renewable.

'But you two were getting closer and closer.' I pointed out.

'People will think I want to get things from him.'

'What things?' I asked.

'People? Which people?' Esmay asked in an angry voice.

'Somebody stopped me and said, 'Go for it. Don't be stupid.' He said it's the done thing. Youth go for old big fish and get what they want.'

'Don't tell me. It's that Andre. I'll kill the bastard!' Esmay bellowed.

'Don't listen to that Andre. He's the master troublemaker on campus.' I advised, being calmer than Esmay.

'It wasn't Andre. He's harmless that one. I ignore him whenever he stops me with his nonsense.'

'Tell big sister who it is, let me go give him one in the groin.' Esmay fumed.

'Aggression never helped any one. Listen, your Dr Alexis is not a big fish. No big fish come teaching in college for pennies.'

'Good Ms Elena Peterson, you're right. Ignore the gossips.' Esmay took her leave then.

It was after Esmay's departure that I got Chris to pour out the cause his distress.

'I don't want nothing from him, I love...err...I like him,' Chris said in the voice of a hurt puppy, 'even if he was an old woman wobbling on a stick or a smelly tramp.'

'Have you told him what you just told me?'

'Not really. I now keep me distance, that's all.'

'Is he aware that there was, you know, something different in your behaviour?'

'Yesterday he asked if he did something to upset me.'

'And what did you say?'

'I said no, he didn't. Only thing was that I got lots of work do that's all.'

'Did he believe you?' I asked

'Don't know.' Chris shrugged, 'he looked a bit sad, like he used to look in the old days when I first work for him. He never used to smile, even.'

'Look,' I took one of Chris's hands gently in my own. 'Talk to your man.'

It felt strange. I was actually advising someone I'd like for myself to make up with his friend. I felt that his hand was cold and clammy. So I rubbed it as if it were the hand of a baby you were trying to reassure.

'I can't, I don't have yours and Esmay's guts. She would've gone straight out and say it. Believe me Elle, I just like him a lot, I don't want nothing, I swear!'

I didn't have the heart to point out his use of double negatives, as I had been doing indirectly to help him. Anyway, it was his way of speaking, so what? I lifted his hand, and without meaning to, placed the palm against one side of my face. 'You'll be fine. Go tell or write him, but let him know of your fear.'

'Thanks, Elena. Don't know why, but you and Esmay like the two big sisters I never had. I'll find a way and the right time to let him know what people might be thinking and saying but that they're wrong.'

With those parting words, Chris left for the Computer Help office where he worked part of the week.

Can it be that he was aware of my feelings for him and that's why he brings up that big sister business? Nah! I doubt it. He was not exactly what you call very streetwise where girls are concerned. When nosy-parker Esmay once asked him he said no, he had no girlfriend outside or inside college. Never saw anyone he was interested in. Perhaps it was because at school, girls as well as boys bullied him. There was this one girl; she stood up for him more than once at school. When Esmay probed him he told us the story and we laughed. It was about a girl whom he was petrified of, even though she had stood up for him. She was a black girl and powerful looking. Afterwards, he was very afraid that she'd ask him for a date and he wouldn't have dared say no to her. That day I stayed seated on the bench and watched Chris until he got out of my sight. But if he had no experience with girls and I had no experience with boys then we'll be like the blind leading the blind across the road; not that love meant sex of course.

I wandered to the library, and still thinking that if Chris was macho, like Andre and his lot, I probably wouldn't have given him a second thought Even Anthony, who was decent and seemed kind, had nothing to match what Chris had I thought, feeling a strange longing for his touch. In the library I had a book open in front of me but was not reading from the pages. I tormented myself. I had no doubt that Alexis cared sincerely about Chris. If he didn't and only wanted a quickie with him he would've made a move by now. He was instead wooing him the way I would have done were I a man. I image holding him and snogging him, inhaling the cologne he could be using.

For a moment I began to think that there might be something wrong with me. I didn't appear to be thinking straight. Instead, I allowed things to go round and round, to and fro, in my head. Why, until now, you never had a man, eh? Those words seemed to be shouting in my head. You should be a mother by now with a couple of kids from at least two absentee fathers. What's wrong with you? Why you fancy a very, almost feminine beauty instead of a macho or even illegible bachelor like Anthony, who would sweep you off to a throne of a kind in Africa somewhere? Yeah! I thought. A golden throne encircled by a barbwire fence preventing you getting out. No thanks. It has to be in England and no one else but gentle Chris, with or without Alexis...

'You okay?' A voice broke into me thoughts.

'Oh sorry, I was...'I began.

'We've been mentally rehearsing our poem for the Jazzarama, haven't we?' Andre was his usual funny self.

'We, who, and what poem?' was my reply. 'Anyway you shouldn't be sneaking up on people like that.'

Andre had come to sit by me and I didn't even realise it at first.

'I heard the poetry group was planning to do its bit at the launching of this year's Jazzarama.' He explained.

'I'm not. Got too much to do. Shit, look at the time!' I began to pack my things.

'Rumour has it that you and Esmay split up.'

'Oh yes?' I got up and he followed, smiling at me like a lizard trying to entice its next supper.

In your dreams, I thought, as I rushed on my way.

'I could've given you a ride home but didn't bring my spare helmet.'

'Look Andre, give up will you? I'm really not interested. Try your luck elsewhere.' I grinned, but secretly I was thinking...you bastard, this is one woman that you won't ever get to stick your over used so-and-so in.

One thing Andre was right about was that 'Poetry by Jazz' event. In fact, everyone seemed to be talking Jazz during the days leading to the end of spring and the welcomed arrival of the Easter break. The music department and the dance class were combining for the event. At least the dance group were allowed to use the first evening of the launch to display their skills as part of their dance finals. I didn't feel that I could cope with going to the music department to practise poetry with Jazz, on top of my heavy workload, not to mention my love life, or rather lack of it. First it was Joy who asked if I would like to take part. I could read a Spanish poem. I declined. I said that I was behind with my Spanish project that turned out to be much more work than I had expected. Then a suggestion came from Chris, who was still going around like zombie. We met, by arrangement, for lunch. He still had not made things up with his Dr Alexis. Instead he had met with the head of 'Return to study and equal opportunity' and she saw that he was unhappy. She invited him to the first evening of the launch.

'Ah, your going to read!' I was very pleased to see him and gave him a hug.

'Me? I can't read aloud with or without music and certainly not in front of an audience.'

'Neither can I. Anyway, got lots to do. I am analysing a parallel text, English/Spanish, set in Costa Rica, where they speak Latin-America Spanish, ugh!'

'Poor you.'

'Chris, I hate to see you unhappy. It hurts me to see you so miserable.'

I hadn't meant to utter those words they merely leapt out from my soul.

'Sorry...didn't, err...I don't want any one else to be unhappy.'

'Well do something to make things up. Have you managed to say or write him something yet?'

'Not really,' He shrugged. 'Anyway, I have been invited to the first night of the Jazzarama. That first night is by invitation only.'

'Aha, that's when the 'big shots', as my mom calls them, will be present, and our Chris with them, eh?' I said, feeling happy for him.

I had no doubt that he would, if he kept with Alexis, be going places I could never tread.

'If you and Esmay want to come I can ask Dr Forester, who invited me, if she could get you two tickets.'

'Nah! I'll go on the nights open to everyone. But you can ask Esmay if she wanted to go to that launch night.'

'Esmay wouldn't go without you.'

'Can't see why not! Anyhow, thanks all the same. The 'open door' ones are good enough for me.'

'Those 'open door' nights will be madness. People coming from all over the place. Tom, Dick and Harry will mingle with us here. That's why Dr Forester got me an invitation card for the first night. Please come.' He pleaded.

'I can cope with madness. Anyway, you go. Your Dr Alexis would certainly be there if this other doctor, whatever her name, was going.'

'No, she's going with her partner and said that I would sit at their table.'

Chris couldn't hide the wish for his man to be there from me. After all, I felt about him the same way that he felt about his boss, friend and mentor.

'If he's there, just go up and say something, like 'nice evening' eh?'

'What if it's pouring down with rain.'

Chris managed a smile then said, *Hasta luego*, and went off.

If college had gone mad with exams and the coming Jazzarama, my home life was worse, in my opinion. Mom got more and more involved with Anthony's family. Mom was planning her first club meeting to encourage friends and neighbours to order African materials; some were birthday or anniversary cards. Others were small trinkets.

'Mom,' I tried to argue with her, 'our neighbours, except for the Ahmed family, are white folk. What makes you think they'll be interested in African stuff and anniversary cards with pictures of black people?'

'We'll have to see.'

Mom continued folding slips of paper invitations that Kevin had written for her on his school computer.

Anyway, she explained that for any order that went through she'd get a small commission. Mom's involvement with his business auntie gave Anthony the excuse to be more often at our house. I felt trapped. I was sure that I would begin to hate him and might not be able to continue to be polite and pretending to be shy but smiling at the stupid jokes he told Kevin. Why can't he take the hint that I did not want to be his fiancée or wife? If the pressure continued I'd have to leave again. At the same time where else can I go? Back to Esmay? No chance! Somehow, I no longer wanted that relationship. But if I stayed, Mom and I would quarrel over Anthony. It was then that African-American woman, what's her name, sprang to my head. We had discussed her work in Comparative Lit. Class. The title was, 'I know why the caged bird sings.' I felt trapped like her caged bird; symbolically used, of course. It was probably due to the feeling of being trapped, that I agreed reluctantly to go to Paella day lunchtime event. When Esmay first texted and asked if I was coming to the Paella lunch I said no, I wasn't. She texted again to say that she had asked Chris as well. I wasn't sure what she was up to but agreed to go along. So on

111

the Paella day, which this time was the Thursday before we officially broke up for Easter term, I made my way there. The place was already packed, as it usually was when a special dish was on. Esmay was waiting for me by the main entrance. We waited for Chris. Joy was not coming after all, Esmay explained. But I had that nagging feeling though that she was telling porkies. She probably didn't ask Joy at all. She wanted me to come, had invited Chris because she wanted to note my secret longing, which Chris was oblivious to but she, being street wise, was not.

'Shame.' I said. But I was planning that if Esmay as much as opened her mouth with sniping remarks about Chris and me, I'd splash her with ice water from the jug on the table. Luckily for her, Esmay did not make remarks about Chris and me when he went to get us drinks. Nor did she ask questions about Alexis. Instead we talked about the forthcoming Jazzarama, which everyone was raving about. Apparently, it was to be the biggest and grandest of all the Jazzarama events. Jazz fans were coming from outside of London and from overseas.

'A lot of 'big names' in Jazz coming.' said someone on the table next to ours.

We ate and chatted. It was just polite conversation. Chris was full of anticipation. I could tell that from the way he spoke. He was to be the special guest of the head of Return to Study and her partner. He was looking forward to the readings with Jazz in the background. He'd never experienced anything like that before.

I was the first to notice Dr Alexis Sylvere walk in. I was sure that he saw us but he went straight to the section at the counter for 'Take-a-ways.' On these special days many of our lecturers and senior staff came to purchase food but usually took it back to their offices. We students often muttered about that and agreed that the lecturers were not allowed to mingle socially with us students.

'Just in case we had flies, and flies do jump about.' we used to joke.

I nudged Esmay's foot under the table. She looked up and I indicated towards the counter.

'Don't look now Chris, but your friend is here.' she whispered.

Chris glanced across then almost instantly buried his nose into his plate of Paella, the special for that day.

Dr Sylvere got his container of Paella which was placed in a bag for him. He left without a glance in our direction.

'He's gone! You can stop burying your face in that plate of food.' I teased.

'You think he saw us?' Chris asked in a whisper.

'No, he didn't. He's suddenly gone blind.' Esmay mocked.

'I lied to him. I said I was now eating in the Help Office with the others.'

'Yes, so you been saying.' Esmay reminded him that he had told us before. To be frank I could not recall Chris telling us about that lie before; I was too busy wondering what my life would be like if I had to stop seeing him altogether. The whole thing was getting increasingly confusing. On one hand I wanted him and badly, on the other I wanted him to make up with his Dr Alexis. Pure madness and a confused mind!

I rebuked myself before saying, 'Look Chris, you got to resolve this thing. The longer you...' I began, but Esmay did not let me continue the sentence.

'This Jazzarama gig might be your big change to make up. Music always brings people together.' she pointed out.

'It's too late. He could've seen me and knows that I lied about having a sandwich lunch with the others at the Help Centre.'

'Never too late. You want him, go get him.' I said, but was not sure if I meant Christ going for Alexis or for me to get Chris.

'Mm...Esmay grunted getting up to leave. See you folks.'

'I'd better get back as well.' said Chris.

'Yeah, and I'd better get to the photocopying room.'

We parted and agreed to enjoy the Jazzarama launch over the weekend though we would all be going on different days.

8

The Jazzarama launch weekend arrived. It was really mad; music, dancing with some of it taking place outside of the hall, drinking and snogging. Luckily, I didn't touch alcohol; instead I fed myself with juices and lots of ice-cold mineral water. Later that night Mom heard me going to the bathroom several times. Next morning she asked if I had been drinking stuff. After assuring my Mom that I did not touch alcohol, I went for my bath. While in the bathroom I heard her shout.

'*Adiós,* Lena.' Mom was in a good mood and on those occasions she used her pet name for me. She left for work.

I heard her slam the front door. Then Kevin left for school but he had left the radio on as usual though he was told not to. With the light music from the radio in the background I climbed into the bath. I felt that I'd like to spend the rest of the day sitting in that hot tub and thinking. News on the grapevine was about who was at the launch on Friday night. I let my imagination run wild as to what could have been a romantic scene between the two. I didn't get very far however because I heard the ring tone of my mobile that I had placed on the chair near the bathtub. At first I let it ring because I felt sure that it was no one else but Esmay. But the ring tone continued on and off, on and off. Eventually, I picked up the phone and said in an angry tone, 'Yes!'

This time it wasn't Esmay it was Chris.

'Ah! Chris, *Buenos Días! Que Tal*?' I said it with an emotion I found difficult to hide whenever I heard his voice.

'*Bien e Tu*?' He replied.

'*Así, Así*' I wanted him to continue practising for his forthcoming oral.

'Listen, can I meet up with you and Esmay today? It's urgent.'

'*Qué arriba*?' I asked.

'Can't talk on the phone. Lunchtime okay? Got to talk to you and quick.'

Chris sounded concerned therefore I didn't correct his grammar to point out that it should be quickly, not quick.

'Okay then, usual place about twelve, right?'

At twelve noon I was at our usual meeting place behind the Tapas Bar. I had texted Esmay that Chris wanted to meet us both.

I also said that he sounded a bit distressed. Esmay arrived before Chris did. We were both concerned that it could be that Alexis had 'come on' to Chris, as it was referred to on campus, and upset him.

'All he had to do was say no!' Esmay shrugged.

'There he is now,' I said, noticing Chris approaching, 'Let him do the talking, right?'

'Want a drinky?' Asked Esmay in one of her phoney voices.

'*La Agua mineral sin gas.*'

'Mineral water, no gas, right?'

'Teacher Elle wants me to practice talking.'

He laughed but I could see that he was worried about something.

'Good. And you?' I looked at Esmay, and then took my purse out.

'My turn, you pay next time.' Esmay left us and I was sure that she felt that Chris wanted to talk to me alone.

Esmay was wrong. Chris said that he wanted both of us to be there in case there was trouble. We waited until Esmay returned with a small tray on which sat three glasses, one bottle of cola-light, one mineral water and one so called non-alcoholic, something or other. We sipped drinks and waited briefly to give Chris a chance to speak.

'We might need your support.' Chris said without looking up at either of us.

'We! Who?' asked Esmay, though I'm sure she had guessed to whom Chris was referring.

'It's...err...well...' Chris stammered, 'I...It was at the Jazzarama gig, I did something terrible but I don't know how I had the nerve to do it.'

'What did you do?' I asked, dying to know.

'Mm...You threw beer in someone's face?' Esmay looked enquiringly at Chris.

'Okay, okay, this is what happened, yea? He did come in.'

'He! Who's he?'

'I wish people would stop being *tonto*.' I snapped.

'I wish people would swear in English so that I could reply. I don't know bloody Spanish.' Esmay barked.

It means being 'silly' that's all. And I wish you two would stop fighting, I came for support and now you two fighting.'

'Sorry, go on. What happened that's so bad that you need support?'

I sipped my drink trying to look casual.

'He, that is Alexis, walked in with that gold-toothed rattlesnake! He said things to me about Alexis and then he comes in with him.'

'Gold toothed rattle what, who?' I really wanted to know.

'His name is Terry, something Scottish.' Chris supplied.

'What did he say to you?' Esmay frowned.

'He suggested I took things from Alexis. Don't be a fool he told me, everybody doing it. Things like that he had said to me. Then he turned up with Alexis. I saw red and wanted to go up and kill him.'

Chris went on to relate to us the night of the Jazzarama. Apparently he had to rescue his Dr Alexis. He had gone up and lied that Dr Alexis had an early job and it was getting late. What followed was amazing, even to Chris. But it was the way he told it and the innocence on his face that made me laugh and made Esmay grin like a Cheshire cat.

'Good fo-you!' Esmay congratulated him.

'I made him take me home,' Chris's voice trembled as he said it, 'It was late and he didn't want me to go on the late bus.'

'Mm...Did you ask him in for coffee?' Asked Esmay, which made Chris blush.

'What? You joking! Let him near that dump where I live? He, err...I made him take me to his house. I said I'd catch an early bus home?'

'You made him? You, little Chris, made him do what he didn't want to do?'

Esmay continued to pressurise Chris into telling more but I warned him, 'Chris, be careful. Don't go saying things. That man could loose his job.'

'I don't want to cause no trouble for him I...' Chris began but did not get any further because Esmay suddenly shrieked, 'Bloody hell!'

Esmay grabbed hold of Chris's left hand. 'What the heck's that?'

My heart sank. Had things got as far as a ring already? Of course, there are such things as friendship rings. But even a friendship ring was serious and I might as well drop dead, or worse, marry, and become a prisoner in the golden cage that would be Anthony and his aunt's home. I felt sick, even though I had often told myself that it would not matter if he went with Alexis, I still had strong feelings for him.

'A...a ring.' Said Chris

'I can see it's a ring. How did it get there?' Esmay continued pressing.

'Don't say anything more.' I warned Chris again.

'Okay...I bought it.' Chris began, but the laughter from Esmay stopped him continuing to lie.

'Yes, you can play it that way. It was your first pay packet so you got something to remember it by.' I found myself advising.

'Jesus, it looks blinking real. It ain't is it?' Esmay said, slightly breathless. 'Mm...Since when do men buy themselves diamond rings?'

'Okay, you're my sisters. I can trust you. Well, we went shopping at that posh place...was like out of this world. I saw lots of things that I thought were nice. I liked the rings in that sale place. I tried to stop him but he insisted, so I choose the ring with the cheapest tag. Anyway, he said I worked more than I got paid for.'

'Mm...shopping in the middle of the night, were you?' Esmay continued.

'No, on the Saturday morning.' Chris blushed.

'*Bastante*, Chris, anyway, I have to pick something up at the library.'

I hinted at ending the conversation. I was still worried that Esmay, if left alone with Chris, might push him into giving more intimate details.

'Is alright, Elle. I stay the weekend to help him with his computer work.'

'And you slept on the sofa.' I was warning Chris because I could tell that Esmay's mind was running wild.

'Not exactly! Is a big house, had four bedrooms and a Granny flat. All the big houses got one for granny or Au pairs and people like that.'

'Good, so you slept in the spare room.' Esmay remarked with a tone of sarcasm.

'Say no more Chris, nobody's business where you slept or spent your weekend. Let's go.'

I had to take Chris away from Esmay's probing.

'You engaged then?' Esmay refused to give up.

'Is not like that, only a gift. Not the kinda thing he'd buy for his engagement, I'm sure.' Chris laughed.

I dragged Chris away in spite of the angry look on Esmay's face.

Once alone with Chris and walking towards the library, I gave him some advice. He should keep his mouth shut about all things related to Alexis. That man stands to lose a lot. Anyway, it was no business of anyone's, not even Esmay and I, what did or did not happen between him and Alexis. That Jazzarama incident will be gossiped about for some time given the grape vines on the Campus, I was sure.

'You don't go talking 'bout your boss's affairs. Them lot at work might see the ring and tease you. Tell them to mind their own bloody business.' I warned.

He smiled and kissed me lightly on the check.

'You is the bestest sister in the world.' He said, using his brand of English as he often did when he consciously or subconsciously 'code switched' as our tutor of English called it.

His kiss felt warm and moist. How I wished it were a kiss on my lips.

'Make up with your Esmay, please. I want you to be as happy as me.' He said, then left, looking back and waving to me with that boyish smile of his.

My God, I thought, he knows. Nah!...Is your imagination that he knows, that's why he's pushing you towards Esmay, he merely wants you to be happy.

I convinced myself that Chris only wanted me to be happy. It was at that stage that I began to think of a way of finding out once and for all if Chris felt anything for me. But I had to get him on his own and longer than only a half hour for lunch or when he came for support with his Spanish oral, which was worrying him a little. But where and how would I get him there? If it weren't for that Anthony who was still hanging around our house for his food prepared for him by a motherly woman. Or maybe Anthony sincerely wanted me for a wife. My own thinking was to find out once and for all how I stood with Chris. Maybe, with luck, he would be bisexual or better still he was not gay at all. He could be merely responding to the first person that showed him kindness and love. Not like Esmay who showed me kindness but was incapable of showing love to anyone. But more like the case of Ms Jolly. Perhaps if good old Ms. Jolly didn't cut me off when I was leaving the House of our Lady of Grace, I too would've thought that I was in love with her.

It was wicked and self-centred of me to do so but I wanted it to be so that Chris only thought he was in love with Alexis. I had changed my mind once again to thinking that I would not have minded if he were sincerely in love with Alexis. Women do marry men who are openly gay, which Alexis Sylvere was not. Well...he didn't go out of his way to parade his gayness though his negative response to all female attention on campus gave people the impression he was gay. In fact, it might well be that I fancied Chris because I thought that he was gay, or at least not macho. Well, whatever the why's or wherefores to what Chris was or wasn't I had to have a plan to find out once and for all if that *Chico bonito* felt anything but sisterly love for me. No! No way shall I let you, my overtly feminine but not macho being get away from me. Not if I can help it.

With those thoughts I jumped on to my bus for the ride home. All along during that ride the sound of the bus and the traffic seemed to be saying: 'Plan, you, must plan...you must know one way or the other. Be prepared to hear a NO. Prepare to suffer the pain which comes with rejections.'

I opened my front door to the sound of the telephone. But, as was often the case, as my hand got near the handset, the ringing stopped. Shit! I swore and pulled a face at the phone. Anyway, I thought, it was either one of Kevin's music mates or Esmay, not taking the hint that I no longer wanted a relationship with her.

The phone rang again and on that occasion I was in time to pick up the handset. It was Esmay. I sucked my teeth, as my mom called that rude Guyanese sound made between ones teeth. I then pressed the hands free button, left the handset off the hook, and went to the kitchen. I had no interest in what Esmay had to say.

In the kitchen I prepared my family a typical Guyanese meal of sweet potatoes, cassava, green plantains and salted cod steamed in coconut milk. It was what Mom called 'hard food' and was her favourite. Kevin often gulped it all down though he complained about the strong smell of salt fish. While we ate, I looked at Mom and wanted to tell her of my love life. I had no one with whom to discuss my intimate feelings. At college, everyone seemed to be talking about some love story or the other. I could not, certainly not to Mom, who obviously had Anthony in mind for me. I could not possibly go up and say, 'you know what Mom, there is this student at college I fancy like mad but he's getting close to an older man. He might be gay Mom but I love him and wouldn't mind if he were.'

I could picture my Mom's face turning tomato-red. She'd stare at me with bulging eyes. She'd utter a loud and long scream then slide onto the floor in a faint.

Mom must have noticed my smile because she asked with a broad grin, 'had a good day at College or did Anthony pay you a visit there?'

'Oh no,' I replied, 'we'd agreed that he would not hang around me at college.'

'Don't keep him waiting too long. Some other young woman will grab him.'

Hurrah! Hurry up young woman, come along and rescue me,' but aloud I said, 'I'll have a long talk with him after my results are out. For the moment I want to concentrate on my work, Mom.'

Actually, I was thinking that I didn't want to get into any argument either with Anthony or with my Mom, which might hamper my changes of a good grade in the exams. I needed at least a 2.1 to get anywhere.

'That Mr. Anthony, he'll make a good husband to some young woman, good grades or not!'

'Oh yes, he'll make any woman a good husband.' I said, while thinking, any woman, but not Elena Peterson.

After our dinner, I reminded Kevin that it was his turn to do the washing up. I went to my room. In my room I did my studies, as Mom called it, in peace. Once in my room, my college work got interrupted with me thinking of my life and the man I badly wanted in it. I wandered from my books to Chris. I got back to that ring on his finger. It was only three or was it four tiny diamond stones sitting in a white gold band. Yet it was symbolic for his entering into what might be a serious relationship and a New World to him. Or can it be a gift to him for having lost his innocence to love? Would I ever get a gift when I do lose mine, proper? Or had Esmay already taken it? Yes and no. I still never had experienced a man. And I never will neither. It would either be Chris or no one. Yet, if I forced myself on a man who did not love me but loved someone else, then I would've thrown away my honour for nothing.

Once again I got myself on an emotional seesaw. I couldn't get that face and warm smile from my mind. But if I didn't, I might go bonkers and end up, not back at that House of Correction, but a loony bin. I have to know. He could only tell me to clear off. But knowing him he'd more than likely say something polite like...you're a lovely young woman, kind and very good looking. I love you like a sister...you'll find a good man or woman which ever you want...blah...blah...blah!

I must have dozed off because I sensed, rather than heard, Mom enter my room as she often did. I smelt her hand cream, which she used after hard work. She came close to me. I kept my eyes closed, though. Mom did not speak. But she pulled up the cover from where I had rolled it down. She switched off the light and went away as quietly as she had entered, no doubt thinking that I was fast asleep. That woman loves me. I began to distress myself once more, this time about Mom. I'd never want to hurt her. But she would be hurt when I made it clear that I had no feelings for Anthony, the man she felt was good for me. In fact, it would break her heart if her only daughter whom she thought so highly off, rejected someone who could make her a princess then went and fell for a man who had an affair with another man. Heaven and brimstone will fall not only on my head but my Mom's head as well. She'd blame herself for my behaviour. I've got to keep my trap shut about Chris. I'll say that the NO to Anthony was only because I wanted to be an independent woman with a profession, a smart car, smart designer clothes and a flashy apartment. Also, I wanted to help my brother with his dream. That's all that Mom would know.

The following days were very difficult ones for me. I had regular phone calls from Chris. At times I suspected that he really wanted to talk about Alexis rather than asking about Spanish irregular verbs. Alexis, he related, had kept his lawyers in the pictures, just in case there was trouble. Meanwhile, Alexis was helping him by speaking to him, sometimes in Spanish. It was during one of those discussions that Chris brought up the promise from Alexis that, after we had finished our exams, he'd take us for a treat. He'll treat us to a meal because we all worked hard.

Actually, he'll be taking Chris but is inviting Esmay and me along. I dreaded it. I wanted to break away from Esmay, not go on a foursome with her. But I had to admit to myself that if Alexis took only Chris and me, it might look strange. People watching and seeing them two look lovingly at each other, which I'm sure they would, bound to wonder what I was doing there.

'He'll take us to some fancy Mexican restaurant and bar. It's in the tourist heart of Greenwich near the Cutty Sark. People had been shouting praises about that place.'

Chris talked like a little boy, who had all he had asked for from Santa.

One afternoon we had met and were walking along to the library. He again brought up that after exam treat thing.

I sighed, pointing out, 'I'm not sure Chris. Wouldn't Alexis want, well, just the two of you to be there? A sort of romantic date?'

I succeeded in not looking at the ring on his finger. Truth was that I didn't have too. That ring was lodged in my mind like a heavy rock.

'Nah! We're, well...where not serious about our relationship. We're not two sixteen-year-olds staring goggle eyed at each other.' He laughed.

'Chris, Esmay and I are not together any more...I want to move on.'

'Doesn't matter, we're all pals, first there were three of us, now we're four.'

'Well, we'll see. Talk to you later.'

He planted that usual ceremonial peck on my cheek and we parted.

Time flew by and suddenly, with much relief, it was all over with studying, at least for a while.

It was when all our work was handed in, and the three-hour papers in a hot and stuffy room were completed, that I had a confrontation with Esmay. Chris had told her about that suggested treat and my reservations. Until then, I had been very polite, even friendly, though I made it clear that I had moved on. She first said that Chris had told her, but she wasn't sure that she wanted to be in the way. She went on to suggest that Alexis might be trying to use us two as a smoke screen, in public.

'You think everybody got your devious mind.' I barked at her.

'Call it what the hell you want. But it makes sense. Here at college it's okay, no one cares a baloney. But outside, I'm not sure.'

'That man wouldn't care one damn what outsiders think?'

'Sorry, I was only thinking. I saw your Chris...' she deliberately emphasised 'your Chris, 'he was carrying shopping to the car. He's probably staying...'

'Esmay, piss off, will you?' I cut in and began to walk away.

'Mm...' She grinned at me in the way she always did when she succeeded in annoying someone.

I read her thoughts which made me give her a venomous look. If she thought that if Chris rejected me I would go back to her, she better not hold her breath. I wanted more from life than what she had to offer. And I was thinking, whether Chris or no Chris, you're history, mate. You were nothing much to write home about anyway. A good friend, that's all. Anything else rated zero as far as I'm concerned. With those thoughts I went and collected my reserved books from the library and made my way home.

On the bus I was angry with myself. That was why, when my mobile played its funny ring tone, I silently cursed it, feeling sure that it was Esmay, and I simply switched it off. I hated myself for pining over someone who might not want me because his heart belonged to someone else. At the same time I was rejecting someone who my Mom believed might take me away and turn me into a princes. Ugh!...The Princes in a Golden Cage. Mm...might make a good Opera!

I arrived home to the ringing of the house phone. I angrily rehearsed what I would say if it were Esmay. I'd tell her in no uncertain terms to leave me to get on with my work. Was she deliberately trying to make me fail my exam?

'Hey!' I said.

As it turned out it wasn't Esmay, it was Chris.

'What's wrong? Esse said you ran off. I rang your mobile but you'd switched it off.' He enquired.

'I didn't want to be pestered again.'

'Who's been pestering you?'

'Esmay, who you think?'

'What is it between you two? Tell baby brother,' he said in his usual humorous tone of voice.

'Nothing really.' I said, but thinking, I've got to stop him seeing me as his sister. I got to tell him straight .I'll make it clear to him that I wasn't his sister. I'll begin with, 'Listen Chris...I have to...'

The words, 'I'm not your sister. I'm in love with you, damn it', were about to leap out when I heard Mom's voice from the door with the usual moan she gave when she'd had a bad day, using her mixing of languages, 'What a day! Día muy malo.' she said.

'Got to go! I whispered down the phone, we talk later, okay?' Resisting the temptation of throwing a kiss down the phone line, I hung up.

'Was that Anthony?' Mom enquired.

'No. Why?'

'He was to ring 'bout his aunt's things. Mind you, think you're right Lena. People don't want to order African things from a pale skin Venezuelan woman.'

'Ah, letters!' I changed the subject abruptly, referring to the letters still in our little letterbox by the front door.

'Every machine chose to break down today.' Mom began to take off her coat.

The crisis had, for the time being, passed. I didn't have to let Chris know there and then that I had feelings for him and that I wanted him to be the one to see me through what would be my personal choice of 'Rite of Passage'. What made me think of this so-called 'Rite of Passage' so suddenly? It was 'old days' stuff. I was thinking about Mom's daily ritual where she comes in from work. She always moans about what a bad day it was, takes off her shoes first since in our house, especially since we moved in our new home, we never enter with our street shoes on, puts her indoor slipper shoes on, then takes off her coat.

I had one letter. It was from the House of Our Lady of Grace about having a reunion. The rest were bills. Two from those people who tell you you might already have won £20,000. You had to phone to hear and how to claim.

'Yeah! Right! At a premium rate of £1.50 a minute? They keep you talking for ten minutes then say you've won a spoon.' I muttered as I tore up the letter.

'Think we're all jackasses.' Kevin added.

'We do not swear in this house. I warned you before.' Mom told him off.

'Jackass is not swearing Mom. A Jackass is an animal with big ears and is regarded as *tonto*.'

'You'll get a big ear and go stupid if I catch you using bad words.' Mom replied.

I didn't contact Chris as I had promised. I wanted to talk to him while I was alone at home. This was to make sure that I could speak freely to him in private and that meant without Mom and Kevin around. After we had eaten that evening Mom talked at lot. She was in one of her moods when she went on and on, nostalgically, about back home as she still called Venezuela and sometimes Guyana. I was sure that she was thinking of me. I wondered if it was anything to do with Anthony. Had she been discussing me with him? Or were her mates at work talking about her 20-year old daughter still not married or at least giving her a grandchild? Or was she on about my dad again who was supposed to get his family in Canada to send for him, then for her and us?

'In Venezuela or even in parts of Guyana like in the villages up the river...' Mom began.

I closed her voice out. I had heard it all before. As good a girl as I was I would've been showered with gifts for what, in the old days, was called 'Rite of Passage ' whatever that was. Maybe it was the fact that my 21st birthday was around the corner that was beginning to worry her. Except for Anthony, not taking the hint that I was not interested, Mom didn't think that there was a young man in my thoughts. She must have been concerned about me. What if my dad's relatives were to actually send for him to go to Canada and he wanted to send for her, what would she do about me? She'd take Kevin with her. But she could not force me to go with them. Thus marrying me off would be the best alternative.

After a while Mom's voice jerked me back to her talking.

'You alright, Lena?' She asked, using one of her pet names for me.

'Brain tired! All that reading and writing.'

I lied that it was only my studies on my mind.

'It soon it be over, my Lena, soon be all over. We go away then. You find a cheap day trip.' Mom suggested.

'Yippy! Can we go to France for the day? All the others at the club been to France.' Kevin remarked excitably, showing some envy of his friends who had been.

'We can't afford that at the moment.' Mom pointed out to Kevin.

'We will when I pass my exam. I promise you that. We shall all be going on family holidays.'

After that I excused myself and went to my room 'to work', I said.

Once in my room, I flung myself on my back onto the bed, my book and pencil in hand. I forced myself to concentrate and go over one of the short stories in the Duncan Parallel Text collection. I was asked by my tutor to go over it again before official submission. I had taken one story to look at in detail. My tutor loved my study of it: I had chosen to give as one reason for my choice that the story was a symbolic tale. It might have even been recreated from an old folk tale. According to Duncan the story was that of two male friends, DUELO ENTRE AMIGOS / Duel between two friends.

One was a pure blooded Jamaican who was very jovial and drank rum with evaporated milk. The other was a man from the Carthage province and was as white as milk. He drank beer. The two men were always seen together. They both drank heavily and got drunk together. People could not understand the friendship between those two men especially at a time when Jamaicans and people of Carthage did not mix. One night the men got very drunk on a bottle of pure rum, which the Jamaican had been given. The man, white as milk, made a mistake when he spat on floor of the Jamaican. They argued and were not seen together again. Then one night a noise was heard coming from the beach. People rushed as they heard knife blades clicking. The two men were having a duel. Before anyone could stop them they attacked each other. Both fell dead on the ground, their blood flowing. A wave from the sea came in and took them both away.

I was told that I must give my source. I gave that as from the Duncan short stories complied by Delita Marten and published by Editorial, Costa Rica, San Jose 1995.

While reading, I underlined sentences and decided my approach to tackle the discourse on the story from either the point of view of (i), folklore about two nations fighting then destroying each other, or (ii), about two men, first friends, who fell out, couldn't live without each other, fought, and then destroyed each other.

At that stage, two people from real life came into my head and made me wonder if I would want to be like that bottle of rum, which led to them splitting and self-destructing?

I must have dozed off because then I became aware of Mom again, tiptoeing into my room. I felt her taking the book, which had fallen out my hands and then covering me, fully clothed. I heard her click the light off; turning my room into darkness. She then quietly left me to sleep. Surely, Mom wasn't much different to other Moms I thought. She'd want to see her only daughter walk up the aisle, a white dress and a white veil covering her daughter's face? She'd be beaming under an expansive hat which we could ill afford, and flouncing around like a peacock. She'd be indicating, though not actually saying it in so many words, that her daughter was a 'good girl'. No babbies, as she called them and absentee dads by the age of fourteen. She'd be telling without words, to her Venezuelan pals, how good her daughter was until her husband left. Not that they'll believe her. A young woman of twenty who never ever..., not even secretly? Lies, they'd be thinking...what of the story about the intruder in the house when she cracked his head which led to her being in trouble? When did she crack his head, before or after...unless of course something was wrong with her? They would patronise Mom and say. *Si, si,* good girl she was, your Elena. They'll be nodding agreement. The bloody hypocrites!

Sorry Mom, I'll try not to hurt you but I will never walk down that bridal aisle. I don't want to go that way. My dreams were away from all that housewifery and babies. Maybe there's something wrong with me, but I can't see myself in that role. Sorry Mom, sorry holy mother of God...sorry if I'm a disappointment to you. Where and why this sudden thought of holy mother of God? Thoughts must be wandering off to the invitation of the reunion at the House of Our Lady of Grace.

The days leading to the week of sat papers seemed to have flown. Projects were handed in. All that was left was the sitting around in a hot room for three hours to answer questions in writing. The oral exam for candidates taking languages was to be on the last day of college in May. I had arranged to meet with Chris because, from his text and voice on the phone, I could tell that my little darling was in a mad panic.

We met, and as soon as we were seated he started moaning, 'It's not our own tutor doing the oral and only now she tells us. It's some clever Spanish person straight off the plane from Spain.'

We were in one of corners of the students' union hall. Since I was no longer living with Esmay, it was either a union or at the back of Tapas Bar on campus for Chris and me to meet. I could not possibly take him home, not with Anthony hanging around.

'They're only allowed to ask questions under the topics listed, for example, under Environment, leisure, that sort of thing.'

'What? I don't know nothin' 'bout all that environment stuff for a start.'

'You do! What about diesel fumes from cars and trucks? Under music they might ask what your favourite music is and why, or do you like disco, that sort of stuff.'

'Oh, I don't know. I'm so scared I can't sleep. I just lay there thinking about the exam. If I fail, I'll let you and Alexis down.'

'Listen, there bound to ask why you want to learn Spanish. They always ask that if you're a beginner or foundation year student.'

'I...,' he shrugged, 'need a second language. And I was told that Spanish was easier than French.'

'Wrong,' I laughed, 'Say that and they'll give you a negative mark.'

'Oh!' he grunted, 'see wha' yah mean?' He reverted to his brand of East End street talk.

'You did some Spanish at school and liked it but had to move to a new area. There weren't any Spanish classes at the new school. You are now studying Spanish and want to go on to advance level.'

'Bloody hell! I couldn't say all that in Spanish, no way!'

'There you have Past, Present and Future tense of the most commonly used verbs such as, to be, to like and to want. I'll prepare something for you to memorise.'

'Can you pretend to be an examiner for oral and test me for twenty minutes?'

'I don't know...' I said hesitantly. This closeness was becoming difficult for me to stand. I might lose control and burst out how I felt about him.

Chris misunderstood. He thought that it was my workload that I was thinking about. Sometimes I wondered if he did realise how I felt. Surely he couldn't be that naive? True he had no experience with women. I could tell from his innocent behaviour with Esmay and me, also with other female students such as Joy. He was almost like 'one of the girls'.

'Sorry,' he said softly, 'I shouldn't ask so much of you. Alexis is helping with English. He really made me polish up my English project about a poor East London lad speaking cockney. How he laughed when I said that if I was better at English I'd turn it into an opera called *The Gentleman and the Tramp*'.

I stopped him. His happiness when he talked about Alexis was getting very painful at times though I was making myself believe that I didn't have a problem with him and his Alexis.

'It's okay. I'll give you an hour, say next Wednesday.'

'*Gracias.*' He gave me the ceremonious peck on the cheek and left.

As Chris walked out the door, Esmay walked in. Her comment as she came towards me made it clear that she'd been watching me.

'Mm…That man is either blind or stupid or is he pretending to be blind and stupid.'

'Some people just can't move on.' I muttered loud enough for Esmay to hear and walked past her.

Time went by during which I did my own revision as well as helping Chris. Then it was all over. No more exam papers thank heavens. All that was left was the long; agonising and nail biting, wait until the results. While waiting, some of us applied for jobs. I applied at the library near where I lived. Chris already had a job at the Computer Help Centre. He was asked to work full time during the vacation so he could be trained by an international IT company in the use of its high tech system and software shortly to be installed in the college's Communication Centre. There was to be an elaborate opening of the New extension to the college the following October. Chris told me with pride of his moving to a sub-office of three young specially trained IT personnel, who will be specialists in the new system. Chris was ever so proud and I shared his pride and happiness. He would be moving into his own space right at the top of the Communication Centre. He would be sharing the space with two other young IT personnel, one of whom was female. He told me some fancy name the three of them would be called. He even tried to explain to me how the three of them would be working with some of what was happening around the college's offices and linked to other Institutions having the same system. But poor me, I hadn't a clue what he was talking about.

As promised Chris and his Alexis, as we were by then calling Dr Sylvere, took us to that highly praised New Mexican restaurant. I reluctantly went because I didn't want Esmay involved. Chris insisted, however, we went as a foursome because we were still friends.

The 'Mexicana' was packed, the Latin American sound was loud and heart pounding, but Chris was very happy. We ate peppery *Arroz-con-Carne*, Paella, Mexican style, avocado dips and *Beber-Mexicana* and more!

By the time we were ready for home Esmay appeared to be a bit tipsy. She had become quite giggly. We drove her home first. Chris asked if I was going to stay with her but I said I wouldn't. Alexis agreed to that and said that Esmay would just fall asleep, that was all. She was not drunk. She could not be incapacitated on the little bit of drink she had had. It occurred to me then that Esmay might've been putting on her tipsy condition to get me to stay the night at her place. No thanks, I thought, as I was being driven to my home. I was in the back seat with Chris and his Alexis in the front. Both Chris and Alexis had gone very quiet yet I could sense that they were communicating with each other without a word being spoken. It was the same in the restaurant and on the way to the car park.

Suddenly it struck me. What if Alexis was aware of my feelings for Chris? He was an older and experienced man. He wasn't stupid. The way he smiles at you with his eyes rather than his lips. It was if he was secretly reading your inner thoughts. But if he knew, what would he do about that? Maybe he was so sure of himself with Chris that he was not afraid of me being a rival. We got to my house. They waited by the road until I waved and shouted *Buenas Noches* and went in doors. I wanted a good sleep because the next morning I would be starting my job at the library while waiting for my result.

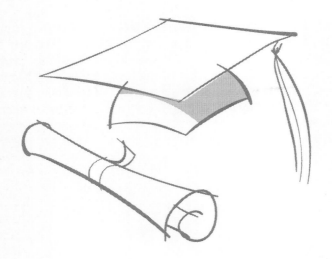

9

Time passed by almost unnoticeably then suddenly, the results were out. I arrived at college that Monday morning to find a great commotion in the Great Hall. I had to push my way through a mass of students. Long lists were pinned along the walls around the hall. We had to check for our names under our individual departments. Only the general results were listed. Breakdown by subject areas, which made up the degree and 'Deferrals', the metaphor used by the college for 'Failed', were to be sent to the students privately. Since I had left home early that morning, if I had a 'deferral' I would have missed the letter. I only had the list on that wall in front of me to tell me if I had passed. With a terrible cramp in my belly, and shaking hands, I nervously checked under the Language and Cultural Studies list. It seemed as if hours were going by while I read down the long list before I came to the 'Ps'. If I don't get to Peterson soon I'm gonna drop! The suspense was making me feel faint. Jesus, please, mother of God, Our lady of Grace, you got me here in the first place, please, I can't fail, I just can't. I worked myself flat out for this exam. There you are! I saw Peterson. Three of them! First, Peterson, Aidan, whoever he was. Then… it hit me in the face like a ball and chain on a demolition site. I saw my name, PETERSON, Elena Carmelita. I gasped at what I saw as I stared at my name under 'BA Honours'. By then other students had already found their names. Soon mayhem burst out. People were laughing, kissing, hugging, jumping up and down; men hugged and patted each other on the back. Two male students openly kissed each other on the lips. I couldn't believe it. Were my eyes tricking me or had I fallen asleep and dreamt it all? Me! Who joined the International University College as an Alternative Entrant through a Baccalaureate and not through the more respected 'A' Levels of the UK? That qualification of mine and a handful of others were at times sneered at by those who came through the 'A' level system. But I've done it! I passed and what a pass!

As if I was shocked into a near trance, I went out of the hall and phoned my Mom on her mobile, before remembering that she was not allowed to receive phone calls during working hours. Urgent messages during those hours went to the main office, which where then passed on. I didn't think that a daughter's exam result would be considered an emergency. My only choice was to wait until Mom's lunch break. Then I thought of my brother. He sometimes rode his bike home to makes himself a quick bite to eat. I left him the news on the home phone and told him not to say a word to anyone, until Mom heard about it. My next step was to check the Foundation year list. But

131

the mass of heads there didn't include Chris's. I decided to go and find him. He was usually very early at college on Monday mornings because he came in with Alexis. I found him at our usual meeting place.

'*Hola. Como estas?*'

He shrugged and showed me a long and miserable face.

'Omigod!' I used an expression that Kevin had begun to use to avoid using the name of God in vain.

I went to sit by Chris.

'What happened? They couldn't fail you!'

'Fail is called deferred, I believe.' He moaned.

'I know that. But they can't fail you, whatever fancy name they want to use. It must be a mistake. You can't fail, not after all that hard work you did, plus all the support you got.'

'Sorry to disappoint you both.'

He said it so sadly that my own result suddenly meant nothing.

'Look, students can appeal. Alexis will tell you how to go about it.'

'No use.'

'Didn't you get a letter? They usually send a letter to explain things.'

'Got a letter alright.' Chris took an envelope out of his pocket.

'Here!' He handed the envelope to me.

I opened the letter ready to explode at whatever excuses the college might have for failing him. Then I saw it and shouted, 'wow, wow!'

I threw my arms around his neck.

'You lying toad, you tricked me...wah!'

I playfully punched him on the chest, then I embraced him, slapped him on the back as men do, then hit him some more.

He laughed and dislodged himself from me.

'You devil, you trying to give me a heart attack, or what?'

I went to place a ceremonial peck on his cheek. Somehow my face moved aside and my lips landed firmly on his. I couldn't stop myself pressing hard on his lips and would have gone further if he hadn't gently pushed me aside with the words, 'Got you going, didn't I?'

He winked at me as if that stray kiss didn't happen.

'Congratulations,' I said, forcing a smile to hide my embarrassment at making a fool of myself, 'Foundation Student of the Year, well done!' I continued, unable to look him in the eyes.

'It's thanks to you and Alexis who helped me on my first step up the ladder?'

He then added softly, 'Alexis is the love of my life but you are my best friend.'

He knows! He's breaking it gently to me that he knows how I felt but wanted to point out that he was not available. Had I spoilt what was a beautiful friendship? He's going to keep his distance from me now. I'm sure he would. He might even tell Alexis that I'd made a pass at him. He doesn't need my help now and won't have to meet with me anymore. We did agree that if he got through the Foundation year, he'd go for the BA Communications Culture or whatever that course was. It was part of some new 'Earn as you Learn in the Workplace' programme.

'Did you trick Alexis as well?' I forced myself to calmly enquire.

'Nah! Could never trick him. I bet ya he knew long before I did.'

Chris said it with such love for Alexis in his voice that I felt a touch of shame. The thought of how bad it would be if I were to come between him and his Dr Alexis went through my mind again. But I didn't want to come between them. I could almost hear myself thinking those words. Yet the longing to hold Chris in my arms was so bad that it hurt. His next words made my agony harder to hide.

'You know, sometimes I get frightened.'

'About what? You've passed, you'll move onto your BA, any…'

'Not about exams,' He interrupted, 'about Alexis. What if I get really hooked on him and then he dumps me.'

'Why would he? You're lovely, probably untouched by human hands.' I chuckled.

'Ah! There's Esse! Wonder how she got on.' He changed the subject abruptly.

I was pleased in a way to see Esmay approaching. She came out of the Tapas Bar. I hadn't seen her go in and wondered whether she'd seen Chris and me in that close encounter.

'She doesn't look happy, unless she's trying to trick us.' Chris nudged me playfully.

Esmay was going to walk past us. I stopped her.

'How did you get on?'

'Bad. We can't all have brains.' She said angrily.

'Yeah, Chris caught me with that already. Now the truth, what did you get?'

'Who cares?' Esmay shrugged.

'We do, we're mates, ain't we Elle?' Chris pecked Esmay on the cheek.

At first I didn't believe her but after a while Chris and I realised that she was genuinely unhappy. We invited her to sit.

Looking really miserable, she sat down while Chris went for more drinks.

'Look, what happened? You did pass, didn't you?' I probed.

'As if you care.'

'Of course I care. We are mates, just as Chris said.'

'Ahem…,' She grunted, 'saw you two lovebirds. Poor Alexis!'

'Forget that. What 'bout your exam? You worked so damned hard.'

'Fat lot of good it did me. All them bastards gave me was a 2.2. What the blinking hell can I do with a lower second class, eh? I've asked to do my MBA studies somewhere else. I want to set up my own business but them other lot they wouldn't have me with only a 2.2. Is my bloody fault! I should've have taken my tutor's advice, stuck to looking at black boys under achieving in school for my special project. It would've got me 40 percent of the total. Instead, like a blinking jackass, me with my stupid ideas, I'd gone looking at white boys doing badly. Who cares two damn if white boys do badly?' She moaned pitifully.

I placed my hand on her arm. That alone couldn't give you a lower grade. What about your exams, did you get nervous? I did for the first paper. I had like a bad cramp in my stomach.'

'Drinks for my two sisters.'

Chris had returned with a small tray on which sat three glasses and three bottles as well as some snacks.

After that we both tried to cheer Esmay up. We hopefully, succeeded in reminding her that she had had work to pay her way. Both Chris and me had financial banking. Chris, by working at the college itself, even though it was for peanuts, me, thanks to a bursary, did not have to slug my guts out in order to pay my way. We encouraged Esmay to think more positively. We pointed out to her that there was a new scheme of learning in the work place. There was bound to be one on teaching or running your own business.

Chris explained that he was going on something like that and that there was bound to be a scheme that would take her with a 2.2. After all, he only had a Foundation Year Certificate. They might pay her something, if not a full salary, and she wouldn't have to work so hard to finance herself if she still wanted to do an MBA. We left her with those thoughts and went our separate ways. I went straight home.

I arrived home to a commotion. Kevin had gone home for lunch and found my message left on the answering machine. Mom got his call during her lunchtime. For once Mom's grumpy boss said she could go home early but she had to work on the following Saturday, her normal day off. Mom was excited. I was sure that she was bursting to tell everyone in the street, in fact the whole of Kent, about her daughter, but waited until I got home.

'I known it, I know my Lena is clever girl.' She put on her heavy Venezuelan accent looking up at the ceiling.

'Holy mother of God, thank you for helping my Lena...'

She gave me a hug then began crying.

'Why are you crying, Mom?' I asked as if I didn't know why.

'Because she's happy,' Kevin replied, 'women cry when happy.'

'*Si, cuando contento yo lloro*, I am so proud of me Lena.'

Mom was thinking in both Venezuelan and English, she was so excited. She made the sign of the cross on herself.

'Now our God in heaven, he gives you a break. That's all I ask; break for my Lena and my Kevy.'

'Actually, it was me who did the hard work, Mom and when last we bin to visit your God?'

I made a joke to stop her weeping. But it was true. We were what was known as lapsed Catholics. But since that Anthony business, Mom had gone religious again.

'Don't make fun, Elena, you, we, get help now from above.' Mom insisted.

'Let's hope your man above,' Kevin joined in the usual family light-hearted bantering, 'help me with my grade four *clarinete!*'

'We must tell Anthony. He phoned asking if you had your result.'

The mention of Anthony was like a bolt of lightening hitting my chest and rather spoilt the afternoon for me. It made me remember what I had said to Anthony about wanting to concentrate on my studies. After my exams I'd decide what to do and let him know. He was not very happy about that suggestion but agreed to let me work towards my exam without any pressure. His family would be proud that he was bringing into the family the type of bride they wanted.

'Lena,' Mom broke into my thoughts, 'we must tell Mrs. Kirsty.'

'Ok then, but no fuss, please!'

But there was fuss. First, Mrs Kirsty from next door arrived. She brought a potted plant from her garden. Then two of Mom's friends who also brought gifts.

These friends had introduced Anthony to us. They had brought a small basket of fruit including a fresh pineapple. One brought a glass-beaded rosary and said that I had entered a new phase in my life. I thanked everyone, took the rosary and the fruit, and placed them on the table. I smiled politely but, looking at the fruit, I felt that there might be some sort of cultural meaning to the presents. So, while the women chatted in Latin American Spanish, and from Mom's expression I knew that she was bragging about me, I tried to analyse the situation. Was the rosary for me to go back to religion seeing that Anthony's family was Catholic? And was the red apple symbolism for the 'forbidden fruit' of the old and probably outdated Catholic rule of no sex before marriage? If only you knew, I smiled nicely in the direction of the women, what my forbidden fruit was. You'd have a shock if you knew about a double forbidden fruit. Well, you see, I long for this beauty who already gave his heart to someone, well, not only someone, but to another man. So there you are. Double forbidden fruit, don't you think?

I heard the women burst out laughing. I laughed as well though I hadn't the foggiest what they were laughing about. My thoughts wandered back to the fruit. That pineapple strangely attracted my attention. Was it symbolic of something? I wondered if there was some special meaning in a pineapple. Could it be the dangerously similar *la Pina* (fruit) and *el Pene* (male sexual organ) that could confuse a student of Spanish? Was that pineapple a sly suggestion of something erotic? Poor Chris, he got it wrong in one of his pieces. I'll never forget his blushes when I pointed out that the Senora could not possible have bought *un pene* in the supermarket no more than a little girl could not have lost her *pero* (but) but she could lose her *perro* (dog). We both laughed, and then went on to find similar but different words from his Spanish dictionary. We were so happy together. Now I had gone and spoilt it all. Oh, why did I let me lips touch his...?

'Lena, what's that diploma you getting soon?' It was Mom's voice that brought me back to reality and the chatter of the visitors.

'Degree Mom, not a diploma.'

'*Si, Si*, but it's special,' she said, turning to her friends, 'Not everybody got them.'

Mom's bragging was getting embarrassing but I grinned dutifully then asked if anyone wanted another drink. Yes, they all agreed, and I went to the kitchen.

I took as long as I could to make the cups of tea and coffee before I returned to the living room. As I was handing round the cups of steaming liquid the doorbell rang. Kevin went to answer it and returned with Anthony. I managed not to gasp, but thought, Jesus Christ! He's had a shave. I can smell it. Unless it was the case that he had a bath in a tub full of cologne, after all, as the story goes, Cleopatra bathed in Ass's milk. Anthony had a bigger than usual bunch of flowers. My God! I wondered if his family owned a florist shop on top of everything else. After all, we had seen that thing on telly about how a lot of the flowers on the market got here through cheap slave labour in Africa somewhere. I heard Anthony ask Mom if he could give me a small gift to congratulate me on my exam result.

A very proud Mom said yes. Mom's friends seemed pleased about Anthony's action and nodded their approval. Anthony handed me the flowers and a nicely wrapped box. I suspected that it was a box of chocolates. All this was under the watchful and approving eyes of Mom and her friends. I accepted my gifts while thinking. Oh, what am I going do. I have to tell him and soon. I'll say he's a gentleman and I respect him but I don't love him. I have no intention of going out with anyone. This was a lie of course. I'd love to go out with a young man, but not Anthony.

That afternoon, which turned into an evening, seemed to go on forever. Anthony was asked questions about his own studies. Did he also take an exam? He explained that he didn't need exams. He was going to work in his family business. He was only interested in the knowledge of how businesses work in Europe. His tutor had advised that he tried the Masters in Business Studies in October. But he didn't really need it. I was glad when Mom said that I looked tired.

'Lena, yu go rest!'

She turned to her friends, 'My Lena, she work hard.'

'Yeah! I could do with an early night. *Buenos Noches* everyone,' I said humbly while thinking, you lot going to discuss me behind my back.

I left them to it.

In my room, something which I had not thought of before came into my head. How strange? Anthony never once talked about his studies, as did other students. This evening was the first time that he had mentioned anything about an MBA. Students talked a great deal about the politics of the world, the heavy work load of reading and writing essays, especially those who had to work for a bit of cash in order to survive. But from Anthony, not a word about study or world politics only about his family and the great things they do, and of his angelic sisters and cousins.

It didn't take long for Kevin to tiptoe into my room.

'You asleep?' he whispered, 'can I come in?'

'Yes, ok, seeing that you're already in.' He came and sat on my bed.

'Elle, what you going to do?'

'Do? Do what, if I may ask?'

'They've already married you off to Anthony. Them friends and Mom, already making your wedding dress and things in their head.'

'As long as they keep them things in their head.'

I gave Kevin a hug. My brother and my Mom were my best friends. I wouldn't want to hurt Mom, but no wedding for me!

D Day came the following Wednesday evening. Anthony arrived with more flowers. Bloody hell I thought, any more flowers and I'll scream!

Aloud I said, 'Do come in,' shouting out, 'Mom. It's Anthony. Mom!'

I didn't need to look around the room to see how many bunches of flowers there were. I could smell them. Blinking hell, I thought. The place looked like those roadsides floral tributes to someone who'd had a fatal accident at that spot. It was like a shrine. I could almost see myself as a statue in the middle of it. Ugh!

Anthony was smartly dressed. Mom suggested that Kevin should go up and do his homework. She had to go next door for a moment. Actually, I knew that Mom wanted to leave Anthony and me alone but with a chaperone in the shape of my brother upstairs. Well, he was supposed to be upstairs but I had no doubt that Kevin would be sitting on top of the stairs, listening. Anyway, Mom was being a bit too old fashioned. In this day and age, young women my age were already mothers themselves and she a grandmother several times over...chaperone...they'd all laugh their heads off.

Anthony and I sat on opposite sides of the table in the living room. After what felt like a long silence, he took a small presentation box from his jacket pocket. He handed me the box. For moment I felt a sharp pain in my chest. I heard my inner thoughts shouting, 'No! No! No!' My heart was pulsing.

Omigod, don't let it be what I think it is. His next words made me sigh with relief.

'This is your congratulation present. You have done so well in your exam,' he said, handing me the box, 'Auntie and the rest of us are so proud of you.'

I took it but hesitated, until he told me to open it. When I did I found not what I feared, but an elegant gold chain with a heart shaped pendant.

'It's beautiful,' I placed the chain gently back in its box. 'I can't...'

'The shop lady,' he interrupted, 'said I could exchange it, if my young lady didn't like this one.'

'Anthony, my Mom brought us up not to accept presents from anyone.' I handed the box back to him.

'Ah!' He waved his hand, dismissing my suggestion of expense, 'It's not expensive and I'm not just anyone.'

'Maybe so, but I'd rather not, I mean, I couldn't accept it, sorry.'

He made no attempt to take the box from my hand so I placed it gently on the table.

'I know you expected something better. You say the word and my father will see that you get something big on those fingers.'

He stretched his hand out to touch mine. I quickly pulled my hand away and said, 'Anthony, there's something I'm trying to say.'

'I know.' A very broad smile spread across his lips.

'I can't accept your gifts because I don't want to go out with you.'

'You said after your exam you'd tell me.'

He looked surprised at first but then grinned broadly.

'I know you're nervous, like my sister and cousins, it's okay, young ladies supposed to be cautious and shy.'

Blinking hell, I thought, if I hear about your family once more, I'll go over there and blow up your family's palace.

Aloud, I reminded him about what I'd said and that I'd think about things. Now I had decided that I didn't want to go out with anyone.

'What are you trying to say?' He drifted back into his version of English.

'What I'm trying to say is that I have no interest in a relationship, I mean a boyfriend.'

It was a lie of course, because there was someone I fancied.

'You mean you don't want me. Is it because I am an African?'

'Don't be daft! Even if you were French, Danish or Eskimo, I'd still say no.'

'You comparing me to an Eskimo? Wherever we come from, we are all Africans!'

'Actually, my mother is from South America with Indian roots and my father has Asian roots. I don't see where this African bit comes in the discussion.'

'Everybody in the world is African, which was where civilisation began...'

I thought here is a contradiction; he just said we were all Africans, how stupid.

'Anthony, I couldn't give a toss. All I am saying is, I don't want a man friend.'

I was beginning to get annoyed and wished that he'd leave, so that I could phone Chris.

'Why don't you be honest? You prefer Jamaican. Thing is, you might only end up with a fatherless child.'

'If that's what I want in the end, so what? And you shouldn't bad-mouth others. You'd be shouting blue murder if others bad-talked you.'

He rose from the chair.

'You been stringing me along all these months. You made a fool of my family and me. My auntie took the time to visit your mother. All the time you knew you don't want me; you see me as an African man living on trees.'

'Any man...remember?'

'Every woman wants a man, that's normal. Say you don't want me. But don't pretend you don't want any man. What am I to tell my family now? That a young Jamaican woman made fools of us?'

'Anthony,' I rose to my feet, 'for one thing, I am not a Jamaican woman. Even if I were, I'd have the right to choose what I want.'

'Elena, I love you. I want to make you the princess of my family.'

'Thank you. You're very kind, but I'm not in love with you, sorry.'

'Elena,' he sat down again. 'you will grow to love me. You might not love me now, but you will. What about Asian arranged marriages? Their love grows.'

'And you know all about that, do you? Anyway, you are a nice man; you need someone who loves you now, not someone who might grow to love you ten years hence.'

On and on we argued but I stuck to my decision. I did not want Anthony as a suitor no matter what he told his family or how well he got on with Mom. He wasn't happy with my rebuff and insisted that he would not give up. He left, insisting that he would make me his, come what may.

Mom must have spotted him leaving because she came in soon after. She was not pleased to hear that I had turned down Anthony. He was a perfect young man for me, she was sure, but she would not press me. He could continue to come on Sundays and who knows, I might get to love him. I told my Mom that she didn't have to marry me off in order to go to Canada if that offer still stood. It emerged then that she hadn't heard from dad for several months about the Canada thing. She assured me that she was not trying to get rid of me so that she could go to Canada. She only wanted my happiness and it was normal for me to have a young man and get married. I would be twenty-one soon. By that age she was long since married to my father and had me, her second child. It was when I was very ill with a bad attack of flu and Mom was worried about me that she talked to me. We talked about all sorts of things then. Now she was again concerned about me. Shouldn't we talk about everything now?

Kevin came down stairs. He had heard everything between Anthony and me.

'He really wanted to marry her Mom. What if he got his friends to kidnap our Elena and take her away?'

'Don't talk mad!' Mom shouted angrily at him. 'Get yourself up those stairs!'

In bed that night I felt miserable. I was not a person to hurt anyone's feelings. Yet the prospect of going out with Anthony only made me think more and more about Chris. I had to say no to Anthony. I didn't really want Chris turned into Anthony by some magic wand. I did not want Chris to pursue me. I would've wanted it to be the other way round. That was what made me think that there must be something wrong with me after all. Anthony was right, of course, to be angry, because I should've made it clear from the start that I didn't want to go out with him. I didn't want what he had to offer. But what did I want? I told Esmay the same: I didn't want what she had to offer either. Mates, yes, pals, yes, but bed partners, definitely not! If it was no to Esmay, no to Anthony and certainly a big no to Andre, the campus's self-appointed stallion, yet, at the same time walking with my whole soul after a man who might, or was becoming gay, what's the matter with me then? Was there such a thing as becoming gay? Nah, Chris adores that man. Anyway, Chris's not clever enough to go with a man simply because the man can offer him at least a leg up the ladder to a better life. My Chris, without meaning to, begs you to take him in your arms and cuddle him. That's what he used to hook Alexis, a more experienced and well-educated man. Chris Newman invites, indirectly invites you, either by gesture or spoken words, to go for him. Grab him and throw him down even. With Anthony he'd offer a golden cage and only once mentioned love and then only briefly. He'll enter that golden cage when he feels like it. He'll do whatever he wants to you. Ugh, the thought of having him on top of me night after night! The whole idea of being tongue kissed by a man you don't love, that to me was sickening. But what in Christ's name was wrong with Elena Peterson? All those things were normal. What was not normal were my strong feelings for a young man who I knew was with another man and I didn't seem to care that he was. But worse was that I didn't even want him to leap on me. If anything, I should be doing the leaping and taking him. Wouldn't that be just as wrong as me forcing myself on him? It's madness, all these crazy thoughts spinning around in my head!

My only sounding board would've been Chris, yet I could not bring myself to tell him about my real feelings. I couldn't tell my Mom either. She'd go ape, as they say, if I said I had rejected Anthony but loved another young man, who himself loved a man. I can image the name she would use to describe Chris. She'd chain me to a chair if she had to or take me for counselling until I agreed to go with Anthony. She'd bring in the priest to sprinkle holy water all over the house to chase away the demons influencing me. She'd ask her friends to light a candle in church and pray for me. Why do I have these strange feelings? Who can I discuss them with? I could not admit to Esmay that her suspicions about my feelings for Chris were correct. She'd only give me more hassle and say that I should see a psychiatrist. Worse still, what if she was malicious enough to tell Alexis?

'And what makes you think that Alexis, an experienced man, head of a large department and all that has no idea about your thoughts about Chris?' so asked the other Elena, the one who lived in my head and often argued with me.

'Nah! Alexis hasn't a clue, he trusts and worships Chris and is wooing him, as virgin or at least a novice, into his bed.' Those thoughts spun round and round in my head like a spin dryer.

I tossed and turned in bed, trying to get myself to go to sleep because I had promised Mom that I'd get up early to clean the house from top to bottom. Poor Mom, she'd been doing a lot of overtime to get a bit more money for us. It meant that she had title time to do any extensive house cleaning.

I must have slept because it was morning and I heard myself shouting, 'No! No! You shouldn't come when Mom is out.'

I was on the floor and Anthony was pinning me down trying to kiss me. He came when Mom and Kevin were out. He rang the bell and I stupidly let him in. The event of the intruder in Hackney came back to me. I kicked and struggled. My hand closed on something. I held it up high, while I heard my voice still shouting, 'No!' I brought down whatever it was that I had grabbed hold of hard. I heard a crash...

'Elena! Mom! It's Elena!'

I heard my brother's shouts as if coming from a long way away.

Footsteps came rushing in. Then I heard Mom's voice.

'What happened?'

Oh!'

I was not sure if I was still asleep or had woken up and gone downstairs. Both Mom and Kevin were in my room.

'You had a bad nightmare,' said Kevin, 'I heard you screaming. I thought a burglar got in through your window.'

'You broke your lamp.' Mom glanced in the direction of my reading lamp now lying shattered on the floor.

'Did I?' I was half-sitting on my bed.

'I must've knocked it over.'

'Picked it up and smashed more like!'

Kevin began to carefully pick up the larger pieces.

'You had one bad dream; maybe you ate dinner too late *anoche*,' Mom came to sit by me and put her arm across my shoulder. She pulled me towards her chest, 'or maybe you think about Hackney, but that don't happen here.'

'Yes, guess it was just a dream. Nobody can get in from the back window. How would they get in the back garden in the first place?'

142

Kevin had come to sit on the other side of the bed and placed his arm around me.

'It could be an anti-climax after all the work towards the exams.' I lied, because I could not admit what my nightmare was really about. I saw no point in worrying Mom that I was worried that Anthony might come when she was at work and Kevin at school.

'You go away for a week, cheap seaside holiday. We can manage a weekend.'

'No thanks,' I said, 'I'd prefer the Art Galleries and a curry somewhere.'

That curry trip never did take place. Chris had phoned and said to meet at the usual place at college. His Alexis had had a brilliant idea, to use his own words. I arrived at the given time and found him already there. He was beaming with excitement and I could see that he had something special to tell me.

'Hi, why for art thou with such broad smile?' I tried my own version of Shakespeare.

'Café o, Frisco?' he asked, after the usual peck on the cheek.

'Mm... Apple juice and one of them stuffed plantain things.'

'For madam, apple juice and Columbia fried plantain coming up.' He mimicked.

I watched him leave to get us snacks and drinks.

What's this all about I thought? Why is he so radiantly happy? Let me guess. Alexis is taking him away on some romantic holiday somewhere. Paris perhaps? That's it, going to introduce the young man to his family in Paris?

Chris returned with drinks and Tapas. Only then did he relate the news.

'He, I mean Alexis, wants to take us out for a typical English high tea.'

'Where would he find a place in London serving English high tea? They're all Italian, French, Chinese and Indian.'

'There are some posh English places but they've got dress codes and things like that. And have the right to say who can come in.'

'They're sure to keep the likes of us out. Can we afford it?'

'Don't ask *tonto* questions. He's treating us.'

'You can't let him pay for four of us, Oh! I'm assuming Esmay's invited?'

'Yes, he said to invite her as well.'

'You think it's what Esmay once said that maybe he wants us two as cover up.'

'Cover up?' He frowned.

'Maybe he wants people to think that maybe I am with you and Esmay's with him.'

'Esmay with Alexis? Don't make me laugh!' He laughed heartily.

'What's so funny?' I said, as if I didn't know that Esmay wouldn't go near a man in that way.

We discussed the plan for the high tea outing. The dress code meant no trainers, hoods or jeans. A lot of people in the arts, like writers and politicians, go there. The hotel restaurant was open to non-residents but it reserved the right to refuse entry. Tables <u>had</u> to be booked in advance.

'I'm not wearing any dress! And what about Esmay? You'll never get her into a frock. You did ask her didn't you?'

'Yes. Like you, she thought that it was really my idea. I had to laugh when she said that Alexis worships me like demy-god. If I was to ask him to go on all fours and bark like a dog, he'd do it.'

'And was it your idea and not his, to invite both Esmay and me?'

'Well, I mentioned that Esmay was sad because she didn't get the grades she wanted.'

We went on talking happily and without any mention of <u>that</u> kiss and which might have gone further had he not gently pushed me aside. While Chris went on to talk about the forthcoming event and going all soppy whenever Alexis's name came up, my own feelings and desires were tearing at my heart. How badly I wanted it to be me in Alexis's position. Again confusion! I might want him because of that relationship. I didn't want to change him, making him non-gay, as society would've wanted. How crazy the whole thing was. How mental!

When I finally got back to the discussion about the high tea, it was to talk about a shop somewhere in Greenwich. They sold what they called designer garb that had seen better days or had minor faults. They were then sold at the store as 'Shop Soiled'. I might be able to get something nice, but plain. Chris said he wouldn't mind coming along with Esmay and me to find him something simple, nothing fancy.

'Wait a minute! Got an idea.' I suddenly remembered something.

'Wha?' He said in typical southeast Cockney street talk.

'Esmay can wear an African wrap. They'll think she's some African studying here at Oxford.' I pointed out.

'Oxford is well outside London, you know.' He reminded me.

'My mom had some wraps to sell but none of her friends wanted any. They all said how nice they were but weren't buying any.'

'Here! You could dress like a Venezuelan native, those Indian people. Yeah! You could pass for one of them.'

'Oh! Did Alexis say it was a fancy-dress high tea, then?' I sneered.

'No, but if it was I'd go as an east London tramp, I suppose!' He said seriously.

'No! Reckon you'd go as one of them Londoners who sew buttons all over their jackets.'

I was trying to take him away from the negative image he sometimes had about his background.

'Yeah! Right! I could go as the Pearly King.' He did a funny walk and wriggled his hips.

We were both very happy in each other's company. Yet secretly, I was wishing that I could've shared my inner thoughts with him. If only I could talk to him about the Anthony saga and the nightmare afterwards.

On the way back home I returned to my self-tormenting mode. One minute I'd convince myself that Alexis hadn't a clue that I had feelings for his young man. The next minute I could almost hear the words ringing in my ears, 'that man knows'. He's a mystery man, but not a stupid one. The shade of his skin, and his eyes when he smiled at you, made me think of something Esmay once said. Something like, 'don't you go take that man for a fool, he no hidiot!'

She had gone into her make up Jamaican talk.

Even Chris pointed to Alexis's dark, hypnotic eyes; almost as if he had another layer behind the one's he showed. Chris had said it with great affection. Also, sometimes, it is as if he can see you even with his eyes closed. He described how Alexis once had his eyes closed, leaning back in his chair. Chris was looking up at him and longing to go up and give him a kiss. Alexis opened his eyes, smiled as if he knew not only that he was being watched but that he could also read Chris's romantics thoughts about him at that moment.

'Strange man!' I thought, as I arrived back home.

My mom thought that it was very kind of the head of department to take his bright students for a treat. And so the days leading up to the high-tea event just flew by. Anthony still came for his Sunday lunch but apparently took Mom's advice not to put pressure on me. As time went by she told me that she had reassured him, that left in peace, I might change my mind. The day before the outing, I washed and set my hair myself rather than going to Essay's aunt's Hair Centre or having it done by Esmay as she had been doing. In any case, my hair was long and easy to manage, thanks to my mixed blood. I pulled a face at my image in the mirror. I even decided that on the day of the high-tea outing I'd use hair chopsticks and do it up to look like one of those oriental young men I'd seen in books.

The day arrived and I was nervous. I'd never been to anywhere posh before. I had never been in the same room with the kind of people who take high tea in hotel restaurants. What if I made a mistake? What if I dropped my fork? Would they have a fork at high tea?

'What do people eat at high tea?' I asked Mom.

'No idea, but watch what the other people do.'

'They hold the tea cup with two fingers and stick the little finger up in the air, saw it on telly.' Kevin joined in.

'Yeah, knowing my luck, I'm bound to drop the cup and break it.'

'Oh! My Lena, she be aright.'

Mom helped to put the final touches to my hair.

I took a deep breath and muttered, 'Well, English high tea, here comes Elena Peterson.'

I left the house to get on the bus and then a train, and met Esmay at Charring Cross Station as agreed.

10

Esmay and I arrived at the Royal Crown Hotel a little earlier than arranged and walked around to the main entrance as we were instructed. We both looked at each other. We didn't need to say a word about feeling out of place. A man in uniform stood like a guard outside on the pavement. He looked at us without a smile. I was sure that he could tell that we did not belong. He knew, I was sure, that the clothes we had on were purchased or even rented for the occasion. We didn't appear to be the type who could afford to be there. It was not evening dress. It was casual but smart, Chris had explained to us. In other words, we looked a bit over-dressed, I was sure. Chris had said that Alexis advised that if we got there before them, which was unlikely, just walk in. Tell the person at the door that we are Dr Sylvere's guests.

'Let's wait a few minutes for Alexis and Chris.' I whispered to Esmay.

'You're right. In fact, I don't think I really want to go in such an unfriendly posh place.'

Many people arrived by cars, got out, and the cars were driven away. The man in uniform quickly went up each time and gave them broad grins, even bowing slightly.

'There all 'milky'.' Esmay muttered between her teeth.

'So what? They wouldn't dare turn people away because of colour or race... It's more our purse they'd worry about....ah! See?'

'Let's go in. It's twenty-five to eight now. Chris did say 7.30, perhaps they were early.' I suggested.

'Yes, we better or that man will call the old bill.' Esmay agreed with me.

'Elena, Esmay!' Chris called out our names as he rushed up to meet us.

'Didn't Chris tell you to go in?' Alexis asked, following just behind.

'We only just arrived.' I lied.

'We had trouble finding a parking space round here,' Chris walked along side us with Alexis in front, 'and the hotel one said FULL.'

I couldn't help noting the different response to us by the uniformed man as soon as he saw that we were with Alexis.

Informally dressed, Alexis had a long white scarf slung around his neck. He looked very handsome I thought, no wonder Chris had fallen for him. We were welcomed at the door of the building and led inside.

Once inside, I tried not to stare. It was so beautiful inside but I didn't want to give away the fact that I had never been inside such a place.

I will some day but at present I could not afford anything like it. Everything around was white and glittering. A woman was playing one of those light classics on a large piano. It was like walking into an imaginary land, like the ones you see on the telly but never in real life. I thought, 'this is the life I want.'

Someone came and took our coats giving the tickets to retrieve them to Alexis. Another, smartly dressed, member of staff came up and confirmed Alexis's reservation. He said that our table would be ready in about five minutes. We sat in a corner of the foyer and immediately a waiter came to take our drinks order. Alexis spoke to him in French and whatever was said, the waiter nodded and went on his way. Soon after that our table was ready. Both Esmay and I had gone very quiet with Chris doing most of the talking. He seemed very much at ease as if he had been to such places before with Alexis. I felt like how a real princess might feel as waiters held out the chairs for each one of us. I smiled a thank you and so did Esmay and Chris, but Alexis said 'merci'.

I noticed that a group of women, mainly black with two whites, sat nearby at a round, larger table. The women already had a waiter serving them. I was sure from the way they were elegantly dressed, that they were bound to be from the professional class, or that emerging group of middle class black people the newspapers and television were going on about. The women chatted and laughed happily. I wondered what sort of jobs they were doing to enable them to come to a place likes this on their own. No men with them, I thought, they were obviously paying their own way. Whatever their jobs were, they were obviously the kind that I'd like. In general, I was very pleased to see the black women there, after the 'all milk' here statement that Esmay made when we were waiting outside for Chris and Alexis.

A waiter came with a tray of four glasses of champagne. Alexis proposed a toast to us as the best entry into the world of academia. We in turn toasted the best Head of Department at our university. Alexis reminded us that he was only acting head and that we might soon see him sitting with a begging bowl by the train station.

'With a dog,' Chris joked, 'don't forget the dog.'

'What's this about a dog?' I asked.

'Well, never seen a beggar without a dog?' Chris was in a joyful mood.

And so our very pleasant evening continued. Two 'towers' of goodies arrived, one with sandwiches, another with delicious scones and other delicacies.

After we had eaten and Esmay certainly couldn't have eaten anymore, we moved from the table to a corner that had apparently been reserved for us in the foyer.

As soon as we took our seats, a drinks waiter came over, his notebook ready. Alexis ordered some sort of pineapple drink with a fancy name for himself and told us to order anything we wanted. I had no idea what some of the drinks on the list on the table were. I played safe and asked for wine, so did Esmay. Chris ordered orange juice and some mineral water.

Esmay cleared her throat briefly before suggesting, 'Shall we have a toast to Chris and Alexis?'

'Hey!' I glanced nervously around but if anyone heard what Esmay said, they did not show it.

'To Chris and Alexis.' I said, raising my glass and clinking with theirs in the time-honoured fashion.

After the 'toast' we chatted about college politics, the bad food in the students' canteen, and what our long-term plans were. What strategies we had if things didn't go as planned. I said that I didn't have any plans other than to do my MA and find well-paid employment with job satisfaction. Chris wanted to travel. He wanted to go St. Marten, Alexis's place of birth, and where he had spent his childhood. Esmay said she had no idea, she hadn't made any plans, and she was going to take things as they came. But, she said, it would be nice to have her own hair and beauty business.

At about eleven, the waiters quietly told us that the bar would be closing in ten minutes. I noticed that there were no shouts of 'last orders' as heard in pub bars or in the soaps. We made ready to leave and asked for direction to the ladies restroom. Once there, Esmay, who I knew was bursting to ask questions, whispered, 'Listen, this place must be very expensive. Four of us, how can he afford it on his salary?'

'He's acting head of that large department, remember?' I reminded her.

'Yeh!' Esmay looked round then spoke softly. 'Even so, if he can afford this place, why the hell is he slugging his guts out at a college which takes in dumb kids? What if he's some sort of Mafia in disguise or something?' She asked seriously.'

'Don't be stupid! He's not from Italy; he's from the French-Caribbean.'

'Ah! Now we're being racist, are we? What makes you think only Italians can be Mafia? Why can't there be Mafia in the French Caribbean or Timbuktu come to that?'

'Let's go, we'll talk tomorrow.' I pushed her out of the lady's room area.

We left the Hotel behind. Alexis was driving us home. Soon Esmay dozed off next to me in the backseat. I tried to make conversation.

'Chris, you should've taken French instead of Spanish.' I chuckled.

'Yep! Looks like all waiters are French speaking.'

'Some are no more French than you are darling.' Alexis has been in a good humour all evening.

'Hear that, Chris? You better learn French if you want to sound posh.' I teased.

'I don't know about being posh but he will learn. And he had better learn some basics in time for this Christmas.'

'What's happening this Christmas, then?' I asked, but I already had the feeling that a Christmas introduction to the French speaking Sylvere clan was arranged to take place.

It was not that Chris needed French to speak to them. They probably spoke better English than the English do themselves. God knows how often we hear the statement that foreigners speak better English than the English do. Of course, it's only a saying, perhaps to annoy the English folk. All these unimportant things went through my head as I found myself dozing off.

We drove along, talking of nothing in particular. Then, as had been agreed, we dropped Esmay home first. She thanked Alexis for a wonderful evening and went inside.

We finally got to my street and drew up outside my front gate. Chris, like a true gentleman, opened the back door and helped me get out. I thanked Alexis for such a lovely evening.

'Have a good sleep.' Alexis replied, nodding in my direction.

Chris walked me to my door, gave me the ceremonial peck on each cheek, and then said, 'I love him very much, you know that don't you?'

I couldn't reply in words but nodded that I knew. I was thinking that Chris knew and was letting me down as gently as I had done to Anthony not so long ago. He waited until I had turned my key in the door and gone in before he returned to the car. It was not the kind of car to make a noise when it drove away. I peeped from behind the curtains to watch it disappear down the road. Then I saw something else and gasped!

Omigod, no! A figure was standing across the road, facing my house.

The figure stood a little away from the dim streetlight. I therefore could not say if it was male or female, since both wore trousers and long coats nowadays. I quickly moved away from the window and went to wake Mom in the armchair where she had fallen asleep while waiting up for me.

'Come on sleepy head. I'm home; you can go to bed now.'

'Had good time?' She asked in a sleepy voice.

'Yes, tell you all 'bout it tomorrow.' I gave a long yawn.

The days and weeks following that evening and leading to graduation day, were hectic. All sorts of things seemed to be happening, either one after the other or all at once. Metaphorically speaking, someone had opened the floodgates, which then let items of all kinds come tumbling down.

First, there was Esmay, who came uninvited to my house after that night out and gave me a shock, then Anthony, with his a long face which made me feel guilty for turning him down, then came Alexis's text asking me to drop by his office.

But first, Esmay.

She came just after midday when I was getting ready to go out to take a walk across the park to the library. I wanted to work out how long it would take me to walk across the park. I wanted to save money on bus fares. When the doorbell rang it had startled me. Was it Anthony? Was he the shadow I had seen across the road the other night? Was he coming to have it out with me when he knew that both Mom and Kevin would be away? Was this going to be a repeat of that event in the damp basement? Or could it be the post woman, probably with a large parcel. I dragged my nervous legs to the door and called out, 'Who is it?'

'Santa Clause, who you think?'

I opened the door to Esmay. 'Sorry, was in the back.' I lied.

I didn't see the point in letting Esmay know that I was scared. I hadn't gone into too much detail with her about Anthony, except to say as a matter of conversation, that there was this young man eating Sunday meals at our house that wanted to take me out but I had declined. I had said that my mom liked him for me but I didn't. Esmay had suggested I talked to my mom about how I felt.

'Mm… was passing and I said I'd look you up after that place.'

'I was about to go out.'

'Come on! You're talking to Esmay who knows that excuse backwards.'

'But it's true. I am thinking of walking to work rather than taking a bus. I want to know how long it would take.'

'Mm… what you make of that place last night?'

'I thought, it's good to see how the other half live and be part of it, rather than only watching it on telly.' I replied.

'Mm… aright for some people, not for me. A lot of…'

'Hey, don't use the 'S' word, we don't swear in this house.'

'Sorry milady,' she mocked, 'milady is already posh.'

'Yeah! Anything not down the dump or whatever is called posh and not desirable to some people with a chip on their shoulder. Thing is, it's a matter of choices. All that Alexis is doing is giving Chris choices.'

'Mm...' Esmay grunted, helping herself from Mom's fruit bowl.

'Apple, called the forbidden fruit. Eve, or was it Adam, who went for the apple? Some people do go after the forbidden.'

'You sure you're not still drunk from last night?' I watched her take some grapes on top of the half-eaten apple in her hand, some of it still in her mouth.

And so began a long disagreement between us. She accused me of trying to put my hat where I couldn't reach it. I was very surprised to say the least that she was so negative about the evening before. I really thought that she was enjoying it all, especially the scones. She must have eaten at least ten, some with cream, and others with jam. She seemed to think that those black women at the nearby table snubbed us. She was sure that one of those women was a television presenter. When she smiled at her, the women looked right through her.

'But she doesn't know you. She was having her own private party.'

Esmay then started on Alexis.

'For all we know he was some secret loan shark. Being a head of department at a college can be a cover up. And what of his dark eyes and black hair, maybe he coloured it?'

Then it was Chris's turn.

'He's not stupid,' she said, why would he leave what Alexis had to offer to come to you?'

On and on she went, like some demented person. In the end, I asked her to leave but not before I threatened to tell Alexis never to invite her to anything again.

'Sorry! Sorry! It's only that it really gets to me, seeing you make a fool of yourself. Chris doesn't want you, can't you see?'

'Whatever! I must go. See you sometime.'

I walked to where I had hung my jacket to put on for that long walk across the park.

'You don't have to go out just to get me to leave.'

'Esmay, why don't you do yourself a favour and go to hell, eh?'

At the door, Esmay barred my way.

'I miss you, damn it! And as long as you keep hankering after that forbidden fruit...'

I gave her a long hard look, frowned, and then thought, 'what a strange woman?'

'Please come back. I miss you. We were such good friends.'

'I see! You want me to come back to live together and this is the way you go about it? Slagging off my two best friends?' I shook my head from side to side in disbelief.

'Sorry I badmouth your other friends. I don't know if I'm going or coming.'

We left the house and headed for the park close by. We walked in silence through the park. I timed the journey on my watch and noted that it would take a twenty-minute stroll, or about fifteen minutes or less if I made a dash for it. We got to the place where I was to start as a general library assistant in the multicultural sub-branch. It was in an old Victorian type, three storey building, linked to the 'Learning in the Workplace' section of our own university library. We walked around and I was pleased to note the shelves were stacked with books in languages other than English. Some captions said Bengali, others said Mandarin, French, Spanish, there was even Japanese and Latin. After wandering around the two-storey building with its various sections, including newspapers in community languages, I spoke to Esmay.

'We can have a cuppa in the basement snack bar.'

'Mm,' she grunted,' didn't know that libraries had snack bars.'

'That's part of the Community friendly project starting here.'

'They couldn't have a better person to help develop things.'

After we had some freshly brewed tea from real tea cups not that 'plastic' machine stuff, we walked into the sunshine. I took Esmay to the bus stop and told her where to change to get home. I watched her get on a bus. I sighed, what a clumsy way of trying to revive a dead relationship!

Anthony was not that easy to get rid of. He had come for his usual Sunday lunch. I was sure then that he was the figure I had seen across the road. Was he going to be stalking me, or hanging around to see if I was with anyone or who I came home with? What if he turned violent against someone he saw me with? Nah! He's not the type. Never-the-less, I decided to have a woman-to-woman talk with Mom. I had to make her see why I didn't want to be around for a cosy lunch of which Anthony was part. He made me feel uncomfortable with his long sad expression. I got my chance for that talk one evening when Kevin was away practising music with his mates.

We were sitting in front of the telly. I went and turned it off, then began a lengthy presentation, as if I was at college and facing a professor testing me.

'Mom, we got to talk.'

'*Que pasar?*'

'Well, it's like this Mom. I shall always be your little girl. But I am a young woman now. You must let me choose what I want to do. And one thing I don't want just now is to go out with a man. I know you worry about Kevin and me. But if you want to go to Canada and join your man, if that time ever comes, you must go, although, I can't understand a woman wanting to get back with a man who dumped her with their young kids.'

'I told you hundreds of times. Your father did not dump us. I wanted to stay behind. I didn't care what others said about how bad England was. I knew my two kids have a better chance in England. I say to your daddy, not so much chance in Guyana or Maracaibo in Venezuela. Your daddy, not like the people, they're unhappy here but still they stay. Your daddy was unhappy, that's why he pack his bag and leave. He promised to send what he can. And try to get to America. He had many friends there. Later he'd send for us, so don't condemn him to hell fire.'

'Of course, he went when we were tiny and he's still waiting to go to America. Tell that to the Marines…! He dumped you with us kids or you had a big fuss and he packed his bag and cleared off!' I kept my thoughts to myself and tried to reassure Mom.

'I know Mom, you made great sacrifice for your kids. I can never repay you. And I don't want to hurt you. But please don't try to push me into that marrying lark, which is something I don't want. I'll work for myself and to help Kevin. And if you leave for Canada, Kevin and me, we stay in this house and look after each other, Okay?'

I took Mom's hand and placed it on my cheek. Her palm felt very cold.

She spoke softly, 'Promise me, if you, well, find a young man, when you ready you tell me, bring him home. Keep your head, don't let any good-fo-nothing come stick a baby in you and disappear, hear now?'

'No chance.' I assured Mom. With that I went and turned on the telly.

After that, Mom and I agreed that I need not be around when Anthony came. I'd be in my room reading or watching my own telly or I'd be out. From that moment, Mom and I chatted like two grown women. But I still could not tell her of my feelings for Chris. Mom knew about Esmay but only that she was a mature student who had befriended me. Now we were both befriending others. For example, Chris, I told her, had lost his Mom when he was only twelve years old and had a rough time since then and needed lots of support with his studies.

The days went by. I was looking forward to the graduation ceremony. Mom was frantically preparing and buying stuff for us all, in spite of my protests. Mom argued that she didn't want us to look different to the other students and their families. We're poor but we don't have to look poor. Most of what we got came from the pay-later catalogue, except for shoes and an expensive hat for Mom. I got a white-lace blouse to match a long white skirt.

'I'll look like some bride.' I laughed.

'White is usual for purity that's why for first communion you dress in white.' Mom explained.

'And wedding,' Kevin joined in, 'But only if she's a virgin.'

'I warned you 'bout that talk you pick up!' Mom went on, 'back home in the old days, you get your mouth and tongue scrubbed with soap.'

'I suppose I'm a bride of the muse of academia.' I continued the conversation with my happy family.

'The what?' Mom frowned.

'Never mind Mom. You try on that fancy hat.'

Mom was beaming with pride while preparing and at the thought of her daughter's graduation ceremony. She had told everyone who would listen, including the post woman and the Bassets at the Corner shop, of her daughter's success in the exams.

During those preparation days I saw little of Chris. We talked on the telephone but all he could talk about was Alexis. He made Alexis look like an angel dropped from the clouds. Chris was oblivious to the nine years he said that there was between them. For example, would Alexis look good on a disco dance floor, and would Chris be content to just have high tea at an expensive hotel or listen to jazz at home? I began to think about those issues because Chris was going on and on about how good his relationship with Alexis was, and that was beginning to irritate me. It was Alexis did this or Alexis said that. Alexis would be taking him to France for the usual Christmas family gathering. The Sylvere clan will arrive from as far away as St. Marten and the Spanish speaking Dominican Republic, even from French Guyana, wherever that was. Occasionally, he asked about Esmay and me. Had we sorted our differences, whatever they were? It was about that time that I began to see the situation clearly. It was worse than those love triangles and soppy romances. My own saga, if I could call it that, was like a long line where A wants B who wants C who wants D, then in the background, E who wants B where E prepared to go to any length to keep B from C. What a blinking complication! Why can't life be straight forward for Christ's sake?

Two days before the big day, Alexis rang and asked me to meet him in his office when I had a moment, but before the graduation ceremony. Thinking that it was to do with the Masters degree I had signed up for, part of which would take place in the Languages department, I rushed over there. I arrived somewhat apprehensive. What if Alexis, as acting head, were to say that my grades weren't good enough to work towards a Masters in his department? Nervously, I knocked at his study door and he called me in. I thought how different he looked compared to when we went out informally as a foursome. And I also noticed how ordered his office or study, whatever he called it, was. Chris, no doubt, was doing a good job keeping his Dr Alexis's place in order. I sat down and nervously placed my hands together on my lap.

'How are you?' He asked.

'I'm okay. Been preparing for the big day.'

'That is what I wanted to talk to you about. What are your plans for after the ceremony, I mean, after students tired themselves out, yelling and going berserk?'

'Nothing special. I'd go home for a family meal, maybe have drink.'

'I am planning a surprise gathering for Chris, just a couple of close friends and my neighbour, to have a bite to eat and a drink at my house. I would be honoured if you and your mother would come along.'

'I don't... Sorry, I'd love to come and so would my Mom, but we can't leave Kevin behind, he's my baby brother, you know,' I said, laughing, 'actually, he's fifteen.'

'Kevin is also invited. He can meet my own baby brother, he's twenty plus.'

'Thank you very much for the invite Dr Sylvere. I'll speak to my Mom and let you know.'

'What about Esmay, could she keep it a secret?'

'I'll talk to her about it and warn her.'

As promised, I discussed the matter with Esmay but warned her. If she let one word out to Chris I'd hate her and never speak to her again. She promised to keep her mouth shut because she wouldn't want us two to never speak again. But it would be better if Alexis invited her and her mother personally. I passed the message to Alexis and he sent a text invitation to Esmay saying that she could bring her mother as well.

Esmay and her mother both accepted and it was all settled. But Esmay had concerns .She wanted to know whether or not she and her Mom should take a bottle, as was the custom when invited to a party. I didn't think that Alexis would care one way or the other and told Esmay so. But Mom and I would take something because my Mom didn't want us to appear to be so poor that we couldn't even afford a bottle of wine from the supermarket.

Esmay's other concern was that Alexis's friends and neighbour might look down their noses at us. I put her straight. Alexis wouldn't have invited us if he thought that his friends and neighbour were snobs. She went on about high places giving her the creeps, until I told her not to go if she was so nervous about it all.

'Who say I'm nervous? I can go anywhere.'

'Good.' I smirked; my comment about her being nervous had the intended effect.

Suddenly my first graduation day arrived. We had to get to college early to prepare. Mom stretched her finances to the limit by taking a bus to the bus station then from there, a mini-cab for the long ride to the college. She was amazed to see other students and their families getting off the bus at the stop by the college.

'We could've saved the cab fare.' Kevin said, looking very smart in his catalogue suit.

I left Mom and Kevin by the main entrance where families were gathering, and went to my own department. There, we were to dress in black gowns with bright red capes and funny hats.

'We look like penguins.' Some of us said, giggling nervously.

Some candidates, as we were now referred to, felt sure that they would forget their instructions or get them mixed up. A couple of us complained that some hats didn't fit properly. I think it was Joy who said that her hat would fall over her eyes and cause her to trip when going up the podium. The woman from the drama department costume section, who was helping us to dress, was telling us to take deep breaths. I could not understand what taking a deep breath had to do with hats that didn't fit properly. My own thoughts were to look out for Chris. What would he look like in his penguin robe and funny hat? I had often felt sorry for him. I, at least, had Mom and Kevin; poor Chris had no family and only had Alexis. All the more reason why I shouldn't make things difficult for him with Alexis. Not that I had any intention of doing such a thing. For some reason that I still could not explain, I loved him with his Alexis, or perhaps because of his Alexis, madness I suppose on my part.

After what seemed like ages, we, the BA's, were led out first because we had the front row seats. After us would be the Diplomas of all sorts then the Certificates. The long wait for the ceremony to begin gave me time to glance around and admire our Great Hall. The hall had been transformed into something like a strange Fantasyland. Blue and yellow flowers greeted us from everywhere. Our own orchestra from the music department gleamed from one side of the hall. The players stood out in their white and gold trimmed regalia. The Hall was either sprayed with something or it could have been the fragrance of the female candidates, mixed with the aftershave of the male students that hit our senses. I was in a different world. But it would have to be a dream. It could not be me. I was only dreaming the whole thing. It could not be Elena Peterson, that girl from the notorious 'sink school' near her run down council estate, slumming it in a dark and damp basement with its rat infested back yard. Not the same Elena who went to schools where you were a hero if you'd done badly in your schoolwork and were in constant conflict with the teachers. Doing well was not the done thing. Not that Elena, who could not go on school outings because she couldn't pay. The only time she went on an outing, she had so little to eat that she had to get some green apples from someone's garden to eat, while others munched their fancy sandwiches. No, it couldn't possibly be Elena Peterson now waiting at a University to be awarded not merely a BA, but a first class Honours degree at that!

The music started up and along came a procession of dignitaries in their gowns of blazing colours and various shades. We had already been told that Doctors and Professors wore the colours of the university from where they got their post-graduate degrees. Most beautiful I thought, and one day you, Elena Peterson, will be part of such a procession.

We sat like statues looking straight ahead as we had been instructed. The podium filled in from the back, which meant that the 'Royal', who we were told was one of the patrons of the college, and all the rest at the back of the procession, would be seated in the front row. The Royal person, flanked by two officials, stepped onto the podium and took the front seats. On one side of the Royal was, to my surprise, Dr Sylvere, and on the other, the Dean. I looked disbelievingly at the scene and wondered how, I, Elena was part of it all. I felt my eyes filling with tears though I didn't know why. Alexis must be someone very important at the college, probably much more than merely an acting head. The music stopped. Our Dean rose to her feet.

And so the lengthy three-hour ceremony began and set my own thoughts wandering. That man being in such a high place could be ruined by any scandal. That man, who looked so much like some general or more than that, almost like some Maya Indian chief with his light olive white, if there is such a thing, skin. He was the same man, who took us out as a foursome and held Chris in his arms at night; arms that I wished were mine. Omigod, I can't do anything that would cause a scandal for this great looking person on the one hand, and an ordinary human, on the other. Why, oh why, was life so complicated and me so mixed up and...

Ouch! The candidate next to me kicked me in the shin because I was so wrapped up in my own thoughts that I nearly missed starting the fourth line of the BA group. My thoughts instantly came back to the ceremony. I was at the start of the next line which had begun with 'P's'. Like walking penguins, we filed up to the podium, where the Royal smiled, shook each of our hands with a glove covered hand, and whispered 'congratulations.'

I couldn't pick Chris out in the mass of black robes until the prize giving when individual names were called out. All sort of prizes were called out before the Student of the Year ones. First, there was one from the Bachelor degrees, then one from the Diplomas, and then finally from the Foundation Year Certificates.

I saw him walk up when his name was called. He had been transformed from a shy, skinny young man with low esteem, who referred to himself as 'white trash', because that was what some others had called him, into a Prince. He took a pile of books and an envelope that I suspected was his award certificate and a cheque. He bowed a thank you. Our Dean called for applause for all of the winners who stood side-by-side on the podium. We all clapped loudly. I must have clapped more vigorously than anyone else, especially when Chris came past, because the now, Bachelor of Arts next to me whispered, 'That one your man?'

'Well not exactly.' I replied.

'Shush!' Another new Bachelor of Arts reminded us that we were told not to talk or whisper during the ceremony, which I felt had become like a temple to the gods and their disciples.

And so, after the ceremony ended and the Royal and the rest of the officials paraded out, the bachelors, followed by the Diplomas and the Certificates, left the Temple of the Gods to the Postgraduates, who would have their own ceremony the next day.

The best part of the day for me began when we got outside.

Colourful Marquees and the aroma of food, plus African drummers, greeted us. The Drama and Design department went overboard, so to speak, to transfer our cold country into the blazing sun of somewhere tropical. It was as if we were taken, perhaps by our overseas students, on holiday to some North African country. The African drummers were no doubt from the Music department's special percussion group. Things were getting wilder. First people merely shook hands, patting each other on the back, girls hugged and kissed anyone who happened to be nearby. People who I had never met before were shaking my hand and congratulating me.

Chris came along with a, 'Hi, Bachelors! You look smashing, I wouldn't have recognised you.'

I gave him a hug and a kiss before I introduced him to my mom.

He had already met Essay's mom, who was standing nearby.

'Mom, Chris is one of the students who are learning Spanish that I told you about. Chris, this is my Mom and Kevin.'

'Hello Chris, *Felicidades*.' Mom greeted him in Spanish.

'*Buenos Días, Señora. Soy amigo de Elena*.' Chris tried his Spanish.

Mom hugged Chris and used her Maracaibo greeting, '*Encantado*.'

By the look in my mom's eyes and the tone of her voice, I could almost read her mind. My Mom had found me another wedding partner. Poor Mom, if only she knew.

'Err...err!' Stammered Chris, '*Yo no hable muchos Castellano*.'

I knew that he meant that he didn't know much Catalan, said to be standard Spanish, but I didn't have the heart to correct him in case he got embarrassed.

'So!' Mom shrugged, 'We talk English. My Elena said you have no mamma, I be your mama now, *si*?'

Oh no! Mom, why are you so desperate to see me off? I kept that thought to myself. After that everything went crazy. A group of scantily dressed African dancers, probably from the Dance Study option, appeared from behind one of the Marquees.

'Look at that!' Chris pointed in amazement towards the young dancers.

The dancers were wriggling their bottoms while the rest of their bodies hardly moved.

'And they are only my first year.' A tutor, standing nearby, replied in a proud tone of voice.

'That dance comes from Ghana. But I don't remember the name.' Someone else offered.

The dancers, danced among themselves to begin with, then they moved into the crowd and began to drag people to join in the dancing. Then everything went mad. People seemed to be performing their own version of an African dance and the spectacle of people in suits or saris doing African bottom wriggling looked ridiculous to say the least. Suddenly, two dancers tried to drag Chris into the dance area causing him to run away. He waved to us as he ran. 'Will text tomorrow.' He shouted.

'Where is he going now?' Mom asked.

'To Dr Sylvere's office to wait for him.' I said.

As far as Chris knew, we were all going to spend the evening privately with our families, Esmay with her mom and I with Kevin and mine. He said that he was not worried about not having any family. Alexis and he were planning to have a private evening together. They would have a bite to eat somewhere and a drink, and then go home to have an early night.

'Mm...how romantic!' Esmay had teased, when Chris explained.

'Poor devil, he has no idea of what is waiting for him.' I muttered softly after Chris left us.

'Do we know what is awaiting him?' Esmay's mom enquired.

'I wasn't sure if Mom taking a bottle would be offensive to those high-brow people.' Esmay was still somewhat concerned about meeting Alexis's friends, who she was sure would be snobs.

I said that I'd take people as I found them and my mom agreed with me.

As soon as it was safe to do so we made a dash for the car park where Esmay's mom's car was waiting. I had no doubt that we were at the start of what would be an interesting evening. Interesting in what way? I had no idea.

11

Soon we were on our way. Esmay's mom had invited Kevin to sit next to her where he proceeded to 'give her an ear bashing' with everything he could think of about orchestras, and which instrument drowned out which. Mom sat next to Esmay who was by the side of the window. She talked to her about how sometimes we did something else, not what we really had in mind. Often, what we actually wanted to do came in another form, which we did not even think of. We soon left the inner London streets with their many shops, most boarded up, and rubbish piled up all along the road. To be frank, this was mainly because Esmay's mom took the back streets in order to avoid the afternoon traffic. We began to notice the difference as we left inner London. The streets were cleaner, and the houses mainly semi-detached with cars and flowers in the front. Esmay's mom had studied how to find Alexis's place on the map. We eventually arrived to find that there was a barrier, which I expected to open as we got near to it, but it did not!

Esmay's mom hooted the horn to alert the man who was sitting in a small hut by the gate.

'He's ignoring us, too busy watching television.' said Mom.

'Not telly he's watching,' Kevin replied, 'he can see everything that's happening around him. It's called a monitor.'

Kevin was right, because the barrier opened and let us in under the large archway that read in fancy letters, 'RIVERSIDE VILLAGE'.

'Wow!' Kevin exclaimed as we drove through, 'Some place! I could live here forever, thank you very much!' He joked.

'It's been on television. It's some kind of private development for middle-management or business's, I believe.' said Esmay's mom, winking in the direction of a gentleman, probably from overseas given his skin colour, with a bulging tummy and smart formal dress, getting into his car.

'Or those that can afford it!'

Mom joined in the conversation.

'I don't get excited about those things. Them not real, its fantasy Island stuff.' sneered Esmay.

'Jacko lives in one like it in America.' Kevin was still excited about what he was seeing around him.

We continued driving until we came to a children's play area.

'Must be round here somewhere, Chris did mention a children's play area.' I said.

'Ah, there is it!' Esmay's mom turned into what looked like a cul-de-sac.

'Ah! Number seven!' I leaned over Mom's shoulder and pointed to a house with a strange roof.

'Chris was right, it's just like two houses stuck together under one slanting roof.'

We pulled up by number seven. There was a small space between two cars parked outside. We had to squeeze in between them.

'That was some parking!'

Kevin praised the driving skill of Esmay's mom.

We came to an outer door, which was already ajar, and stepped into a short passageway full of shoes, umbrellas and other stuff like that. I walked towards the inner door. Instantly, a loud jingle sound greeted us, so loud, that it startled me. The door opened and I gasped. There before us stood, not Alexis's baby brother as Chris called him, but Alexis himself. It was if we had travelled back in time and come face-to-face with a young, twenty-one or twenty two-year-old Alexis. With a cheeky smile, as if he was laughing at a joke only he knew, the young Alexis stretched out a hand.

'*Bonjour mademoiselle*,' he said, taking my right hand and kissing the back of it.

'I am sorry, we don't speak French.' I said as the young Alexis went to place a kiss on the back of my Mom's hand, and everyone else except for Kevin, who got a hug and a pat on the back.

To Mom, he said, '*Bonjour Madame.*'

He first kissed the back of Mom's hand and then did the same with Esmay's Mom.

'Come and meet everyone.' invited Young Alexis.

There were around eight or so guests in the room and a series of introductions followed.

'Hi!' A little boy, not much older than about ten, came up, 'Ali Baba the second, friend of Ali Baba the first.'

A man, who I suspected was the boy's dad, explained, 'That's a game he plays with Alexis, in it, they rename each other.'

'Hi! I'm Kevin, Elena's brother.'

'What computer you got? I have an Apple...' the boy began.

'What would you like?' Someone led us towards a bar.

The two Moms found a couple to chat with. One of them, I was sure, had to be the florist from nearby our college, where Chris had once asked me if I wanted a Saturday job, helping the poor man. Chris was right. The poor man looked overweight and his young wife, or whoever she was, was seeing to it that he had nothing else but mineral water. The two Moms humbly handed the two bottles of wine we had brought to a young man who appeared to be acting as bartender. He thanked us with a broad smile. We gathered from his accent he was from either a Hispanic or Portuguese speaking country, Brazil more like, I thought.

That was how the evening began as we waited for Alexis and Chris to arrive. Young Alexis announced that Alexis had rung to say that he was 'held up' but would be with us soon. I spent the time looking around the large room. There was booze at one end, a spread of Tapas at the other. In between, a piano, and there was also a large stack of what appeared to be CDs. High up across the back of the room was a banner, which said, 'CONGRATULATIONS'.

Chris was in for a surprise, lucky devil. I felt that there seemed to be an air of anticipation. I actually overheard two guests whispering that Alexis had something more than exam results up his sleeve. Meanwhile, I looked around until I managed to get young Alexis by himself and apologised.

'I'm sorry I stared. It was rude of me.'

Young Alexis laughed heartily.

'Don't be sorry. It happens all the time. Alexis's friends, they meet me for the first time and they have big shock. And my friends meet Alexis for the first time; they get a big shock also.'

'It's amazing, almost spooky!'

Esmay, glass in hand, came to stand by us.

'Spooky?' Young Alexis frowned.

'Like ghosts of the other.'

'No, not ghosts. One day you might meet *Mon père*, eh, my father, and then you can say you gone forward in science fiction, maybe.'

He laughed aloud, obviously enjoying people's reaction to the likeness between him and his brother, and they weren't even twins.

Someone's ring tone sounded, he listened then said, 'They're here. That was Paddy at the gate. Quick! Lights out.'

'Not a sound!' said someone else as all the lights went out. We all seemed to stop breathing.

We heard a key turn in the door. There was not the usual jingle sound because Young Alexis had switched off the contraption. Then two shadows appeared and we all shouted, 'Surprise!' All the lights came on.

There was a loud gasp. Alexis's shirt had a bloodstain on the collar. On one side of his face, near his eye and nose, there was an injury of some sort. Chris had obviously been crying. Young Alexis rushed to his brother and began speaking rapidly in French to him.

'Everyone wanted to know what happened?

'A drinking brawl in the students bar, I bet.' A guest suggested.

'I am sorry everyone. It is not as bad as it looks. Please, continue with your drinks, I'll be with you soon.'

Alexis began to leave the room with Chris following him.

'I'm sorry; I didn't mean to, it was an accident.' Chris pleaded tearfully.

'You, you hit my brother?' exclaimed young Alexis going for Chris, 'You try me!'

Alexis stepped in and held his young brother back, though not in time to prevent the kick young Alexis was about to deliver. The kick landed against one of Chris's legs but Chris's only response was that he kept saying how sorry he was and that it was an accident.

'It's alright. The young man is leaving.' said Alexis before he went to change.

It was an embarrassing time for all of us. We kept looking at each other. We were not sure what we should make of it.

'Ah! They'll make up.' said John, who had introduced himself as one of Alexis's oldest friends, as he got himself another drink.

'Orly should let his brother and the young man sort things out between themselves.' someone else suggested.

Left alone we couldn't decide what to do. Should we stay or should we leave? Just then, Alexis returned in a clean shirt. He asked us to stay and not let the food go to waste. He then explained that things had got out of hand.

Alexis had had some good news and had been held up. Chris had waited alone in the office. When Alexis finally managed to get away from an impromptu meeting, he went to find Chris. Alexis had no idea that Chris had seen him with someone, got the wrong end of the stick, and gone wild. Apparently, Chris had a foul temper. Alexis said that he did not condone violence of any sort and that next thing we know, Chris might see Alexis close to someone, maybe the postman at the door, and get the wrong idea again, 'next thing you know, I get a baseball bat across my head.' said Alexis, quite seriously.

'He wouldn't do that, would he?' asked John, who was on his second glass of wine, equally serious.

'He's gone very quiet wherever he is,' said Esmay's mom,' shouldn't someone go to him?'

'No, leave him to stew.' Alexis shrugged.

'He's maybe crying his eyes out. He did say he was sorry.' Some one suggested.

Young Alexis, whose real name was Orly, was still furious. He was fuming as he stood by a window looking out onto the street.

'He is so lucky it's not bad. Or I would have to break his arm.' Said Orly

Chris, the person for whom the gathering was intended, was somewhere, suffering misery for what he had done.

'Now who is having what? 'Alexis, by now sporting a shiner, rubbed his hands together, trying to rescue the situation.

No one replied, so Young Alexis picked up a tray of goodies and began to pass them around. I thought that was futile because the person for who the event was for, was alone, somewhere else in the house.

'I still think that someone should go get that young man and let him explain himself.' Esmay's Mom insisted.

'Come Essy. Let's go get him.' I took Esmay by the hand.

We went the way Chris had gone and came to a small, self-contained section of the house. Some sort of 'granny' flat?

It was very quiet there so I called out, 'Chris, is us, Elena and Esmay.'

There was no reply.

'Chris, you aright?' Esmay called.

'I'm sure you can sort things out, you and Alexis.'

I encouraged a reply but none came.

We came to a door, which had a postcard of a little boy doing a wee on it and a sign saying, 'Manneken Piss'. I guessed that it was a door to a toilet.

'You in there, Chris?' Something made me push the door slightly.

I looked in. That's when I heard a voice, similar to mine, scream out, 'Blood!' Then everything went black.

When I opened my eyes again, for a moment thought that I was dreaming. Was I experiencing some sort of replay of the scene that happened many years ago in Hackney? People were all talking at once.

'One of us should take him in a car. The ambulance won't get here until next Xmas.' some said sarcastically.

'No, they'll get here when there's an emergency.'

'Yes, and they'll be paramedics as well.'

'Still think that we should wait. Orly has already done the best he can.'

Everyone had a suggestion about what was best. While all that talking and advising was going on, Alexis was muttering to Chris.

Please...No! No! Not again. Why did you go and do something so stupid?'

'He's dead.' I heard a voice similar to my own saying.

'Don't talk stupid.'

Esmay shouted at me and brought me back to the real world.

I was not dreaming. Chris was hurt. He must have hurt himself because of what happened between him and Alexis. What if he dies? Oh my God, what if he dies? I couldn't take it. I didn't mind if I had to play second fiddle to Alexis but I could not face losing him to Mr. Death. Please God! Anyone! Don't take him away. Don't let him die.

There was blood, and lots of it. But people do live after loss of blood. I watched as young Alexis, helped by Esmay, tended to Chris who was lying so very quiet on the floor. Someone had fetched something from the linen cupboard and that was being torn and used as a bandage.

My mom was sitting on the floor next to me trying to reassure me.

'He be aright once they get him to hospital.' She said.

'Where's that damn ambulance, eh?'

I had never heard Alexis use strong language before. He sounded very upset and was kneeling alongside Chris, holding his good hand. Chris's other hand was now heavily bandaged.

To me Chris looked dead. Was he so sorry, that he would rather die than break up with Alexis? If his feelings were that strong what right had I to even think about him? Why don't I just make up with Esmay Miss-love-no-one and leave Chris in peace; if he lives that is! He had such a sad look on his poor face, and he was shivering, even with a cover placed over him.

'I'm calling the private Health Centre.'

Alexis rose angrily from the floor and spoke to his brother in their own language.

'In fact, we'll drive him there ourselves.' said John.

'Wait! Wait, he's coming round.' someone observed.

'No he's not, he's having a fit.'

'He's fitting alright; I knew we should have rushed the lad to the hospital by car.'

'It's shock. There is always shock after a trauma like that.'

'I still think that we should take him in ourselves. National Health? You could be dead by the time they get to you.'

Chris's body was shaking quite violently and we all stood by feeling helpless. I felt the tears running down my face but could not stop them, not even when John gave me a strange look. I couldn't bear to see Chris's body rocking and shaking.

'I'll get them to hurry. I know what I must tell them.' young Alexis said.

It was Esmay's mom who frowned then said, 'Wait a moment. That's no fit.'

She stepped forward to kneel by Chris and began to talk strangely to him, stroking his shaking body.

'Get me a glass of water. A plain glass, please.' she asked.

'Don't give him water, he'll choke.' someone shouted.

'Lift this head up.'

No, leave him flat.'

'Esmay, go get me some cold water girl. You know what I want.' demanded Esmay's mom.

Esmay went straight away.

I pleaded, 'Please don't die on us, Chrissie, please don't...'

'It'll be alright, whoever you are, everything will be alright,' continued Esmay's mum in that softly spoken voice.

We all looked on bewildered at the event which was supposed to have been a happy occasion but had gone so terribly wrong.

Esmay returned with a glass of water and it soon became obvious that her mom had no intention of giving Chris a drink. Instead she sprinkled a few drops of water on the floor by the side of Chris's head. She began to mutter strangely, sometimes in a deep dialect, which I could not understand then in English, though none of what she was saying made much sense.

'Don't be so angry. This young man is part of us now. He is the love of one who is part of us. The one who was brought up by us. Hush...'

Suddenly, all the lights went out at once. There was a unified gasp of 'OOH'!

'Them fuses can't all go at the same time.' I heard Esmay say.

'Candles, where do you keep them?' someone asked Alexis.

'I do not have any candles. I have never needed them in this house.' replied Alexis.

'You must have, don't you have candlelit dinners?'

'Oh! Those candles!' Alexis said, in what sounded like a silly voice.

'Damn, where is your fuse box?' a voice came from the dark.

Suddenly, there was the noise of loud banging from somewhere. I screamed out loud.

'It's only the door! Must be the ambulance at last!' John said.

Some guests stumbled over each other's legs to get to the door, leaving Esmay's mom, Esmay and myself, to stay with Chris and Alexis.

'He'll be alright, now,' Esmay's mom reassured us, 'they'll look after his hand and arm. He'll be fine but for the scars.'

The lights came on again as suddenly as they had gone out. The ambulance had arrived and with it, two paramedics.

'Sorry, we went to Orchid Road.' said one of the two paramedics.

'What on earth was going on in the dark?' asked the second.

The first one, who was younger, said to Chris, 'And what happened to you then?'

'Well, he was upset and hurt himself.' Alexis said.

'And you are?' enquired the other paramedic in a suspicious tone of voice.

'Alexis Sylvere, Dr Alexis Sylvere.'

'Doctor?'

'Of Philosophy. My brother is the medical student.'

'I am Bashier. What's your name?'

'Mr Newman, Chris Newman.' Alexis replied.

'Let the lad speak for himself, please.'

'You were partying in the dark then?'

The older paramedic looked strangely at Esmay's mom as if accusing her of something.

'Are we going to get this young man some medical attention or stand here answering questions?' John, Alexis's best friend demanded angrily.

'We have to establish what's wrong before we can move him sir.' the younger man pointed out.

'He taken something or what?' asked the older man, obviously suspicious of the circumstances.

'Such as may I ask?' Alexis responded angrily.

'Chris, you in pain?' The younger man asked.

Idiot! I thought. I was sure that the older man was asking if Chris took drugs. And us all looking like a mixed group of friends and in the dark; we must've been doing something fishy.

The way he looked at Esmay's mom, bet he's thinking she did a bit of voodoo. Racist! Why Esmay's mom got that look and not my mom? Of course not! My mom too pale skinned to be thought of as a voodooist, while Esmay's dark indigo skin, well, she must be a voodooist. Stupid stereotyping.

Finally, they got Chris to the ambulance and Alexis reassured his neighbours, who bye now had gathered around the entrance to his house.

'Graduation day celebration got out of hand a bit?' The younger Medic retorted.

'Yes, we've all had them, haven't we?'

John made light of the situation while we all followed Chris to the ambulance.

I lied to get myself into the ambulance. I said that I was the patient's half sister. I didn't mean to tell a white lie. The words simply sprang out of my mouth as I watched Chris being put into the back. The older paramedic said that Alexis was also needed. And that he could only take one other person. The others could follow by car.

Orly wanted to be the one to get in but my lie made him give me a strange frown, then he gave way for me to step in with Chris and Alexis to the hospital.

In the ambulance, the younger paramedic came to sit with us at the back while the older man drove us on our way with sirens blaring. The younger Paramedic told us that though my brother had a lost of blood he should be fine once he got attention. He was a healthy young man; he shouldn't have trouble making up the lost blood.

At the hospital, Chris was rushed immediately to the emergency treatment rooms with Alexis in tow. I tried to go along with them but a nurse stopped me. She told me to take a seat and that I would be called a little later.

Oh, no! It suddenly occurred to me. What if they asked me for Chris's details? After all, I had said he was my brother? Just then the other guests arrived. First Orly, he came in with John and the barman, followed by Esmay, Mom, and Kevin, with Esmay's Mom at the back as she had had to park the car.

We had what seemed like a long wait before Alexis eventually appeared. It was obvious that he had had his eye seen to while they were attending to Chris.

'How is he?' we all asked in unison.

'He cut a tendon on one of the fingers on his right hand.' Alexis informed us.

'Oh no!' I was horrified. 'He'll lose a finger.'

'No, it will not be lost. We fly him to Paris tonight.' Orly then went on to explain that Chris could be flown to Paris that night and that Alexis could arrange everything.

'That will not be necessary.' Alexis said, shaking his head from side to side.

'Can we see him?' I enquired.

Alexis went back to ask if we could. He quickly returned to say that we could, but only two at time. Don't get him talking and only for a brief moment.

Chris was sedated. Orly and I were the first by Chris's bedside. He wasn't in a proper ward but some sort of side room. I held Chris's good hand. He looked so very ill. Orly read my thoughts. He said softly, 'He was given something for the pain and to make him sleep.'

'Get well soon. We all love you and we're all here for you.'

Those words just came out; I had no control over them.

Alexis had permission to stay the night. He thanked the rest of us for our support but said we should go now. He would keep us posted. Orly was to take care of the house. He was to make sure that the alarm was on when he went to bed or left the house. Alexis spoke in English for our benefit.

The night that Chris was in the hospital was very bad for me. I had two worries; one being about Chris's welfare, the other was that Mom would come to suspect that my feelings for Chris were more than just being mates at college. How would she react? She must realise by now or at least suspect what the relationship between Chris and Alexis was.

What a disastrous end to a day that started with such happiness, fanfare, dance and music.

All that secret planning for Chris's event, the event that I was sure would've brought Chris out to Alexis's close friends and his young brother. All the preparation that must have gone into it! The food alone could have fed a large family. What could Chris have seen that made him go for Alexis? True, Alexis had insisted that it was an accident and so did Chris, but somehow we all knew that the two had had a fight. And that small cut under Alexis's eye was probably from the diamond ring he had placed on Chris's finger when they spent their first weekend together. Now Chris was laying there, his own blood spilt. Was their relationship going to be based on blood spilling?

I hardly slept, my thoughts ran amok, going from one thing to another. Could it have been some sort of blood spilling ceremony? If it was, where did I fit in, after all, I was still intact where blood spilling was concerned within the realms of sex and love? Actually, there was something on telly about people who harm themselves called cutters. Apparently, they cut only to punish, not to take their own life. How can loved ones prevent it? The first thing I'd do when I started at the library would be to see if there were any books about this problem and how family and friends can help. There must be stuff on the subject, if so they should have them on the library shelves. Another thing I'd like to look up but must be careful about that one. Was my thinking my individual fantasy, or are there others like me? People who fancy someone like mad even though they knew what he was? Was there such a thing as platonic love? Got to be careful though, not to start asking those questions or be caught looking them up on the web. I'll be under suspicion as to why I wanted to know all those things. No, I must keep my trap shut, that's all. That's bloody all! I turned and twisted in bed unable to fall asleep.

The day after the tragic event was horrible for me. Mom noticed that I was walking around in my dressing gown like a zombie. I was feeling extremely tired and had a splitting headache because I had not slept after such a along day. At nine o'clock, I could not stop myself phoning the hospital. After the phone kept ringing for at least ten minutes there was a message. It was the usual 'press 1 for this', then 2 for that, then '3 for the other, and then it turned out to be the wrong number anyway. Another recorded message said, 'For information about a patient try the individual ward or unit!'

In the end I gave up on the hospital and tried Alexis's mobile. It was switched off.

I made myself find things to do around the house; dusting and polishing, shining the cooking pans which were beginning to get black from Kevin's cooking or rather his burning. I even washed my black knickers, which were piling up because they could not be washed with other non-black clothes. I then tried Alexis again. There was no reply until after midnight when I tried again and he replied.

'What is happening, I tried several time to get information but your phone was turned off or something?'

'I am sorry. All mobiles have to be turned off when inside the hospital and I did not want to leave his bed side.'

'How is he?' I asked sadly, feeling that I was an outsider.

'He is doing quite well actually. We were asked all sorts of questions. I had to fill in some forms for him because he had things done to his right hand. And like many of us, being right-handed, he cannot use his left hand very well. Anyway, main thing is, I am trying to get them to let him go home to recover.'

'Home? He can't look after himself, he's on his own!'

'Hmm… not any more. Anyway, contact Orly for the latest. I must go back in now. He will begin to think that I have gone away and left him.'

'Keep me posted…please.' I pleaded.

'I will.' And the line went dead.

It was late afternoon that the message from young Alexis came. I had dozed off after working myself flat out like a demented person doing the housework. The shrill ring tone of my mobile woke me up.

'What's happened?' I asked.

'Chris is allowed to come home this afternoon. We are going to collect them. He sees one more official to collect his medication and then out he comes. *Bien* eh?'

Young Alexis sounded excited.

'Thanks for letting me know. I'll see him when he gets better and comes back to college.'

I must have sounded sad because young Alexis invited Esmay and me along.

'No, you <u>and</u> Esmay, she can come.'

He actually said Esme which some people said was the correct way to say it.

'You don't mind if we come to see him home then?'

'Of course not. You are his, how you say, his mates from college?'

'Yes, we are his mates.'

Esmay and I arrived at the hospital in time to see at least two carloads of people.

They had all come to help take Chris and Alexis home, that was, to the 'Orchid'. Chris was in clean clothing and so was Alexis. The two sat in the back of the car driven by Alexis's friend, John with his barman friend next to him. Esmay and I got into the back seat of the second car, which was driven by one of the members of staff from college, who was at the event the evening before. Sitting beside her was young Alexis. We were soon on our way to Riverside Village.

As we drove along I could not help wondering whether Chris was well enough to be taken home. Of course, it was clear that Alexis had an abundance of friends who supported him, but they all had to go to work. Who would look after Chris when Alexis was away all day at the college? Perhaps that's where I could come in. I could delay my start at the library for a couple of weeks. I visualised myself nursing Chris and then we arrived at number 7 Orchid Place.

We all went indoors and young Alexis, obviously now in charge, offered drinks to welcome Chris home. He also said he'd made real French onion soup and had bought baguettes. But the friends that had brought us declined, saying that they had to get back but they would call the next day. Esmay and I wanted to leave as well and catch a train if someone could drop us off at the nearest train station. However, young Alexis insisted that we stay and keep him company. Big brother would get us a taxi home when we were ready. Big brother would not want us two pretty Mademoiselles travelling on trains late at night. We accepted the invitation.

First, we gathered around the kitchen table and fed ourselves on French onion soup with baguette. It was noticeable, the loving care with which Alexis fed Chris, who wanted to feed himself but could not use his left hand very well. And the right was so heavily bandage that it resembled the hand of an Egyptian mummy. Esmay and I said no thanks to the garlic bread because it would make our breath smell. After our feast of soup and bread, Chris sat up for a short while but looked so tired that Alexis took him to rest in the large room. We watched them leave.

'All that care,' Esmay of course had to comment, 'wish we all had someone to care like that for us.'

'You and Elena got each other.' young Alexis pointed out as he began to clear the table.

I helped with rinsing dishes and cutlery before placing them in the dishwasher. While we worked, Esmay was standing idly by the kitchen window and admiring the garden. At least, so it appeared, but I knew her better than that. She was weighing up the situation. Sure enough, when we went back to the room that I suspected was the real dining room, her thoughts came out. It started with something I said.

'What's going to happen? Alexis has got to go to work.' I heard my voice saying, as though it had a life of its own.

'Oh, our Elena wants to stay and nurse the patient.' she said sarcastically.

'That is very kind of you Elena. But if big brother got to work, he'll bring somebody in to care for his young man.' said young Alexis, equally sarcastically, which seemed to put Esmay in her place.

'I'm sure Alexis will. You have to excuse Esmay, she means well.'

'Don't you mind Esmay,' he shrugged, 'big brother has already arranged for Chris to register with the Estuary Health Centre?'

'Oh! We better hit the road now.' said Esmay.

'No you stay and talk a while. Tell me how you work at English university. Many pretty girls, eh?'

Deep down I felt the need to stay, anyway. What if Chris is in pain during the night? I was glad that Esmay agreed that we could stay a bit longer but we must let our moms know where we were, even though Esmay no longer lived at home. I had my suspicions that Esmay wanted to stay for a reason different to mine. She wanted to keep an eye on me and analyse the situation. I was secretly sure that she was wondering, as I was, if Orly was aware of my feelings for Chris. Orly came over; during the short time we had known him, as probably more streetwise than his big brother.

We chatted about nothing in particular. Suddenly, young Alexis suggested, 'What about cinema? I love the English cinema. How you say it in my mother language eh! *me gusto muchés.*'

He said it in the funny way of talking that he put on sometimes. But I was sure that he spoke Spanish as well as he did English.

'Let's check the journal.' he said, picking up one of the newspapers.

'That's not a journal, that's a newspaper.' Esmay laughed.

Once more she looked foolish when young Alexis said, 'We French much stupid, we say *journal*, you say newspaper, *Mon mère*, she always says *périodique.*'

We found a cheap show among those listed, '£5 for students' it said. An International Film Theatre was showcasing experimental short films over two weeks. We decided to check that one out. We agreed that Alexis and Chris would prefer to be left alone for a couple of hours. Young Alexis went to fetch his jacket, and came back putting a wad of notes in his wallet.

'Big brother gave us money for film and for taxis. He never let anyone drive his car. Horrible man my big brother is!'

'Hi, you take money from your brother!'

I was horrified.

'We pay for ourselves. I have £10 for me and Elena.'

'No, is OK. I borrow from big brother. I pay back later. He has got plenty anyway. Our *grand-mère*, she gives him everything and I borrow from him.' He said with such a broad grin that told me that he never pays back anything.

'You sound like a spoilt brat.' said Esmay, as we all walked out the door.

'Brat, what is brat?' Young Alexis was in a jovial mood.

In an almost childish humour he told us a little of Alexis being the lucky one.

Alexis was not only the first-born once, but twice, in addition, he was a first-born boy. He was the first-born boy of his parents, and the first-born boy of his grandparents. And for the Sylvere's that meant a great deal. A word of warning rang in my ears. Apparently, there existed a Sylvere network, a sort of dynasty I suspected.

'If someone makes one Sylvere happy, all Sylvere's are happy, and that person will be happy also. But anyone mess up one Sylvere will be much unhappy.' He sounded very serious.

Of course, it could've been my imagination but I felt that the information being given was also meant as a warning to me. If that was the case, then young Alexis suspected that I had feelings for Chris and how hurt Alexis would be if I were to come between them.

The film, dealing with sexism in a Community in a village in India, was most enjoyable. There was beautiful scenery and Indian music, which Young Alexis seemed to enjoy immensely. After the sixty-minute film we went to the Cinema cafe where young Alexis burnt his tongue with a hot curry. For every two or three spoons of rice and curry, he had to take a drink of the iced water provided on the tables. People nearby first laughed then felt sorry for him. He was advised that the more water he drank the more his tongue will burn. He should eat some plain rice instead. We ordered a bowl of plain rice for us, which helped. It was already late into the evening when we left the café.

It was Orly's idea that we bus it both ways and keep the taxi money to use in the cafe. He said he remembered the stop we took a bus from and knew how to get back. Anyway, he had seen the bus stop more than once every time they had driven past. But, after we walked a while, Esmay had to ask, 'Orly, you sure you know where that bus stop is?'

'Of course I am sure. It was here near those funny looking trees.'

'Orly, there are thousands of trees like those in England.' said Esmay, pointing to some weeping willow trees across the poorly lit road.

'The local council must have moved it!'

I was laughing and crying at the same time.

Finally, we got to a stop. After a short wait the bus came. We sat down happily, only to find out after a while that it was going in the opposite direction to the Riverside Village. Orly insisted that we stay on the bus until the last stop then come back with it. The driver overheard us and advised that we get off at the next stop, cross the green to another bus stop where we could get the 101A which goes up past the Riverside Village. We had taken the 101B going away from the Village.

'Why you not tell us?'

Orly then said something in French which the driver appeared to understand. He responded with, 'And the same to you mate! Its them frogs you lot eat…gets in your brains.'

'You lot, you come my country, I feeds you lots frog-curry, you skinny English man!'

Orly put on his phoney English that he was so good at.

'He'll give you a big frog in a minute.' Esmay joked.

Laughter all round, except from the driver who was shaking his head from side to side.

'Foreign students!' He muttered with a sneer.

We stood up ready to get off but from the IN doors rather than the OUT exit of the single-decker bus. We waved to the driver with an *Adiós* and *Bonsoir*.

'You keep away from our English beer, got it?' he shouted after us.

We laughed our way back to the Orchid. By the time we finally got there it was after midnight. We tiptoed in only to find that Alexis had waited up. He had put Chris to bed, given him his medication, and then waited for us to return safely. I felt guilty. He must have been worried sick about Chris and there we were, out enjoying ourselves, laughing as if nothing had happened.

'I'm so sorry, we got lost getting back.' I said, apologetically.

Young Alexis apologised in French. He probably repeated the joke of us going the wrong way.

'Your mother rang. You have not been home since early afternoon!'

'Oh! I did tell her that I'd be coming here with Esmay after the hospital.'

'It's all right. I explained that my brother took you two to the local cinema. Should you get back late I will keep you here for a 'sleepover'.'

I rang my mom, though it was late, because I knew that she would sit down stairs until she heard from me. I assured her that we were safe and that there was lots of spare space for guests. Alexis took the phone from me and told Mom that we were in safe hands. His brother was leaving and wanted us to show him where young people go. Alexis then went and set the alarms, which assured that no one could enter now without the alarm going off. And it also sent an alarm to the security gate as well as the police.

We were put in the extension side of the building which Esmay said was called a 'granny flat', she had seen houses advertising on the 'for sale' window and saying that there was a 'Granny Flat' with the house. It could also be used for Alexis's family coming to stay from overseas. I was pleased that there were two single beds instead of one double. I took one bed and Esmay took the other.

Next morning, I was woken by the sound of voices, movement and a strong smell of coffee. Everyone else was already up and about. Orly was preparing a continental breakfast.

'Good morning everyone.'

I heard a weak voice.

'What you think that you are doing out of bed?' Alexis rebuked.

'That's right; you should still be in bed.' I said but pleased that I was there when he got up the second day after his ordeal.

'I'm no invalid, please.' Chris protested.

'Invalid or not, back to bed with you!' said Alexis in a manly voice, 'we will bring you your breakfast.'

'But…'

'No buts. Orly will prepare a tray. Someone will bring it up, please.' He ushered Chris away.

'I'll take it.'

I wanted to see upstairs and perhaps the bedroom that Alexis shared with Chris. I took the tray from Alexis.

When I got there a strange feeling came over me. The room was large and smartly furnished, with a large bed, in which Chris was half sat like he was a prince or demigod being worshipped. My mind began to think erotically but painfully. Was this where it all took place that weekend after the Jazz event? A bedside table sat near to the bed.

Alexis apologised and said that he would get a bed-tray.

'No,' Chris interrupted. 'Please don't try to make me an invalid.'

He turned sideways and tried to pick up the cup of coffee using his left hand, but he could not hold it.

'I will use my left hand even if it kills me.'

The frustration in his voice was obvious.

'You will darling but for now, let me help.'

With a heavy heart I went back downstairs and found Esmay and Orly chatting happily.

Esmay was saying, 'Yes, we will come over for a weekend.'

'We! Who! And going where?'

'Our friend Orly has invited us over to Provence. It's in France, in case you didn't know.'

I ignored Esmay's sarcastic remark.

12

The days following the Chris incident were difficult ones for me. I could not get him out my head. Sometimes I only wondered how he felt, was he getting better and things like that. Sometime I cursed myself for going to the cinema and enjoying myself while he was resting, sedated, perhaps, to stop him feeling pain. During those days I rang in the morning and in the early evening but each time it was Alexis that answered and reported on Chris. He was doing well but slept a lot. Alexis's own GP had already visited him. It emerged that the reason why Alexis was anxious to take Chris home so soon was a concern based on reports of people going into hospital with one illness and coming out with either two more or even ending up in a coffin. In any case, the Health Centre near the village, though privately run, did take National Health patients. Alexis had arranged with the hospital for Chris to be registered with Alexis's GP at the centre.

Once, I phoned at midday, because secretly, and without shame, I was trying to find out if Chris was ever left all alone in the house. A woman answered. I was careful to ask for Dr Sylvere, not Alexis, and lied that I was to be his MA student. The woman said Dr Sylvere was not available but I could leave my name and number. I picked up courage and asked if Mr Newman was there, he was going to work with me on my project.

'There is no one else available, please leave your name and number!' came the response, the woman sounded agitated by then.

I hung up, knowing that I had no choice but to wallow in my own misery. Was Alexis trying to keep Chris from me? If so, why? Or could it be that he wanted Chris to rest and not be pestered by phone calls. They could have gone to the hospital? Shall I ring again; maybe Chris had taken a turn for the worse? Nah! You would be stalking Chris if you kept phoning. Christ, Chris, what can I do? Who can I talk to? Who can help? Maybe I should see a psychiatrist. Blast, why the hell can't I love a man. Oh my God! Not a man! I couldn't bear having a man on top of me, perhaps stinking of fags or stale ale, no thank you very much! But what is Chris, what is he then? He is different. He is more like me in a way. Wouldn't it be nice if some magic fairy could turn Esmay into

Chris, or Chris into Esmay? God! No! Cold Esmay and an entity herself, no thanks magic fairy. Not a single word of affection out her mouth. No, good fairy godmother, don't change my Chris into Esmay, please.

I thought of jumping on a bus, then a train to the Riverside village, but was unsure if I should turn up uninvited at number 7 Orchid Place. I tried, but failed, to get Esmay to come along. At least then there would be two of us. She was very rude about it. She shouted at me on the line and said that I wanted to use her as a smoke screen.

She barked, 'You want the man, go get him. You're becoming a bore with this Chris thing. Go get your man, and stop going round in circles, Yes, No, Yes, No. Go get him for Christ sake and if Alexis gets hurt that's his blinking business.' She slammed the phone down on me.

'You cow! Don't you worry? This is the end between you and me.' I muttered onto the line now gone dead.

My Mom tried to help but ended up saying the wrong thing. She said that I shouldn't worry so much about my college friend, 'that young man has fallen, not exactly into a gold mine, but well, let's face it, he is into a good thing there.'

'You saying that Chris's relationship with Alexis is for material things?' I asked angrily.

'Well...' Mom shrugged.' That Dr man is in a position to make a difference.'

'That's horrible! If that's how you see Chris.'

I sighed. Why can't people believe that there can be true love without any material gain? I want nothing from Chris and have nothing to give him, yet I love him and hope that he feels something for me, even if I have to play second fiddle.

Some comic relief came from Anthony nearly three weeks after the graduation day events. I had forgotten all about the Anthony saga by then. That Sunday, he had turned up late with a female about 18 years old or so. Anthony introduced her as Nathalie, a friend from college. The two were in the park nearby and he had been telling her how good Mom and her family were to him so he brought her along and hoped that Mom didn't mind.

What a clumsy lie! Even Mom, who was not exactly street-wise, would realise that the poor girl was being used. Me, jealous over Anthony? What a laugh.

'Hello, I'm Elena.'

I shook hands with her, thinking that she was pretty and most suitable for being a princess in a golden cage. She had blue eyes and, though her hair was not naturally blond, she was white. But what if we are not dealing here with a trip to a golden cage but to a British Passport? But still, I mustn't be so suspicious. I should give people the benefit of the doubt until I can prove otherwise. Wasn't I angry when Mom was suspicious about Chris with Alexis?

Mom welcomed the two guests as she always did. She offered snacks and soft drinks. Lunchtime was over so it was bits of cold chicken, slices of bread and Jamaican ginger cake. While we ate, Anthony told Nathalie about my exam success then went on about his father's business.

'What about you Nathalie, what are you reading?'

I changed the subject because I was sure that poor Nathalie must be bored hearing about Anthony's successful family.

'All sorts, but I like romances best.' She replied, looking with glittering eyes at Anthony.

Poor you, I thought, that's the jargon used in university circles darling. When someone asks you what you are reading, they mean 'what are you studying', for example, history, law, or whatever. Mind you I'd never heard anyone say I'm reading Business Studies. I kept my thoughts to myself.

I carried on with small talk at the same time admiring Nathalie's hairstyle. I told her about the Hair Centre of my friend's auntie where I sometimes got mine done. While talking nonsense to Nathalie my thoughts wandered. I was sure that Nathalie was not stupid. She could sense that there was something about Anthony and me like I was his 'ex'. After about two hours or so, Anthony announced that they had to leave. He wanted to take Nathalie to meet another family who had befriended him in London. The pair said their goodbyes and I followed them to the front door.

At the door I kissed both of them on the cheek and said, 'I am happy for you both. Perhaps we could go out as a foursome when you two settle down.'

Nathalie's eyes lit up when she smiled and she said, 'that would be great, wouldn't it Tony?'

'Yes, sure.' said poor Anthony.

When I returned inside, Mom was clearing up the glasses and saucers. 'You got a nasty streak in you. You know he trying the jealousy tactic.'

'Oh, that's what it was?' I replied as innocently as I could.

Kevin joined in.' You knew alright and Anthony knew that you knew.'

'Actually, I'm happy he found someone. He is good looking and a very decent young man.'

After that Anthony saga I waited and walked around with a heavy heart.

Another week went by when suddenly Chris's voice came over the phone. I had given The Orchid a ring and left a message on the answering machine. I said that we were only enquiring if Chris was getting on all right. I had little hope of getting a reply from him. When he did I could not hide my delight at hearing his voice.

'It's Chrissie, Mom!' I shouted, though my Mom was standing close by.

'*Hola! Como estas*?' I greeted him.

'Bien, pero tengo pocos problemas con los dedos a me mano derecha.'

'Well done!' I praised his attempt, though I had often told him not to take one word at time.

'I been reading a lot, when not sleeping.'

'Good! I tried many time to get you on the phone...'

'I heard.' he interrupted, 'Alexis wanted me to rest. He took my mobile away. And that Mrs Moor, she wouldn't let me near the house phones. Anyway, I'm okay now, been to the Clinic today.'

'And? What did they say?'

'That I was making a miraculous recovery. The bandage gone now but my right hand and left arm look terrible. The cuts weren't deep but the scars long and ugly. I'll never be able to wear short sleeves ever again. Oh! Why the hell I gone and do something so stupid.' he moaned.

'Hey! Hey! Come on baby, its early days.' I tried to soothe him because his voice had gone sad. 'Take a deep breath. And don't worry, you'll be fine.'

'Sorry I come moaning to you. I messed things up. Not for me, I don't care about me, but for Alexis.'

'Come now, none of that sadness. It's not like you to give up.'

'Alexis's been preparing me, I know he was. He wanted me to be ready to take to meet his friends. He wanted a nice, smartly dressed young man with his hair done and a diamond on his finger, on his arm, to meet his friends. They'll call that young man 'scar-hand' behind Alexis's back.'

'Scar what?'

'You know? There was a gangster called scarface, I believe. Me, I'm scarhand.'

After we both stopped laughing at what was really a serious matter of people harming themselves, I suggested we met and he could fill me in. At first I suggested I went up on the Sunday to the Orchid, but he said that I'd better not. On Sundays, he and Alexis always spent the day quietly at home or they would probably drive around a bit. I then suggested one weekday. We could meet at the train station nearby. We could sit in the coffee bar and talk. Again he declined and I got the message. He wanted to be left alone with his Alexis, while I was being evil in suggesting a meeting behind Alexis's back. Chris put it that he wanted to get better first. He was still getting bouts of depression, especially when Alexis was away, even though Mrs Moor was always at the house when Alexis was out. That Mrs Moor, he explained, used to be the cleaner who came in twice a week for few hours, but now there was some other arrangement, he believed. Now Mrs Moor did more than just the dusting. He assured me that we would meet as soon as he returned from a weeks break in Somerset where Alexis was taking him. John, who I had met at the party, had a cottage high up in a small mountain village. Friends often went there to recoup or for their honeymoon. Alexis said that it was beautiful place, when you stood by the back window you could see right across to Wales.

'I'll have a rest, read a bit, and listen to a bit of music and things.' he concluded.

Oh Yeah? Probably spending most of your time in bed or in each other's arms. Aloud I wished him luck.

'Well, have a good rest or drive around. We'll meet for *tapas* when you get back.'

'Thanks, and tell Esmay she's not to worry about me. Us three will meet for *tapas* soon.'

'I will.' I lied once more.

For a moment I felt ashamed of myself. I was becoming a liar and a good one at that. Blind idiot, I want you, not Esmay! She could be a friend that's all. Intimate relations with a woman, not for me, with all due respect to others for whom it is.

'*Adiós, y un beso.*' He sounded a little more cheerful.

'Adiós, un abrazo y un beso.'

We both hung up and I promised to throw myself into my work.

Work was very challenging but interesting. My direct line manager was a young woman who referred to herself as a third generation Guyanese. We had something in common, so she reckoned, though I was only a second generation and only from part Guyanese parentage. She said that she had nothing good to say about Venezuelan people, no offence to my mother she apologised. At least my mother had lived for some years in Guyana which made her different. My line manager had apparently read newspaper reports on how Venezuela wanted to grab a large part of Guyana's land. By the time them Suriname hooligans also grabbed land on the other side of Guyana, the people there would be left with only a strip of land. But let them try! My line manager went on to state that she had no interest in politics. Her background was visual arts, but she became a librarian and hoped to get more Arts books and a variety of newspapers, including non-English ones, in the library. She did not disagree with the big boss who was director of the Library service for the South East and dropped in whenever he felt like it. He wanted more computers and E-books, at the same time she wanted more books, which people can actually see and touch. What about people who are computer illiterate; shouldn't they have books as well?

On and on my manager went like a tape on repeat. If she had the power, she pointed out; she'd have a mobile library, not only for that dreadful council estate not far away but also across the whole of the south east, like they had for dentistry and opticians in parts of Africa. She went further, but by then I had lost track of what she was saying, though I was sure that she was a nice caring women. I was thinking that I'd have to be prepared to work with her as a professional but one with ill feelings about her family's Venezuela neighbours. I was relieved when that first working lunch with my line manager was over. Before we parted for the day she reminded me, yet again, to write down any vision or plans I wanted to put forward and she'd do the rest.

I got home that day and Mom asked how I'd got on so far. First, I told her about lunch with my line manager and her thoughts about Venezuela. It was a mistake. Mom saw red. She told me her thoughts about Guyana and told the whole story of the thieving Guyanese people coming over to Venezuela. While I helped prepare our supper, Mom gave me at least two examples of the thieving Guyanese. Many of them who went over to Venezuela were murderers on the run from their own police.

'And they shoot you dead; I read about it somewhere that they shoot you if they caught you steeling fish in Guyana waters.' I said light-heartedly.

'Is the lord's fish, not some Guyanese soldier's?'

Mom was seriously annoyed.

'What sort of person kill someone over a fish?' Kevin asked.

'Shoot 'em back, that's what I say!'

I was amused at the negative views held on both sides. In fact, my Mom, who often claimed to be a 'live-and-let-live' type of person, not interested in politics, held the same views as my line manager, who also claimed to be non-political.

After we had our evening meal as a family and were relaxing, I shared the ideas I had for my job in the library with Mom. I said how I could combine it, to save me doing two projects, with my study at college. Mom did not understand it all but gave me her blessing and said to go for it.

I spent the time waiting for Chris to return, writing down my vision and suggested outline. Under contents, I listed the mobile library for bilingual books. That would help those non-English speakers to learn or improve their command of English and speakers of English as their first language who are learning another language would be able to improve on the use of that other language. I braced myself for condemnation for suggesting that the 'romance' shelves should include same-sex romances and our 'religious' section should include books not only about Christianity, but also Islam, Judaism, and Buddhism. In other words 'The World's Religions', which should include Voodoo, and other Caribbean and South American religions as described by Ninian Smart.

Mom threw her hands up in despair.'

Don't, Lena! You be thrown out the library job and the college. Is that what you want? Don't do it Lena, don't.'

'And why not? I was asked to present my vision.'

Of course, I couldn't tell Mom about other ideas I had but wouldn't dare put it in my vision for progress in the library. Instead, I told my Mom that it was inevitable that the library work would be linked with my college project and that I had no intention of spending my whole life stamping and handing out books to people.

Chris returned from Somerset and we talked on the phone a couple of times. It was the end of August by the time he came to college and we met up. Alexis had driven him in and for a moment I feared that Alexis would sit with us two after he saw that Esmay was not present. Luckily he did not. He left us both alone and Chris filled me in with most of what had been happening. He did have a fabulous week in Somerset.

'Ah! estupendo!' he declared, 'If it wasn't for me damn hand.'

I looked at his right hand. It did look healed but was heavily scarred. The knuckles, for one thing, but also inside his palm had been cut. He had grabbed a piece of glass from the mirror he'd smashed with his fist. The glass had slashed across his fingers, especially his little finger. I had to be honest with him.

'It does look bad now but it will get better. Alexis bound to know of any possibility of the scars being removed or disguised or something. The medical profession does amazing things these days, especially if you can pay.'

'Maybe you're right. Anyway what about you? I been bursting your eardrums with my story.'

'Not much to tell. Library work is interesting and challenging. At least I wasn't told off about my presentation of my vision for advancement in the library.'

After a while, we went for a stroll along the lane and continued chatting. First we talked about my library job and preparation for my Masters, then about Chris's own job and planned studies. He was currently on sick leave until the middle of September when he went for an assessment. If he had made good progress, his doctor would sign him off as fit to resume work. Alexis wanted him to study full time and get a job later but he preferred to earn a bit of money and pay his way. But how much would he be able to do with that hand of his? For a moment he returned to his depressed state. He'd be wearing only long-sleeved shirts in order to cover those scars on his left arm. But he couldn't hide the palm of his right hand.

'Nosy parker people will ask questions.'

That was when I came up with another of my little lies.

'If anyone asks, why not say that you were washing a glass jar and it shattered, cutting your palm.'

I tried desperately to find something to ease his discomfort, not the physical but the emotional one. I so wanted it to be possible for me to take him into my arms and 'kiss' everything better. But here, in the grounds of our college, where you only have to spit and it gets on the grape vine, I dared not.

'What about Esmay is she okay?' he said, changing the subject.

'We don't see much of each other at the moment. We're both work hard to get a bit of money together during the hols and before our post grad work.'

'Is that the only reason?'

He frowned and stopped walking to look at me.

'That and the fact that we both want to move on in our chosen direction.'

'Then you don't know that she phoned Orly?'

'No! Why the hell she do that?'

'Well, Orly did invite you two over.'

'And what did Orly do when she rang him?'

'He was away from home. Apparently he gave her his sister's number in Provence.'

'What's that blasted Esmay up to?'

'I don't know, but there will be disappointment if she tries to take up that invite on her own. The Sylvere family are serious people and will want to know what's going on.'

'I apologise for her and her stupidity. I shall have to have a word with that Ms Esmay!'

'Please, don't say nothing. Anyway, Alexis already knows. The brothers have no secrets from each other.'

'What did Alexis think of it then?'

'He said that, if at all, you should both go, not only Esmay. Any case, Orly, the big joker, always invites people to Provence when he is seldom there himself.'

'And what happens when people get there?'

'His sister's family's in-laws got space for short stay guests. Selected people go there and pay to stay. And Alexis said that Provence is one of the most beautiful areas of France.'

We wandered around campus for a while longer before going back to the Tapas Bar and had Chris's favourite, which was the Columbia fried plantains dish, then went to the reading rooms where I advised him on the books he could take home to read. There he showed particular interest in the Spanish/English bilingual romances. I explained to him the difference between a bilingual text and a parallel text.

'You becoming a first class teacher.' He commented.

'Me, a teacher? No thanks, no school kids going to drive me to the nut-house.'

Chris led me to the building that we once called the Library which was being upgraded and renamed. From the following September we were to have some fancy, but to me ridiculous, name, for any building in England, something like 'EDIFICIO INTERNACIONAL COMUNICACIÓN, UK'.

'I hope that the lifts never break down.' I teased, as we went higher and higher.

'The engineers got back up stuff that you and me know nothing about.'

He took me up to the top floor of the twelve storey concrete and glass tower, where he would be working when well enough to return to work. He pointed out that things were still being prepared. There he would be sharing with four other young members under the watchful eyes of a manager who would be returning from wherever he was being trained in all that high-tech stuff.

Chris pointed to and explained about things in a large room which he called the 'Control Room.' There, they will monitor everything we do downstairs like reading, borrowing, listening to CDs and so. To me it looked like the set of a science fiction story. There were flat-faced computers and contraptions everywhere of which I understood very little. Everything he was explaining sounded like gobbledegook, but I was proud of him, and silently wished him well and that he would soon get over the embarrassment of those scars. Even with those scars he was getting prettier day-by-day, and smart, though casually dressed, compared to that first day when he walked into my life. I was sure that Alexis could afford to take him somewhere and pay to have his hand seen too. That was one of the things Alexis had to offer which I could not. Of course, I would say it over and over again, I wouldn't want to come between them, and split them up. I'd never do that. And yet the situation was getting more confusing in my head.

All too soon, that pleasant afternoon went by and it was soon four-o-clock. Alexis would want to return home in order to beat the heavy traffic. We went to Alexis's office and I watched while Chris cleared some stuff off his desk and placed them into a container in readiness for them to be taken to the new place high up the tower block. He said that a lot of bits and pieces would be remaining in Alexis's office anyway. About four thirty, Alexis arrived.

'I've brought him back safe and sound.'

The words flew out before I could stop them. I realised too late how what I said might have sounded.

'You two had a good *charla*?' Alexis asked jovially.

Again that nasty thought. If this man was aware of my feelings for Chris he was very good at hiding it.

'*Si, charlamos muchos.*' I replied with a grin, hoping that I'd said it correctly.

After all, his mother, I had learnt, was really from the Spanish speaking Dominican republic and that only his father was from France and he himself French-Caribbean born and raised. In addition he was a linguist proper, and you don't mess with them when it comes to languages. Any case, I wandered off again, what if he knows about my feelings but had such confidence in the relation between him and Chris that he had no fear of me?

'We better make a move, darling if we are to avoid the worse of the traffic.'

Alexis indicated that he was ready to leave.

I followed them to Alexis's car, said *Adiós* and watched them drive off.

'See you mid-September.' Chris shouted from the window of the car.

Mid September came and preparation began for us who would be doing Masters Degrees .We were meeting our individual supervisor's for pep talks. Mine was a pleasant little man, who spoke English with a definite Latin-American accent though I could not place it and dared not ask. I presented what I had been doing, and what I hoped to do. He wanted to know if I had done any extra-curriculum work. I couldn't think of anything else and said that I was helping a foundation year student with his Spanish homework. It was mistake. My intended supervisor began rattling away in Spanish. I couldn't understand half of it because he spoke so fast. We both laughed. He said that if I wanted to help then I had to be at least three steps ahead of the person I was helping. It was at that stage that Chris's name came up. He will still need my help because part of his BA Communication will be in Spanish.

My supervisor to be was pleased to hear about my support for a student at a lower level than I was. He nodded and said that helping others could improve ones own progress, at least that was what I understood him to have said. When I said that my Mom was from Venezuela. His eyes lit up but he said that to learn standard Spanish, I must go to the Salamanca in the Lyon area where proper Spanish was spoken.

Aha! I thought, that's where you're from, eh? It was at that stage that he told me about the trip, which took just over 10 days, for intensive fieldwork on language and culture. It was only for those students who would be taking Spanish further and already with a good level of Spanish. Only Spanish will be spoken once we set foot in Spain. None of the people involved with us, apart from the drivers, *Amas de casas* and families, to secretaries, were allowed to speak to us in any language other than Spanish. Wow! I thought. That's going to be sheer hell. Yet a plan was already forming in my head. Of course it could be wishful thinking, his man didn't like letting him out of his sight for ten minutes let alone10 days. As for me, even if I was selected based on references, there was the cost. We would all have to pay 25 percent of the cost covering tuition in a university setting which included free use of all the state-of-the-art high-tech facilities, and our room with two meals a day. Chris would have to pay the whole of the cost. Another idea entered my head. Mm… I thought, 'high Tech' eh! Now whom do I know who would benefit? The department where Chris would be working, that's who.

My supervisor to be, advised that I let him know as soon as possible because the funds raised by the department covered only 12 post-grads, so it would be on a first come, first served basis, even with the right references. The trip would be towards the last week of October, which was half-term for schools, and reading week for Higher Ed. Institutions. I mentioned that I had to speak to my Mom and the library where I would be working four days a week during that time.

I rushed back home and told Mom. She was delighted.

'First time to a Spanish speaking country. That's a start. Later, you go Venezuela, yes? You help your people there.'

'Mom, I'm not going to be a social worker extraordinaire.'

'No, but you give them education. Maybe you set up your own school in Maracaibo Village?'

'Yeah, give them a good English education and a set of computers.' Kevin joined in with his usual brand of humour.

'Stop talking dumb. You always got to be so *tonto*?' Mom rebuked him.

'I'm not being silly Mom; we discuss these things in social studies. Our teacher says those poor people badly need food and we give them boxes full of books to show how well fed we are in London. That's why they all want to come here to...'

'Don't you have home work?' Mom interrupted.

'Yes Mom,' Kevin made to leave.

'He's a member of the family, Mom,' I pointed out, 'he should stay.'

We then discussed the matter as a family. Mom would do all she could. She would do some more overtime at work. I would need some spending money. Kevin said he'd do more around the house and he would cook proper meals not just beans on toast. Mom could work all day on Saturdays. But I had a better idea. Maybe I could get my line manager at the library to support that trip as part of my library work. In any case, I have to ask to have that time off.

When I later put the idea to my line manager she said that it was a fantastic idea. Equipment such as a digital camera would be no trouble; they even had a camcorder which no one used. She had to put it to the director but was sure he would agree. She would sell him the line that I will visit the Salamanca general library, also the university's own library. I would be returning with information useful for our library.

With the promise of help from home and from my part time work, I quickly e-mailed my supervisor. He suggested I asked the library to give me a letter of support, which could be sent to him via the internal email system. He also suggested that an independent reference from a senior person at the college would also be helpful because there would be a lot of competition for the twelve places given the funds available.

I didn't know of anyone more senior than Dr Alexis Sylvere but first I had to ask his permission. When I called his private office number I got an answering machine. I left a brief message explaining the situation and the urgency of it. I asked if I could give his name as a reference to Dr Fernandez, my supervisor-to-be.

My next discussion was with Chris. He too was delighted for me. Showing me his English literature lessons he told me that's where Shakespeare got the information for Othello. They had tried to read the extracts brought in to class by their English tutor but they 'the foundation study' lot, couldn't manage 'Shakespeare's cockney', as he called it, and kept laughing, which made the tutor angry. He went on to tell me about the North Africans who had invaded Spain in the 10th century and ruled it for three centuries, trying to force their religion on the people. Chris went on and on about all the stuff he'd been learning as background to the English classics. While he talked, I was thinking, not about all that political history stuff, but how beautiful he'd look in period costume, standing on stage performing Shakespeare, in the original language but with a cockney accent.

'Listen, what if you could go as well, on the Spain trip I mean?' I interrupted.

'What! Me? I can just about order me a meal in Spanish.'

'My mom would prefer to see me as a teacher. So why not practice on you?'

'But you hate teaching! The kids would send you mental, you said.'

'You're not a kid. Anyway, if I were to teach at all it would be post 16. They'd come to college because they wanted to, those not interested in after compulsory education would keep away.'

'Oh, I don't know, Elle. Anyway I'm not really a post grad.'

'Listen, let's meet and talk about things, okay?

'*Vale*, let's!'

'I'll have to visit my supervisor to see if he got my references and things. We can meet afterwards.' I suggested.

As soon as I hung up it struck me. Oh no! *Idiota*! He'll tell Alexis about the conversation we had on the phone and Alexis will reveal that I asked for a reference. Stupid Jackass...there goes your good reference. Why couldn't you keep your blasted mouth shut? That man would think that you want to take Chris away with you and come asking him for a reference to enable you to do so. You're insulting that man's intelligence? Serve you right if he did think you want to use him then

197

take his young man away. Serve you right! No Spanish, Salamanca or whatever, for you, stupid brainless girl.

Two days had passed and I still hadn't heard anything from my supervisor so I resigned myself to the reality that I must have blown it. I told Mom that there were perhaps too many people and I was among the ones that got left out. Mom was sad and said that if she had the money she'd pay for me to go. She was sure that some people would pay their way and go along. I pointed out that anyone can go to Spain but not anyone can go on the official trip, pay or not. I still had to be accepted. Maybe I was recommended but was at the bottom of the list. Or maybe I was not even recommended.

I should not have worried. I came home during the afternoon of the third day since I'd first discussed the matter with my supervisor and found a message on our answering machine.

I was one of the 12. I should meet with Dr Fernandez the next morning at 10am. Oh no! I was on duty at the library that morning! I began to panic. I couldn't tell Dr Fernandez, my supervisor, that I couldn't make it, therefore it had to be the library. I quickly tried to get my line manager but she had already left. I left a message saying that I could not be there because I had an urgent meeting to do with the Spanish trip. My next call was to Chris. I sent only a text message to say, 'I'm in. I'll be at college. C U after 12.

Mom came home to find me very excited.

'I'm in! I'm in!' I shouted as soon as she came through the front door. I danced around her. Kevin was also pleased for me. We hugged and danced around like two school kids. Mom rushed out and I was sure that she was going next door to tell our neighbours. Then she would tell the postman, the bin men, in fact anyone who wanted to listen about her Elena's trip. She was one of the chosen 12.

My meeting with Dr Fernandez was to discuss last minute things. There were lots of documents to read. Passport, did I have one? Oh, no! I never had to have a passport before.

It turned out, seeing that we were part of Europe, we didn't need one. Only the students not born in the UK had to produce passports or other documents. Lucky for me I was English by birth. Dr Fernandez nodded. All that I needed to show the office was my birth certificate and the college would sort things out for us; personal travel insurance was advised to cover our belongings. We did not need health insurance but should sign a document the college will get for each of us from the post office. All that discussing and going over documents nearly made me forget to ask if I could take a student, I have been helping, along. I said that I might consider teaching Spanish but to 16+. I was fibbing again of course.

To my surprise my supervisor agreed, saying that it was good idea but the student would have to pay his/her own way and that would be expensive. I explained that the student was part of the college's 'learning in the workplace scheme' hence he gets a bit of a salary. He might have to have time off, I pointed out. But he will bring back info useful for his work.

'*Vale.*' Dr Fernandez nodded.

I couldn't hide my excitement when I met with Chris later that day. His doctor had said he was well enough to do light work. In fact, the Health Centre's physio wanted him to use his hand and not keep it protected like a baby. But when I told him that my supervisor said he could come along, Chris hesitated. For one thing, he'd need approval from his head of department to be away for ten days. He'd already had a lengthy sick leave. I suggested he pointed out that he will be able to see how the university there uses its computers for the benefit of the students who were not doing computer studies or something to that effect. The trip might be useful as part of his ongoing training in communications. Chris had other concerns though.

'What about Alexis, even if my boss said yes? Alexis protects me like a mother hen. Would he agree for me to go?' Chris shook his head from side to side.

'Discuss it with him.'

'He'd be scared that something bad would happen to me.'

'Like what?'

'Like I might have a relapse, then there are them mad bulls that run down the streets. People tease them and get butted. It's been on telly.'

'But you're not going to tease any mad bulls, surely?' I chuckled.

'No, but what if one caught me in a side street and butted me in me bum!'

'Oh Chrissie. You make people laugh. I can almost see you teasing the bulls but then you're not fast enough to get away.'

'It's not funny! With my luck, someone else tease him but he goes for my bum.'

The time I waited to hear whether Chris could come along with us was sheer torture. I became almost obsessed with having Chris going with us to Spain. I'd imagine how we would walk around looking at monuments, art galleries and taking photos of cultural places. I could see him being silly, sticking out his tongue and pulling faces while he stood in front of some building, making me take a photograph of him for Alexis.

The days of September and leading into October when we were to leave were hectic ones. Mom was going over the top ordering stuff from the catalogue .She went to some shop and got me two packets of knickers. Each packet held seven knickers, all black. But they were going cheap so Mom got them. So those fourteen black knickers, together with my old ones, gave me enough underwear to last for two weeks, using at least two knickers per day. At the same time Mom was doing all the overtime she could get and working10 to 3pm on Saturdays. Kevin was very helpful. He did the dishes and cooked basic rice and greens or white cabbage stewed with bacon pieces. He even took to ironing his shirts once I had put them through the wash for him. I promised him that once I got through and began earning real money he would be next. He wouldn't have to go to no Canada, even if that Canada business wasn't only a dream in Mom's head. For my part, I prepared the usual Sunday chicken and rice and did the laundry so that Mom could rest a little. I was delighted that Anthony rarely visited us now that he had found another interest. Yet, I was not happy, but tried not to show it and must have succeeded. Then one morning when I least expected it a text came from Chris. It simply said, IT'S YES!

I kissed my mobile and texted a reply on my way to the library, DELIGHTED!

After that the days flew past. Plans finalised, we, the chosen 12, met at college, but were informed that three other people would be joining us. One was the other half of the engaged student in our midst and two were students to people on the trip, who would be teaching Spanish to young adults. Those three were paying their own way.

Suddenly that Sunday afternoon was on us and we were all at Gatwick airport with our luggage. Friends and families came to see us off. We checked in and were ready to go through to the Passengers only area. There came hugs and kisses. Mom was not the kissing type but she gave me a hug and said to look after myself then she rubbed her eyes. Kevin was there but felt that he was too grown up to be kissed in public by his big sister. He shook my hand instead. Chris didn't have parents or friends, he only had Alexis. I waited to see if Alexis would kiss Chris in public but he didn't. But the way they looked at each other was if they didn't need to kiss. But Chris went up and gave Alexis a hug.

I went up and gave Alexis a sisterly kiss on each cheek.

Alexis's words came, but barely audible. 'Take good care of him and bring him safely back to me, please.'

'Will do.' I promised thinking, if he knows, why is he allowing him to go away with me? Nah, he sees me as a big sister for Chris who had no relatives he knew of.

'And remind him to take his air sickness tablets and drink water...they're in his bag...and if he needs anything...'

'Don't worry!' I interrupted, 'he'll be fine. I'll see that he behaves himself.'

I noticed then that Chris was standing with his back to us as if he daren't look at Alexis being left behind.

After the usual long delay at the airport we were finally on the two hour flight to Barajas aeropuerto in Madrid, where we were to be met for another two hour ride, this time by special coach to Salamanca on the border side with Portugal.

At first, Chris showed signs of nervousness, especially when the 'seat belts' light came on and we began to speed down the runway. He clasped my hand tightly and muttering, 'never been on an aeroplane.'

'Nor me.' I said back.

'Ah! Once you're in the air it's just like being on a bus.' said the student sitting in the same row as us.

Soon there was loud laughter and jokes. There was talk of the those good-looking Spanish *Chicas* and *Chicos* followed by disagreement on whether the *Chicas* were prettier than the *Chicos*, then came the correction that we were long past that age group and might end up in a Spanish jail if we went around saying we were looking for pretty *Chicas* and *Chicos*. Then the reminder that we were going there to learn about Spanish language and culture, not in search of Latino lovers Bonita, *Guapo* or *Feo*. Hey, who ever seen an ugly Latino? I have, no you have not, I have...and I had a Latino boyfriend... liar! Boyfriend, Latino, English or whichever, you? Hey, careful maybe it's rude to say Latino in Spain though they say it in US where you came from, Coriander, my name is not bleeding Coriander!

We soon became noisy but all in good spirit. Chris had by then become relaxed and joined in the laughter at all sorts of ridiculous things that were being shouted across the plane.

The two-hour flight came to an end and we began our descent into Barajas aeropuerto, a gigantic complex.

A welcome party met us and led us to two mini coaches. Each bright sky blue with the golden letters inscription, 'SINDICATO DE ESTUDIANTE / SALAMANCA de LYON.'

We had arrived.

Chris took my suitcase which was heavier and I took his bag to the coaches. We were placed by name onto the two coaches depending where we were to stay. Soon we noticed that neither our driver nor the two Spanish students who came to welcome us spoke, perhaps by choice, a word of English. We got on our way at nine, Spanish time. We were too tired to do anything else but sleep all the way until the welcome student sitting by our driver called out, 'Salamanca!'

I opened my eyes and I saw the Art Work and a sign carved on what looked like a rainbow showing that we were entering our destination.

'Greeting Mother Salamanca. We come in peace.' I muttered.

'What's that?' Asked Chris, by now also awake.

'Where my Mom comes from, you greet the new territory when you enter it for the first time.' I explained.

We drove through a lively town centre for short while, and then continued for nearly two hours. Three students were dropped off somewhere. Chris and me, together with another student were taken a couple of minute's drive further. Our driver, who was in constant contact with wherever we were going to stay, spoke into his contraption. We stopped, were helped out with our luggage and led to the entrance of what looked like an upmarket tower block. A pleasant woman of about sixty met us. She at once began to fuss over us and spoke rapidly in Spanish. We smiled said *muchos gracias*, even when we didn't understand what she had said. This is going to be fun; I said with a smile, looking sideways at Chris.

13

We woke up the next morning to the sound of a Spanish radio and smell of coffee.

I noticed then that we were in a truly Catholic home; not like my own family in London. In my family we got baptised, but the only time we went to Church was for a wedding or christening. Here, in this place, which was to be our home for two weeks, there was evidence of our Ama being a good Catholic. Thing is, for me it was my own fault. I did say Catholic under religion on the form we had to fill in. I didn't want to jeopardise my chances of getting on this all paid for trip by saying, 'None' or 'Agnostic'. But what did Chris put under religion to get him placed in this house? I was sure that like me he did not attend mass, though his mother would have christened him at one time or the other.

Anyway, here we were together in one house. Chris and me, with Aneesja of course. In my room was the picture of the Virgin Mary with her baby in her arms. I frowned; because in the picture she looked a bit dark skinned and her dress different to the one of our Lady of Grace where my recovery had begun. In fact, the pictures of the Virgin Mary and baby I saw in my life were blue-eyed blonds. This one was brown, not black, but a yellowish brown and her dress made her look more like some Gypsy. Did the Spanish people pray to a different Mary asking her to intervene between them and her son Jesus? Mm! I thought, looking at her image from where I was on my back in bed. Yours is a big mystery. Your son is also the Son of God then you must have had an affair of some kind with God, his father. Or are you his stepmother? But such thoughts are heresy aren't they? Forgive me Holy mother, but you were a virgin when you gave birth. Am I getting more and more confused with these things, and why now? Maybe it's because my own life is such a mystery. Am I going mad, or am I already mad? Some women do go to bed with women; something that I'm not sure was really for me. Women do marry gay men, at least so I've noted from my web site, but usually it's to try out non-gay, my own coined phrase. I don't want to change anyone so why then do I hang on like a love sick teenager longing so much for the arms of a young man I knew was gay? I have no one I dare ask. Esmay started as my best friend, now she has ideas of her own. Pity they don't teach those things in college, unless perhaps on psychology courses. My mom should be my best psychologist but I wouldn't dare go to her with the questions that were spinning around in my head like dirty clothes in a washing machine. But did Esmay suspect something about Chris also going to Salamanca? Nah, she couldn't know that I manipulated the whole thing. Chris was a student and students do go on field trips. Some poor students got sponsorship, others pay their own way. And as Mom heard when Esmay's mom mentioned it that time, Chris would be well catered for, financially. Anyway, we're here now, Chris and me, so what happens next? True we came for Spanish language and culture history. And stupid me, never been with a man, I wouldn't have a clue how to make a move on him, even if I wanted to. Anyway, I just like to be near him. There were platonic relations, so I read. You can be friends without crawling under the bed sheet.

Chris had gone to his room that was next door to mine. I knew that he wanted to be alone to sneak a phone call to London even though we were warned that phoning from Spain was extremely expensive. I wasn't sure if that applied to mobiles as well. We had agreed to phone London only in emergencies. The idea was for us to submerse ourselves in Spanish for two weeks and cut ourselves off from any other language. But I wasn't that naive to believe that Chris wouldn't secretly contact Alexis.

After a much needed sleep, I staggered, still barely awake, out of my room to the corridor leading to the showers. In the corridor we came down the evening before there was a religious statue, one of those things you buy on stalls for tourists, standing by the telephone. Was all that religious stuff a daily routine or put there for our benefit? The women must have had details of the three students coming to live with her as a family.

After a much needed, cooling down shower, I went to the kitchen/diner to find others already dressed and waiting for me.

'Sorry, err...*Lo siento!*'

I remembered that we were not to speak anything else but Spanish while we were there.

We tucked into a huge continental breakfast. There was a variety of cheeses, juices, salami and freshly baked bread, which I later learnt, was delivered to the door the same as most of us get our newspaper in London. The early morning news blared from the radio in the background. Our 'Ama de Casa' was eating with us and occasionally pulled a face at something the speaker had said. She would shake her head and mutter in Spanish that the man speaking was stupid. On one occasion she shook her fist in the direction of the radio and said that the speaker was a lunatic.

I noted even then that Chris had an effect on the Ama. She was going to fuss over him, I was sure of that. She began to hold up items like a fork, knife, and glass and telling him the name of them in Spanish. When we were ready to rush off to class, she wrapped up a slice of cake and a pear for Chris to take for break. She told us two girls to take something for our *pausa*.

'She's got a son his age, probably.' Aneesja whispered when we were briefly left alone.

The Ama had gone to her room to put on outdoor shoes and Chris went to his to get his things.

'Chris got that effect on people. Without meaning to he makes people love him.' I whispered back.

'You better keep an eye on him then. I would if he was my man.'

I could sense the question in Aneesja's words and thought; you keep your paws off him. Go near him and you'll get your hair ripped out your scalp.

Our Ama decided to take us to class for the first day, to show us the best way. She sneered at the map we were each given. She knew a short and nicer way, about five minutes and we would be there. In reality, it took us much more than ten minutes because of Aneesja shoes. Poor Aneesja, her high heels were not made for going down cobblestones and steep hills. I became concerned, looking at poor Aneesja hobbling along on that hill, what if she fell and broke her ankle? Some people going up or down passed us and glanced in our direction with amusement. Even a street cleaner that was coming uphill on the pavement waited to let us

207

come down past him and his trolley thing. I guess the poor man was scared that Aneesja might come tumbling down on top of him.

Our college, according to our Ama's explanation, was in the old part of Salamanca. I had no doubt that it was made by the sweat of the brows of Spanish workers, who hacked into rocks under slave-like conditions for their North African masters who had invaded their country in the 12th century. I noticed, however, one positive aspect of that invasion. It was the beautiful architecture left behind by the invaders, or copied, after they had been chased out.

We finally got to a building by a monument. At the entrance we went down some steps to where it said, 'Piz Santo Domingo'. Down another dip and we came to, 'LA FACULTAD ESPAÑOL LENGUA EXTRANJERA'.

There we were for the beginning of our ten days of intensive Spanish. Four hours each morning in class. In the afternoon, after siesta, a series of culture activities to choose from was laid on. The events included visits to museums, art galleries, open air poetry reading, watching flamenco dance in Plaza Mayor, fireworks, bull fighting and of course numerous bars scattered around and an excursion outside of Salamanca. These visits were partly for fun and finding out about the Spanish cultural history .We had notes for presentations at college and to report back when we returned our own country. How will Chris cope with all of that? Did I selfishly drag him into something too big for him at present? After all it was only just over 3 months ago that he had his problem.

The test, which was to place us into groups, began. At least 80 of us, most from various parts of Europe but also from Caribbean countries and Brazil, buried our heads into, what looked like, endless sheets of papers with boxes to fill in. The flags of all the countries we came from greeting us along the walls of the hall didn't help much. Everything was explained in Spanish. Poor Chris, I could tell from the expressions on his face that he was petrified and struggling. We were told in Spanish to answer what we could and skip the rest. Did Chris really understand that instruction?

After the ordeal of the test we were taken to a room for refreshment while our test papers were being examined. When we returned I found out that as I had predicted Chris and I went in separate groups. My group was one below the top, which would be doing 5 hours instead of 4 every morning. Chris went in to the group just above the bottom. Luckily, he would be doing 4 hours a morning like the rest of us below the top group. I could see the look of concern on Chris's face as he was being taken away with about nine others. I winked at him for reassurance. We saw nothing more of each other until one-o-clock at the end of the first day because we had our break at different times. We met outside the classroom and found that our Ama had come to fetch us, to make sure that we knew how to get back and could use the front door key.

Back at the house we had a huge lunch laid out; there was so much of it that we each said we would keep some for dinner. We had booked for two meals a day. We had all chosen breakfast and lunch, and had planned to have snacks in the evening. Before going to our individual rooms I went to see Aneesja's. It was there that she said that she was glad that we had enough food left for dinner because she didn't bring much spending money. I told her that made two of us. I did not tell her, but was thinking that Chris might be the only one of us who probably brought lots of euros, plus his credit card, for spending money. That was one of the things I would be depriving him of if I were to make a move and got him in trouble with his Alexis. After lunch we each ended up in our room for siesta until four o clock when we were to meet for various culture visits. We couldn't all go out to the same place. So we went with our own study class, each to a different place. That meant that Chris went to look at buildings while my group joined the top group for a lecture. That's when the green eyed monster showed his face. I could almost see Chris smiling at someone and them seeing it as an invitation. They'll go for him. Would he be strong enough to resist? If it were a man, I would've failed to look after him as I promised Alexis. If it were a female, someone's eyes would be scratched out. I tormented myself during the lecture about some culture event and why. The speaker spoke so rapidly and in such a strange accent that most of what he said went over my head. Anyway, my thoughts were with my young man at Plaza Mayor with other people.

We returned home by 8:30 in time for our evening snack. Our snack consisted of cold salad and lots of bread. Our Ama had gone out with her friend from the apartment above. She left us a note and instructions. While we ate, Aneesja had a lot to say, as did Chris, about their visits. But soon, Chris indicated that he had a lot of *Tareas de casa*.

The grin on my face led him to say, 'Can't get my tongue around this here Spanish lingua.'

He put on his funny talk. We first went to my room where we spent a long time chatting. First we talked about the picture in my room. He thought that it wasn't the Holy Mary, as we knew it as school kids in London. The London one was definitely not dark and not dressed like that. We laughed a lot, especially when I said that I must get my Mom a postcard showing a picture of a light, brown skinned, Holy Mary. It was Chris who then came up with the idea that our Ama may have overdone the catholic thing. She probably had a stack of images and statuettes. If Jewish students were expected, she'd take down Holy Mary at the double and replace it with Jewish stuff.

'And the Israeli flag.' I joined in.

'And when it is Muslim students coming she show the Islam religion icon.' he continued, mocking.

'Don't know about that. The Africans who invaded and stayed in Spain for 200 years were Muslim.' I reminded him.

We giggled happily with me laying on my bed and him sitting by my little desk. I was thinking, wouldn't it be nice to just go up and hold him? He was displaying that provocative laughter of his again. While he sat on the chair, his legs crossed, hands folded behind his head, oblivious to my thoughts, I visualised kissing him. I wouldn't ask for anything more, only a kiss. Surely nothing wrong with that?

'Well sister, its homework time.'

He rose ready to leave.

'If you need help, you only got to bang on the wall.'

He made his way out and I followed to get a cup of water. I saw Aneesja in the corridor. She was looking at the objects on the side table. The look on her face said it all. She had been listening at the door of my room. Nosy parker!

Next day we had breakfast together, again with the Spanish news on the radio. Our Ama said that we know the way now so we could go alone. We took the way as shown on the map given to us, which was along the main road. For a while we were fine then the side streets and more cobblestones. With those stones poor Aneesja's shoes couldn't cope. We saw a turning that we thought would take us to the Arabian looking tower near the college. We got to an Arabian looking building alright but it was nowhere near our college. We were lost.

'They probably got dozens of Arabian looking towers.' Chris moaned.

'Why the hell they still have cobblestones to break people's blinking ankles?' Aneesja cursed.

With two people moaning by my side I had to keep my head. I asked a woman but she had no idea where the college was. Only a third passer-by knew that we were out of our way. We were going in the wrong direction. The woman went a short way with us. She took us across some traffic lights on a busy road which she said led to the area where we were heading. She explained that the whole area was Castilla y León but various outsiders within it. At least I think that was what she said. By the time we got to college, classes had begun and we got a telling off. We must try to get to classes in time. This was an intensive course for academic purposes. We apologised and said that we got lost but were told we couldn't be lost because we had all been provided with maps. We worked hard that day. I had never realised that there was more than one version of Spanish past and future tenses. At least Chris's group played card games and looked at leaflets from shops trying to sell their goods.

Even so Chris still felt uneasy, 'Not sure I can cope, Elle.'

Chris's spirit was low.

'You will,' I said, placing my arm around him, 'you will, trust me!'

'I'm to be a shop assistant, eh! I mean a *dependiente*, tomorrow. They'll laugh at me if I get it wrong.'

'Don't worry, everybody laughs at everybody else. I was laughed at today.'

I lied to reassure him.

'Maybe I shouldn't have come. Things too high for me. And I'm sure they notice my hand but nobody said anything about it.'

'You're missing Alexis, that's what it is, isn't it?'

'Badly! But he wanted me out of the way for two weeks. Why eh?'

'Chrissie, Chrissie, that man adores you! He worships you!'

'Maybe he....'

'He what?'

'Maybe he wanted a break from me. Perhaps I was stifling him.'

'*Que Va!*' I was thinking. I wish you would suffocate me!

'What's that? You not learning bad language in Spanish, are you?'

'It means, 'What nonsense', that's all.'

We got home, refreshed, and waited for Aneesja to get in and then we had lunch like a family. Our Ama again did her bit in helping with our Spanish. She told us that Lunch wasn't a Spanish word even though young Spanish people used it. She told Chris, her baby boy, what the word for midday meal was. Poor Chris, he'd never remember '*Almuerzo*' or he's bound get it mixed up with some other word.

After lunch, or *almuerzo*, whatever our Ama called it, we went to our rooms for siesta. Chris and I spent most of our siesta time in my room. We were leaning over books and so close together that I could smell garlic mixed with the peppermint flavour mouthwash on his breath. We looked up some Spanish vocabulary which he needed more than I did because in my class we had gone past the stage of buying souvenirs for granny, or meals in restaurants. We were at the stage of reading and analysing Spanish literature. When he got up and stretched, I told him to take a break in his room.

'Lie down and count sheep.'

He laughed and asked, 'Why sheep, not cats or dogs, or even pigeons.

He gave me my usual ceremonial kiss and went to his room.

At five-o-clock, we gathered in front of our college. A number of local students came to take us to various places of interest we had signed up for to visit but Chris wanted to change to be in the same group as me.

'Ah! *novio, si?*' One of the local students, acting as group leader, said with a big grin on her face.

'*Si, nueve.*' Chris grinned back, but using the wrong word. In fact, I was not sure he understood what *novio* even meant.

'Woo…!' Came the sniggering cry from other students.

It had been agreed that if someone from our group wanted to swap then it would be all right. Someone offered and Chris came into our group. Some others also wanted to swap round. There was lots of swapping around and the lists were being thrown out of order, much to the dismay of the student leaders. In the end, the leader of our group hurried us away in case yet another student tried to join us. We followed like sheep to a square where there were at least four street bars side by side, one next to a church, all blaring music.

The one next door to a church was at the bottom of the steep hill that led to the main campus and the famous Cathedral that is said to be a 'magnificent building'.

The bar was named El Toro and had a huge cut-out picture of a big black bull with gleaming white horns. Our group leader informed us that it was a special breed for fighting. I was thinking, how unequal, unarmed bull against a man armed with a sword. But I dared not voice my thoughts. You don't go to another country and criticise their way of life. We were introduced to other young people and listened to loud music. First, one male person tried to chat me up and then a young female, then a man tried chatting up Chris. When Chris struggled to respond in Spanish the young man spoke to him in English and was told off by our leader. The young people were told to speak to us in Spanish. Soon people were dancing in front of the El Toro to the latest hits. Chris's provocative movements took me by surprise. The way he danced made me wonder who or what he was thinking of at the time. Was he actually teasing or enticing, mentally dancing with his Alexis?

'Corr…can he move!' Aneesja whispered into my ear,' 'I'd take him home if he were mine.'

I did just that.

The attention from that Romeo was getting a bit dangerous. I wasn't sure if Chris knew how to tease then pull back. Or maybe he wasn't even teasing. He was only enjoying himself unaware of the thinking of anyone around him.

It was the same back in London. He didn't seem to be aware of the effect he was having on some people, both male and female.

I went to dance with him and then led him away, leaving the 'Romeo' staring after us. By eight, we gathered as planned by the steps of the church by the El Toro. From there our group leader walked us back to the college's gate where we dispersed in various directions. Chris, Aneesja and me, decided we'd go home for supper, rather than spending money at a restaurant where some others were going. We made our way home with Aneesja being very talkative. She said that the Latin Romeo fancied me but played up to Chris to get to me. She had overheard Chris telling the Romeo, as we had named him, that I was his sister.

'Well that was one of Chris's big jokes.' I informed her.

'Aha! So Chris didn't want Latin Romeo to know that you're his *novia.*'

Aneesja's chat and laughter caused the Ama to ask if we had taken alcohol. We admitted we were invited by the young locals to take small drinks with them. We couldn't possibly refuse. She advised us to be careful. She said that Spanish young people drank, sometimes too much. Even some girls had been drinking behind their fathers' back. We must concentrate on our homework in order to master Spanish. At least that's what I think she was saying, because she spoke even faster when excited or annoyed about something. It was then Aneesja came up with an idea. She'd say that she had forgotten what we had to do and we could say the same.

Back in my room, Chris thought it was Aneesja that was stupid and not the Spanish professors. He was sitting on the edge of my bed, his legs dangling.

'What a ridiculous excuse she had in mind.' He grunted.

Watching Chris sitting there, his hand folded on his lap, something he unconsciously did when he was deep in thought, I again had a pang of guilt. I noticed something I had forgotten. He was doing so well that I had forgotten what had happened three months ago. This should've been a convalescent holiday. I didn't expect him to have so much written homework. I thought he'd be there as my companion, disguised as my student.

'Your hand, all that writing! Sorry Chris, I didn't dream they'd give you so much to do.'

I took his right hand in mine and inspected it. The doctors had done an excellent job. But the scars on his right palm were still visible and ugly.

'It doesn't hurt but others noticed it, I'm sure. I can cover me arm with long sleeves but can't go round with my right hand gloved. Nobody said anything though, but I'm sure they suspect what it was. There are things about such issues on the web.'

'Oh! Chris.' I lifted his injured hand and pressed the palm against my face.

'Is Ok, don't want you to worry about me.'

'I'm one selfish cow. I didn't think. How could I bring you here?'

'It was a good thing for me. If anyone asks I'd say I had an accident which I would rather not talk about.'

'I'm sure you can get a proper skin graft or something.'

I let go of his hand. I dared not hold on to it much longer encase I made a fool of myself.

'Alexis bin finding things out. If nothing can be done in England, he'll take me to Paris.'

'I'm sure they're places in England for people able to pay, as I said before.'

'That's just it. If it going to cost lots of money then I don't want it done. Don't want Alexis paying out money because of me stupidity.'

Those words were like a sharp knife rammed into my heart. Every time he mentions Alexis in that soft tone, I remind myself of what Alexis could do for him. That reminder always made me feel dreadful about my secret longing for him. It was like the forbidden fruit. God, if you believe in the bible, placed a juicy apple in front of Adam but warned him not to touch it. Again, I silently swore that I would never come between the two of them. Looking at him sitting there on my bed I couldn't believe that he didn't know how I feel. Surely he must know by now. Was he merely stringing me along?

Chris, at times, appeared to be settling in. He had sent three postcards to Alexis. On one of them he wrote in Spanish and started it with *Estimada* Alex. I laughed at that very formal address he used for his boyfriend. He in turn grinned at the card with a picture of the dark version of Virgin Mary, referred to on the back as, '*Virgin Románica*'. I had a sudden strong feeling for my Mom which made me send that card to her, the women who brought me into the world and cared for me almost single handed. I signed the card 'Your baby'.

'You! A baby?'

'To my Mom, I'd always be her baby.'

I had suddenly become emotional. The end of our first week in Salamanca came and Chris became restless again. He woke up depressed. Our Ama noticed and made a great fuss of him. She placed an arm around Chris and said that her own youngest son was not much older than him. That young son was away in a foreign land and perhaps missing his mamma. She said it in such rapid Spanish that I wasn't sure that Chris understood it. She gave him an extra slice of her almond cake, pinched his arm, and muttered '*flaco*'.

He grinned weakly because he understood the word to mean skinny.

Usually, we three students went in the lift together. But on this occasion, I told Aneesja to go along. We'll follow in a bit. Aneesja understood, grinned at us and left.

'*Que pasa*?' I asked when a few minutes later we got in the lift. I managed to stop the word, darling, which was tumbling in my head, 'Tell your Elle what's wrong.'

Oh me god, if the lift didn't go down soon I would've kissed him and not in a sisterly fashion either.

'Nothing, honest, I'm okay.' He sighed.

'Look, if it's too much for you this intensive four hour Spanish lesson…'

'No, we have fun in our class; we play word-cards and card games. We match names with card and pictures. We do things on the computer. I come top in the computer lab. I even helped that student from Holland. He's ever so funny!'

'What is it then? Home sick?'

'He never even bothered to answer my texts.'

216

'He's got your cards or soon will. He wants you to settle down.'

'Nah! He's with his old friend, the one we had that trouble with on that awful night.' He said miserably.

'Look, stop that nonsense, okay? Anyhow, we'll talk after college.'

That afternoon, instead of our siesta in our cool apartment which was air-conditioned, I suggested we go for a walk. We went alongside the great park, which was once a huge religious complex, so we were told in class. There we had trees to protect us a little from getting sunburnt. We wandered along, without a mention of Alexis. Instead we talked about the culture of Spain as we were told. After a long stroll we came to a huge sign indicating that we were now at the start of Castilla y León area. We joined a line of people by a shop purporting to sell only Italian ice cream of which there was at least fifty varieties, some one in the queue said. We decided on vanilla for Chris and chocolate for me, since those where the only two words we could remember in relation to varieties of ice cream. As we sat on a bench away from the sun and eating our ice cream I listened to Chris who was talking like a little boy. I felt sure that the babbling was to avoid talking about Alexis. While I listened to him, my thoughts were elsewhere. I was imaging myself in a tight embrace with him. At the same time I was feeling a sense of shame of even thinking of betraying Alexis. What on earth was I to do?

'Let's go, *vamos*, I'm boring you.' Chris said, after eating our own and licking bits off each other's ice cream.

Chris had talked endlessly.

Next day was the Madrid excursion, open to everyone from the school, regardless of which class and tutors. Our Ama packed us a lunch so that we could save money. Eating in Madrid was expensive so she said. She loaned Chris a hat from her own children, who had now left home, to keep the sun off his face. He was getting brown, she told him. She also suggested that Chris could borrow a couple of short-sleeve shirts that belonged to one of her son's. Chris politely thanked her but said he had to stay in long sleeves. To my surprise he showed the Ama his arm. She said to wait a moment and disappeared to her own room. She quickly returned with a flimsy and baggy shirt with long sleeves.

That Saturday I went on the trip, but somehow my heart was not into wandering around streets and taking photos of buildings. Perhaps the only compensation was that I was with Chris. I had him to myself and he had me, because everyone by then thought that we were an item. That night we all returned to our Ama with sore feet and sweaty bodies. We didn't even think of eating at that time of night. It was just shower, bed and dreams. We had a late lay in on the Sunday and had to make our own breakfast because our Ama had gone out. Over breakfast we talked of the coming week. It was going to be hard because of the test at the end of the week. Then it would be party time. It was also the end of the week's festival of Saint whoever. We were told about so many Saints that we got mixed up. A street theatre group had already invited us English speakers to a Saturday evening event.

On that second Monday of our stay in Salamanca, Chris had a computer printout handed to him by the office. It was an e-mail, written in Spanish, sent by Professor Sylvere. He sent a reply immediately and said we were doing fine. Please tell Elena's Mom. What else but Chris's delight at the e-mail from his Alexis did I expect? I felt alone once again and left out. Everyone else had by then paired off. Even silly little Aneesja had got cosy with that Dutch lad, just as giggly and comical. During the excursion the previous Saturday, they were seen to be holding hands. No one had attempted to pair off with me or with Chris, for obvious reasons.

That second and last week in Salamanca was as hectic as we had thought. It was homework on top of homework, revision until way past midnight. Our Ama was concerned that we were given too much writing to do. However, we had to do the work because of the exam on Friday morning. Our results would be given to us and copies would be sent to our college back home. Some of us needed a good result in order to get on a higher-level course. Luckily for me, my MA was not a Spanish main nor was Chris's Communication studies degree depending on Spanish. Yet we had to work. Chris buried his head in a pile of books. He moaned, however, that the more books he studied the more confused he was getting. Even in English, all that stuff of past perfect and non-perfect was doing his head in. Spanish was worse. He couldn't even remember if it was the table that was feminine and the tablecloth masculine. Or was it the other way round? He was sure that he'd do badly in the exam. If he had known that there would be an exam he wouldn't have come. He did not want to bother me because I had my own revision. But he badly wanted to do well. He had to move up the ladder so as not to embarrass Alexis when he was with his intellectual friends.

'So, he only wants lovers for their brain, eh?' I sneered, making 'suck teeth' as my mom calls.

Mercifully, Friday morning came and we sat a two-hour examination on various aspects of Spanish language and culture. We had the afternoon free to do as we wished while our papers were being marked. We were to return at noon on Saturday for results. It was going to be the longest Friday night and Saturday morning. I wasn't unduly concerned about me doing well but had to comfort Chris. He was in a great panic so that's why I pretended that we all were secretly panicking and I too might not have done well.

'You've got nothing to loose.' He insisted.

'And you? What do you have to loose?'

'The man I love, that's what!'

'Wait a moment. You mean to tell me that if you don't do well that man will dump you?'

'No, but...'

'Look Chris, get to bleeding bed, will you?'

I shoved him out of my room.

'Sorry to anger you, you're me only mate.' he said, before he left.

Damn him. I threw myself backwards on the bed, damn you, Chris. Damn you. I swore at the white ceiling. He had no idea how it made me feel when he went on and on about his man. He blinking goes on and on about doing well to keep hold of his man. Blast, you pass your exam to get a posh job, not to hold on to no man, as my Mom would say, or women for that matter. Stupid *tonto* that's what you are Chris and you can drop dead for all I care. And don't you dare come into my dream. But he did. It was one of those erotic, or was it erratic, dreams, because it was kind of crazy. You're in bed on top of him and pumping up and down, and it is terrific and you scream out his name. It's only a dream yet you're left sticky. Then, your energy spent, you roll back off him. You're exhausted.

The light ring tone from my travellers' alarm clock by the side of my bed woke me up. It was daylight already and I hadn't even undressed for bed.

That Saturday morning was uneventful. We were all very tense, though Chris and I still went for a long walk after breakfast. I apologised for chucking him out of my room so rudely. He understood.

'I was going on too much and you had your own exam and well...'

He did not finish that sentence but I knew what he was thinking. He was thinking of a name we had agreed would never be mentioned. To me that person by the name of Esmay was dead and that was all there was to it.

Saturday noon came and we filled the hall of the college. We could smell exotic food and there were a lot of people moving about in the background. Speakers got on the podium. The speeches were lengthy, some at a level of Spanish too difficult for some of us to understand. We could only guess what was being said. Our professors were congratulated for their leadership and us for responding so well. For that we must be congratulated. The countries where we came from were listed one by one in alphabetical order, and were congratulated for preparing us for what was an intensive course. On and on the congratulations went, and in Catalan, which, we were told, was the standard version of Spanish and which the Salamanca people were so proud. I heard the words *familias* and Ama mentioned and guessed that they were being congratulated as well. I supposed that the way they looked after us helped us to do well in our studies. I thought that they would soon be congratulating our mothers for giving birth to us, and our fathers for planting such a good seed in our mothers and the midwives who delivered us etcetera, etcetera! At long last the congratulations ended and we went up one-by-one to collect our diplomas. The diplomas were all the same except for the fact that the level of Spanish achieved so far was printed on each.

Outside the hall there were lots of hugging and kissing and the exchange of telephone numbers and e-mail addresses. Everyone was eating and drinking. Later, Chris and I dashed home to freshen up and change before meeting the others at the pre-arranged time.

We arrived at seven and met the others near the magnificent building of the Church of San Sebastian at the Plaza Anaya. There were already young people in character and costume gathering by the steps of the Anaya College. A group represented the bulls by dressing in black, with shining white horns. The other group were the matadors. Strangely, the bulls were all female and the matadors' male. To my amazement, the bulls were set to chase the matadors instead of the other way around. Soon, the craziest drama I had ever seen began. Matadors were running for their lives down the road leading to the Plaza Major. The bulls were chasing the matadors. Even people not in character were chasing or being chased. I held on tightly to Chris in case someone grabbed him and we got separated. It was as if the whole place had gone berserk. There seemed to be young people everywhere, running, laughing, shouting and teasing the matadors, while older people kept out of their way. The open-air bars along the roadside provided the background sound and plenty of booze.

'Never seen anything so mad!'

Chris had to shout above the noise.

'Hold on to me so we don't lose each other.' I told him.

My holding on to him didn't help much. Someone tried to grab him. I shouted, 'he's mine!' and dragged Chris away.

We actually ran down the hill past the park where we met up with a young couple that had also run away from the bull-chasing crowd. The couple told us of a place where young people from all parts of the country get together, especially during the festival weeks. That place was La Sahara and was a bar with a performing area. Because of the festival there was to be live music from college or university bands that were given a platform to showcase their work. A group from Cuba was expected, also a college group from the Basque country and there would also be Salamanca's own group.

'That's cool.' said the teenager with her boy friend.

'Here we say *muchos beber*.'

The boyfriend did not speak much English.

It all sounded great, Chris and I thought, and we went along with the couple. It was quite a long walk into the Castilla-León's main area of the Arts. By the time we got there, La Sahara was packed and people were spilling out onto the pavement outside. The noise was almost deafening. We had to push our way to the bar to get some drinks. Then a new group came up on stage to a rapturous applause and whistling. As soon as the band started, the crowd went wild. People began to dance, or rather move their heads and shoulders, since there was not really enough room for dancing. Couples were either laying their heads on each other's shoulders or snuggling. Chris was obviously enjoying it all. It was our last day in Spain, at least for now. We might as well 'let our hair down' as they say. I threw my arms around Chris's shoulder and moved our bodies from side-to-side with others doing the same, like sardines squeezed into a tin.

We needed more drinks but there was no way we could get back to the bar so we went outside where there were now tables and waiter service. It was there that things went horribly wrong. A sort of Karaoke session started where people went up and sang or an amateur group played the music of their favourite group. One particular group of percussion instrumentalists began playing something I recognised from our Tapas bar in London. It was a track from The Gypsy Kings.

The youngsters first tried Bamboleo and that got people jumping up and down. It was when the band began Tu Quieres Volver that Chris got very emotional. He'd had three drinks but that wasn't enough to get him drunk enough to want to weep in public. I didn't want him to embarrass himself, that's why I took him away.

'What's wrong?' I asked when we got on the road back home.

He was still weeping and was obviously still distressed and the cool night air didn't seem to have much effect.

'I feel so alone!'

'You're not alone. Don't I count?'

'You're me best mate. But, he…he took me to his bed. Now…can't you see?

Why would he let me go away unless he's politely dumping me?' he whimpered.

'He's not. He wanted you to be free, to spend some time on your own, like he doesn't want to hold you in prison.'

I placed an arm around his waist. 'Don't be sad.'

'Thanks for trying to comfort me, but I know what I know. It's over between us. I've bin dumped. It was his way of softening the blow.'

'Chris, that song, that last one…did it upset you?'

'That's the one when we had our first special dinner and when…when we agreed…you know, to be an item, and when we first…nah, don't worry. I'm making an ass of myself. *Vamos*!'

He rubbed the back of his shaking palm across his eyes.

'Yes let's go.' I chanted, happy that he appeared to be little less distressed.

Walking with our arms around each other we managed to find our way back home. There we found a concerned Ama. She had gone wandering around looking for us after Aneesja came home alone and said that we had been separated during the festivities.

We apologised and said we'd had difficulty finding our way back. After Ama gave us a good telling off and said that she was responsible for us, she said we might as well go to our rooms. If we were hungry, she said angrily, we were quite capable of making something ourselves.

'Like when we were little kids.' Chris whispered when we were alone in my room.

Chris was in low spirits again. This time it could have been the fact that he wasn't exactly accustomed to alcohol. He flung himself backwards into the armchair and said, 'He used to say that I had beautiful hands. Now one got ugly, he dumping me. Well Professor Sylvere, you dumping me, yeah? Well you can go to hell, see if I care,' he moaned, ' I love him, he taught me things, not only books, but about love…and he gone and dumped me.'

He whimpered like a baby, 'I miss him so badly and want him here.'

'Shush! Chris…Ama will hear you. And you'll only make yourself ill.'

I went and closed my door pushing the bolt quietly. I didn't want our Ama to hear him saying things about Alexis or see him weeping. I wasn't sure how she would react if she did or thought that he was drunk. I began to wipe his tears away. Then things got out of hand. I didn't mean to kiss him, not that way. I had meant to kiss him on the cheek as I had often done. And he had planted a ceremonial peck on my cheek. This time the kiss went further than it was intended. At first he whispered…,'No', but that no got weaker as I fumbled with his pants. Next moment, with the door locked, I was taking from him what I had so badly wanted after several months of 'soul searching'. The months of yes, then no, and yes again, left my head. The name, Alexis, was far away from my thoughts now. Not that there was time to think. The evil action on my part was over in what seemed like a split second. It was nothing more than thrust, enter, and then it was all over.

I had taken advantage of a friend when he was at his lowest.

Chris, realising what we had just done, was furious with himself. He got up and smashed his fist so hard against the wall that the picture of the Virgin and her baby fell off onto the desk. Luckily it wasn't real glass in the frame. It was sort of imitation glass material whatever the name of it was. Chris quickly arranged his pants and stormed out of my room. I heard him slam his door shut. I would never forget the look of hatred in his eyes before he left. I had lost a good friend. I felt terrible, as if a bucket of ice water had been poured over my head. I had never, in my life, experienced anything like it; in fact, the entry hurt. For months I had wanted to take him into my arms. And what did I get? Nothing! No, that's not exactly true. I did get something. I got a broken friendship, that's what I was left with. And if that's what it is with a man, then no thank you very much. Mind you neither of us had experience with the opposite sex. Yeah! That's it; blame the disappointment on lack of experience. Round and round things went in my head, from positive to negative, from guilt to excuses; after all, he was a man and stronger for that! He could've pushed me away if he had wanted. He did say no, half-heartedly. Perhaps he said no, but meant yes! Nah! I had him cornered and after all he was flesh and blood. He couldn't push me away. Lust, I suppose, lack of control got the better of us both. Now we're left with our guilt. Would Alexis suspect just by looking at us? He's experienced and not stupid. Maybe he wanted Chris to be with me and make up his mind about what he really wants. And what of Mom, my God, she'll kill me. What if she suspects? I had overheard her and her mates saying that you can tell when a girl had begun with 'them things'.

What if Mom could tell as soon as she looked at me? How would I explain turning down Anthony and the idea of marriage to go for Chris, a gay man.

I found myself in the bathroom. I had to wash. I felt dirty and sticky. Another problem was the stain on my knickers, which I had not taken the trouble to pull away properly. I washed and washed, and the blood went but a stain spot remained. I wrapped them up in a bag, meaning to secretly chuck it in one of those large bins on the road. I couldn't risk Mom finding it during her enthusiasm to put things in the washing machine.

Oh my God! No! I hadn't taken any precautions. The whole deed was spontaneous and unplanned. Ok, there must be that morning-after pill in Salamanca. But do I know enough Spanish to go to the chemist nearby and ask for the morning after pill? I don't even know the Spanish for morning-after pill. Anyway, would that brief encounter of 'thrust-enter-nothing' be enough to need those pills? Of course, I could get that pill back in London. It would only be two days after and if anything does go wrong there is always termination. Oh, my mom will go mad twice, once for getting in trouble, another for contemplating the murder of an innocent baby. We had not been attending mass but were still Catholics, and once a catholic, always a Catholic, as the saying goes. Good Catholic girls were not supposed to go round murdering unborn babies. So hurry up and come along my period, for once I shall welcome you, cramp or no cramp.

I went to bed still feeling awful. Again I cursed myself. I had taken advantage of a friend, that I was supposed to love and respect, when he was at his most vulnerable. I tossed and turned in bed, unable to fall asleep. I even got up and managed to put the picture of the Virgin Mother and Child back in the frame. I prayed, which was something I hadn't done for years, and got back into bed. Still I couldn't get to sleep, even though I closed my eyes tightly and forced my thoughts to go blank. I must not think of past events. That had been a mistake and must be forgotten.

I opened my eyes again and that's when I saw him. A man was standing by my bedside, watching me. He looked horrible, tall and skinny, almost like he had crawled out of a tomb or something like that. He was more creature than man. He opened his mouth to speak, and with arms outstretched, walked towards me. That's when I screamed. At least I believe I screamed. Then came a chilly silence and I was scared to go to the bathroom. Did I dream it all or did someone die in the room? Did Ama hear me scream? That's if I did scream?

Next morning was Sunday and the day we were travelling back to London. We had the morning free. Chris and I left the house together, only this time in silence. We got to the Plaza Mayor and found our classmates already there. The usual flamenco dance to entertain the tourists had already begun. After watching two dances, I got bored. I liked the various costumes but the dances all looked the same.

'I'm going to Saint Martin, something going on in there.' I pointed to people going in and out of the Church.

Without a word Chris followed me inside. It was a magnificent 12th-century church, well decorated with colourful decor and fresh flowers. Some people were wandering around admiring the beautiful decor. A small number were on their knees, obviously praying or simply reflecting. I sat on a pew near an altar devoted to the Virgin Mother and Child. I silently admitted that I had done something very bad. Not only the bit that people do sometimes as young as nine, but I forced myself onto a good friend. If it had been the other way round, him forcing himself on me, it would've been a criminal offence. I could only pray and ask that my action did not divide two people who dearly love each other. I rose and put a few Euros in the box by the candles, took one, lit it, then placed it in the holder alongside many other lit candles. I walked out with Chris following me, his face still expressionless.

Once outside, we noticed that a procession was forming. Musicians, dressed in black and wearing medieval hats, played what looked like Scottish bagpipes. A group of men and women in colourful traditional dress followed the musicians, followed by little girls in white. That scene took me back to my childhood. Then, I was dressed in white for purity and veiled as a bride for my first communion at the age of seven. Again, I was dressed in white at the age of ten, for my Confirmation. For some inexplicable reason, that religious procession had a strange effect on my emotions. My legs, as if they had a life of their own, took me to the back of the procession alongside other people not in costume who could have just been curious tourists. I was sure that this was an enactment of some event that took place many years ago.

The procession, protected by police on motorbikes, went from the Plaza Mayor, down the steep hills alongside a park that was called, I believe, de Fonseca. Once there, it was clear that I had walked in on an open air mass. I should have left then but my legs wouldn't let me. I joined in the mass while at a distance away Chris sat on a stone wall. I had not attended mass for many years and could not remember the hymns that on this occasion were accompanied by guitars, violins and drums, instead of an organist. The service was either in Latin or at the level of Catalan that I could not clearly understand. I heard the name of Santa Clara mentioned several times but for me to be there seemed to be the main thing. When it was time to respond to the Holy Father's prayer I simply moved my lips and muttered. When people began to line up for Holy Communion, I joined them. True, the rule was that you had to go to confession before communion. But there was also your own conscience. When my turn came, I opened my mouth and the priest helping with the communion placed the small circle of bread, which was blessed and represented the body of Christ, on my tongue. The representation of the blood of Christ was the wine in the chalice that was first blessed then the bread was dipped into it. I remembered all that from my catechism classes as a child.

The service ended and the music of the young musicians saw the congregation out. We made our way towards our temporary home. On the way there I repented and confessed to Chris.

'Chris!'

I made to take his hand as I often did but he pulled away.

'I'm so sorry about last night. I took advantage of your moment of unhappiness and need.'

227

'Doesn't matter, it was my fault, my weakness.'

'I love you Chris and I always will but I let things get out of hand again.'

He shrugged and said, 'Forget it! It will never happen again, that's what matters.'

He said it coldly. And we said nothing more about the matter and got home to begin packing.

At four in the afternoon a minibus arrived to take us together with the other students to Madrid's Barajas airport. We kissed our Ama and thanked her for looking after us. We each gave her a small present. I got her some perfume. Chris got her some fancy chocolates and Aneesja got her some hand cream. We waved goodbye at the door and again from the mini bus when it drove off.

I was leaving Salamanca and that event behind.

14

We arrived at Gatwick airport where Mom and Kevin were waiting. I spotted Alexis s from a distance standing by a kiosk. He had, so I thought, a rather blank look on his face. He did not seem to be as excited as the others who came to collect us. Surely Chris would not have sneaked him a text? He wouldn't say what happened on a mobile? I noted Chris looking around frantically.

I pointed, 'There he is!' and watched Chris rush to Alexis and throw his arms around his neck.

It did not escape my notice that Alexis did not hug him. I also felt that Alexis looked at me in a strange manner but that could've been my guilty conscience at having betrayed a friend.

Don't tell him now; I silently tried to transmit that to Chris. If you must tell him, wait until you get home, and at an ideal moment. If you must tell him, blame everything on me. You desperately wanted him and I took advantage. Yes, blame me, and keep your man. I love you that much to let you go where you'll find what I cannot give you.

Meanwhile, Alexis's offered to take us home.

'We be aright from London Bridge but thank you very much.' said Mom.

'It would not be a problem, I've brought the saloon.' He explained to no avail.

Mom was adamant, and we made our own way home.

On the way, Mom was very quiet while Kevin bombarded me with questions about the trip. I answered, but my thoughts were elsewhere. He made jokes and I laughed even when I didn't find them funny. We got home and Mom warmed up some soup she had made for me. After gulping down as much as I could of that Creole soup, as Mom called it, I took Mom's advice and went to my room to rest. It had been a very long day. In fact, looking back on it all, it had been a long road from the damp basement to exotic Salamanca and my entry into womanhood on my own terms.

In spite of thinking that I was too tired to sleep, I slept until Mom came to my room with a cup of tea and the words: '*Buenas Dias Princesa.*'

Mom was in a happy mood all of a sudden.

Christ, did she find that paper bag with my knickers in it? Didn't I throw it in the street bin in Salamanca? I couldn't even remember if I had. If I hadn't and Mom found them when she to put my stuff in the washing machine. Nah! If she had she wouldn't have brought me a cup of tea in bed. She'd more likely come up with a broom handle and demand to know who it was. Anyway, Mom left for work and I went downstairs to find that she had not unpacked my things. She left it to me to unpack and put what I need to be washed in the machine myself. Thank goodness, I sighed.

I spent the rest of the day working hard but couldn't take my mind off Chris. Had he told Alexis? Had he got in trouble and had his things chucked out on the pavement? I cooked, cleaned, put the coloured things in the washing machine, and found out to my relief that I must have thrown the knickers away because they weren't in my suitcase or bag. In the afternoon I phoned work to say that I was back and would be in next morning. After that, my hand took itself to the phone and my fingers dialled Chris's number of their own accord. I prepared what I was going to say when or if he answered. I'd say something like, 'How are you or did you get a good rest and…' Nah! Too long winded. I'd just say 'Hi, did you have a good rest?' And he would probably say 'and why shouldn't I …? I changed my mind several times. His number was ringing but in the end I couldn't decide what to say and hung up. I waited for Chris to phone or text me but, as I half suspected, he did neither. I was sure he'd told Alexis and they had split up and it was my fault.

At work on Tuesday, I had to answer all sorts of questions, even though I said that I'd write a report about the trip. I had to admit that it was mainly the university library that we visited. I did go to a small public library and made a list of storybooks in bilingual Spanish /English for our young readers. We had also taken shots of Old Spanish architecture that we could exhibit in the children's area.

'Ah! Well done!' My supervisor was pleased.

By Tuesday evening I could bear the silence no longer. I had to phone Chris. His mobile was off and that made me more miserable. He knew that I was going to ring so he had switched it off. I soon developed a bad headache and a sick feeling in my stomach.

Mom blamed it on the jet lag and said, 'If god wanted us to fly he would've given us wings.'

In a way I was relieved that Mom saw it as jet lag. But I had the sneaking feeling that she was dying to ask, as usual, was there a nice Spanish gentleman paying me attention? If only she knew that I was weird. I didn't want any Anthony nor did I want any Esmay, instead I was eating my heart out for this Chris, even knowing what he was. Poor Mom, she would be delighted if I'd got married to a Spanish speaker, having rejected Anthony. She had no idea that she would never see me going up the altar in a white veil, well, except perhaps for the one I wore at the age of seven for my first holy communion to take 'the body of Christ' for the first time.

That night, alone in bed, I dialled Chris's mobile again. This time I got through and left a message - just to ask if you are okay or are you also having trouble with jet lag - then hung up. Those words were all I could bring myself to say. I hoped that he would read between the lines that I was enquiring if he had got into trouble over the Salamanca affair. Chris replied to my message - I'm okay, will be in touch – end of message. There was an air of, 'don't call us we'll call you' in the tone of his text. I desperately wanted to know if Alexis knew and if they had split up. After all, Alexis was my head of department and I might have to meet with him at some point. I must know how to react if I had to attend one of his lectures. I remembered what Alexis had said when we were leaving for Salamanca. He said, 'Look after him and bring him back to me safe,' or words to that effect. But what exactly did he mean by that? On and on I punished what I considered the evil side of me .My headache got worse as I battled with my guilt. If they split up, was that a good thing for me? Surely there is no guarantee that he would turn to me. In fact he'd hate me for causing him to lose a person who not only adored him but also could have made a difference to his life. Before we went to Salamanca he did say that Alexis would be taking him to France to meet the Sylvere clan, especially his grandmother, who apparently doted on him and would give him anything, even though she'd prefer him to marry a pretty French maiden from a rich family.

Wednesday came and we MA students had to meet for a post-mortem of the trip. But my need was to meet Chris face-to-face. If he were around, I'd find a way of finding out what happened at home. On that first day back at college, I met and chatted with a number of the new MAs from other colleges. I was pleased to notice that Esmay was not among the MAs. She had gone on the teacher's course and they worked separately because a great deal of their time was spent in schools. I toyed with the idea of hanging around in the car park until five when both Alexis and Chris, if they were still together, were bound to turn up. If they did not come out together then I'd know they'd broken up. So deep was I in thought that I didn't notice Esmay coming towards me until I nearly bumped into her.

'Sorry, I was miles away.'

'Ahem! I could see that.' She said, her gaze digging at me.

'Anyway, how you getting on?' I had to say something.

'I did leave a message a few days ago. Your Mom said that you were still in Spain.'

'I was and we had a fantastic time.'

I paused briefly then said, 'You should move on Esmay.'

'As you have?'

'Yes, as I have.'

'Mmh…what 'bout you and those two?' She pointed her shoulder in the direction of the staff car park car.

I was stunned into silence. It wasn't those two as she said. It was Chris with bags of shopping. I watched him open the boot of the car. Chris obviously had his own key; I couldn't take my gaze away as he packed the shopping in the boot then closed it. I could sense Esmay watching me, watching Chris's movements.

I was not going to give Esmay pleasure by letting her note that Chris and I had apparently fallen out. I called out, 'Hi, Chris.' and walked towards the car. For a moment, I expected him to ignore me, leap into the car and drive off. He did not. He stopped, waited until I got near and said, 'Hi.' but without the usual infectious smile.

He walked towards me but he had obviously seen Esmay watching. Esmay remained in the distance.

'How are you?' I could not think of anything else to say.

'*Bien y Tu?*' He replied in Spanish.

'Your BA going OK?' I asked, as causally as I could.

I dared not enquire if he had told Alexis about us but he seemed all right.

'Yes. A lot of work, but its Ok, Alexis has been very helpful.' He said, glancing in the direction of Alexis's office. Then he walked to the front of the car, opened the passenger side, waved to me, and got in.

'See you around.'

I'll never be sure if I actually uttered those words or only thought of them.

His movements and the coldness in his voice said it all. I had not only lost him as a lover, which was a one-sided affair anyway, but also as a friend. I walked back feeling dejected. I went in the direction of the bus stop to take me home.

'You OK?' I heard Esmay's voice behind me.

'Yes,' I said, without turning round, 'why shouldn't I be?'

'I could come to the library when you have a break and we could go for a snack.'

'Please don't. I meant it when I said that you should move on.'

I walked way from her and didn't look back.

From then on I threw myself into my work even though I wasn't feeling very well. I had my period, and for once, I welcomed it. It meant that I might not have to worry about ending up with something inside me that I didn't want. To my delight, my period, which I had not seen for at least two months, came with a vengeance. On top of it I had a very sore throat, a nasty headache and was sneezing. Mom got worried because of the fear about Asian or bird flu or even both at the same time. Mom suggested the doctor be called. I told her not to fuss. It was only a bad cold. Mom went on to blame it on the contrast of climate, 'You coming from that blazing heat of Spain to chilly and damp London.' She insisted.

Mom began to pamper me and tried to drown me with ginger tea and Pineapple juice. Then she blamed too much work. The library, setting up my project plus my studies at college was all too much. Mom couldn't understand why I needed any more studies. I had much more than she had and far more than many of the young women who can barely write their own names. Why was I pushing myself so hard? Poor Mom, if only you knew that it wasn't a MA or library work that was the trouble. Your daughter is broken hearted; your daughter is weird, Mom.

After a week at home I dragged myself back to the library. My line manager said that I looked dreadful. And I might pass on my cold to other colleagues.

'Go home, keep warm and rest.' She demanded. 'I saw you and I will record it that you were ill and sent you home.'

Another week went past before I went back to work at the library, even though I wasn't feeling fantastic. I began to avoid Chris when I went to college on Wednesday's. Yet I could not get him out of my head and feared I'd bump into him. In order not to come face-to-face with Chris or Esmay I purposely kept away from the Tapas Bar and took my own sandwiches and a soft drink. I became a lonely soul avoiding everyone I knew, except for the ones I had to be with in the research method class. I often swore silently at the thought of the break-up of my friendships. I didn't give a damn! Lots of people have 'one night stands', so it's no big deal! But if I didn't give a damn why did I feel so sad and unhappy?

Christmas was approaching and we were very busy. We decorated the library with photographs and cuttings under the theme of 'Christmas around the World'. There was a 'Happy Christmas' sign in several modern languages starting with FELIZ NAVIDAD, all in fancy letters that Kevin had done. But at home, I told Mom not to bother with an elaborate Xmas tree and decorations. Kevin and I had grown up and there was no need for all that fuss. I felt also that it was such a waste of money. Mom agreed, then immediately spoilt things with a snide remark, 'Yu right, got to start putting a bit by for when m'baby get herself taken to the altar.'

Don't hold your breath mama, this young woman is not for the sacrificial altar I thought, but grinned to please her. Meanwhile, Carol singing time came with carols blasting our eardrum not only from the television and radio, but also from door-knocking singers. I too made use of the Christmas card time and the season of good will. I sent a card addressed to Mr Chris Newman c/o Professor Alexis Sylvere, 7 Orchid Place. But inside the card I wished them both Merry Christmas and a successful New Year. The moment I put the card in the post box I regretted it. What would Alexis think? If Alexis knew about Salamanca would he see that card as rubbing his nose in it? I toyed with the idea of standing by the box and when the postman came to empty it, asking him to give it back to me. I had to agree to myself not to waste my time and that of the postman who could not possibly hand over the card. Meanwhile, I waited hopefully for 'that card', at the same time fearing that it would not come. And it didn't. That card that I so badly wanted was never among the pile of cards coming through our door. I reminded myself of the talk of taking Chris to France to meet the Sylvere clan. But surely there are Christmas cards for sale in France?

A large card came from Esmay to me, and smaller one from Anthony to our family. With the card from Anthony was an invitation to his engagement party on New Year's Eve. Now, I thought, who is rubbing whose nose in it? Mom got cards from Guyana and from her family, including her two brothers in Venezuela, who had not spoken to her for years. Mom was very happy that her brothers had relented and contacted her after a long and bitter family feud.

Christmas dinner was a Guyanese speciality; rice with Pepper pot that lived up to its name. It burns people's tongues off if they weren't used to it. As a special treat Mom had ordered a dozen roties from a nearby Indo-Caribbean Restaurant. She also made her own Chicken Curry, Indo-Guyanese style, to go with it. I had all my favourites yet I didn't feel like eating. Too many mince pies at work, then I was snacking at home, I couldn't manage more than a small bite. Mom understood. She always craved for black cake after the Xmas festivities but by then most of it had gone. Black cake is something that was made after mixed fruit was soaked for several months in 90 plus percent proof rum. I took a small piece and warned Kevin not to eat too much of it as he'd have a hangover in the morning if he did. We laughed and were generally happy as a family. We didn't have much money but we were together.

Boxing Day came; we had lunch made from leftovers, and then went for the traditional Boxing Day walk in the park as did many others. Families with their kids, people with their dogs and an old couple taking one step at a time. When our legs got tired and Mom eventually managed to persuade Kevin that he could not have a dog just to throw sticks and tell it to fetch, we went back home. We walked in to find the red light on the phone flashing. I pressed 'Play Message' and got a shock. I instantly recognised the voice, though so angry it could not be the Chris I knew, unless he had become possessed by some demon. What could have upset him so much? He was half-weeping, half-shouting. I had trouble understanding clearly what he was saying.

'You liar, what you think you're doing? You spoiling some one else Xmas, eh? You trying to cause trouble? Well, all you'll get is my blood on your hands...your evil...'

The message came to an abrupt stop as though someone on the other end had put the phone down. Quickly and angrily I pressed delete. Mom was aghast and stared at the phone.

Kevin broke the stifling silence. 'What was that?' he asked with his mouth wide open.

It could not be the Chris I knew, unless someone had prompted him to do so. He was not the person to be so rude on the telephone, especially to me.

Mom found her voice. 'Who the devil was that?'

'It was Chris.' I said, still puzzled about what he had been going on about. He must have been really angry to phone me in such a tone of voice. Saying things like evil, was I evil? How would his blood be on my hands?

We just stared at the phone trying to make some sense of all that ranting, and that's what it was. Chris hadn't even called me on my mobile to ask me to give him a call, which would have been more private. He just burst out about something I was supposed to have done!

'What was that all about?' Kevin asked again.

'Sound like devil, how dare he?' Mom was furious.

'Chris was accusing me of something?' My God! He must have told Alexis.

'How dare that trash?' Mom's eyes were bulging with anger. 'How dare he treat us with such disrespect?'

'Mom, don't call people names that you don't want them to call you.' I warned her.

'He sure went mental 'bout something.' said Kevin.

'Get me his number. He'll get the sharp end of my tongue.'

'No, Mom.' I insisted.

'Don't you NO me! That man was out of order. Anthony would not speak to us like that, phone or otherwise! Anthony is a well-brought up gentleman, your so-called friend grew up wild in the back streets of London and we all know what some black people call his lot. We might be poor but I brought you children up proper.'

Now it was Mom who was ranting and raving.

'Mom, leave it, please. Let me deal with things?'

Mom kept her eye on me as I phoned Chris. First I tried his mobile; it was turned off, then his flat at the run down council estate where he lived. Number not available said a recorded voice. The only number left to ring was 'The Orchid' which I reluctantly dialled. A voice saying the usual, - Sorry, we are unable to take your call at the moment. Please leave a short message and we will get back to you.- came down the line The 'we' in the message left me with little doubt that Chris had officially moved in to 'The Orchid'.

'Was happening?' Mom inquired.

'Can't get hold of him.' I muttered.

'Of course you can't. He damn well knows we try calling him back!'

'Please Mom, no 'we'. Let me handle this.'

'What is it with him? Tried it on and you say no?'

'Mom, it's nothing like that.'

If Mom knew the whole story she'd probably kill me. I kept that thought to myself but decided that it was time I talked to her; after all, a girl's Mom should be her best confidant.

'Mom,' I began, 'I have something to talk to you about.'

'Kevin, wasn't you to go to, what's her name, Eugenia house?' Mom suggested that Kevin left us.

'Why can't I listen as well? Am I not part of the family?' Kevin put on what he thought was posh talk.

'You'll be bored with woman's talk.' I gave him a sniggering wink.
'I can go to Paul's. What's it worth?'
'You'd bleed your own sister.' I sneered. 'Is it Paul or his sister
Eugenia?'
After I promised to give Kevin money to take his friend Eugenia to
the cinema, he made himself scarce.

First, Mom went to the kitchen for a couple of glasses of juice. She
returned and sat opposite me at the table. I folded my hands in my lap
and took a deep breath. The words in my head filtered through my lips.
'Mom, you know I'm twenty one soon...' I paused.
Mom took a sip from her glass without taking her eyes off me.
'Well..., got something to share with you. Remember, I am nearly
twenty one,' I kept repeating my age, 'so please, don't hit the roof.'
Mom's silence was deafening. She just glared at me and waited. It
was as if her cheeks would burst at any time and blood would spring out.
'Well, when we were in Salamanca, things got out of hand. It was
the last night of the festival of Saint Clara and well, people went raving
mad and we all went to the bullfighting dramatisation and we found
ourselves at the border of the Leon region, which is where Salamanca is
... well people were messing about, you know how it is with young
people, and we got lost getting back...' I found myself stammering and
telling Mom a long-winded story until she stopped me.
'You done things with a young man?' Mom asked.
'Something like that.' I couldn't help thinking how Mom
automatically thought of a man, as if 'doing things' could only be with a
man.
'Was he a decent man who respects you? Was he clean?'
'It was a decent healthy man.'
'If you sure!' Mom shrugged.' What gwan happen next?'
'Nothing. He's with someone else.'
'He's what? And you let him...! Yu turned down a single man and
let a married man have you?'
'Well...actually...he's not married, but....'

'He living with someone who don't understand him, eh? Oh, Lena, Lena, they all say dat so to get inside you panty. And that poor woman at home, slaving in the house after a hard days work in some factory.'

'It's not a woman Mom and he's not from factory class.' I had no idea what a factory class was but said it anyway.

'Well…Oh my!'

Suddenly Mom gasped. She rose from the chair, her eyes looked as if they were about to pop out. She muttered. 'Awhah yu just seh?' drifting into Creolese.

'Sorry, Mom, should've told you. It's Chris. You know Chris, don't you?'

Mom threw her hands up in the air, then held her head and began shaking it from side to side as if wanting to yank it off. She stared at the ceiling, her chest rose, before a loud howl, like wounded animal, came from her mouth. 'No…not my daughter, no…!' She made the sign of the cross on herself like a true catholic but something she had stopped doing a long time ago.

'It's no big deal and you did say yourself that you're not prejudiced.'

'Not when he brang his filth on my daughter…. the dirty pig…'

Mom began ranting in a mixture of various dialects from her background. She rushed like a mad women to the drawer where we kept telephone messages and numbers on a pad.

'Mom, calm down. I mean, no crime committed. Anyway, it's over, he wants nothing more to do with me, you heard it yourself on the phone message.'

Mom found Chris's number and went to the phone.

I grabbed the phone to take it from her. 'You're not phoning him.' I said.

That's when Mom pushed me and I fell sideways against a nearby armchair.

'You make me hurt my side.' I shouted.

Mom waited and watched me get up.

'I'm OK but no need for you to go mad. I love him and it was I who went for him!'

'You stupid girl! *Idiota*! He made you think you wanted it to happen. He conned you, Lena. You have no experience and easy to trick...*un truco*, Lena!'

'Mom, he didn't trick me. Actually, he's the victim here. I'm the guilty one.'

'Don't worry; I make him big victim! If your uncle's were here them beat his brains out.'

Mum again went to fumble in the drawer by the telephone. We also kept an exercise book there for messages and addresses. While fumbling, she swore in every language from Guyanese English to Venezuelan Spanish and listed all the things that should happen to Chris. If only her brothers were here.

'I'd hate you for life if you phone and blame him. I'll never speak to you again, that I swear...'

'Why you defending him?'

'Because I love him and because he is innocent.'

'Lena, you been to college, your *madre* she never been. But I know, I hear say what those men do. You must know. You must talk about things at your college? And what 'bout Esmay, doesn't she tell you things?'

'Yes, Esmay told me lots of things.' Poor Mom you ain't got a clue do you? But I love that man. I would never come between him and his love. That I did promise.

Mom ranted some more in her various dialects, calling Chris all the things she could think of, from sinner to filthy scum, before she announced, 'I'm going to vomit. That man with my only daughter.'

Mom rushed to the bathroom, still calling men like Chris all the horrible words in the world she could think of.

I went upstairs and imagined Mom shoving her fingers down her throat to make her self vomit. I didn't have to stick my fingers down my throat. I was violently sick.

Next morning both Mom and Kevin gave me the silent treatment.

Mom must have told Kevin something because he could not look me in the eyes. The phone rang and I rushed towards it but Mom was nearest and got there first.

'Look, you phone this house...' She began.

I snatched the phone from her and shouted into it, 'Look, Chris...'

'It's Alexis. I wish to speak Mrs Peterson if I may.'

'What about? Your Chris...' I didn't get further because this time it was Mom who grabbed the phone, while Kevin looked on.

'Look! No...you listen! We're decent and clean people in this house. We don't have your money but we're not trash...hello! Hello!'

Mom slammed the phone down. 'He hang up!' She muttered with a nasty look and marched off.

It took me some time to pick up courage to dial the Orchid number. When I did I heard a new message, 'Message from Alexis and Chris, we will get back to you as soon as we can.'

I frowned, when was that new message put on? And that voice wasn't that of Alexis or Chris, what was going on?

I remembered then that Alexis had given me his mobile number when Chris was going with us on the Salamanca trip in case of emergency, he had said. I called that number. It was a bad line but I finally got through to Alexis. He answered and said they were in France. He had tried to apologise to my mother for Chris's out of character behaviour. He was very upset but should not have phoned and left a message. He was beside himself with anger at what had happened.

'What upset him so much that he can insult my family like that on the phone?'

'He has to talk to you himself about that. Just apologise to your mother and Kevin for me.'

I had no intention of dialling Chris to find out because I had my pride. Yet the words 'his blood on my hands' worried me. What could I have done for him to say that? True, he had hurt himself when he thought that Alexis was sending him packing. Unless, just unless, the event in Salamanca had only now come out and he felt that he'd cut himself again if he had to lose his lover because of Salamanca.

Anyway, I passed on the apology from Alexis but Mom ignored it.

Mom stopped speaking to me, and Kevin tried to avoid me. It was horrible. Once, we were a happy family laughing and being together on all things, now I was being ignored and it was my fault. Kevin was now taking his meals in the kitchen. Mom, even though eating at the same table as me, would not say a word. She wouldn't even touch anything thing I had prepared. New Year's Eve came and still the silent treatment from my family. I tried to break through that silence by bringing up the multi-faith service to which all residences were invited.

'Mom, is about that midnight multi-faith service, are we going?' Mom shrugged and walked away.

That afternoon, for some unclear reason, I got on a bus and found myself in the area of the House of Our lady of Grace. I stopped at the corner shop and got come fruit juice, including Pineapple, now my great favourite, and four packets of biscuits. I arrived at The House of Our Lady of Grace and hardly recognised the place. The old screeching Iron Gate had gone and a new one, with a security camera, was in its place. I tried to go in but the gate was locked and had an arrow pointing to the building itself. I got there to find that the name had changed to: 'Our Lady of Grace, Centre for Intermediate Education', what a mouthful I thought, then rang the bell.

'Yes?' came a voice from somewhere. I could be seen standing at the door, I was sure of that.

'I'm Elena, Elena Peterson, an old girl from here. I brought some donation for the New Year Eve's party we used to have.' I tried laughter for relaxation.

The door opened very slowly, like in a horror movie when you see no one, only a door moving. I entered into a small office and waited. A young female, no more than fourteen years old and obviously pregnant, came out.

'I'm Brenda, duty junior tonight. How can we help you?'

'Not sure really. I lived here for three year. It looked different then.' I wondered why the young person, with such a pleasant and intelligent voice, was she doing here with her stomach sticking out?

'Wait here.' As she left I heard her calling out to someone.

I was alone briefly then Brenda returned with someone.

I gasped, and then I heard my own voice screaming, 'Betty, mad Betty!' I threw myself at her.

'Elena, Saint Elena!' she hugged me back. 'What you doing here?' Brenda was watching and grinning from ear to ear.

'Come in, come in.' Betty was practically dragging me to a room that had been a living room in my day, but was now a television room.

A group of young females, some watching television, others reading magazines, continued with what they were doing until Betty said, 'Everyone, meet Saint Elena, that's what we called her.'

'Loow, Saint Elena!' The girls said in union, and carried on as if I wasn't there.

'Louisa! Betty called out. 'Manners!'

'Oh! Sorry! You want hot or cold drink?' A rebellious looking teenager grudgingly slammed down the magazine she was reading and rose to get me a drink.

'Cold would be okay, thank you.'

'We take turn for special duties.' Betty explained with a broad smile.

My drink arrived quickly enough and Betty took me to her office. Once there I said, 'That Louisa girl...'

'She's had a rough time. She, like many of them here, badly need people like you and me.'

'Not me, thank you! For me it would be a top job with lots of money, car and house and stuff like that. No troubled teenage girls going to kick me in the shin, thank you very much.'

After that, Betty and I exchanged tales of the past and present and plans which did not go as expected. Like me, Betty had dreamt of a good job with lots of cash. But her punishment for trying to burn down 'The House' was two years of probation and community service. Ms Jolly arranged for her do her community service in the same house that she tried to burn down. They worked her like a slave just for food and accommodation, she moaned. Even her social-benefit went straight to the house and they gave her a few pennies pocket money and she had to sign for it.

'The crazy thing was,' Betty explained, 'after those two years, I was free to leave but, for some mad reason, I stayed on as a paid worker.'

Now with Ms Jolly as her mentor, Betty went to college one day a week for a degree in Youth and Community Education. We then went on to talk about our love lives.

'There was someone. The lying toad.' Betty sneered. 'I found out he had a wife back in Scotland, that white scum bag and he wasn't even that good looking!'

Betty made me laugh the way she said it.

'Careful, that's racist.' I pointed out.

'Is all right. I am half white. I can call whites bastard and half black; I call the black ones bastards also…that's one advantage of being a zebra.' She winked.

'Zebra? Oh! Zebras. I see. A new insult tag, eh?'

'That's what they call you if you dare mention you got white roots too. Anyway, what of your love life?' She asked.

'Mine wasn't a liar. I knew he was in a gay relationship but I still love him. Anyway, he's history now.'

We talked, laughed, got sad, laughed again, and then suddenly, midnight 2005 was with us. We realised that Betty wouldn't be able to get me a minicab on New Year's Eve so I had to stay.

'Is OK. I'll phone Mom.'

When I finally did get Mom to come to the phone, she was very sharp with me. 'You big woman now, do what you like!' and hung up.

'What did she say?' asked Betty.

'She said it was all right.' I lied.

'Listen, everyone. I've invited our visitor, an old girl of Our Lady of Grace, to welcome the New Year with us. And she accepted.'

'Yeah, Saint Elena staying, let the fun begin.' someone shouted and the rest cheered.

'Ah! Double-O-six nearly here…Three…Four…we counted with the Hogmanay merry-makers of Scotland beamed onto the telly in London. On the stroke of twelve came madness.

'Happy New Year.' Everyone was jumping up and down.

Whatever the difficulties that had brought them to this special residential place of learning were forgotten for that moment. Now, away from their families, they were hugging and kissing each other. One tried to do a waltz with Betty.

'Bang! Bang!' Betty had to bang hard on the coffee table before she managed to bring some order in the room.

'I'm sure that Elena would like to say a few words.'

'I'd like to say that I wish for you all that you wish for yourself. I have spent three New Year Eve's here without my Mom and brother, my only family, then this year, by some strange power, my legs brought me here. I can assure you it wasn't planned. I came, and once again entered the New Year away from my family and I have no regrets. Nor will my family when I tell them where I spent it.'

Mom showed no interest when I got home and told her of the changes at Our Lady of Grace and how Betty would need a lot of help with what she was trying to do. All that stuff about a library with a Reading/Writing club would need lots of helpers. When I got tired talking to myself I shut up and decided to keep out of Mom's way. I began to support the Our Lady of Grace young women and helping Betty.

The start of spring term soon arrived. My first day back was to be Wednesday, 18th January. That morning, I got a text message from Chris, 'Must meet, very important.' A strange feeling came over me. Had they split up and he was turning to me? But was it what I wanted? In my text back I suggested the Greasy Spoon Cafe near the library that Thursday lunchtime. I couldn't bear having Esmay spying on me if I met him at college.

What Chris had to say when we met was nothing like what I had expected. Instead, he gave me such a shock that for a long time I sat numb, holding my head in my hands.

'I did write to your Mother and you to apologise for my behaviour. I was out of order.'

'You wrote to us both! When?'

'About three weeks ago. As soon as I realised what I done.'

'Got no letter from you. And Mom said nothing about one!'

'Oh well, lost in the post I suppose.' Chris said, but we both knew that both letters could not have been lost.

'Anyway, Mom and me going through the silent treatment at the moment.'

'I'm sorry. Is my fault. Alexis said it could be the blow on my head. But I say it ain't no excuse.'

'Blow on your head, what blow?'

'Orly! He threw a punch at me. I turned sideways to avoid it and it landed on the side of my head. Made me stagger! Worse place to get punched.'

'Of course it is. But don't tell me, he was drunk and you two got into a fight?'

'When he got the phone call, supposedly from you, to say that we were lovers, he lost it. He made me follow him to the garden and lay into me like a mad man.'

'What phone call? What you talking about?'

What Chris then related to me was nothing short of a horror story. No one could be so evil as to spoil a family's Xmas by telling such a lie.

'It's a bloody lie! I know nothing about a phone call. Besides we never were and never will be lovers. My feelings for you were and always will be a one-sided thing. Salamanca was a one-off; I can assure you, and Alexis.'

'I'm flattered, and will always see you as loving sister and a best friend.'

'Surely Orly would've recognised my voice. And Alexis could've traced the number?'

'Orly thought you disguised your voice. Anyway, he'd had a few glasses of wine! Alexis did think of tracing the number but got the 'caller's number withheld' message. And unless it was a police matter there's no way he could get the caller's number.'

'But who…?' It suddenly dawned on me. There was only one person who had the motive and opportunity and had Orly's number from a past meeting.

'I know who it was and she's a dead woman.'

'Please don't do anything to bring more bad publicity. I felt that you should know that someone might be pretending to be you, but please, no more publicity. Alexis is professor at the college. He's not supposed to get involved with students. He already had some explaining to do over this and they're watching him.' said Chris.

'I know that person so frustrated that she'll make trouble for others.'

'Alexis's family is highly respected in the French community. His grandmother is like the queen of a clan. Only the night before, Alexis had introduced me to her, then to other members of the clan. Then, the next day, their family, some all the way from the Dominica Republic, heard of the fight between Orly and me and the reason why, it was terrible. No wonder I went berserk and called your house, shouting into the phone.'

With that, Chris paid for the soft drinks we had and left, leaving me stunned.

'I can image how it must have been. That poor man, he had just introduced his lover to the family.' Betty said, when later that afternoon I retold the story of Chris to her.

'I'm ready for a show down with that wicked witch taking her own frustration out on others but Chris doesn't want to risk having any bad publicity for his gentleman friend.'

'I don't get it! What did that Esmay woman hope to gain?'

'I could only think that she got it in her confused head that if she split them up I'd have a chance with Chris, then he would reject me and I'd turn to her.'

'You mean, she fancy you?'

'Well, we did get close but she wasn't what I wanted.'

'Oh dear, still, you know what they say about all is fair in love and in war.'

'You don't hurt someone you love.'

'Anyway, what you going to do now?'

'Nothing, for Chris's sake, given the way he feels 'bout his man, I'll do nothing. I could of course talk to Esmay's mother. She's a very nice, respectable woman.'

Betty agreed that that was probably best and I was grateful. It was the first time that I had someone with whom I could discuss such a personal matter. I could not possibly discuss these things with my Mom. Just when I came to breaking point it appeared that some unseen power led me to someone I could trust to discuss my troubles with without fear of being ridiculed. Strange how I was led back to Betty, an old friend.

15

Time passed and I still felt downhearted and wanted to go somewhere in the back garden and bawl my head off. I had no communication with either Esmay or Chris. Mom was now talking to me when she had to, usually, when I asked her something or said that I might 'sleep over' at the Centre if it got late. I'd been spending lot of time helping Betty to turn a junk room into a small in-house library. I became a pineapple juice and sardine sandwich freak.

February came and Valentine's Day was fast approaching. The girls, who had by then labelled themselves, 'Daughters of Our Lady of Grace', as I had once called myself, were making cards. I was aware that not all the daughters of our Lady of Grace would have someone outside to send a valentine card to. 'No sweat,' I said, 'we each make a card to 'To Love', and use them to decorate the room in bounty style for the party.'

We did just that and the Valentine party started with people reading from their cards before hanging them up. I had encouraged the girls to make up verses but some of them had been very saucy and went further and wrote, 'Roses are red. I will meet you in Bed'. We had fun. Even grumpy Louisa gradually joined in. We had lots of snacks and drinks donated by well-wishers, including Ms Jolly living nearby. Poor me, the greasy and highly spiced snack someone's relative had donated didn't agree with me.

I was sick through that night. The next morning, I still felt terrible and even though it was Wednesday and my study day off work, I couldn't face going to college. Instead, I decided to stay at home to read and write notes. Mom had gone to work and Kevin to his sixth form college. I made myself the usual sardine paste ready to smear it on bread. I put in extra lemon juice as well as extra pepper and onion, cut up in the hope that the extra lemon mixed with the sardine would help with the sickly feeling I had in my stomach. I made myself comfortable with a thick sardine sandwich and textbook in hand. But because of the unusually stifling heat of that February day, I had left the front door ajar before I sat myself in that comfy chair. I was not sure how long I had been reading and eating when I looked up and saw her.

'What you here for? If you come to apologise for your witch of a daughter...'

I didn't get further. Esmay's mom spoke strangely as she did when Chris had had his accident and she had been talking him out of a fit.

'You were chosen. And it's a boy. You'll be the birth mother of a great man.'

'Who left the door open?' came Kevin's shout. 'Mom said not to leave the front door open, if you too hot you open the windows.'

'Hi Kev! Sorry, I was stifling, had to open the door and I dozed off.'

Thanks heaven, I thought, it was only a dream; there was no Esmay's mom.

After that day I continued to work flat out. I was helping Betty develop her in-house library; worked at my library, plus my MA studies. It was beginning to tell on me. I began to get terrible cramp around my ankles, no doubt from spending long hours sitting with my legs dangling, by the IN or the OUT counter at the library and the long walk to and from work, in order to save money. Also, Mom's continued coldness made me very unhappy and no amount of hard work was helping to ease the pain and feeling from having lost all the people I loved. It was Betty who suggested I saw my doctor for something because I could be run down. I probably wasn't eating properly.

'Nah, I'm fine. I'm sure that my doctor has enough on her hands with all the threat of flu epidemics and other real illnesses.'

'There's been a lot about African-Caribbean's and diabetics. I'm not saying that your diabetic but I noticed how you swallow a lot of that sugary and acidy pineapple juice and I worry.'

'OK! Ok preacher Betty, I'll go waste my doctor's time. As far as I know there are no diabetics in my family.'

To please Betty I made an appointment for my next study day off work which was on the Wednesday. I arrived at the surgery and found that I had to see the duty doctor because our family doctor was off-duty on Wednesdays. The duty doctor, a very young Asian woman, made some small talk to put me at ease I suppose. Given her youth, she had probably only recently qualified.

'Now, what can I do for you today?'

'Not much. I've been working very hard in our local library plus my part time MA studies at Uni…'

'What are you working on? Let me look at your eyes.' She pulled my eyelids slightly down while speaking. 'Have you been dieting?' She did not wait for me to explain what I was studying.

'It's an interdisciplinary study of language and culture. Yes I do eat, but of late I have lost my appetite.'

'I see. Shall we start with a good look at you?' It wasn't a question, she pointed to a screen opposite.

After a brief examination I went back to my chair and waited while she tapped things into her computer. She turned to me with a smile and said, 'You are a little anaemic, something we'll have to tackle. Good news though, your baby seems fine. Strange thing, there appears to be no record here.' she said seriously, 'You haven't been in for quite a long time.'

For a moment I was speechless. Had I heard her correctly? I couldn't possibly be punished that way. Nah! Is a guilt dream like the one when Esmay's Mom came to my house?

'You said baby?' I heard those words coming out as if from someone else. 'I can't be. You must have got it wrong.'

Suddenly, some latent prejudices sprang out the cupboard. This one was Ageism. Baby me foot, you're straight from medical school I bet. What the hell do you know? Would you know the different perhaps between fibroid and baby?

'I'm sorry if this was not good news for you at the moment, but you are definitely carrying. You must see your own doctor as soon as possible.'

'I'm more regular than I have ever been. And even without that terrible period cramp I usually get.'

'Happens sometimes. The little prince, or little princess, is playing a trick on us but he's not fooling anyone! I've made an appointment for you.'

Her voice faded away. From then on, nothing more of either what she explained or the leaflets pushed into my cold and clammy hands, registered. It can't be, no chance, it can't be, was all that went round my head. She's made a mistake. It's that fibroid thing sometime mistaken for a baby I'd heard about and there's also a high incidence, so they say, among African-Caribbean women, which I'm not, so must be something else. It's my punishment. I betrayed a friend, I've 'coveted my neighbour's goods', which was forbidden, and for that I must be punished. Poor Mom, if the doctor was correct, I'd bring shame to her door. She would never again be able to face her neighbours or friends and work mates. Not after the way she always praised me to them. Her daughter Elena was everything good and clever. As for me, the same me who always condemned those who 'only sit and produce kids' as being loose, or stupid or both. How clever I've been, eh? Not clever enough to stay out of this mess! Mind you, I still felt that the doctor could be wrong. I'd heard of the medical world making wrong diagnoses. That's it, I'll wait a few days and if my period don't make its appearance then I'll go to see my doctor. If it does make its appearance and is normal then that doctor has it wrong.

I had no idea how long I sat at the bus stop as bus after bus came and went. My mind got tired of trying to work things out. I certainly could not go home that night after what the doctor had said. I could not face Mom, not yet. I rang her and said that it was late and I would stay overnight at the centre.

Betty was already in her private quarters because although she wasn't on duty, she was on call. The night staff let me in and I went to Betty's room.

'You look dreadful, what happened?' She greeted me with concern.

'Only very tired. I've been to the doctor's. She said I was very anaemic, that's why I get that feeling of tiredness. And sometimes my head feels light.'

'Of course you're anaemic. Sardines have oil but you need other things.'

'You're right. I must force myself to eat properly.'

Having satisfied Betty with my fib of what happened at the doctors, I settled down to wait for the end of the month. But, when the end of March came and went and nothing, at first I wept then consoled myself that I often missed a month. I still could not tell my mom so I turned to Betty but begged her not to tell the girls. It may only be a false alarm. After Betty's promise not to tell I went back to the doctor's. This time I went not only about my health but also to ask if there were any homes outside of London for someone in my situation. Secretly I was hoping for a miscarriage.

'Yes, there are such places,' My doctor explained, 'but they are not as rosy as you might think.'

After that, it was as if my head was full of buzzing bees. There were scans, blood pressure too high, rest, eat, rest then eat, then rest, baby, baby, baby...on and on they gaggled. Then I remembered something on telly about linguists saying that a baby can hear and understand even when it's still in the womb. That's when I began to talk to mine while alone in my room at night. Look, go where you're wanted. Many happy couples want you. You're not wanted here. But I wouldn't commit murder. So do us both a favour and go...go... and before Mom has to be told.

Days went by and no matter how hard I worked I still couldn't get the situation that I had brought on myself out of my head. Also, I was beginning to wonder if Mom had suspected something about me, though I was as skinny as ever.

One Wednesday in early April the need to tell my mother was forced on me. I had to go to college for a special text I needed to work on during the Easter break. I needed to get there before the college closed at 5 PM. I arrived secretly, hoping, but at the same time fearing, that I might bump into Chris. But the person I bumped into was Joy, not Chris. We hugged and laughed because we had not seen each other for some time. She was also on an MA but a different area of study. Soon I was getting all the gossip straight off the college's grape vine. Joy had all the latest news, especially the juicy bits.

'Ah, and have you heard? You'll be getting a new head of the language department.'

'What?'

'Your head, he's going. Jumping before he's pushed. Gone on sabbatical, not returning, of course you haven't heard it from joy.'

'How come you know all this?'

253

'My dear! You ought to be friendlier with office staff, they hear things.'

'Nah, probably just malicious gossip.'

'Well, gossip or not, rumour has it that some scandal might be brewing and he got wind of it and jumped!'

'I'm sure he'll have got legal advice.'

I left Joy by pointing out that I had to go before the library closed.

On the way a home I made up my mind. If that man had to leave his well-paid job because of my action, then any punishment meted out to me will be well deserved. With that in mind I got home and later had supper. When Kevin finished his meal he left with his clarinet case in hand. After I cleared the table, I returned to our living room to face the music, so to speak.

'Mom, please sit down.' I held out a chair by the table for her, which she took and sat down.

'Remember I told you about Salamanca? I believe it's caused trouble. That Esmay could've been spiteful because I wouldn't talk to her. She may have been spreading tales. Now Alexis, the professor, err...Chris's friend, err...partner...' I stammered and my hands shook so much that I had to fold them together.

Mom said nothing; she just glared at me in a strange way.

'Err...you're going to be a grandmother. But is Ok, I'll go away.'

The words that I never thought I'd ever have to say came out. I waited for the blows to rain down on me. And when Mom rose I was sure that she was going for the broom handle.

What came was worse than a broom handle. My mother folded her hands over her head and cried out like wounded wolf. She cried out to the ceiling.

'I tried, Jesus in heaven *tu sabes* how hard I tried. I work hard to protect my children and yet some dirty man get my daughter.'

'Mom, please don't badmouth him. I went for him. I love him.'

My words only made Mom cry more and she became hysterical.

'Is Ok Mom, I wouldn't bring shame for you around here.'

She cried louder and I hugged her to calm her but ended up crying as well. I don't know how long we stood there weeping uncontrollably, before Mom dislodged herself from my arms. She composed herself and sat down.

'I suspect something wrong but I couldn't believe it. Not you, other girls perhaps, but not my Elena.'

'There're places outside London for this sort of thing...' I didn't get to complete the sentence.

'You not going, not running away nowhere.' Mom interrupted.

'Is you I'm thinking about, Mom. If I stay, them lot here going to mock you.'

Mom shrugged. 'Let them. But what about the Chris filth. It was him?'

'Yes! But it's my responsibility. I went for what I wanted and got more than I'd bargained for. I have to deal with that.'

'I can't believe it! Thought you had your head on. But we stay a family.'

'I'm sorry Mom. I wanted to tell you, but I was terrified after the way you reacted you about Salamanca.'

'I suppose the doctor can give you blood test and things. You hear about things when is between...' Mom stammered, but I knew what she was thinking.

'Stop right there, please Mom. Chris is a healthy man, never been around. Please Mom, I love and need you but please don't go thinking bad 'bout Chris.'

I wasn't due back at work until the Tuesday after Easter, which left me to spend time at the centre to colour-tag books that had been donated. Mum was not exactly over the moon about the situation but at least we were on speaking terms.

When I came back from my lunch break, I was told that I had a visitor in the boardroom. I nervously went up the flight of stairs. Who could it be? It must be someone important for them to be sent to the boardroom to wait for me. When I finally got to the boardroom, I found the door already open and someone was standing with their back to me. I must have gasped because there stood the last person I had expected to visit me. Even with his back to me I knew who it was.

'*Buenas Tardes.*' He came up and shook my hand.

'Good afternoon, professor.' I said professor instead of Alexis because it seemed appropriate given his formal appearance and his French accent.

'I was told that this would be your long lunch break.' He pointed to a chair and I sat down.

'Yes it is, but I'm not bothered. An apple or a sandwich on a park bench is good enough for me.'

'Park bench it is then.' He pointed to the door.

I took out an apple though I still had a sandwich in my bag because I had not bothered to eat yet. To be honest, I was too embarrassed to bring out a sandwich stinking of sardines.

'You should eat more than that my dear!'

'Is something wrong, why are you here?'

'I am concerned about Chris. I think he is heading for a breakdown.'

'Why you think that?'

'He is working as if possessed. He slaves on the computer, polishes my shoes until they look like mirrors; dusts around the house, getting under the feet of the person paid to look after the house, and in so doing causes the poor woman to feel that he does not want her around. He has been purchasing more plants than we have garden space...'

'When did he begin to behave like that?'

'I am not sure. It was some weeks ago that I noticed how exhausted he appeared at night and he was beginning to have recurrent nightmares.'

'Maybe you should seek counselling for him.'

'Actually, I have toyed with the thought that you could have a reassuring word with him.'

'Me? Why would he listen to me?'

'I was unable to make out his nightmare, except that it could be his guilt about Salamanca.'

'What guilt?' I heard my voice asking.

'I do know about Salamanca you know! Sitting here now with you, I can understand the possible meaning of those dreams that frightened him so much.'

'You been talking to my mom?'

He shrugged, gave me a brief look, smiled, then suggested, 'Why don't we meet and discuss things like civilised people?'

'I don't see the point of that.' I replied.

'I can. We both love him and neither would want him to 'crack' up.'

I hesitated.

'I don't want to interfere.'

Actually, I didn't feel that I wanted to go crawling to The Orchid as if I was begging for something.

'Look, why not give us a call or just drop in. We are usually home in the evening and on Sundays. On Saturdays we go out and do our 'big shopping', as Chris calls it.'

The word 'we' made it very clear to me where I stood. The two were still together and not even my stupidity in doing what I had done could change that.

On Labour Day, the public holiday and two Sundays after that Easter meeting with Alexis, I was sitting in his drawing room at The Orchid. I had told Mom that I would be away for the day. I was going down town to see the parade and then I'd be at the Centre to applaud the girls showing off their bonnets. I didn't tell Mom that I'd be at The Orchid because that was not my plan. But once on the road it seemed that my legs took me in the direction of the River Side Village then The Orchid. Twice I thought of turning back but couldn't. I suddenly had a strong need to be at The Orchid and perhaps to try and reassure Chris that he need not be afraid that I'd want support of any kind from him: I could sign documents to say so.

I had rehearsed what I would say, yet once I got to The Orchid, and was sitting down with a glass of ice-cold juice in my hand, all I could think of saying was that I was sorry.

'I understand why Chris made sure he was away when I came. I'm ever so sorry about all of this. I didn't plan it. But it was my fault not

Chris's. I let my feelings run away with me. We were partying and drinking stuff.'

'There is no need for anyone to be blamed. These things do happen. You were both inexperienced when it came to the opposite sex and got carried away. What happens now is all that matters.'

As Alexis spoke, I was thinking how confident he was in his relationship with Chris. He didn't see me as a rival and for that I was grateful but at the same time I was embarrassed that I had made a fool of myself.

'I didn't set out to cause trouble between you and Chris, I swear.'

'I know that. But if Chris wanted to be with you, I would step down and move on. His happiness is paramount. That was what I told him after I learnt about that Salamanca affair.'

'You told him that?'

Again I felt ashamed that what happened in Salamanca was discussed. It made me feel cheap.

'I did and I meant it. He must feel free to choose. I will not chain him down.'

'No wonder he's going to pieces .He does not want me. You're all he wants. But what you told him made him feel that you pushing him away.'

'I am not pushing him away. But now he is one worried young man. He fears that he will have to pay for years for that brief moment in Salamanca.'

'I wouldn't ask him for anything.'

Suddenly, something, perhaps brought on by Alexis's confidence in his relationship with Chris, prompted me to say. 'Was I used to test Chris loyalty?'

The words just sprung out of my mouth.

'Don't ever think of me as someone capable of doing such a thing.' Alexis said angrily.

'I'm sorry, it's just that it's all such so strange… so strange. I do love him and no one, not even I myself could stop that but…'

'I also feel that there appears to be something strange, almost supernatural, going on. Of course, I have been brought up; probably even breast fed by French Caribbean black women, and might have

258

inherited their belief system. But there is also Chris who seems to have an extra sense.'

While Alexis spoke about Chris's strange nightmares of seeing a small human like creature crawling on the floor and in the back garden, I was thinking of my own. Starting with the spectre of a naked, white-faced man, as if he'd been in tomb, standing by my bed, then walking, arms outstretched, towards me. As for the one of Esmay's mom telling me that 'I had been elected'. Guilt dream! Or was it?

'Hello Chris!' I hoped that I sounded distant enough.

He'd arrived late, probably hoping that I'd left. He stood at the door of the room. The fear and worry on his face must have done something to my system because what happened next was nothing short of a vivid nightmare.

Chris did not reply to my greeting, instead, his fear turned to what I saw as disgust. Alexis calmly walked out of the room, obviously to leave us alone to talk.

After he'd left I said, 'Is Ok Chris. Alexis and I talked. I'll go now. I shouldn't have come.'

I went to get up but a sharp pain on one side of my stomach made me sit back down with a groan!

Chris said nothing. He didn't even ask if I was all right.

I got up again and began to walk out of the room. Chris silently stood aside for me to pass. Then that sharp cramp pain again. Could it be my monthly? I'd be delighted if it was. Another stabbing pain!

'Alexis!' I shouted out while holding on to my stomach

'What's wrong?' asked Alexis, rushing to my side.

'It's must be wind. I haven't been eating…Ahhh…' By then I was doubled up with pain, now coming from the lower part of my back through to my stomach.

'Come sit down. We will get you something to eat.' Alexis helped me back to the sofa.

'No! No thanks! I can't stand the smell of food being cooked, ugh!'

'Don't just stand there! Get a blanket or something!' Alexis sounded confused.

'Or maybe a doctor?' Chris said coldly.

'No doctor, please. It's only a bad case of wind and…Oh! I need the toilet.'

I felt myself leaking as if I had lost control of my bladder. I made for the guest bathroom rather than try to go upstairs but I never made it!

My water broke outside the door. I knew then that I might be losing 'it', which I didn't want in the first place. Hurrah, I thought, even though I was in such pain.

After that it was like a repeat of when Chris had self-harmed himself and almost on the same spot. They were both talking at once. Meanwhile, I was still in terrible pain. It was not unlike my period pain when I had missed a month or two, only this time it was much worse. I heard Alexis arguing with someone on the phone and saying that 'yes, this is an emergency'.

Chris was blaming Alexis for dumping rubbish in the guest room. Between them they helped me back to the drawing room. I was beginning to feel cold and a cover was brought. I found that the only position that eased the pain a little was when I went on my knees in a praying position but face down on the sofa. I felt Alexis placing the blanket across my shoulder and back while he tried to reassure me.

'Should she be like that?' I overheard Chris whispering to Alexis as if I was not in the room.

'Where is that damn ambulance? And they call themselves a private company.' Alexis bellowed.

Just then the front door bell rang.

Alexis made to rise but I grabbed hold of his hand.

'Don't leave me. You're older!'

'I'll go.' Chris, obviously glad not to be with me, rushed to answer the door.

After he left I said, 'he's petrified. Don't tell him off too much. None of this was his fault.' I said in his defence.

I felt a pressure which made me say that I was going to mess myself if I didn't get to the bathroom.

'You are all right. Help is here.'

I didn't get there; it felt like something was coming out of me.

I was having a miscarriage. Good, thank God! I thought with joy.

I delivered and Alexis caught 'it' in his hand just as the help walked in.

'Cynthia, midwife from the Health Centre. What have ...' the voice of a young woman began to fade away.

I vaguely heard the tingle of the front door again. Footsteps, voices, all coming from a distance, some doctor apologising because it was his day off, he didn't get the message...about twenty-five weeks no more, private...I had passed into a twilight world.

In that world, people were doing things to my body. Once, they tried to make me look at a bundle all swaddled up, with a tiny, very white and stained face showing. I turned my own face away. I didn't want to look at such a creature. I kept going to and fro, in and out of that world. I kept seeing people, Alexis, Mom, Betty, Chris, even people I didn't know. Those people were talking about me, sometimes too me, and I was answering back, but I don't think they heard me. I heard Mom's voice in the distance and it reminded me about *Duennes*, which I had heard of before. *Duennes*, sometimes called *Duendes*, the spirits of children who had died before they were baptised. After that came a man in the regalia of a priest and talking in tongue.

On and on I went, in and out that dreamlike twilight world, which I would never be able to explain.

'Good morning! You're back with us then?'

'What's happening? Where am I?'

'In Riverside Hospital, I am Dr Ashmed.' she said, taking my hand.

'You have been very sick and drifting in and out of dreamland.' said someone with a strong American accent.

'You have a visitor.'

A third person carrying a bundle came into the room. She put on a baby voice.

'Good morning, Mummy.' and placed a bundle in my arms.

I held the bundle, and took a long look at the tiny face .I felt nothing, no feeling of guilt, no motherly love either. I was thinking 'this poor thing, alive yet so small'. It was all wrapped up like a mummy. It opened its tiny eyes, which I thought looked like two black and scary pebbles. I held its tiny body for a short while then handed the tiny bundle over to someone called Wanda, who said she was his special nurse. She explained that he'd be in my room from now on. Doctor had cleared him. And he no longer needed to be in an incubator

'We're a fighter aren't we my little A.C.?' she said.

'A.C.? What's an A.C.?' I asked.

'I'm sorry. I spoke out of turn; I understood that the family asked baptism to be arranged because he was so desperately weak. But then he rapidly picked up.'

'He is our miracle baby.' The doctor came up and joined in.

'It's Ok! I'll have a word with my family about the baptism.'

Other visitors arrived. Mom, Betty, Chris. Alexis sat by me for a long while. He explained that the Riverside was a private hospital but with all the recourses for special care such as needed by A.C. short for Alexander Christopher. In addition, Riverside had a much better patient/nurse and medical support staff ratio than the general hospitals, with which it often collaborates. Actually I was thinking in terms of money but I dozed off again.

The month of May came and went, and soon it was August and the early afternoon sun was greeting A.C. like a prince into the wider world. In his white lace gown, once worn by his godfather, and a bonnet, too large for his tiny head, held in place by blue ribbons tied under his chin, he rested peacefully in the arms of his godfather. He yawned, oblivious of the cameras and the two cars waiting for close relatives and friends who came to whisk him away and into that new world where his personal bibliography had already begun.

What would happen now?

A.C didn't know; I didn't know either, only time would tell.